Tell Me Who You Go With

Archer & Bethany

Darla J. Michaels

To my daughter, Stella. Never forget that you are magic.

Content Note

This book tells the story of a polyamorous relationship. And contains consensual non-consent, drug use, and attempted sexual assault. Reader discretion advised.

The Brotherhood Order of Entry

The Brotherhood is a secret society built on legacy, power and choice. Each pair is inducted in turn, bound to both the society and to one another. This roster reflects their order of entry.

I.   Dr. Braden Hart & Linea Whitfield-Hart **

II.   Dr. Jonathan Patino & Grace Fontaine **

III.   Landon Moreau & Kelly Sinclair

IV.   Tyler Maddox & Lexi Sloane **

V.   Maverick (Mav) DuPont & Emmerson Montrose

VI.   Graham Langley & Morgan Hale

VII.   Archer Jackson & Bethany Everly-Jackson

VIII.   Cooper Wescott & Marlowe Pierce

IX.   Callan Graves & Taylor Fairchild

X.   Harlan Rothwell & Francesca Vescari

XI.   Emerick Blackmoor & Elena Marcelline

XII.   Micah A Stevenson & Hadley "Joanna" McAfferty **

*** Founding Member of The Brotherhood*

Your words have power. They hold magic some say. Speak carefully for every word that parts your lips will come back to you someday.

Bethany Jackson-

Kitchen & Green Witch…they mix together…

Prologue
Archer

I've always wanted a wife. I know it sounds strange, especially coming from a man and a young man at that. But there's something that's always appealed to me about choosing a woman and caring for her.

I guess you could say I probably wanted to care for a woman because my own mom wasn't cared for. She did it all by herself. And the only thanks she ever got was chasing around after her own kids. She wanted them to go out into the world and make something of themselves. Didn't seem like much thanks to me.

Looking back, she deserved more. She was a saint...still is a saint. I wanted a woman who I could show off to her. Who I could shower in affection, bring nice things and have fun working hard together to make a great life.

And I swore to myself that when I found this woman, I'd give her everything she ever needed and never let one harmful thing come her way if I could help it. While things haven't been perfect and I've made some decisions I regret to this day, one of my Brothers has it far worse. His Lady wasn't so lucky.

It's why I'm sitting at Micah's dining room table with Jonathan, Micah and Harlan, brainstorming. Because Linea is as much mine as Bethany is. And someone hurt her. Someone did the most monstrous things a person could do to another.

I'm going to help return the favor.

"What's the third thing?" We have assembled at Micah's house in secret on a Saturday morning while Braden works in clinic. When the guys look confused, I clarify. "Linea said there were three things a woman could be. A virgin, a helper and…" I let the last part hang there because either I missed it, or she didn't say it.

"She never said. I…" Micah looks pained. "I should have asked. I was just so stunned with everything…"

"Why does that matter", Harlan pipes in.

"With a case like this, everything matters." Micah's voice is so solemn. I know he doesn't want to be involved in this without Braden. He hates these secret meetings. "The objective is to know more than people think you do. And the strategy that has always served me well is to assume the other side knows what you do. We need the information. At the very least it won't matter but at the most, it could be the key to finding justice for her."

"Well Micah, since you and Linea are thick as thieves, I think you'd be the best person to get this from her, don't you?"

Jonathan and Micah are in a silent standoff at the dining room table. I don't know what's gotten into them, but they've been at each other since the night I came for Jonathan's car keys.

"Braden should be involved in this." It's Micah's answer to Jonathan's demand.

"But he's not. So, just ask her", Jonathan deadpans.

"You two need to fix your shit." I look between Micah and Jonathan so there's no question about who I'm talking to. "I don't know what's going on here but whatever it is, squash it. I thought the point of this was to send these creeps to jail or hell…whichever one we can accomplish. We won't be able to do either of those things if we lose or get caught. And we will have destroyed part of The Brotherhood if either of those things happen. The only option is to put these assholes away so they can't hurt anyone else. Get your fucking heads on straight right God damned now."

Bethany

Well, this is awkward. Linea and Grace are at my kitchen table. Hawk is on the couch. He can see and hear everything. I know he's listening even though he's thumbing through his phone and drinking the coffee I offered him.

"How do you deal with...that", I ask Linea, shifting my eyes to Hawk so she understands what I'm talking about.

"I have my fun. Trust me."

Hawk snorts and then glances up at me.

"Sometimes towels fall down", she explains in an overly cheerful tone, even for her. "On accident of course."

I make eye contact with Hawk and my eyes go wide when I see him glaring at the back of Linea's head. She winks at me, and I laugh. It's clear she's trying to get under his skin. I wonder how she was punished for that little stunt.

"How mad was Braden?"

"Mad", Hawk answers on Linea's behalf.

Linea shrugs playfully.

"Who cares. It's not like Hawk's never seen a tit before, right, Hawk?" I smile at how Grace provokes him. He doesn't take the bait.

"So, what can I do for you", I ask them, trying to steer us into territory that may not get me punished this afternoon.

"You've been married to Archer for a while." Linea lets the statement just hang there. I'm not sure where she's going with this.

"Four years. Five this July."

"Five years", Linea says quietly to herself before she continues. "I don't know how to do this." She looks across the table at me with watery eyes. "I've been married for a few weeks, and it seems…"

"Unnecessary", Grace finishes her sentence, in the dry way that Grace has about her.

"It's a kink", I tell them. I don't want them thinking this was a situation where Archer and I dated, fell in love and married before all of this. They look back at me, confused. "We didn't come to The Brotherhood married. We married to get into The Brotherhood."

Linea's eyes get wide in shock. I laugh and Grace just shakes her head.

"Why does this matter", I ask, reluctantly.

"I just want to know how you do it. Five years is a long time." Linea chews on her lip and furrows her brow, clearly unsettled by the thought of marriage.

"I don't know if you want to take notes from me." I can see her deflate at the table.

Grace laughs. "You can't be a worse wife than I was", she challenges.

"I've done much worse than take off my top for a stranger." Linea's eyes widen at my response. "I know I may not look like it, but trust me, I'm a strong contender for wife of the year.

5 Years Earlier- Mid July

Chapter 1
Archer

I reach up to tug at the collar of my dress shirt but it's as open as it gets. We decided on a casual wedding. I'm not wearing a tie. The sleeves of my dress shirt are rolled up just below my elbows. Whatever sweat the pits of my dress shirt miss, the inside of the cuffs are sure to catch.

Bringing my hand down from my collar, I catch Bethany looking me over. She looks nervous. I get it. We've had three dates...if you can even call them that. And the amount of trust she's placing in me is enormous.

I told her I was looking for a wife because I joined this brotherhood and nothing gets me harder than making my wife service others. And I'm not talking about acts of service in the form of baking and cleaning. I'm talking about true acts of service like giving a world class blowjob or fucking my new friends while I watch. She didn't bat an eye. She just nodded. She. Nodded.

When I told her I was looking for a wife fast, as in a week or so, she just picked up her phone and started looking at her calendar. I wanted to ask her if she was serious because I couldn't believe my eyes. I thought this would be a much harder sell. She wouldn't even answer the one question I'd asked her every time we met. Kitchen or green? But now, she was going to marry me? The only question she asked was if this would be a real marriage.

My response? You bet your ass it will be.

The next day, I called Tyler and told him I'd found my Lady. He told me Micah would be sending out a list of documents that I was required to send them before we were officially in. At the top was to send pictures. I messaged Tyler about this, and he said they weren't fucking any uggos and reminded me that this was a commitment. I couldn't just dump her if I rolled over one day and realized I made a mistake. He wouldn't have to worry about that. I don't believe in divorce. Once Bethany had my ring on her finger that was it as far as I was concerned. We were it...for eternity.

I wink at Bethany, and she smiles at me but it's still all nerves. You know the kind of smile. A little too wide showing a little too much teeth. I start to walk over to her but Jonathan steps up next to me, stopping me from going to my bride.

"Ready?"

"Yes, sir", I tell him, glad he is only ordained and not a real religious figure. He won't give me shit about church and all that other stuff.

"You know at some point, I'm going to have my cock down Bethany's throat, don't you?" I smile at how he says it out the side of his mouth so my little brother, Marvin, can't hear. "Don't call me sir. I just took the class, paid the fee and lucky for you, haven't gotten paged yet. It's hot as balls in here."

I laugh. It is hot as balls in here. And the fact that a world class trauma surgeon just said that to me as a founding member of The Brotherhood makes me feel right at home. It's like I found my people. He's just one of the guys and I like him more and more each time we meet.

"We're gonna cut some corners...if it's okay with the groom."

"Let's do it." It's three in the afternoon. I know what I want to do after everyone leaves. I'm sure Jonathan knows too.

"Grace", Jonathan calls behind him and a woman steps up next to him. "Have you two met?" Jonathan nods to Bethany.

"No." Her voice is as cold as her face. She's impeccably dressed, not a hair out of place and makeup that makes her skin look flawless. But she looks like she could give two fucks about being here. I wonder if she looks that way all the time. I wonder if she'll look that way while I'm railing her.

"Grace." Jonathan uses a little softer tone with her. It's gentle. Not quite a whisper. Not quite a request. It's a polite order only by using her name.

Grace gives Jonathan the side eye, let's out a barely audible exhale and walks over to Bethany. Bethany looks concerned. I try to stifle my smile. One of the nicest ladies is meeting someone who might be able to kill with her eyes alone.

"She gives phenomenal head", Jonathan murmurs next to me.

I chuckle. "I'm sure she does", I tell him, trying to look natural but failing. God damn. I'm so fucking excited. This is it. After this ceremony I'm in. I'm on the schedule. We're on the schedule.

Grace and Marvin look our way, the need for instruction written on their faces.

"Stand wherever the fuck you want. It doesn't matter", Jonathan tells them. Grace smirks and Marvin raises his brows. We were raised not to swear. As the youngest, he catches hell if he swears so he's shocked to hear someone ordained throw out an f-bomb.

Now that Grace and Bethany have met, I cross the room to bring her to us. Her living room is eclectic and homey. There's a burnt orange velvet couch against the wall with some dark blue velvet throw pillows, some with patterns and some without. A large dark wood coffee table sits in front of it holding an antique brass candelabra. The cream-colored candles have been lit as indicated by the dried wax that drips down the candles and onto the metal holder. A few smaller tables hold plants. Apothecary jars line the mantel above the fireplace. Some hold candles and what appear to be various dried herbs. Others are empty. There's a bookshelf filled with books that look like they're about a hundred years old...her home is really a site to see so far.

My boots are heavy on the hardwood floor as I cross the space to her. Grace falls back, standing on the opposite side of the room as Marvin. She's only there to sign as a witness for Bethany. Bethany's only concern was who she'd find to stand up for her. She wasn't interested in inviting someone from her family. I didn't press her. My own family was pretty open minded but even they would have trouble with this.

"Darlin'"?" I reach my hand out for Bethany, and she puts her delicate hand in mine. The comparison is striking. My hand is much larger than hers. Tan. Strong. Hers is fair and dainty. No flashy fingernails or jewelry. Not even for this occasion.

"Ready?" She nods and gives me a small smile. "Nervous?"

Darla J Michaels

"A little." Bethany looks down at the floor, then focuses on Jonathan when he calls out to her.

"It'll be quick and painless. I promise." Jonathan doesn't hold anything. Not even a bible.

"Are you one of the..." Bethany lets the question die on her lips before she can finish it. I realize she doesn't know what they're called. It's sweet.

"Yeah. We'll have some time together later." Jonathan doesn't say any more than that. I'm not sure if it's because he isn't sure of what Marvin knows or if he just wants to move this along. Maybe it's both.

"Marriage is a commitment in life, where two people can find and bring out the very best in each other. It offers opportunities for sharing and growth that no other human relationship can equal, a physical and emotional joining that has the promise of a lifetime.

Today signifies the creation of a new home and a new family for you both. May you be fulfilled by each other's love and friendship. May you be overjoyed by the promises you are about to make and the life together you will create. May the promises you make to one another today, be lived out to the end of your lives. Tomorrow can bring you the greatest of joys, but today is the day it all begins.

Archer and Bethany, do you, present yourselves willingly and of your own accord to be joined in marriage?"

"We do", Bethany and I answer in unison.

"Will you promise to care for each other in the joys and sorrows of life, come what may, and to share the responsibility for growth and enrichment of your life together?

"We do."

Jonathan turns to me.

"Repeat after me...

Tell Me Who You Go With- Archer & Bethany

I, Archer, take you Bethany, to be my lawful wedded wife
I give to you in the presence of God and these witnesses
My promise to stay by your side,
In sickness and in health, in joy and in sorrow,
As well as through the good times and the bad.
I promise to love you without reservation,
Comfort you in times of distress
Encourage you to achieve all your goals,
Laugh with you and cry with you,
Grow with you in mind and spirit
Always be open and honest with you,
And cherish you for as long as we both shall live."
When I'm finished with my vows, he has Bethany repeat
the same ones.

"Hold hands", Jonathan directs us, almost as if he's bored
with this ceremony. I'm astounded that he's doing all this by
memory. He hasn't tripped up once. I find myself wondering if
he could do a full ceremony this easily. I'd gather it'd be harder
to do the abbreviated version, having to know what you'd cut
out and all.

Once we join hands, he continues. "These are the hands
that are holding yours on your wedding day as you promise to
love each other today, tomorrow, and forever. These are the
hands that will countlessly wipe tears from your eyes, tears of
joy and sorrow. These are the hands that will passionately love
you and cherish you through the years. These are the hands that
will help hold your family together as one as you overcome
adversity. These are the hands that will give you strength when
you need it. These are the hands that will work alongside yours
as together you build your future."

Jonathan scans the room and lands on Marvin. "Rings?".
Marvin reaches in his pocket and pulls out a black velvet box. I

smirk, recalling the conversation I had with Bethany after she accepted my indecent proposal.

Why would I want diamonds? I don't need them. Diamonds don't make a marriage.

And that right there is one of the many things Momma would love about her. Diamonds don't make a marriage. Even still, I could get her much more.

"Go ahead and slide the rings on", Jonathan prompts.

"Having this love in your hearts, you have chosen to seal your vows by exchanging rings. Having pledged their fidelity to one another." Jonathan pauses, turning his gaze on me with the smallest smirk on his lips knowing fidelity has such a different meaning to me. "To love, honor and cherish one another in the presence of this gathering and by the authority vested in me by the constitution and the laws of this state, it is my honor to now pronounce you husband and wife. You may kiss the bride."

And kiss the bride I do. Bethany is so sweet. Her face is flushed from the heat. Her hair seems to have a few extra curls to it, framing her face. I grip Bethany by the chin and look her in the eyes.

"Wife", I murmur to her before pressing my mouth to hers and sliding my tongue into it. We've only kissed a few times but every time we do, I don't want to stop. It's like some invisible force is locking us together. I can't get enough of her, and I'd venture to say she feels the same way about me.

Before allowing us to finish, Jonathan announces us for the first time. "It is my honor to be the first to introduce you to: Mr. and Mrs. Archer and Bethany Jackson.

There is no clapping like there would be in a big ceremony. It's quiet. The only sound is Grace's heels, confidently crossing the floor to deliver the leather portfolio to Jonathan. Jonathan thanks her and brushes a kiss across her cheek before casually opening the folder and sliding out a piece of crisp white paper. The final step is the paperwork part. He points to where we sign, and it takes a matter of minutes to get everything in order.

Jonathan reaches across me and shakes Marvin's hand. Then steps forward and embraces Bethany, giving her a brief kiss on the cheek before pulling back and shaking my hand.

"Congratulations", he tells me. "We'll call you." He winks at Bethany and when I turn to her, her face reddens more.

"Sounds good. Thanks man." I hold my hand out for him to shake, but he pulls me forward and hugs me instead. "We'll take good care of her. Do the same."

"I plan on it."

Jonathan chuckles. He knows where my mind is at. Sex. I want sex with my wife. My. Wife. God damn. I'm married.

Marvin clears his throat as Jonathan and Grace exit on their own. I'm so caught up in the promise of what's next I forget I haven't said goodbye to my own brother yet.

"Thank you", I tell him, pulling him in for a hug.

Sweat drips down his dark face and when we pull back from the hug, he's fishing in the suit coat he's wearing, grabbing out a handkerchief to wipe his brow.

"You gotta get out of here and take that jacket off. I told you this wasn't formal", I razz him a bit.

"It's your wedding Arch", he counters but I waive him off.

"The number one thing is..." He cuts me off before I can finish.

"Oh, I know what the number one thing is. I'm not saying a word."

I laugh hard. I'm not scared of Momma, but I'd never want to disappoint her. She was the best thing that's ever happened to me. She adopted me with eight kids of her own and did it all by herself. She is literally the most amazing woman I've ever known. And she's going to be pissed if she finds out what I'm going to do with Bethany.

"Alright. Go on and get out of here. I got plans with my wife." I look over at Bethany and wink at her.

"Thank you, Marvin", she tells my brother, her voice so soft and sweet I just want to scoop her up and haul her off to her bedroom...of which I haven't even seen yet.

"No problem", Marvin waives awkwardly, not sure if he should hug her or not. We come from a family of huggers. This is a hugging occasion. I nod towards the door, making the decision for him.

As soon as the door closes, there's one thing I have to do before anything else. Get the hell out of these clothes.

Bethany's looks at me, eyes wide in surprise when I slide my suspenders off my shoulders and start unbuttoning my starched white shirt.

"I've never done this before. Not the marriage part...I mean...I haven't done the marriage part either, but I mean...what comes after the marriage part." Bethany starts to pace with soft footsteps across the room. Her feet barely make a sound on the hardwood, I note, while I try to focus on not passing out from heat stroke.

"Maybe I should have told you. But I thought it would be a good thing. And you didn't ask. In all the time we've spent together you didn't ask once. I mean, all you cared about was kitchen or green."

I shrug my shirt off, tossing it to the floor. Manners have left me. I'm going to die in these clothes. I glance at her, and she looks nervous. Or turned on. Or both? My only goal is getting undressed now that Jonathan and Marvin have left. I think I need a shower. Christ. I hope she has one of those. No air. A wood burner for the winter. I'm surprised she has electricity. I bet she barely even uses it; I muse to myself.

"It's both. Mostly kitchen with some green. It's hard not to be both. They kind of mix together sometimes."

I nod and give her a small smile. Glad to have the answer I've been looking for over the last month. We'd gone on three dates, most of which you couldn't even call a date. They were random meetings that turned into more. And now, here we are. Her nervously telling me something that sounds important but that I don't quite understand while I'm sweating my balls off. I've literally got sweat running down my ass crack.

"But I do more. I mean...I did more. And then this happened." I glance up to find her motioning between us as I toe off my boots. "I didn't think it would work. My mother doesn't think it works but when my grandmother was dying, she told me to do it on my twenty-third birthday. So, I did because I was just so very lonely. And then there you were...all the time. And you asked and I...how could I say no to you? I mean...look at you?"

Yeah...look at me. I'm stripping in your living room in the middle of a hot July day because I can't take the heat in this place. We are not living here. As this woman's husband I am putting my foot down. Bethany starts pacing as I shed my pants. I stand there, my skin glistening with sweat in my boxers, so uncomfortable I don't care one bit how ridiculous I might look right now. Her white sundress flows behind her as she walks back and forth in front of me.

"Say something". She sounds desperate but I don't know why.

"Bethany, darlin', I would say something, but I have no idea what you're talking about. I do appreciate the clarification on kitchen and green though. Finally solving that mystery is the least you could do since becoming my wife."

Bethany stops in front of me, pulls her bottom lip under her teeth and furrows her brows. I smirk as I notice a bead of sweat sliding down her neck from her hairline where she's carefully piled her long locks on top of her head with what I'm guessing to be about a hundred hair pins. I want to lick that bead of sweat. But I also want to watch it slide down her porcelain skin. I want to see where it travels. Maybe remove her clothing as it slowly slides down her body before I take her somewhere with air conditioning and partake in the best part of the wedding day. The wedding night.

"Sex." She says the word like it has the potential to be explosive. I take a step toward her because maybe I could have sex in this sweltering heat. But I stop my advance when she takes a step back. "I haven't had it." I cock my head to the side. Her words aren't computing. "Ever."

Bethany's gaze drops to the wood floor in shame while I'm left standing there like an idiot. Ever? As in never, ever...EVER?

"Are you fuckin' with me?" She shakes her head. God damn. I chuckle. And then I laugh. She looks around the room awkwardly and I shake my head at her, extending my arm out to signal that I'm not laughing at her. I'm the luckiest sonofabitch that ever existed right now. But I wish I would have known so I could have given this a little thought. I would have liked to plan for something like this.

"What have you done?"

Her eyes shift to my boxers and her eyes widen a fraction. My cock is threatening to rip out of my shorts.

"Not much", she answers, after clearing her throat and folding her hands in front of her lap as casually as she can muster. Okay. I hear you loud and clear, Bethany. You're uncomfortable.

"Well why don't we start with what you have done and see where that takes us?" She nods and this time I make her come to me. "C'mon darlin''. Let's see what you've got."

Her teeth come down on the side of her lip as she meets me in the middle of the living room.

"Don't be nervous." She gives me a small smile and then reaches out to trace a bead of sweat rolling down my neck. "That's right. I'm yours to touch now", I encourage her. She reaches up and brushes her fingertips across my stubble, then rises on her tiptoes even though I still have to bend down to kiss her.

It's hard to keep my hands to myself. I want to touch her, but I don't want to interfere with what she's going to show me. So, I only allow myself to put my arm around her. Not tight. Just enough to feel her. Enough so that she knows I've got her.

She lets her hand fall from my face and slide to my chest. Then she drops down to the flats of her feet, breaking the kiss. I look her over as she thinks. But after a few seconds pass than is normal to transition to something else, she doesn't make another move.

"Bethany." She looks up at me, nerves clearly showing on her face.

"That's it."

I narrow my eyes at her, and she pushes out of my hold.

"I should have told you." She turns around letting out an unintelligible grumble. "Why didn't I tell you", she asks herself.

"Bethany." I want her to stop beating herself up. This is a good thing. A really good thing. "If it was important to me, I would have asked."

She lets out a laugh. "No, you wouldn't have."

12

"You're right. Because I assume someone like you isn't a stranger to sex."

Bethany sucks in a sharp breath and whirls around, fiery anger now in her features. "What's that supposed to mean?"

I shake my head. That came out wrong. "You're pretty. You're nice. You have manners. I would have figured any man would want to bring someone like you home. Especially to bed."

There's a knock at the door.

"Shit." I forgot to tell her what I had planned. This whole house without air conditioning and her virginity news threw me off.

"It starts now", I call over my shoulder as I walk to the door, having no time to explain.

She doesn't respond. It doesn't matter. This is what she agreed to.

Chapter 2
Bethany

I start to twirl my grandmother's ring only to remember, her ring isn't there anymore. I replaced it with Archer's just now. In the short time it was off, I felt like the connection had been lost with her. The only person in my entire family who really knew me. And she's missing. What would Gram say now?

She'd probably tell me to follow spirit. Except I don't know how to do that. Not like she did. I asked her if she heard things, considering for a moment that she had some sort of cognitive issue. But she told me it wasn't like that at all. They were thoughts that showed up in her greatest time of need. Answers to things that seemed to have no good solution at all until the solution just dropped into her mind.

I'm having a great time of need. And I have no thoughts. I surely don't have answers. Where are you when I need you spirit? Shit...shit...shit!

Darla J Michaels

"Really", I hear an unfamiliar male voice say to Archer. Heavy footsteps approach us. Thank heavens I have clothes on. But Archer just answered my door in his boxers. What in the...

They enter the living room, and my mouth hangs open. I can't help it. Because the man standing next to Archer is huge. I mean, military, basketball player, linebacker huge. He stops in the center of the living room, feet spread apart, looking me over.

"Pretty", he says to Archer. "Panties?"

"Still on."

"Hmmm..." The stranger motions toward me, indicating Archer should address me.

Archer crosses the room to me and takes my now sweaty palms in his, just like he did during the ceremony. Except they weren't sweaty then. They were certain.

"Bethany." He licks his lips and searches my eyes. I can't take my eyes off his. They're hazel and beautiful. "I asked Tyler to come here because I want something from you and it's all I'll be able to think about until I get it."

The need in Archer's voice takes me by surprise. I thought being married was nothing but a kink to him, but now I'm not so sure.

"As my first official act as your husband, I want you to let Tyler play with you." I try to pull my hands from Archer's, but he only grips them tighter. "Bethany, darlin'' I'll be there the whole time", he croons.

I don't know about this. Now I'm wondering if I made a mistake. This all seemed well and good in theory. Spirit brings me what I ask for and he's gorgeous and funny and kind...but with an infidelity kink.

Archer takes my hand and shoves it right up against his hard cock. "This is for me. Not Tyler. Not even for you. It's for me. After you give for me, I'll give back to you."

He's moving my hand over his length and with no effort at all, he slides through the slit in his boxers. My hand is on him, and he feels so good. Warm and firm with skin like velvet. I almost moan at the feel of him in my hand.

"Okay." I agree, hoping I get to touch him at some point. I've never done any of this. But I gather by his easygoing nature that he'd show me everything I needed to know about pleasing a man.

"Where's your bedroom?"

Words have suddenly escaped me. I'm nervous. Not sure what to expect. What does play with me actually mean?

"Show us, darlin''."

He releases my hand from his boxers but continues holding the other one, lacing our fingers together and nodding for me to lead the way. Heavy footsteps follow behind us. My house isn't very big, so it takes us a matter of seconds to reach my bedroom. I lead us in. Tyler clicks the door closed behind us.

The guys seem to only be focused on one thing. My bed. If this were the other way around, I'd be looking at every tiny detail. But Archer seems to have no interest in my personal space. I suppose I should be flattered. This is how it's supposed to be.

"Take your panties off for Tyler, darlin''." My eyes go wide, and he chuckles, his cock hard as a rock, still sticking out of his boxers. He never even bothered to tuck it back in. "We want to see it. C'mon now. Don't make me ask twice."

There's an edge to his voice. I don't think he'd hurt me but punish me? Yes. For some reason I think he'd be very creative in the punishment department. Maybe it's the twinkle in his eye.

Darla J Michaels

The devil's glimmer. So, I comply. Reaching under my sundress and sliding my panties down my legs. I place them in Archer's outstretched hand and when he brings them to his nose to smell them my mouth falls open. All this is new to me and I'm curious about what's next.

He passes my underwear to who I now know to be Tyler. "Sit."

I sit on the edge of the bed, watching Tyler breath in the scent of me on the piece of fabric that was once between my legs while Archer climbs up on the bed and positions himself behind me. If I weren't so distracted with my new husband sitting behind me, feeling him poke into my back with his hard cock, I would swear Tyler licked the crotch of my panties.

"Is she going to need these today", Tyler asks Archer.

"Nope."

Tyler balls them up and tosses them across the room. I hear them land in my garbage can.

"I'll replace them", Archer tells me with a smirk as Tyler crosses the room to us, kneeling in front of me.

"Bethany, darlin''…The moment you said I do, you became mine. Every part of you. Show me what's mine." He plants a kiss on my neck while he waits for me to get the nerve to pull back the skirt of my dress. "Come on. Don't be shy. Let us see it."

With shaking hands, I grab the hem of my skirt and slowly drag it up my thighs. "Good girl", my husband gently encourages me. "Open your legs", he croons, planting another kiss on my neck. When I don't comply fast enough, Tyler places his large palms on my knees and spreads them open, just as my skirt uncovers my mound.

"Bethany", Archer breathes in awe. "Look at your wet little pussy. Come here", he orders me, as he turns my head so he can get access to my mouth.

Tell Me Who You Go With- Archer & Bethany

This kiss is so different from the few kisses we've shared. It's hungry. Needy. Urgent. And I feel myself getting wetter by the second as Tyler's thumbs gently rub up and down on the inside of my knees.

It's funny that allowing Tyler this access to my body doesn't feel so strange when Archer is kissing me. It's like he's got me, and I know he won't let anything bad happen to me even though this stranger is looking at my most private place.

Archer breaks the kiss and pulls back, his gaze drifting down my body. Sweat trickles from his hairline following his jaw. Our skin sticks together with the humidity. But the temperature is soon forgotten when Archer speaks.

"Look at Tyler's hands." No sooner are the words out of Archer's mouth than Tyler's hands are moving up my thighs. His hands are large and calloused. The hands of a working man.

"No one's ever touched me..." I let the words die as his hands are almost right there. Right where Archer wants them.

"I know. I know", Archer croons as Tyler's left hand moves past the bullseye and up to my waist. He grips me tight and glances up at Archer before he continues. "Let me give him this. Let me give him your first time being touched like this. You look like you need relief. Tyler..."

The tone in Archer's voice when he says Tyler's name is like a gunshot for a race. Contemplation is gone. There's only action.

I watch as Tyler swipes his thumb across my wet slit. When I try to close my legs, Tyler just uses an elbow and the side of his body to stop me.

"Bethany", Archer chastises as Tyler rubs me again.

"Oh..." It's all I can get out. I think my brain is going to explode. My husband, who I know almost nothing about, is letting a man touch me between the legs while he watches...and it feels so fucking good. Better than I could have ever imagined and I'm trying to close my legs. What is wrong with me?

I must be out of my mind. Either because I'm doing this or because I tried to stop it. But if I'm being honest, I'd have no chance of stopping it. Tyler could overpower me with no effort at all, and Archer leaves me speechless with the devil's smile and his gentle commands.

"Look at his hand. How he rubs you so nice. How he takes such good care of you."

There's a lapse in time. No one speaks. There's just breathing and the sound of my wetness on Tyler's fingers.

I'm so close it literally hurts. And the thing that pushes me over the edge is when Tyler reaches down to my opening, slides the tip of his finger inside me just barely and then runs it up and over my mound. With it, he takes my arousal and makes more of a mess over my clit. He haphazardly rubs my wetness over my skin, his own thick fingers covered in my intimacy.

When I orgasm, my legs fall open and I'm limp against Archer.

There's a knock at the door and I roll my head across Archer's chest, delirious with pleasure.

"They can go fuck off", he tells me, and I smile at him because that's all the strength I have right now.

"It's Braden", Tyler tells Archer, still rubbing me. When Archer shifts underneath me, Tyler stops him. He pulls his phone out of his back pocket and makes a call. "It's open." That's all he says before tossing his phone to the side with a clatter.

I can't take my eyes off Tyler as Archer kisses down my shoulder. Hy heart hammers against my chest while I listen to Braden's footsteps get closer.

There's a knock at the door and without waiting for an answer, it slowly opens. Braden is standing there in khaki pants and what looks to be a white linen button down with the sleeves rolled up. Almost like he planned on coming to our wedding but missed it. Or maybe like he's the next groom.

"How is she?" His question is to the room in general.

"Wet", Tyler answers. Braden nods and Tyler continues to gather more wetness from my entrance and slide it over my clit. Almost as if he's trying to tell me he isn't done yet.

"Did she tell you yet?" This time Braden's talking directly to Archer.

"That she's a virgin?" Braden simply nods. "Yeah. But the question I have for you doc, is why you didn't tell me."

Archer has a tone to his voice that I haven't heard him use in the short time that I've known him. He's irritated. I don't even have to look at him to know it.

"I thought maybe you knew. And then I started thinking about the look Bethany gave me during the exam. She looked like she had a secret. A secret that she realized I just found out about. And I picked up the phone to call you but then I thought what if..." Braden's eyes land on mine and travel down to Tyler's hand. "...what if the thought of you giving away your wife's virginity was such a turn-on that you were grateful I didn't tell you about it?"

The air is sucked out of the room. Archer's body tenses beneath me. When I turn to look at him it's as if he doesn't even see me acknowledge him.

"You want my wife's blood on your cock?"

I feel Tyler shift between my legs.

"Very much."

"And you knew about this." It's a statement that he directs at Tyler and this time, I can't tell if he's angry.

Darla J Michaels

"We don't have secrets", Tyler answers, the only justification to this possible betrayal.

"Starting now?" And there it is. The annoyance is back in Archer's voice.

"You'll know everything we know starting now. So, what's it going to be?"

The second I open my mouth to object, Tyler slides his wet fingers inside, shaking his head at me. When I start to move, Tyler secures one wrist and Archer secures the other.

I try to talk around his fingers, but Tyler slides them in deeper, gagging me.

"Right here? In her bed?"

"Anywhere you want." Braden smirks. "Am I forgiven?"

"Yeah."

I moan against Tyler's fingers and struggle in their grasp as Braden walks closer, unbuttoning his shirt.

"Bethany, Bethany, Bethany…" Archer calls my name rapidly, trying to stop my panic but when he doesn't get my attention the way he wants, he sinks his teeth into my earlobe, and I whimper. "Anything you want and then some. Whatever it is. All of it. I'll give it all to you when you give me this."

I say no around Tyler's fingers.

"I said anything Bethany."

I'm trying not to panic. This is not how I thought this would go. I thought it would be me and Archer first.

"Let Braden see her, Tyler." Still keeping a hold on my wrist and his fingers in my mouth, he moves from between my legs. "I'll be here the whole time." Archer turns my head as Tyler's fingers slide from my mouth. Archer's mouth is on mine. I can't object. The choice is taken from me. "He'll start out slow." Archer kisses me again and I moan when Braden starts rubbing me where Tyler left off.

"He'll slide his fingers inside you." I whimper at Braden's intrusion. "I bet he can make you come on the inside, can't you Braden?"

"Bethany relax", Braden gently orders me.

"Look at his hand work you down there." Archer sounds drunk with opportunity. "How he touches my wife just how I've asked him to."

I look down as Archer directs me to, watching Braden's hand moving between my legs in tandem with each wave of pleasure he evokes from me.

"She's tight." Braden doesn't look at anyone when he reports this. His gaze is fixed between my legs.

"It'll be perfect. Me giving Braden something that's supposed to be mine. Watching over you while he takes it. Then having you for myself. Bethany, darlin''...whaddayah think?"

"Kiss me", I whisper, caught up in how dirty this is. How dirty he is.

Archer smiles that smile of wicked delight. Like he knows he's doing something he shouldn't but can't help himself.

"Here she comes boys", Braden announces as I whimper and start spasming on his fingers.

"All you have to do is say yes, darlin'", Archer whispers in my ear before he's kissing me once more.

Here's the thing about the devil. He always presents an offer that's so good, so utterly tempting that you don't even think about how you might end up paying for it later. But you always pay. One way or another. Because the devil always gets what he's due.

Chapter 3
Archer

I've been listening to the sound of everything chirping and buzzing outside for hours. I'm wired. For the first time, I'm not sure what I want to do with a woman. But this is different. Because for the first time, I'm married. Not even twenty-four hours in and I can't sleep.

I'd like to think it's because of the bugs. Or maybe because Bethany doesn't have air conditioning. By choice. Who lives in Connecticut and doesn't have air conditioning? By. Choice.

I chuckle as I think of Marvin looking at me across the living room. My youngest brother stands there, sweating his ass off while Jonathan marries us in Bethany's living room. If there was a thought bubble above his head, it would probably say something like...yo Arch...you for real?

I swore him to secrecy. Momma wouldn't like this one bit. She'd like Bethany. That I have no doubt, but the secret wedding? I'm catching hell for that. I just hope Marvin can keep his mouth shut long enough for me to tell her. If not, I'll know the second she finds out.

My Bethany. I look down, hoping I didn't disappoint her last night. Hoping I didn't make her upset. But I couldn't do it.

There was something about the way she kissed me…I just felt like I didn't know enough about her to give her to someone neither of us barely knew. So, I broke up our little threesome and sent the guys packing. Tyler could have cared less. Braden, however, did not look happy. I'm sure there will be a discussion the next time we meet.

But it doesn't matter. Not really. He can be as pissed as he wants but what happens with Bethany is my decision to make. Just like I don't get a say about their Lady, they don't get a say about mine. The guys made that clear to me when I joined.

I look down at my virgin wife, sprawled out in bed with most of the covers off her. We never went to that hotel. We never left her house. I couldn't fuck her. It felt wrong. Even though she knew why I wanted to marry her, and she still said yes, it felt wrong. I was trying to do the right thing, but I may have disappointed her.

My hand falls between her shoulder blades, covering the tattoo I gave her. Her artist called in sick. I was glad. His image was basic. Bethany deserved better than basic.

She stirs under my touch, stretches and then lets out a little sigh, hands groggily moving over the covers to find my naked body. Her gold band glints in the moonlight.

Mine.

"Are you mad", she asks into the sheets while her hand grazes my cock and stops on my abs, her fingers feeling my taught sweaty skin.

"Right now? Yes. I'm mad at your living situation." She chuckles but I'm serious. "How can you sleep in this humidity", I ask in awe of this woman.

"We didn't have sex", she clarifies, turning to face me. The moon illuminates her face as she looks up at me. "Do you regret this?"

Now I am angry. She thinks I'd regret marrying her because we didn't have sex on our wedding night? I feel the need to demonstrate exactly why I made the choice that I did.

"Don't move, wife." I love saying that. For reasons I don't quite understand, calling her wife makes my cock rock hard.

Bethany huffs out a breath as I move her so she's lying face down onto the bed. I'm not gentle. I'm even less gentle when I spread her legs apart with my knees and lay on top of her. My cock is at her entrance and I'm dead weight on top of her.

She struggles underneath me. "Archer."

"Wife", I warn.

"Get off me." She's struggling but I don't shift my weight to relieve her. Instead, I press the tip of my cock against her entrance. "Archer! Stop!" She's trying to thrash underneath me, but she can't. The size difference alone is enough to have her pinned exactly where I want her.

I take things one step further and slide just the tip inside of her.

"Please", she hiccups, a scared sob threatening to break through.

I pause where I am, still inside her. "Shh, shh, shh", I try to settle her as I move the dark strands that have fallen across her face in the struggle. "I don't want you this way. I want you in every way that you'll allow me to have you, but not like this. Not by force", I grit out, because her pussy feels so good it's killing me. "But to answer your question, no. I'm not mad at you. And no, I don't regret this." I kiss down her neck and shoulder, feeling her soften underneath me. "I didn't know what I wanted to do with you yesterday. And until I do...until I know how I want to rid you of that insignificant piece of skin that you've been holding onto, you'll wait. You'll wait until I'm good and ready to take from my wife…or allow someone else to do it." She doesn't say anything, so I prompt her. "Yes, Archer."

"Yes, Archer", she whispers, as I slide off her and haul her into my arms, unwilling to let her go yet.

Bethany

"My mom is going to lose it", I tell Archer as he pulls me in for a kiss. It's three in the morning. The witching hour. And I'm sitting on my husband's lap of less than twenty-four hours, his cock sliding between my slick folds as he kisses me.

He scared the shit out of me just moments ago. I didn't take him for a rapist but the way he held me there and put just a bit of himself inside me...I didn't know in that moment if I'd love him or hate him.

"I wouldn't have done it", he breaks the silence to tell me before kissing me so thoroughly I'm breathless. "Bethany. Did you hear me? I said I wouldn't have done it."

My eyes drop to the flame tattoo on his chest, flicking up around his collarbone.

"You scared me", I admit, my fingers tracing the flames.

"I meant to."

My eyes snap to his.

"I'm serious, darlin'. Don't you ever throw out regret when it comes to you. Ever. I took vows. We took vows."

"You want a wife you can give to others to fuck. Your proposal wasn't out of love", I remind him. At least that's how he explained it to me.

"You're right. But except for your house, so far, I think we're on the right track for love, don't you?"

I don't answer him because I just don't know.

"Bethany?" Archer's hands palm my face. "Darlin'?" I look into his devilish eyes, not sure what to say, so I decide to tell the truth.

"I spelled you. And you were perfect. I mean...you are perfect. But I'm worried I'm not perfect for you." It's the sincerest thing I've ever said to another adult in the longest time. And he laughs. Not a chuckle. It's the loudest laugh I think I've ever gotten from someone. He's so caught up in laughing that his hands fall from my face.

Tears pool in my eyes. He's laughing at me. It hurts something fierce.

I need some air, so I swing my leg over his lap and start to crawl across my bed to freedom when strong warm hands haul me back, flipping me over so I'm looking at the ceiling. He isn't gentle this time either and I huff out a shocked breath when I land hard in an undignified heap. I don't have time to right myself before he's crawling over me, laying his body on top of mine. This time, I part my legs for him and this time he slides the tip in once more. I don't struggle against him, and I don't tell him to stop.

"I married a quick learner", he muses to himself, looking down at me. But my lips start to quiver because I've never felt more vulnerable in my life. "Now...", he grabs one wrist and brings it up and over my head. "Stay", he warns, pausing to look in my teary eyes before grabbing the other hand and doing the same. He secures my wrist with one hand and then plants a gentle kiss on my lips.

"Let me get this straight." He takes a long moment and looks into my eyes. I suck in a breath and when I let it out, it leaves me as a sob. He watches the tear roll down my cheek and when it makes it down far enough, he kisses the teardrop, then licks his lips.

"You think that because you cast a spell, you brought us together. And because that spell brought me to you, when I asked you to be my wife, that's the only reason you said yes?"

I nod, sniffling, my urge to cry growing quieter by the passing seconds. He doesn't look mad. I thought he'd be mad.

"Wow." He looks away from me, never shifting or releasing his grip. Then he lets out a heavy sigh, shaking his head. "I married a liar", he says to no one in particular. "Bethany", his voice softens. "The first time I met you, it was over for you. The way you blinked at me when I came out to do your tattoo like your vision was bad. Like you weren't sure if I was real...or you had something in your eyes." He smirks at me. "Let me see your mouth", he whispers and closes the distance between us.

What happens between us next is like alchemy. Two unlikely elements coming together, transforming into something unimaginable. Heat. Lust. Love. I could kiss him forever.

"Don't do that", Archer warns when I push up against him where we're just barely joined. "You wouldn't want to give that to someone you aren't perfect for now, would you?"

"You know what I mean", I start to object, even though I love the way he feels inside me just the tiniest bit.

"No. I don't. I kissed every inch of your body last night in this sauna I now own half of." I roll my eyes, and Archer gives me a look of displeasure. I raise my brows at him in challenge, and he bends down, shifting from inside me, taking my nipple into his mouth, biting down. I writhe underneath him as he moves to the other nipple, sucking hard before he bites again. Aside from my screams of shock that he bit me, I'm rubbing up against him because I need release. That little move flooded me with the need to come and I'm hoping he relives me from this sudden ache.

"And that wet little pussy you're rubbing all over me didn't seem to mind my mouth on it last night if I recall correctly." He's sliding his hard length through my wet lips, and I can't take my eyes off him. "I won't lie and say yours is the first pussy I've licked. Practice and all...but yours is the first pussy I'd like to lick forever."

I close my eyes as he runs his hard length back and forth through my wet slit. A moan escapes my mouth, causing me to forget about the terms. To forget that I may have manufactured something that was a disappointment to him as of yesterday after the deed was done.

"I didn't deflower you yesterday because I don't know if I want to." He takes my other nipple in his mouth and sucks, bringing me so close to orgasm I whimper.

I don't understand. He doesn't know if he wants to be the first man to have sex with me? I think I heard him wrong.

"Jesus. You like that don't you. You just got wetter. See, I was close yesterday. Fuck if I want to right now." His lips find my neck and I'm panting beneath him.

"Would you like that? I figure it's yours so you should get a say." I don't answer right away because I need to think. Instead of letting me think, he throws another idea out there. "Maybe I should ask Jonathan to do it. He married us and all."

Archer laughs when my eyes widen in response.

"No?" He peppers my skin with more kisses.

"It's not a fair question."

"I'm always fair...wife." He bites my neck and then takes my earlobe into his mouth.

"I need some air", I tell him, in a breathy voice I'm not used to hearing from myself. He releases my earlobe to let out a hearty laugh.

"Is this how long it takes for you to be fed up with the humidity? Let's go. I'm coming with you." And as quickly as I was pinned onto the mattress, he rolls of me and I'm free...and much cooler. Archer's added body heat is something else.

I watch him leave my room in awe at the site of him. Tall. Muscular. Tan. Tattooed. Pierced. Not who I thought spirit would bring me, but I have to trust they know better than I do.

I relax back onto the bed needing to think. And after a few seconds pass I realize thinking is not what I need. Feeling is what I need. Sensing...just being...

"Are you just trying to get rid of me?"

Archer stands in the doorway with the same pants he took off after we wed. He's got his boots on but no shirt. I can't help but to ogle him. If I didn't need to leave this house and talk with spirit, I'd call him back to bed just so I could keep memorizing his body with my fingertips and my mouth.

I toss the sheets off me and Archer hollers. You know, the kind of exaggerated type of catcall a construction worker or the like would give to a pretty woman. I can't help but laugh. He's funny and charming and I'm so blessed that he's mine.

"You'll want to put a shirt on." I look over my shoulder as he furrows his brow like I've lost my mind. "Mosquitoes", I clarify, pulling a thin long sleep dress from my closet and slipping it on, not bothering with a bra or panties.

"How far outside are we going?" He's amused. I like it and hate it in equal measure. This is the tough part about being who I am. It always has been. But maybe it doesn't need to be like that. I should be able to just let him know me without being embarrassed or self-conscious.

"There's a stream about a half mile through the woods. We'll cross it. You should take your shoes off and roll up your pants", I warn.

I grab my cards from the nightstand and brush past him as he stands there, looking at me confused. I glance at the clock in the kitchen. I'll only have about twenty-five minutes. We're cutting it close.

"Let's go Mr. Jackson. We're going to miss it." And without looking back, I leave through the front door and step out into the moonlight.

Present Day

Chapter 4
Bethany

"You spelled him?" Linea looks at me from across my kitchen table in disbelief.

"I did."

"Like...you wished for him?"

I can tell she's genuinely trying to understand the whole thing, so I cut her some slack. If you aren't someone who grew up believing in spirits and magic the concept can be tough to wrap your mind around.

"Not exactly. I told spirit what I wanted in the form of a spell and spirit brought me Archer."

Grace eyes me like I'm missing some of my marbles. It's not the first time someone has reacted this way. It's why I keep this part of me to myself.

"Explain it", Grace challenges.

My eyes shift to Hawk when he lets out an amused huff. The ladies glance his direction and then back at me.

"Spell him", Grace suggests, tilting her head in Hawk's direction.

Linea's eyes widen. "Can you?"

"Be serious", Grace chastises Linea.

"Yes." It's one word spoken with absolute faith and authority. Hawk sets his phone on his leg and makes eye contact with me. I don't look away. Grace chuckles. She sounds like a villain, and I smile because she reminds me of the female version of my husband.

"So", she prompts in question.

"I have to have intention, or it doesn't work."

"Can I do it", Linea offers. I shrug at her question. I suppose anyone can do it. It depends on how in tune you are with yourself, how badly you want it and what it is you're asking for. "It would be kind. Like...for him to win the lottery or something."

"I'd still keep this job just to get under your skin", Hawk volunteers from across the room. I can see Linea's jaw clench and try not to smile...but I can't help it. I like these two. Linea narrows her eyes at me and scowls. Quite impressive for her. I didn't think someone with her disposition could scowl but perhaps she's evolving.

"Hawk." His eyes dart to mine. "Would you mind just standing up."

"I don't think so."

"I'm not up to anything. I swear."

"I think it's safe for you to stand, Hawk", Grace encourages in a patronizing tone. "No offense", she tells me.

None taken. I get it all the time.

34

Darla J Michaels

I slide my chair out from the kitchen table and cross the small space over to Hawk. When I stop in front of him, he eyes me speculatively like he believes I could bend his will with magic. I simply look him over. He's nice to look at.

"I don't know what your problem is with him", I call out over my shoulder. "He's attractive." Hawk smirks at me and shakes his head. "Is he normally this quiet? I mean, Archer is kind of quiet but sometimes he's a talker and I need silence to work."

"He's always quiet", Linea tells me, irritation clear in her voice. "Always watching. I have no idea what he reports to Braden but it's beyond irritating."

Hawk smiles at Linea's comment. It's a nice smile. A mischievous smile. It kind of reminds me of Archer's smile.

And that's when I hear it. The ringing in my ears. It always happens when spirit is trying to get me to pay attention to something.

"How old are you?" Hawk tilts his head to the side as if he doesn't understand my line of question. "You're a Leo", I tell him. I don't know why. I just feel it. He nods in confirmation.

I step forward and bend down, looking into his eyes. He hasn't said more than five words since the ladies have arrived. Hazel. I look at his brow line, his jaw line and finally his full lips.

"Say my name", I all but command him. "Bethany", I prompt, in case he doesn't know it. I stare into those familiar eyes as he considers my demand.

"Bethany."

"Shit", I whisper.

Archer

I have a client coming into the shop mid-afternoon. It should be just enough time for me to decompress from the meeting with Micah, Jonathan and Harlan. I take an occasional client to keep my skills up. Plus, I have an apprentice. When I work, I like him to shadow. But I can't do any of that until I shake off the morning meeting.

I don't know what has gotten into Micah and Jonathan. Those two can't see eye to eye for the life of them. I'd like to think it has to do with Braden but I'm not so sure. I agree with Jonathan. Keeping Braden out of this is for the best right now. At least until we formulate a plan. Braden works best with all the information. The last thing we'd want is for Braden to think we're going to cause harm to Linea. It won't end well. I do know that for sure.

The most work we got done today was a short list of people to put away, but we all know the list is going to get longer. The more we dig into things the more we'll add to the list. This isn't just avenging Linea. It's evolved to taking this whole twisted thing down. I don't disagree with that either but if we're going to make this bigger than taking down those who wronged Linea, we need to be on the same page.

We all have our assignments. Harlan is going to dig up everything he can find on everyone who makes one of our lists. Based on what we know and what we learn from Harlan, Micah is going to put together a list of things we need to prove so we can put some of these people in prison. He'll also tell us who we're most likely to get a conviction on. Everyone else will end up on the hit list. His legal mind will help us tease this out. He also needs to decide how this is going to go down. The case could wind up with the district attorney, but Micah may be able to have someone in his firm partner on it. Strike a deal of sorts. It's unusual but we all decided we aren't doing all this work just to have someone on the outside fuck it all up.

Jonathan's job is to find out what the third thing women can be in this disgusting arrangement. Micah didn't come through. Jonathan was pissed. He accused Micah of trying to sabotage their work. His comment struck a nerve with Micah. Anything where Linea is concerned seems to strike a nerve with him lately.

And my job? It's to keep us focused and on task.

My phone rings on Bluetooth while I'm pulling into our driveway. Momma. I take a deep breath and pick up the call.

"Hey Momma", I greet her with enthusiasm even though I'm faking it. I'm emotionally drained right now.

"Archer, baby, where have you been. You haven't stopped by to say hello and I want to see that wife of yours. How is she? Are you treating her well?"

"Of course I'm treatin' her well. And she's just fine. Better than fine. How are you Momma?"

"Well, you wouldn't have to ask me that question if you came to visit more often."

I rest my forehead on the steering wheel and take a deep breath.

"I know. You're right. I have no good excuse Momma."

"You'll be married for five years this July." She waits. I know she's still mad about not being invited to the wedding.

"Yes, Momma. Five years." Just thinking about our wedding day warms my heart. Bethany looks as beautiful today as she did when I first met her. Hasn't changed a bit.

"I want to have you two over for dinner."

Tell Me Who You Go With- Archer & Bethany

"We'll look at our calendars and let you know what we have available", I offer.

"For your anniversary. But I expect to see you sooner", she clarifies.

"Well, I'll look at calendars", I tell her again, but she cuts me off.

"You know, I didn't even get to see my baby get married."

I don't apologize. I simply let another heavy sigh speak for itself.

"Momma...I promise you the moment I step foot inside and greet my wife I will look at the calendar and give you a date."

"Mmmmhmmm."

"I love you Momma."

"I love you to, Archer."

I cut the engine to the truck and sit there for a moment watching the rain pelt the windows. It's April and we're in the thick of the rainy season. It's in the mid-fifties and never stops raining. I don't mind it. Bethany on the other hand makes do. She likes to be out in nature when she reads her cards. The closest compromise we've made was building her a little shack to protect her from the rain so she can read without getting her cards wet. Our house is just at the edge of heavily wooded land, which I also own so I had Tyler send some of his guys out to make her a place that would allow her to escape the elements long enough to read. Sometimes I'll go with her but many times, she leaves and comes back, climbing back into bed with me, snuggling her cold wet body up against mine.

Just thinking about her and how different she is from all the women I've met...even those in The Brotherhood makes me smile. I wouldn't trade her for the world.

But I must admit, on top of all my other frustrations, she's at the top of my list right now. I read the report that Hawk sent

Darla J Michaels

out. Bethany kicked them out of her house with no explanation. Why would she do that? It makes no sense.

She has some explaining to do. We don't allow disrespect in The Brotherhood. And Hawk made it sound like the ladies were just as confused as he was. I won't have Bethany start acting out like Linea. Bethany had her turn years ago and we addressed her grievances. I won't tolerate another season of her antics. We're going to shut this down right fucking now.

As soon as I heard about their time together getting cut short, I called her to my house. I call it mine instead of ours because I want nothing to do with her witchy little cabin. She has her turf, and I have mine. We like it that way. Normally we stay the night at my place. Occasionally I'll concede to staying at hers.

The moment I step out of my truck, it rains harder, and I wonder if the universe is trying to tell me not to go in yet. But I don't have time for an invite into my own home. I gotta keep this day moving and if I don't like what I hear from Bethany, she may be coming with me to the shop.

I take my time walking to the back door. The rain feels good even though it's cool out. And maybe I need the rain to recalibrate me. I'm stressed and I hate having important conversations when I'm stressed. So far, it's all I've done today.

The house is open. I hate it when she leaves the doors unlocked when she's alone. Someone would be stupid to break into my house but even still, I'd feel better if she were behind locked doors, even with Spirit there.

I don't make it a secret that I'm home. Scaring her is not my intention, even though it might teach her a lesson about locking doors.

Spirit's deep bark greets me. He nuzzles at my hand as I make my way to my wife. I'm thankful he's not a jumper. We had him trained by a professional when he was a pup. It's made all the difference now.

The moment the door opens, I smell it. Her simmer pot as she calls it. The smell of cinnamon, orange and cloves waft through the air. I'm sure there's other things in her pot too, but I won't ask. As long as it doesn't smell like shit, I'm not concerned about it.

When I enter the kitchen, she's stirring the pot clockwise and murmuring something I can't understand.

"The door was unlocked", I tell her, interrupting her. She pauses for a moment, opens an eye to acknowledge me, then she shuts her eye and keeps stirring. This time, she's quiet. I know what she's doing. She doesn't want me to know what she's up to so she's saying her incantation in her head.

"I don't like magic in my house, Beth", I warn. It's true. I don't. I respect who she is and what she does, but it makes me uncomfortable. I didn't believe in it before her. Then she made me a believer. "Beth", I warn her, sternly.

Slowly her eyes open and all I see there is concern. For what, I'm not sure.

"You're all wet", she tells me, her eyes still sad but looking me over. I realize, she may not have thought a thing of dismissing the ladies. She doesn't sass the ladies. Just us men from time to time. Maybe that's why the report surprised me. Her behavior is unusual.

I reach back and grab my shirt, tugging it over my head and setting the wet material on the counter. She sets the wooden spoon on the stove and turns her full attention to me. And for the first time since I entered the kitchen, I really look at her. She's in the long sleeve black dress she wears when something's wrong. Really wrong. It flows out from her slim waist kind of like you'd see a woman wear in the 1950s. No shoes. Her hair piled high on top of her head.

"Bethany." I softly call her name because I don't want her thinking she's in trouble even though she might be. She steps up to me and looks my face over like she's trying to see something new. Her fingertips brush my jaw, cheekbones and brow line and for a moment she closes her eyes. When she opens them, looking into my eyes, hers widen a fraction before she averts them.

"Darlin'...what's goin' on? Did something happen this morning?"

Her fingers skate down my arms and then she walks behind me, her breath hitching a bit at what I'm not sure.

I want to give her a chance to explain before telling her what I know even though she knows we report out on them. She should know that I'm well aware of the happenings at her house this morning. But when she doesn't say anything, I start firing off questions.

"Did you spell him?"

"No." She steps to the front of me.

"Did you want to?"

"No."

"Did the ladies say something?"

"No."

I grip her by the shoulders and instantly regret it when her eyes snap up to mine. "You were rude", I tell her, trying to soften my approach but failing. I'm frustrated by this day, and my patience is almost gone.

Her eyes well with tears and I feel remorse for how I just handled her.

"What happened", I ask as I back her up to the counter and hoist her up next to where I laid my wet shirt.

The tears start to fall, and she shakes her head. "I'm not going to tell you yet."

"Is that so?" She nods. I get angrier. "Have it your way darlin'." I will not tolerate this. When I ask a question, I expect an answer. And if we're playing games then let's play some games.

"It's not the right time", she tells me, whipping tears from her cheeks and straightening her posture.

"I understand. Let me see your mouth, darlin'." She leans forward and I smirk. No, no...she's got it all wrong.

Her breath hitches when I slide her from the counter and onto her feet. "Knees." It's one word that makes her eyes widen. "Now."

I have had an incredibly long day so far and it's barely half over. If we weren't hiding that we were meeting, I would have messaged one of the women to come over and service me. But no one can know we're meeting but us, so blowing off steam wasn't an option earlier. But now? Steam will be blown, and lessons will be taught.

I slide my phone from my back pocket, opening the app for her implant and setting it on the counter behind her. "I will give you one more opportunity to tell me what happened this morning." When she looks away from me, I snap.

Before I realize what I'm doing, my hand is in her hair and I'm turning her to face the tent in my pants. She grabs at my wrists in what seems like an attempt to get away.

"I'm not punishing you, Beth." Her punishment will be worse.

I work my pants open with one hand while I hold her head with the other. She's nervous that I'll be rough with her. She should be. I haven't seen this kind of defiance from her in a long time. It looks like she needs a reminder of how things work in The Brotherhood.

"Open." She glares at me when her lips part. If I wasn't pierced, I'd shove myself into her mouth. Since I don't want to chip her teeth, I issue one more stern order. "Wide."

I decide I'm going to take my time with her. Why rush? Getting head is such a beautiful act. It should be savored. And with the morning I've had, I am going to enjoy something about this day if it kills me.

I tip my head back the moment I'm inside her mouth. Jesus this is heaven. With my eyes shut, I find a rhythm and pace that works for me. And when it doesn't work for her, she starts to struggle against me.

I simply take my other hand and place it under her chin while I tighten my grip on her hair. She gags as I look down at her. Mouth full of my hard cock, drool dripping down her chin...mascara starting to run down her cheeks.

"I forgot how pretty you are like this, Beth. It's been a while", I grit out. I slide to the back of her throat until she swallows out of reflex when she gags. "You're doin' so good, Bethany." She gags hard but it doesn't deter me. She can take it. I have trained her well over the years. "You're okay...you're okay", I reassure her as I force her to take me deep once more. I like how she presses against my thighs with her palms. If it didn't feel so fucking good, I'd laugh at her attempt to get away from me.

"I thought we were closer than this, Beth." Her eyes roll up to look into mine. They still look sad. "Don't play with me, darlin''." She had the chance to make this right. Even still, I give her another opportunity. I'm still going to cum in her mouth but at least I'll let her get off if she answers my question.

I slide out of her mouth, and she swallows thickly, looking up at me, never breaking eye contact.

"What's it gonna to be?"

5 Years Earlier- Mid-May

Chapter 5
Bethany

I have been staring at the altar I made for hours. The sun is finally beginning to rise and I'm nervous...and skeptical. But I've never known Gram to lie. In fact, she was the most accurate person I think I've ever known. She just knew things...which is why I'm sitting here with sweaty palms and hope in my heart that this will work.

To say I'm feeling desperate is an understatement. I want love. Real love. Like the kind you read in books or see in movies. The kind where you look across the room and make eye contact with the person you're supposed to spend the rest of your life with and that's it. You just know.

She didn't exactly tell me how to do it. I think that would have been wrong. Then it would have been her spell, not mine.

Doubt creeps up my spine as I look at the arrangement. I've got two red tapered candles inside a heart made of pink salt. A bud vase of pink tea roses is on the metal tray. It's near a bundle of cinnamon sticks and vanilla beans.

And for reasons I don't quite understand, I felt called to place some fine tipped drawing markers on the tray, some peppermints and a beer. Brewed Awakening. It's made at a brewhouse in the area.

I'm hesitating. How ridiculous. Spells don't really work...do they? My mother would say they don't, but then again, my mother and I are nothing alike. I'm more like Gram than I am mom. Maybe I'm hesitating because I believe the spell will work too well. Like maybe I'll wish for love and have so many men attracted to me I won't be able to choose. The thought makes me laugh out loud. Be practical Bethany, I mentally chastise myself. That would never happen.

If I don't do this now, I'm going to miss it. I shake my hands out at my sides and wipe my sweaty palms down my nightgown. Closing my eyes, I take a few deep breaths to center myself and just visualize what I want.

Love. Commitment. A man who is sweet, attractive and knows his way around the bedroom. He has to be funny and kind. Not just to me but to everyone. And he has to embrace who I am deep down inside. Accept that my practices aren't like others. That I believe in the healing power of food and nature. That I know there are spirits out there that guide us every day. He has to love me for me even on the days when I'm not so sure who I am. Oooh...and he has to love kids. I love kids. I want kids.

Out of nowhere, the words just come to me.

Find me love
True love that will never leave me
A love so strong that the pull is undeniable

Darla J Michaels

A bond so deep that we're constantly drawn together
through you spirit
Find me the man who is mine forever and who I belong to
Bless me every day with his presence.
Spirit show me how strong you are
Send my soul's match to me
And so it will be done

When I open my eyes the candles flicker brightly. Their flames tall and strong. For some reason I can't explain, I reach out and uncap the beer, taking a hearty swig. Delicious. Just like he'll be, I think. I take a seat on the couch and drink the beer, watching the candles glow.

It's officially dawn. Soon the birthday calls and texts will start coming in. It will be a reminder of how badly I want something different in my life. A true connection, not just a familial one.

I push the thought of going through the motions aside and sip my beer. "Mine", I whisper, just over the bottle's opening before taking a swig. I close my eyes as the suds slide down my throat and inhale the delectable scent at the bottle's opening. He'll smell like this from time to time. When he bends in to kiss me and press his lips against mine, wet with beer, his tongue tasting of mischief.

The hairs on my arms stand up so I continue, assembling who spirit will bring me, resigned to finishing the beer with my eyes closed. Mischief. Yes. He gets into mischief a lot. He breaks twice as many rules as he makes. And he's feisty. Not afraid to put someone in their place.

His smile is a mix of wicked and friendly. Sometimes they blend together and it's hard to tell which is which. He looks intimidating. Maybe a bit of a bad boy. But he'd never be bad to me or anyone else who didn't deserve it.

And he likes affection. When we're together, he wants to feel me near him, and he likes to feel my hands on him too.

And the outdoors! He loves the outdoors. Just spending time sitting on the back porch listening to nature all around us in the moonlight while we snuggle each other and share a beer…And he'll pull me onto his lap and kiss me senseless. My God is he a good kisser. He's such a good kisser that he doesn't have to take. He simply leads and I follow without encouragement.

And that's when I see it. It's a flash of eyes. Beautiful hazel eyes with black eyebrows. I think it was a vision, but I wouldn't know for sure. Maybe that's what the third eye is all about. I'm still learning. But I know what I saw. Hazel eyes. If spirit is sending a man to me with hazel eyes, I'll know exactly who my true love is when I see them.

I finish the beer and bask in how it warms my bones. I don't drink a lot. It probably isn't something I should do before school but by the time I'm in class it will have worn off.

I don't want to do today. A card and cake will be waiting in the teacher's lunch area. No one really cares. It's a date the principal marks on the calendar and alerts everyone to chip in and wish me a happy birthday. The whole thing is awkward really. And the cake is gross. For a moment, I think about calling in…but I won't. I would never do something so irresponsible. Besides, my students are counting on me, and a sub just won't do. And if I took the day off, I'd talk myself out of my after-school appointment. There's no doubt in my mind about it.

I get ready for school, considering turning my phone on do not disturb or maybe turning it off altogether. But I don't. If I don't answer my messages, my mother will be over in a flash and I'd rather she wish me a happy birthday from the comfort of her own home...not mine.

I compromise. I take my phone and put it in my car. Then I set an egg timer for the number of minutes before I would need to leave, minus five so I can quickly respond to any messages that come in before I get to school. After school is out, I don't want to be bothered. That's my time and I'm protecting it. I can call my parents back on the drive to school. This way, I have a defined end time to end the call. And during the call, I'll mention an after-school activity, so they'll think I'm working late on a school night. But really the after-school activity is my activity.

Satisfied with my plan, I get in the shower. I'd love to take a relaxing bath. Ordinarily I'd celebrate my birthday in the evening with some wine and chocolate but I won't be able to do that tonight. The bath will have to wait. I can make peace with that.

I shiver at the chilly morning temperature. Normally, I use the wood burner to heat my small home instead of the heat when the temps don't drop too low. There's something about the crackling of the fire and the ambiance that makes my soul sing. The only downside is that it's a bit chilly when you're getting ready to step into the shower. Getting out can be worse. Still, I like what I like. And wrapping up in a fuzzy robe with a piping hot mug of coffee is worth it. I like the pleasure that comes after the discomfort. Discomfort makes pleasure feel ten times better. I wonder what that says about me.

My mind wanders under the hot spray. Today is going to be wonderful. I can feel it. This birthyear is going to be unlike any other year I have experienced. The hazel eyes I saw in my mind's eye give me faith that my deepest desires are going to manifest right before my very eyes.

Tell Me Who You Go With- Archer & Bethany

I silently thank Gram for her wisdom and influence. I don't know where I'd be without her. Much to my mother's dismay, she taught me so many things about witchcraft and spiritual living. My life has never felt more fulfilled. I think it's a calling. Somehow, she just knew that about me. That I'd take to the practice effortlessly. God, I miss her.

She was a force of nature that never had to raise her voice or a brow. You know the kind. When they walk in a room you feel them before you see them? Silent at the kitchen table yet you turn to them because they compel your attention, so you hear everything they have to share?

I think she freaked my sisters out. Stepping out of the shower I smile at the memories. I would run up to Gram the moment I saw her, but my sisters would stand back and huddle together. Almost like having safety in numbers.

The girls are eight years younger than me. That reminds me. It's been a while since we've seen each other. I'll have to have them over for a sleepover when school is out. I'm so busy with school that I don't get as much time to see them as I'd like. I'm sure they're quite busy with school, friends and boys.

In my fuzzy robe, I sit down at my vanity table. A gift to myself when I bought my cabin in the woods. Dark antique wood, claw feet, ornate handles to match an ornately framed mirror and beautifully carved high back wooden chair to match.

It sounds funny, but I can feel the energy radiate off this piece of furniture. It called to me the moment I saw it. Like it was already mine.

I couldn't leave it there. I also couldn't exactly afford it. But the nice man at the antique shop allowed me to make payments and in a few short months, the piece of furniture was mine.

Sitting at this piece of furniture has become my morning ritual ever since and I couldn't possibly have it any other way.

Darla J Michaels

Getting ready is a simple process for me. I don't wear a lot of makeup. It's just never called to me, and I don't think I need it. After a quick application of tinted moisturizer and some mascara, I'm done.

There's no need for blush because even though I have a fair complexion, I've had rosy cheeks for as long as I can remember. And I'm not a big fan of eyeshadow. It makes my eyes dry. I also think it looks incredibly ridiculous on me.

I swipe some berry tinted lip gloss on my lips although that isn't entirely necessary either. My lips have a natural color to them that is beautiful on their own.

Then I pull the towel down and free my black hair. Pulling my jar of flax gel from my vanity table, I scoop a generous amount of my homemade curl tamer with my fingertips and rub it together between my palms before finger combing my long strands.

My fingers slide easily through my hair without the need for a brush. I decide I'll wear my hair down today, showing off my naturally curly hair. It's not a tight curl until the weather turns humid.

In no time I'm enjoying a cup of coffee in the quiet, shuffling my cards now instead of before sunrise. Something had to give so I could do my love spell. This was it. I prefer to be outside while I'm reading my cards, but since I'm dressed for the day, the kitchen table will have to do. Besides, the cards are going to say what the cards are going to say and at this point, my deck knows me well enough that location likely doesn't matter.

I close my eyes as I shuffle the deck, focusing on the sounds the cards make as they slide against each other and the weight of the deck in my hands. And when I'm confident that spirit is going to tell me what I need to know, I begin pulling cards from the deck.

Today, I'll pull five cards because today, I turn twenty-three and adding the digits in twenty-three makes five.

I do this with my eyes closed. I'm simply feeling. It's intuition and I know when I'm channeling spirit because I get this ringing in my ears. Some would call it tinnitus, but I know better.

Once I have the cards laid out, I flip them over. I do not want to do today.

Every card carries a warning. The moon, the hermit, the nine and ten of wands and finally the sun reversed. So basically, my day is going to be full of negative emotions, drained energy, being on guard, anxiety and loneliness. Fantastic.

Chapter 6
Archer

I flip open today's appointment calendar before Trix gets in. One of my artists called in sick today which means we're either canceling some clients or I'm taking them.

I don't mind taking the clients as long as the flash is done and we're on the same page. Typically, we meet with clients ahead of time for a consult, so we know exactly how much time to schedule and what's involved in getting the artwork finished. That's not the case with my sick artist. Looks like he's got all his consults done except one. Bethany Everly. Five thirty appointment for a witch's knot between the shoulder blades.

It looks like the time was scheduled to give her the tattoo, but she hasn't signed off on the image yet. This could be a problem. I may have to reschedule her. If she doesn't like what she sees, it'll need to be redrawn. It's unusual for one of my artists to schedule this time without the commitment from the client. I wonder why he did that?

I write my name by the clients on my sick artist's calendar, so Trix knows I've got them. He's booked solid today. I didn't take any clients today because this is the day during the week that I decided to get the boring business side of things done. I'll have to push that stuff back to my next admin day, which isn't a problem because I'd rather be tattooing than I would bookkeeping.

Done with today's calendar, I grab the artist's flash folder and head back to my office to study the drawings.

As I head to the back of the shop, I feel a sense of intense gratitude for the life I have. This is more than I ever would have dreamed. If the me of today would have told the me as a child that I'd be a talented tattoo artist with my own shops, I wouldn't have listened.

No one wanted me when I was a kid. Why would anyone want me as an adult?

I push the bad memories aside as I pass each tattoo station. The building is big for a tattoo shop, but I had to make it that way. Once word got around about the tattoos I do, I had a waiting list that I'd never be able to take care of. It's the reason I decided to start my own business. Patrons settled for the honor of getting tattooed in my shop if they couldn't get one from me.

Eight tattoo stations line one side of the wall and eight line the other. My boots thunk across the hardwood floor as I look at the vintage decor I'm walking through to get to my office. It resembles the 1940s.

Vintage light fixtures hang from the ceiling with Edison bulbs. Of course, the artists have spotlights to work with but the place in general is dim.

We have flash art on the walls but it's classy. The best flashes my team has created are framed and put on display. And unlike the ways of the past, if it's in the frame, the artist won't do another like it. It's merely meant as advertisement of the possibilities we can create for our clients. And let me tell you, when you tell a client they can't have something that catches their eye, they get really invested in working with the artist who created the image to have something even better and more personalized than what's displayed.

The color scheme is in reds, greens and blues. Think romance and rebellion. They're a heady mix when combined.

The chairs are barber style chairs, and each station is equipped with everything the artist needs to do their work. They maintain their own station and I make sure everything they need is available to them...which is part of what I won't be getting to today.

The team will be here in about an hour to get ready for their first clients. Trix normally gets here before the artists do. She's a Godsend. She runs our calendars better than anyone I have ever had at the desk. If she left me, I don't know what I'd do without her.

I grab my keys from my pocket and unlock my office door. I specifically asked for a doorknob that took a skeleton key. When I say that I love my building, especially my office space, I do mean just that.

My office has a large antique dark wood desk at the back, and a barber chair sits prominently in the middle of the room with vintage cabinets that house all my art supplies. I have a drafting table next to a large, seeded glass window. It's not the best view because it faces the backs of a few shops downtown, but it's allowed me to get to know those merchants, which has come in handy a time or two.

Among my favorite stores is Sinful. It's a cupcake shop. Gourmet flavors I never could have dreamed up. So good. If I only have time to eat one thing during the day, I'll go in the back and snag a few treats to carry me through. A close second is the coffee shop next door and third would be the flower shop. I cannot begin to count the number of times that flower shop has saved me. Not for women. I've never dated someone long enough to bring them flowers, but for my momma. I bring her flowers when I come to visit. A fresh bouquet is a staple I never leave without now.

I've had a writing tool in my hand to sketch with since I can remember. I'd sketch whatever was on my mind constantly. At first, it started out as doodles. Then, as my propensity to tune out the world became greater, I fell deeper and deeper into my artwork. I think sketching saved me. I know that sounds strange but there were so many things I could have done other than draw to pass the time when my parents abandoned me.

Plenty of trouble to find with the bad kids in the neighborhood. Plenty of things to steal. Just plenty of everything that would have made my dismal situation worse.

So, I stayed in my home alone as long as I could before someone came to seal up the house for lack of payment. By the time they came, the cupboards were bare anyway. The place provided me with shelter but everything else had eventually been cut off.

We had no electricity which meant no running water or temperature control. Thankfully it was spring. I had blankets and sweatshirts to keep me warm.

Sketching was the only thing that made my heart full and gave me purpose. So, I'd sit at the kitchen table no matter the circumstance and pull art supplies my mother had left for me in a dented metal box along with a few pads of paper and just get lost in my artwork.

I run my hand over the box that saved me. It sits prominently on my drafting table, holding some of the tools I sketch with. This box was the only thing I took with me when I was forced to leave the house. I've never been without it. Partly because it was from my biological mother who to this day still causes an ache in my heart when I think about her. But the other part is because this work is what I was called to do. I'm an amazing artist.

When I open my guy's flash folder, I let out a heavy sigh of dissatisfaction. He's newer. Not bad...but not great either. I remind myself that I hired him because he has potential and potential turns into greatness with practice hours.

His work lacks emotion, creativity, dimension...everything a person should have in their image if it's going to live on their physical form for the rest of their life. These flashes are just basic. But the clients signed off on them, so it is what it is. Besides, I won't have time to redraw them but for some, I could add color or maybe a little flourish here or there if they allow it.

It really depends on the client. Some will let you tattoo damn near anything on them, and others want only what they've approved. I close the folder and make a mental note to give my artist some feedback and encouragement when he's feeling better.

A nock sounds at my door. Trix is leaning in the frame with my coffee.

"You are a lifesaver", I groan, taking in the bakery box she's holding.

"I got you six", she tells me, crossing the threshold to set my coffee and cupcakes down on my desk.

Most men drool over Trix. She's gorgeous. Tall, long dark hair, beautiful brown eyes, full lips with a ring right through the center of her lower lip, long dark lashes, porcelain skin...she's a bad boy's wet dream. And her clothes are always dark and tight. I've seen more of her mid-section than I have of any woman in my entire life. And she always wears these heeled black boots that announce her arrival everywhere she goes.

But she does nothing for me. I know she likes me, but I'm not interested. Number one, she works for me. I don't mix business with pleasure. Not only because I don't think it will work out well, but I also need some space. My girl needs to do her thing and let me do mine. That way, when we come together at the end of the day, the only place we want to be is in each other's arms.

And number two, there's no pull between us. She's competent, brings the men back for more by way of her appearance and keeps me updated on the things I need to know around the shop.

"Did you treat yourself?" I smirk at her because I already know the answer.

"No. You did." She winks, turns on her heel, and walks out of my office back to her desk out front.

I laugh hard. She's a spitfire and quick witted. I like it. She keeps me on my toes.

I decide to take the time to drink my coffee hot and relax while I enjoy what is likely going to be the best part of my day. A cupcake, coffee and quiet.

Don't get me wrong, I love tattooing clients...when they're mine. These people are strangers that have won the tattoo lottery by getting me today, but they aren't my clients. I get excited to tattoo the people I have relationships with. These people will likely just come and go.

The day goes by quick. It's the dinner hour and I've never been so grateful my client came in drunk. I sent him home. We don't tattoo people who are high or drunk. Too much liability. Too much regret. Too much drama later.

To be honest, I was thankful for the cancelation. It allowed me to grab some food before my last client gets here. The witch's knot.

Darla J Michaels

I'm fully aware that this client could cancel too. She needs to approve the flash and if she doesn't like it, she's going to need to reschedule. I have nothing left in the tank for her today.

I shove the last bite of my burger into my mouth when I hear Trix's footsteps getting closer to my door. I don't normally eat like shit but there was no saving this day and the greasy food hit the spot.

I'm looking right at the door when she stops in front of it. She cocks her head to the side and smirks.

"Last client is here."

"Thank you, Trix." She looks annoyed. "Everything okay", I prompt, confused because Trix normally isn't one to hold back.

"You're going to have an early evening. Trust me." And with that, she clicks her red fingernails on the door frame, presses her lips together in dissatisfaction and leaves me alone with her cryptic remark.

Chapter 7
Bethany

Well this is just great, I think, while walking behind the receptionist at The Ink Parlor. This woman doesn't want me here. She doesn't have to say it. Her face does. Thankfully, she won't be doing my tattoo.

"Your artist called off. Archer agreed to take you", she informs me, looking over her shoulder, annoyance clear in her features. She tells me that Archer agreed to take me as if he wouldn't have otherwise done it. As if I should consider myself lucky for his generosity. Maybe I should. I've never done this before. But her comment is still rude.

It's not lost on me that she doesn't want me here. It's fine really. This whole experience will just go right along with the rest of my craptastic day. May as well round things out with consistency.

She knocks on the frame of the door, standing in the entryway so I can't see in.

"Bethany", she says my name to this Archer guy in a terse kind of way.

Darla J Michaels

I hear heavy books cross the floor.

"That'll be all Trix. Thank you", the voice with a hint of southern drawl dismisses her kindly.

Trix steps out of the doorway, gives me the side-eye and stalks off.

I look down out of nerves. I'm getting a tattoo today. A permanent addition to my body. It's going to hurt. And now this guy who I have never met will be doing it. I suppose it really doesn't matter. I barely knew the other guy anyway.

"Bethany", his warm voice calls to me, coaxing me to look up and face this man who's going to help me celebrate my twenty-third birthday with this permanent act.

My eyes go wide when they meet his. They're the hazel eyes I saw this morning after my spell while drinking the beer. It can't be. Can it?

"You are Bethany, right", he asks when I don't respond.

"Yes. Sorry." He holds up his hand, signaling for me not to continue.

"No. There's nothing to be sorry about. Your artist called in sick, so you get me if you're okay with it."

I'm nodding because words have escaped me. Could this really be happening? No. It's way too soon. Also, does this stuff really work? Could I have actually done a candle spell for the first time and have gotten what I asked for? It's unlikely. I don't believe it.

"Come on in", he prompts me, when he sees I'm not much farther in the room than I was when Trix saw herself out. "Have a seat." He motions to the chair in front of his desk. "We need to review the design before we get started."

When he turns to lead me to his desk, I take a moment to look him over.

Black hair. Longer on top and shaved in the back. Black henley, bunched up over his forearms exposing sleeves of tattoos on both arms and up his neck. The fabric of his shirt stretches over his muscular form. I've never met someone with enough discipline to have a body like his. Even his backside is toned.

When he rounds his desk, he opens a manilla folder and rummages through it. It gives me more time to look him over.

He's fantastic. Stubble on his jaw with a neatly trimmed beard and mustache. The patch of hair under his lip makes him look kind of dangerous. I follow his jawline up to his ear where a few piercings hang and I notice the deep slant of his brow.

Archer glances up at me and I suck in a breath. I have just been caught checking this man out. I'm mortified. He, however, takes delight in my embarrassment because he smiles and looks my face over before presenting me with the sketch.

Turning the paper to face me, he slides it across the desk for me to view.

A witch's knot. I look up at him and give him a shy smile. Well, looks like one person knows my secret.

"Is this what you asked for?" He asks me the question as though he can't believe I chose this.

"Yes, Archer." I answer him confidently, not understanding where this new voice has come from. I normally wouldn't be this confident. I'd normally just nod or give some quick reply where the words all run together.

He takes the sketch back and runs his fingertips over the drawing. Then he looks up at me and back down at the sketch.

"This is exactly what you requested", he clarifies.

"I asked for a witch's knot. This is a witch's knot." I must be missing something.

"Did you want this witch's knot?"

Darla J Michaels

"It's fine."

He chuckles and shakes his head.

"It's not fine. In fact, I'm going to redraw it."

This is the final straw. The worst end to the most horrible birthday ever.

Normally, I can keep it together, but not today. At first, my nose stings. It always happens before I cry. Then, I get a hot heavy lump in my throat. And finally, I shed the first tear.

"Okay", I choke out, turning for the door to leave without even looking back at him.

"Bethany...Beth", he calls to me sternly, shortening my name. No one has ever shortened my name. It gets my attention. I stop and sniffle as I wipe my cheeks. He lets out a heavy sigh. "Just...can you find something to do for a few hours? Then you can come back and I'll get you squared away?"

I nod without looking at him.

"Darlin'...it'll be just the two of us then. You comfortable with that?"

I pause, realizing that I don't really know this man. But when I look back at him, his eyes soften in that way that makes a person feel at home.

"You can bring a friend", he offers.

I chuckle. A friend? For a witch's knot? He cocks his head to the side, not understanding why I'd be averse to this.

"Seven thirty", I ask, to make sure I don't miss him.

"Seven thirty", he confirms.

I walk out of his shop, refusing to acknowledge Trix. I just can't take anymore of today's punishments.

The bar down the street is the perfect place for me to blow off some steam. As an ode to the man spirit is bringing me, I order the beer I drank this morning. And then I order a few more. Between the beer and greasy bar food, I'm feeling a little better about my day.

By the time I walk back into the tattoo shop, I'm relaxed, well-fed and ready to meet with Archer.

Trix lets out a heavy sigh when I enter and motions for me to follow her. She's quiet but then half-way down the aisle, she looks over her shoulder and says, "He does this with women from time to time. Don't get attached...he sure won't", and then looks straight ahead, paying me no mind. I'm not sure if her knock is more forceful or if it's just me but when she says my name, it sounds like it's dripping with sweetness we both know isn't genuine.

Archer thanks her in his low voice and Trix glares at me as she steps away from the doorway to let me in.

"Alright", he waves to me, and I enter, self-consciously because this is it. This is what I asked for.

"I like this one better, but of course I'm a little biased", he tells me as I cross the room. I give him a small smile but as soon as I get close enough to the table to see what's resting on it, my smile fades.

There, on the table are the exact art supplies I had on my altar this morning. I run my fingertip over one of the fine tipped pens. For some reason, I need to make sure I'm not imagining it.

"Bethany?" I look up at him as if a spell has been broken and I've left my world to enter his. "Are you alright?"

"Yes." The word comes out breathier than I expected and I can literally see the smile start in his eyes and spread to his mouth.

"Okay. You wanna look at the flash or my art supplies? If you're a good girl I'll let you draw with them later", he tells me with a wink. He's teasing me and I like it. I purse my lips

Darla J Michaels

together, trying to hide my smile. I like him. He's funny…and nice…and nice to look at…

I turn my attention to the flash, as he calls it. Its gorgeous. So gorgeous, I reach out to touch it, but Archer grabs my wrist, stopping me.

"No", he tells me, clipping the "o" and with a slight raise to the pitch. "It goes on the wall, darlin'." He nods straight ahead where several framed flashes hang with his signature in the corner. "You like it?"

I nod and step closer. When he releases my wrist, my body misses his touch. Not in a sexual way. More like when someone touches you and they absorb all your burdens. Somehow your body just knows everything is going to be okay.

Archer's image looks like it jumps right off the page. A steel witch's knot on top of a steel circle. Inside each knot is the sign representing the elements.

Around the image in each knot, it's colored to represent the element that the metal circle fails to contain. Flames for fire come outside of the steel ring in a whimsical blaze, turning into smoke and air that mix like clouds in a thunderstorm for the air sign. A beautiful blue ocean that pours out near the water sign and finally a rich green that swirls out like magical fog from the Earth knot.

"I want that."

Archer chuckles. "Good. I want you to have it. Let's get you changed. I'll unlock the front so you can grab your clothes, and we'll get started." He sees my face fall at the mention of changing. I didn't even think to bring a change of clothes, that's how distracted I was by the events of the day.

So here I am, standing in front of him in a dress. A dress that would not allow one to get a tattoo between their shoulder blades.

"So, in this case, we reschedule or improvise", he offers. "Can I see the back?" He holds his hand up in the air, points his index finger down and rotates his hand in a circle indicating I should turn around for him.

I let out a heavy sigh, close my eyes and turn around.

And then his hands are in my hair. No. One hand. One hand that grabs the hair at the nape of my neck...tight. He brings his hand up against the back of my head so he can see my dress.

"Bethany", he starts and lets out a heavy sigh. It won't work. Whatever he had planned feels like it won't work. "Darlin'..."

And suddenly, I don't care. I have had issue after issue all day long and nothing, especially a flimsy piece of fabric is going to get in my way of having this.

With all the liquid courage I have, I improvise. I don't think. I just act. Grabbing my skirt, I lift it up and pull the dress over the top of my head. "I want it", I tell him once more, balling my dress up and shoving the wadded-up material against his chest.

Chapter 8
Archer

I don't do this anymore. It's not worth it and to be honest, it's not as fun as it used to be.

Bethany stands in front of me completely naked except for panties and shoes. Panties that I can see through and heels that make her legs look like a snack.

Do not look at her breasts, Archer. Do NOT look at her breasts.

I realize I'm holding my breath when I let out a long exhale. "Lets...get that table ready for you", I concede.

She doesn't seem fazed at all. I watch as she lifts one foot up to slide off her heel. When I realize I'm clutching her dress in a death grip, I turn my back to her and get the table ready.

The design isn't big, but I prefer the table in a seated position instead of laying down. As an artist, I feel I do a better tattoo between the shoulder blades that way. You get to see your canvas as the world would.

I haven't asked but based on what I've seen of her, she doesn't have any tattoos, so I doubt she'll have any complaints about the way I position her.

I finish wiping the chair down to make sure it's clean for her. She stands there almost naked waiting for instruction.

"You can sit when it's dry. You don't want that chemical on your skin, Beth." Her lips part when I shorten her name. I think she likes it. I never considered asking her how she likes to be addressed. Typically, we just call our clients by the name they give us.

She doesn't seem to object so I don't worry about it and focus on grabbing my supplies that I haven't had time to set up yet.

As I bring my supplies over to the table, I see she's moved across the room to my drafting table. Again, she's sliding her fingertips over my supplies.

"Your fingers better not have been on that flash", I warn her. She turns her head, looking at me in shock as her dark curly locks cascade over her shoulder and fall over her breast.

Fuck. I am a sucker for a woman with dark hair. Especially someone who doesn't know how undeniably beautiful she is.

"I need these for my hair", she tells me, holding up a few sharpies. "You know...to pull it up so you can work", she clarifies. I raise a brow at her. "I didn't touch it", she tells me with more backbone than any woman has ever spoken to me in my life. I don't scare her. I don't seem to even intimidate her.

She takes the sharpies and puts them between her teeth, biting down to hold them there as she gathers her hair and wraps it in a knot at the top of her head. Then she slides one sharpie in and then the other.

She brushes her dark bangs out of her eyes and trains her gaze on me. "Ready." When I don't acknowledge her, she pulls her plump bottom lip under her top teeth and looks at me with uncertainty.

I don't look down her body no matter how badly I'd like to because the natural beauty of her face has me captivated. Her skin is pale and flawless, her hair is black, long and has a curl to it, lips a natural looking deep plumb color with eyes like brilliant blue crystals.

"Can I sit", she motions to the chair, and I realize I just got caught checking her out like she did me just hours ago.

The only difference between her response and mine is that I'm not embarrassed. She's pretty in a natural way. So pretty I'm disappointed I won't be able to see her face when I tattoo her.

"Go ahead", I tell her with a smirk. I watch as she straddles the table. Her feet don't even touch the floor. But it's not her feet that I'm paying the most attention to.

She's in see-through black panties, straddling my tattoo table. If this were happening a year ago, we'd be having sex tonight for sure. But I don't do that anymore. Not because I'm a good guy but because it's the same old thing.

They think I'm a bad boy because of how I look. We fuck. Then we're both disappointed. They want someone that I'm not and I just want a good girl. Not some random hook up.

In truth, I want to spend a lifetime with someone. It has to be the right someone and I'm not so sure the right someone is willing to fuck a stranger at their work. It just doesn't seem right to me.

"Lean forward and try to relax. We're going to need to take some breaks. Your legs will be sore if we don't. The tattoo will take a few hours."

I clean her skin where I'm going to apply the stencil. My hand would look fantastic there, holding her down in bed for my pleasure.

Tell Me Who You Go With- Archer & Bethany

I have got to stop thinking about this woman in my chair. It's not right and besides, I don't hook up with clients anymore. But she's not like the others. The others want to be associated with me because I look like I spend all day intimidating people just to get my way. But I don't. I mean, I have in the past when it mattered but it's not my reputation. She's here for the art, not me and for some reason I respect that so much more.

"The image will go right here", I tell her, cupping my hands and pressing down on her skin so she can feel where the image will land.

"Okay", she consents, looking straight ahead.

"Are you nervous?" I apply the transfer paper and wait for her answer as she considers my question.

"I wish it weren't going to be painful."

"Why?"

"Who likes pain?"

"No one. But pleasure normally comes after pain. It's going to be beautiful Beth." She turns her head to look at me. I allow it for now. When I'm working, she'll have to face straight ahead.

"Do you really believe that or is that what you tell all your first time tattoo customers?"

"This is just a moment. It'll be here and gone before you know it. But what you take away from the moment will last forever if you want it to. You get to choose what you focus on. It's that simple." Momma told me this a lot growing up. When your parents walk out on you without a second thought, it's easy to get caught up in a loss like that instead of focusing on the opportunities and experiences in front of you that never would have been if they had stuck around.

I peel the paper from her skin. "Looks good. If you need a break, you let me know, okay?" She nods. "I know you'll want to face me and talk but you have to look straight ahead." She turns

Darla J Michaels

her head to face forward, resting her chin on the top of the seat back. "Let your arms fall to your sides and try to relax."

She doesn't complain when I get started. I know it doesn't feel good but if she's in a lot of pain she doesn't show it. And she holds still. Thank goodness she isn't a fidgety client.

"Why a witch's knot?" I think I know the answer, though it's hard to imagine she practices witchcraft. I've worked on plenty of people who do. Looking at her I'd never guess she practices. She doesn't have a witchy look to her unless you count her black hair.

Bethany doesn't answer me at first. She waits longer than normal and for a moment, I wonder if she's going to answer me at all.

"I don't know if I want to answer your question. You're going to judge me."

I laugh. Out of anyone in this shop or even in this city, I'm the last one to judge anyone.

"Darlin', I've been judged my entire life. You get used to it when you're different. Can I give you some advice?" She gives me muffled permission. "Fuck em'. Be yourself and if someone doesn't like it, they can go straight to hell."

"Fuck em', huh?"

"Yep. Life is too short to give a damn about what other people think. Me included."

We sit in silence, the only sound between us is the sound of the tattoo gun. She never does answer my question. It's okay though. She doesn't have to. No one gets this tattoo if they aren't practicing. What I'm dying to know is what she practices.

"Is that woman your girlfriend?" It takes me a moment to realize she's referring to Trix.

"No. Just business. She keeps order at the shop and for that I appreciate her. It's nothing more. Never has been. Never will be."

"She seems protective of you."

"Well, I'm protective of her. But it's not like that. We're family at the shop. It's the way I've always run my business. Shit happens. Sometimes people just need a little help and compassion."

"Maybe I should come work for you", she muses.

"Yeah? What do you do?" I wouldn't mind seeing Bethany every day.

"I'm a teacher. Sometimes I think I should have done something else. I don't fit in there and the maturity level is on the floor."

"How's your boss?"

"He was taught to be an educator. Not a leader. There's a big difference."

"What would you do if you weren't a teacher?"

"Sell plants."

"Plants?"

"Yeah. Like...I'd have a huge greenhouse and a place to dry herbs. It would be so peaceful." She lets out a sigh at the thought of it. "Anyway...I'm having raised gardening beds delivered this weekend. It's not a greenhouse and won't be enough to allow me to quit my job but it will be nice for me to try it out and see how I do."

"You've never gardened?"

"No. You?"

"The only thing I ever tried to grow was pot."

"And?"

"As it turns out, I have a very green thumb."

She laughs and its music to my ears. It's a dainty little chuckle. Not a full belly laugh. I'd question whether she was being genuine, but she doesn't strike me as the type that puts on airs.

"Would you quit? If someone came along and they could fund your greenhouses and whatever else you wanted to do, would you leave education?" I ask because I can fund her passion projects, and it wouldn't make one difference if she made a penny. She could run a massive deficit, and I would never be the wiser.

"Yes." She scrambles to defend her answer. "Don't get me wrong, I like educating children. I do a great job. It's just the adults...you know?"

This time I laugh. I do know. It's one of the many reasons I went into business for myself.

"I do. More than you know, Bethany...more than you know..."

Chapter 9
Archer

I'm about to finish up and I have to say, I'm not happy about it. I've been looking at Bethany's backside for almost three hours. It's a view I never want to give up.

She's slender. Toned. And it takes every bit of strength I have inside me not to revert to the man that I was. The man who would make an advance on a woman getting a tattoo knowing full well he'd be on the receiving end of some head...sex...or both.

I don't think her visual appeal is the only thing that gets me though. She's a nice person. Like...a genuinely nice person. She has morals. Do unto others as you want done to you and some shit. That's what the others were missing.

Sure, I could fuck any one of those other women in my studio but rest assured, they'd be chasing some other man the next night. For some reason, I get the feeling that Bethany has standards. Just being in her presence makes me want to have standards too.

Darla J Michaels

I contemplate asking her out as I finish the last of her body art. Would she go out with a man like me? Sure, I have a fortune now, but I came from nothing. I'm not degreed like she is. And I have tattoos covering a large portion of my body. It would be unlikely that a woman like her would go on a date with a man like me.

I wipe a moist cloth over her tattoo once more to make sure everything is as it should be. Her skin has a sheen of sweat on it. There's no doubt she's uncomfortable, but she's done well, considering this is her first tattoo. She hasn't asked for a break once.

"You did good", I tell her as I smooth some balm over her freshly inked skin. "So good."

I don't want our time to end. I like her. She needs to stick around. I need her to stick around.

"Thank you."

She sounds emotional. I get that tattoos are emotional for people, but I've never had someone cry over a witch's knot.

I tattoo people because of the emotion behind it. I suppose you could say that I'm a big softie inside with a tough exterior.

"Can I see it?"

"Yeah." I take off my black gloves and pull my phone from my back pocket. She lays still till she hears my camera phone go off.

When she sits upright from the massage table, she doesn't have a care in the world even though her breasts are till on full display.

"It's beautiful", she breathes out the compliment. Then her eyes meet mine. "I should pay you and go", she tells me shyly, looking away.

"Beth..." Her gaze searches mine. "I can't charge you", I tell her. I set my phone down. "I don't want to be inappropriate...but I really want to be inappropriate."

She laughs. I smile. Then I lean in and am every bit inappropriate that I wasn't going to be. But what I notice is that she leans in too. And when our lips touch it feels like something unreal. Like we're two people who belong together.

Bethany swings her leg over the tattoo table to face me and winces as her muscles protest at their new position.

"I know, Beth. I'm sorry." She chuckles while she leans forward like she's known me all my life. The moment her lips meet mine and her tongue slips in my mouth, I taste it. Beer. That explains why she's sitting here in her panties kissing me in thanks...or whatever this is.

I don't' tattoo people who have been drinking. I didn't even realize she was tipsy when she came back.

But what's done is done so I kiss her back. I really kiss her. With so much affection, I'm pulling her from the tattoo table and onto my lap, pressing her naked chest against mine.

"I shouldn't be doing this", I confess.

"It's my birthday. You're excused", she whispers and then kisses me again.

"Your birthday?" I hold her back, threading my hands into her hair. She tries to nod but is only mildly successful due to my grip.

I kiss her again, this time allowing my hands to untangle from her hair and slide down her back to rest on her hips.

"I have cake for you", I tell her, remembering I have one more of the cupcakes that Trix bought for me. I don't know why but I feel the need to give this woman everything.

"Yeah?" She pulls her bottom lip under her teeth, and it makes me want to fuck her. If she were one of those other women, I'd shove her onto the table, slide her flimsy panties to the side and fuck her till she begged me to stop. But she's not one of those women.

So, I get the cupcake.

Bethany

I look from Archer to the cupcake.

"Is that bacon", I ask, not believing my eyes.

"Candied bacon", Archer clarifies.

I'm still sitting in front of him in only my panties. I'm not sure where he put my dress. I also don't care.

He begins to unwrap the cupcake paper, and I can't take my eyes off his hands. I'm not particularly practiced with sex. I've never had it. I've also never had skilled lovers. But while I don't know exactly what I'm judging, those hands...inked, with what appear to be well manicured fingernails seem to fit the bill.

When my eyes meet his, I smile at his declaration. "This is breakfast. I swear you will crave this cupcake every morning for the rest of your life."

I smile at the thought. There's no way this cupcake tastes like breakfast. I don't buy it.

He holds the tasty treat out to me, allowing me the first taste. As soon as I start chewing, he plucks the piece of candied bacon from the top and holds it out to me. When I hold my hand over my mouth full of chewed food, he furrows his brow and cocks his head to the side as if to say, c'mon now...take a bite. So I do...

And it tastes like breakfast alright. Breakfast I'll crave every morning for the rest of my life.

He raises a brow at me, and I cover my mouth, stifling a smile as I chew.

He takes a bite, and I grab at his wrist, pulling it back to me. Archer throws his head back and laughs with a mouthful of cupcake, not seeming to care that I see him like this.

We eat off the cupcake until there's one bite left, and he kindly concedes to giving the rest to me being it my birthday and all.

I wonder what it would be like to wake up to Archer and have breakfast. I bet it would be heavenly, I think as I chew.

"You're right", I tell him, loving the way his eyes light up when I admit he knows more than I do. "Thank you." I grab his hand because I need him to know I'm so very sincere. "This was the best birthday cake I have ever had."

"Sinful", he tells me with a glimmer in his eye.

"It is", I agree. That cupcake tastes like pancakes, syrup and of course bacon.

"No, no...Sinful is the cupcake shop I got it from", he clarifies. "I saved the best for last."

The way he says that makes me wonder if he's talking about the cupcake, my tattoo or maybe even me. That's so ridiculous. A guy like him interested in me.

"I should get going. It's late. You've stayed way past closing time for me." He nods, then reaches behind him and grabs my dress.

"Sorry", he tells me, handing me the wadded-up material for me to put back on.

He bandages me and gives me some aftercare instructions before I get dressed and then I'm off.

The entire way home all I can think about are his hands on me. How comforting they were even when he was inflicting pain on me at my own request.

Archer is a nice guy I think as I lay my head back against the headrest and realize I left with his sharpies in my hair. I smile thinking of him being so protective over the flash he drew for me. I wonder what it means when he puts them on his wall.

Tell Me Who You Go With- Archer & Bethany

I cannot believe my behavior tonight. I took my dress off for a stranger. I palm my face while I wait at a stop light. Wow, Bethany. Is this what turning twenty-three is going to be like for you? Making all kinds of choices that are beyond inappropriate but story worthy just to get what you want?

And he kissed me. Or did I kiss him? I'm not even sure how it happened but I do know I want to do it again.

How he pulled me on his lap and wrapped his arms around me...I could allow him to do that for the rest of my life.

And he knows what I am. He didn't judge me or run even though he knows I practice witchcraft. He didn't even press me to tell him about it. If this were anyone else, they would have scrutinized me or spoken to me like I had lost my marbles.

I should return his markers. But I'm not going to. The tattoo and his art supplies are the only things I have left of him. It's too bad this is where our story ends.

Present Day

Chapter 10
Archer

I changed our meeting place. Meeting at Jonathan's was a disaster last week. Harlan's place is neutral territory.

I get to his place early. Francesca is still there, saying her goodbyes to Harlan while I help myself to a cup of coffee.

They're in the living room fucking. Whatever Harlan is doing to Francesca, she sounds like she's close to orgasm.

He's got the right idea. We haven't discussed Micah and Jonathan's repeated pissing matches but blowing off steam is smart.

I had Bethany on her knees for me in the shower this morning. Then I took her back to bed.

She was pissed when I left. It's understandable but warranted. She thought I was going to let her come. It's been about a week since she denied me the answer to my question about her rude behavior with Linea and Grace. I haven't let her orgasm since.

What Bethany needs to be reminded of is that if I ask her a question, I'm expecting an answer. And if I tell her to do something she better God damned do it.

The longer she doesn't comply the worse it's going to get for her. If she thinks her pussy aches for release now, this is just the start of it.

I roll the vial around in my palm, not bothering to look at the ingredient label or the warning list. Bethany's name is printed on it as though Harlan filled a prescription for her.

He kind of did. I don't know where he gets this stuff but what I do know is that it's my turn to play with potions now.

I pocket the vials when I hear Francesca quiet down. I don't know what she knows about Harlan but regardless, she doesn't get to know about Bethany. It's not that I don't trust her. I just want this to be a little surprise. And since Francesca and Bethany are on good terms, I can't have Francesca ruining it now, can I?

Bethany was a pent-up mess when I left.

"Archer", she pled with me to get her off. "I said I won't tell you yet", she tries to reason with me.

"And I said I won't allow you to come yet, wife. See how even that is?"

"Please", she begs with desperation in her voice.

"We can try again tonight, Beth", I tell her, then give her a lingering kiss on the lips before I head out.

I look over the top of my coffee cup to see Francesca stroll through the kitchen. She's wearing a matching bra and panty set.

Harlan loves that bougie shit. Not me. I like the women walking around in my t-shirt with no panties on. Easy access.

Darla J Michaels

She stops next to me and reaches up to grab a coffee cup, pouring herself a steaming mug.

"Good morning, Archer."

"Morning darlin'." I turn to her and slide my palm down her bare back and over her lace covered rump.

"You're early", Harlan observes, walking into the kitchen to grab coffee too. "You have time to play with her", he tells me. "We won't need to start reffing for about twenty minutes."

I chuckle at his joke. I do feel like a ref at these meetings.

"Limits", I ask Harlan. I may not be interested depending on what they are.

He lets out a breath and runs a hand through his hair while he thinks about what's on the calendar for Francesca tonight. Harlan looks tired. Harlan never looks tired. So I let him off the hook.

"I just want to touch her pussy while I have my coffee."

"Sure", he answers as though I've asked him for something as benign as borrowing a pen. I suppose to us, it is.

"She's with Mav tonight", I tell him, sliding my hand from the back of Francesca's panties to the front causing her to groan when my fingers find her clit. I'm good with schedules and remembering little details. I could probably tell you who was with who for the next two weeks and not get one detail wrong.

"Oh, my goodness", I remark in wonder. "How'd your pussy get so wet, Fran?"

"Harlan", she whispers as she turns and kisses me.

"Harlan, huh?" She nods and moans her confirmation against my lips. "Can I see it? Hm?" She nods but doesn't move to take her panties off. "Can I make you come while you stand?"

She shakes her head, her coffee long forgotten. When I look over at Harlan, he's already clearing off a spot on the island to make room for her to lay down.

"Fran, darlin'. We're gonna play, okay?" She nods again and I kiss her while I walk her backward to the island where her body will be on display for us. "Up you go", I tell her, hoisting her onto the counter without warning.

She's such a good girl, laying back for us so we can have some fun.

"She goin' in the cage", I ask Harlan while I slide my hand inside her panties.

"She is." The tone in his voice is stern. I know he's not gotten over her betrayal. He would have punished her longer if he could have but the medicine he has is toxic in high doses and we'd never take a risk with one of our women even if we were making a point.

"The only one we have to lock up", I say to myself, wondering how far I'll have to go with Bethany before she tells me what I want to know.

I bring my lips down over hers but don't kiss her. I want her moan. I want to claim it with my mouth.

"Francesca", I whisper onto her lips. "I think I'll fuck you after." I grab her hand and press it against my jeans where my hard cock threatens to break through my zipper. "Want to fuck, darlin'?"

When I slide my fingers inside her, she moans. I kiss her, hoping to hell this meeting doesn't take too long, and we can get next steps figured out. I have a packed day so I might not have time to fuck her before I have to head out.

"It'll take about a week", Harlan tells me while I kiss his girlfriend. He's talking about the meds. He's trying to tell me that if I don't fuck her after the meeting, she's going to be miserable before her date with Mav tonight.

If I use the vials, I'll have to get used to making these kinds of decisions on Bethany. Do I get her wound up and let her suffer or fuck her and let her suffer? From what I understand, it's about the same.

"Was it worth it", I ask Fran. She nods. "You gonna keep secrets again?" She shakes her head. "Stop the sneakin' around?" She nods, her eyes rolling back in her head now that I've slid my fingers inside her.

Footsteps sound in the hallway. It's Jon. Not Micah. Interesting.

"Oooh. A buffet. Harlan you shouldn't have." Harlan chuckles while I kiss Francesca. "May I?"

"Help yourself", Harlan gives Jonathan permission.

"Let's see that mouth sweetheart." I finish my kiss, not wanting to be stingy. Francesca doesn't turn her head towards Jonathan. Instead, she just stares up at me, her eyes hooded with pleasure.

"Come on pretty girl", Jon turns her head towards him and slides his hard cock into her mouth.

"She okay", I ask Harlan as I unclasp the front of her bra, uncaging her perky breasts to do as we please.

"It's normal", is all he tells me. I'm not sure I like that. This doesn't seem like Francesca. At least it doesn't seem like the Francesca I know.

She gags around Jonathan, fucking my fingers taking a backseat at her discomfort. As soon as Jonathan gives her relief, she's back to fucking my hand.

"Did you take her blood yet", Jon asks Harlan.

"Every morning. It's downstairs in the lab."

The last set of footsteps enters the room. Micah.

He doesn't say a word but just stands there taking in the scene. I don't blame him. It's not the first time we've had a woman sprawled out to share between us, but it's not what he was expecting this morning, I'm sure.

Harlan doesn't participate. He just stands there drinking his coffee watching us play with his girl. I look at Micah and motion towards Bethany. "We'll make room", I offer with a smirk.

Micah lets out a heavy sigh and addresses Harlan. "Coffee?"

"Help yourself." Harlan looks at me and raises his brows. Yeah. We're getting that Micah again today. We better make this count.

"Fran be a good girl for me and relax your throat, sweetheart." She gags around Jonathan as I bend down and take one of her nipples in my mouth. "Eyes up here. That's it. Look at me. Look at me while I fuck that mouth of yours." He slides in deeper, and she barely gags this time. "And some women don't like eye contact. See what a difference that makes?"

"I don't get him", Harlan tells the room. "Eye contact doesn't make a gag reflex subside yet when he says it, it shall be done."

"Did you come in here", I ask, sliding her panties down her thighs.

"Back door."

"Perfect." I fuck her with my fingers while I tongue her slit. She moans around Jonathan's cock. Micah stands next to Harlan, still watching.

"I do. Jon's the calm in everyone's storm."

I roll my eyes up to Micah, never moving my mouth from Francesca in shock that he's given Jon a compliment.

"Thanks friend", Jonathan tells Micah before he blows his load down Fran's throat.

I slide my fingers out of Fran and give her a few light pecks on her freshly waxed pussy. "Gotta get started darlin'", I tell her, not bothered in the least that she won't finish with me.

Darla J Michaels

When Jonathan slides out of her mouth, she looks down her body at me as I slide her panties back up her thighs. Micah sets his cup down and snaps her bra closed, sliding his palms into the cups of her bra to comfortably fit her breasts back into it.

I help her sit up and I can tell she's a little dizzy. When Harlan comes around the counter, I move over for him so he can address Francesca without interference.

He's sweet with her even though he's still pissed. "Look at me", he gently orders her. "We won't be long." She nods in understanding against his hand. "Paul will bring you breakfast. I want you to eat and then get some sleep. I'll find you when we're done here."

Harlan helps Francesca from off the counter and kisses her on the lips. She's so out of it, she forgets the expectation for saying goodbye. None of us will likely see her after the meeting. Unless it ends early enough for me to get my dick wet.

Jonathan reaches out and pulls her to him. "Thank you", he murmurs against her neck, kissing her and making her laugh as his stubble tickles her skin.

Micah tips her chin up and gives her a brief kiss on the lips and when she starts to walk away without letting me say goodbye, I use the whistle I call Spirit with. She stops in her tracks, pivots on her bare feet and pads over to me.

"Taste", I order her, kissing her deeply so she can taste her cum on my tongue. "Good?"

"Yeah", she says against my lips and continues the kiss.

Harlan clears his throat. I'm going to make the aftermath worse for her if I keep it up but he's giving me discretion here. Discretion I may need to use with Bethany at some point.

"Go on", I tell a panting Francesca. I nod towards the exit to the kitchen but before she leaves, she raises on her tip toes and

87

kisses me on the cheek. I shake my head as she leaves us. She's sweet. Sassy and sneaky but sweet.

"Paul will bring us breakfast", Harlan tells us, pulling out his phone to access the camera system. We follow him through his monstrous home as he checks on Francesca. His well-manicured fingers tap the screen, and I can see him follow her through the house. She gets to a room that opens when she stands outside of it.

"Her bracelet has a chip in it", he tells me. "She's required to wear it at all times."

"Why do you need to track her?"

"Her implant tells me where she's located on a map. Her bracelet tells me where she's located in my home. It also can give her a little zap if she deserves it."

He shocks her. I didn't know that. I suppose I don't have to know that if it's just for him to use. I couldn't do that to Bethany. I do understand why Harlan has no reservations about serving Francesca up a punishment.

Damn. The meeting we had after Linea told the real story of what happened to her was tense. Harlan was furious. And there's a code among us that allows discipline the way the Lady's owner sees fit. Unless it breaks another rule, the rest of us sit idly by and watch.

"Is that her room?"

"No. It's where I keep her when I need complete privacy."

I watch Francesca step into a large floor to ceiling cage. Harlan taps the screen, and the gate closes behind her. There's a robe that she unhooks from one of the bars and a large beanbag looking chair that she curls up in while she waits for her food. At first, I feel bad for her but when I continue to watch, she looks at home there.

"Don't feel sorry for her. She did it to herself. When she proves she's trustworthy I'll reno the room and this will all be a distant memory." Harlan pockets his phone and slides his finger into an automatic panel.

"No retina scanner", I tease.

"No need. It samples my blood. It's a bit antiquated. I'm testing out a holographic sentience gate. Perhaps since we'll be meeting regularly, you all can get a quick scan before you leave today. So, we don't have any unnecessary technology glitches for when this system is switched out with the new one."

With a gush of air, the door pops open and we all file in behind him. Once we enter, the door shuts automatically, sealing us into the room.

"A what, Ironman?" The guys laugh at my joke.

"A holographic sentience gate. It only grants access to individuals recognized by an adaptive holographic AI that senses intent, emotional state and memory patterns. This room is completely secure. Soundproof and weapon proof", he clarifies.

We take our seats around the board room style table in the center of the room. This place is way too formal for me. A thin piece of glass slides down from a panel in the ceiling.

"Alright, who would like to give their update first", Harlan prompts? As he speaks, the glass illuminates and his words show up on it as we all sit there dumbfounded.

"Before we begin..." Micah watches a transcription of his words file in below Harlan's with his initials and color code off to the side. I laugh when Micah glares at him. Lawyers don't like to be recorded. "What happens to these notes?" He directs the pointed question at Harlan and gets a smile back in return.

"Relax counselor. I use a local air gapped intranet protected by quantum encrypted communication nodes. No data leaves unless it's scrubbed and tagged." Micah raises his brows at

Harlan as though his explanation has fallen short of Micah's expectations. I get it. He doesn't want to go to jail. He's looking out for everyone in this room.

"Nothing is released unless I release it and everything can be destroyed as if it never happened if need be. I'm not an idiot, Micah."

I smirk at the terseness in Harlan's tone.

"Alright. I'm runnin' this since it looks like Tony over here's got us covered." Harlan rolls his eyes at my reference once again to Iron Man. "Who did their homework?"

Jonathan raises his hand indicating he'd like to go first. I nod, interested in what he has to share.

"I got some time alone with Linea and asked her about the third thing. They're watchers. These young little freaks who's only job is to report back if a helper and a virgin get too chummy. If they look like they're sharing secrets or exchanging information, the virgin and the helper are separated."

"That explains the timing for Linea to be pulled from school and be taught at home", I reason.

"How does she even know that", Micah challenges Jonathan.

"I asked her that too. She said one of the watchers apologized to her. She came by the house for something and saw Linea all lonely looking and she felt bad."

"And she just told you this? Just as plain as we're talking today?"

"I made her a deal. It was too good to refuse."

Micah is boring a hole through Jonathan's head with his eyes.

"What's the deal?"

"That's between Linea and me. It doesn't concern you." Jonathan takes a drink of his coffee and then trains his gaze on

Micah. "What's the matter? You thought you'd be the only one who has secrets with Linea?"

"Jonathan she could relapse", Micah warns.

"She won't. She wants what I'm willing to give her for her participation much more than reverting to her old ways. Let's just say I've provided her with incentive no one else here can. By the way...in case you aren't aware, she's still a little upset with you", he goads Micah.

"You two done?" I've about had it with their sparing.

"What happens when they serve their purpose and get older", Harlan asks. I get where he's going with this. It seems like an awful short-term gig unless they're spying for something else later.

"She doesn't know. But she did give me a few names. One for sure is the watcher who apologized. The others are suspects."

"I'll have them followed and see what we can learn from them", Harlan volunteers.

"I'll take the names and see what I can find out about their past. Who they're related to, affiliations, jobs, hobbies...anything that could create links to others involved in the abuse of these girls."

"Let me know what you find out. Like I said, Linea is more than willing to answer my questions", Jonathan tells Micah.

"She shouldn't be involved. If this thing blows up, she'll be named. Have you considered what this could do to her? She could be in the press, be called to testify... We should be protecting her."

"That's what we're here for, Brother. No one in this room will let that happen to her." Even though I make this declaration like I know it to be true, I hope to hell I'm right.

Chapter 11
Bethany

I let my mind wander as I stare out the window in the passenger seat of Archer's Range Rover. He's killing me slowly with sex, I think as his thumb rubs lazy circles on my thigh.

"How angry are you, Beth?"

I let out a heavy exhale and train my gaze on him. "You're not being fair", I start to complain but I stop when he chuckles.

"Fair is all I've ever been with you, darlin'. And I think you'll see that clearer if you don't tell me what I need to know by the date I gave you."

Two shitty weeks. He's giving me two shitty weeks to figure out how to tell him something that will crush him.

"It's not long enough."

"Oh, I beg to differ. It's too long but that's the best we could do."

"What are you going to do to me?" I have to admit that I'm a little scared of the consequences either way. I feel like I'm damned if I do and damned if I don't.

"What we always do to you, Beth. Whatever we want."

I squeeze my legs together, the threat a turn-on that Archer hadn't intended it to be. He throws his head back and laughs before he addresses me once more on the matter.

"Don't romanticize this punishment. If you're angry now, it's about to get worse. Because the longer this takes the more ruthless I'm going to get. And we both know I'm a nice guy, but we also know that I can be a sonofabitch too. Don't we Beth?"

He's right. He is mostly a really nice guy. But when he's pushed to his breaking point all that Mr. Nice Guy stuff goes out the window.

"I apologized. I called them both and apologized." Once more I try and defend myself hoping he sees reason.

"That's good. Thank you for doing that. At least you still have manners. Now all we need to do is address your disrespect for your spouse and Braden's employee."

I huff out a breath, frustrated with how relentless he's being. I suppose I'm not giving in either...but I can't. Not yet.

We pull into Momma Jackson's driveway, right on time.

"Come here", Archer gently beckons to me and crooks his finger towards him to get a kiss. Even though I'm mad at him, his touch feels heavenly. His stubble scratches my lips as I open my mouth for him. The way he kisses me with such reverence...no one has ever kissed me like that.

"Archer", I whisper against his lips.

"Darlin'", he answers me back. "What is it", he prompts me when I don't get on with it.

"Promise me this will never change."

"The kiss?"

He doesn't get it. The kiss is just a vehicle for affection. But his affection is a part of his being. It's who he is. And I worry that what I know might snuff some of that out.

"The way you love."

Archer smirks against my lips and kisses me once more before pulling back to look at me. His fingertips trace my jaw line until he's cupping my chin, forcing me to face him.

"I will always love you this way. I don't know what's got you so freaked, but it must be big for you to question how I show love for you."

I close my eyes and take a long breath before facing him again.

"I love you Mr. Jackson."

"Wife", he says with a wink and a devilish grin before he releases me and exits to open my car door.

When we enter, it's a mad house. Archer's mom is shoeing everyone out of the kitchen. My nieces and nephews are running wild around the house. It smells divine in here.

"Bethany!" Momma Jackson shouts her greeting across the room, cutting through all the noise and moving effortlessly through the chaos to get to me.

"Oh, it's so good to see you." She hugs me. Tight. I hug her back while Archer watches us and smirks. When she finally lets me go, Archer addresses her.

"And me...Momma...is it good to see me?"

"Well, you did drive her here", she concedes in a sassy tone, patting her son's cheek then turning around to resume cooking.

My mouth falls open as he shakes his head at her antics. All this time and she's still upset with him over missing his wedding.

"Geminis", I shrug when a little gremlin slams into my legs almost nocking me over. I gasp at how big Cora has gotten. "Well look at you!" Those big brown eyes look up at me and I smile when I see she's tried out her mother's tinted lip gloss. The red looks beautiful against her dark skin. And her hair has

Darla J Michaels

gotten so long. I hated it when my mom did my hair. I wonder how she does when her mom braids hers. It's pretty but I bet it took a while.

I squat down to get to her eye level. She's turning four in May.

"We're having cake for dinner", Cora exclaims. "Chocolate cake!"

"Now Cora, you know good and well Granny Jackson isn't givin' you chocolate cake for dinner", Archer corrects her.

Cora looks at Archer, doesn't bother responding and turns back to me as if she has no idea what he's talking about.

"Also, Geminis", I tell him, looking over Cora's head, unable to hide my smile.

"Show me the cake, Cora", I tell her in a conspiratorial voice. Her eyes go wide and she's off, racing in the direction she once came from. I shrug and follow her, leaving Archer on his own.

It's been a while since we've been here. When we first got married, I thought the chaos was overwhelming, but now? I like it.

I think I like the people. That must be it. This house is louder than a cafeteria lunchroom on a rainy day after Halloween and if there is something I do not miss about teaching, cafeteria lunchrooms would be it.

I chat with the family during the controlled chaos. Everyone seems to be doing well. Healthy. Happy. And they all have a lot to talk about. This feels like family.

And of course I like it. But the reason I like it more than any ordinary situation is because of Archer. He got the family he needed...no, deserved... when his own couldn't bother to stick around for him.

"All right! If you're hungry have a seat in the dining room! If you're not, then go home!" Momma Jackson's bellow cuts through the room once more. We break out in laughter. She only kind of means it. Well...maybe she mostly means it.

Archer finds me through the sea of his kin. It's not hard. We're the only light skinned people in attendance.

"Thank goodness you aren't vegan", he tells me, grabbing my hand and kissing me on the cheek. I agree with him...only because I'm starving and I'm sure there's butter and cream in most of the dishes Momma Jackson prepared. I'm salivating just thinking about it.

When we enter, Momma Jackson sits at the head of the table. There are two seats open. One on each side of her. Archer motions for me to take the seat next to Cora and she claps her hands with utter joy at this new development.

When Archer's oldest brother, Marshall, finishes lighting the candles on the table, the lights are turned off.

Momma Jackson grabs Archer's and I's hand bowing her head in prayer as the rest of the hands connect around the table in unity. Momma Jackson begins.

"Lord, we gather here today to celebrate all the blessings you have given to us. To not only thank you for bringing us together tonight but for bringing us together when we needed it the most. May you continue to allow us one more day to be in the company of each other until we are returned to you. And may this day and every day after continue to remind us that family, whether found or born is the greatest gift we could ever be given. In God's grace we thank you. Amen."

With a gentle squeeze of my hand, Momma Jackson raises her head to address the room. "Well, what are you waiting for? Let's eat!"

Darla J Michaels

Laughter, chatter and silverware clanking against dishes breaks the silence.

I look at Archer who's laughing along with Cora's mom. He doesn't see me look at him.

I want to throw up. Or storm out of the room. Or maybe even fall to the floor but I can't do any of that because Archer will do whatever he needs to do to move up the incentive he has planned for me and that simply cannot happen.

So instead, I reach for my glass of water, but Momma Jackson's hand, who I now realize has not let go of mine stops me. I turn to her, and I swear she knows.

"Mashed potatoes", Momma Jackson asks me with a wink.

"Yes, please", I tell her, hoping that I can eat them. She releases my hand and turns the bowl, so the spoon is easier for me to reach. Her eyes are still on me and I'm thankful when Cora's little hand that now rests on my arm pulls me away from her gaze.

"Ooooh", Cora says to the bowl of mashed potatoes making googly eyes at them.

She makes me laugh. I'm so grateful for this little girl tonight.

Dishes are passed around the table until the chatter dies down because everyone is eating. I pick up my fork to begin my meal but before I do, I look across the table at Archer. He's staring right at me. His eyes drift down to my plate and then back up to mine. He gives me a stern look and when I don't give him the satisfaction of grabbing more food or starting to eat, his brows furrow in worry.

I can't look at him. I can't bear for him to even look at me for fear that he'll ask a question and I'll answer it, taking us down a rabbit hole I don't want to go down right now.

He nods. It's slight. Imperceptible to the rest of the table. But I know that nod. That nod means he's pissed. That nod might mean he'll be a sonofabitch when we get home.

I force myself to eat what's on my plate and I don't pass on dessert entirely. It would draw attention especially sitting next to Cora. So, I opt for vanilla ice cream instead of the cake.

The meal is long. Too long. And I'm relieved when Momma Jackson excuses everyone from the table after their bellies are full.

"I'd like to help clear the table and do dishes if you don't mind", I volunteer.

"Sure about that, Beth?"

My eyes go wide at Arther's interjection.

"You feelin' okay?"

"Of course."

Momma Jackson looks between us and saves me from Archer's watchful eye.

"You're sweet, Bethany. That's one of the reasons I like you."

I don't wait, I grab my plate and glass, rounding the table opposite of where Archer stands. And I know that as much as he'd like to stop me, he won't. But I still hear his heavy footfalls thudding across the dining room floor and by the time I've made it to the butler doors, he's holding one open for me to get through.

Always the gentleman even when he doesn't want to be. I know this because the look in his eyes makes me think that if he could get away with it, he'd grab me by the neck and pin me to the wall.

"Thank you", I politely whisper and enter the kitchen.

"Kitchen's closed, Archer." Momma Jackson's tone is one of warning as she steps through the door and doesn't look back.

Darla J Michaels

This is Momma Jackson's space. And if she says the kitchen is closed the kitchen is most certainly closed.

The butler door swings when Archer lets go but he doesn't step through it. I don't take my eyes off the door until Momma Jackson addresses me.

"Let's talk and work. You rinse. I'll load."

"I can do it", I tell her, not wanting her to lift another finger.

"I know you can. But you're not." I give her a small smile and do as she tells me, working up the courage to start the conversation that I never even thought about asking before.

When we're almost done with dishes, I finally get up the nerve. "Will you tell me more about Archer's story, Momma Jackson?"

Chapter 12
Archer

"I can't wait two weeks, Harlan. I need options."

"Of course. The drug is as versatile as the person you use it on. I haven't done much testing on it so I can't predict what the effects will be on Bethany. You can use it directly, as an injection but I think you should wait until we're all meeting for her."

"Okay. What are my other options?"

"Slip it into her drinks. Just a few drops throughout the day. It's extremely sweet so you'll have to be careful what you put it in. If she suspects it, then we'll have to use other measures. I think this way is best."

"Then what?"

I can hear his smile. "Then you wait."

"Care to be a little more specific? Is there a stopping point? What's too much? What's too little? I need to know what I'm looking for here."

"Give her one drop tonight..."

"One drop? No. I need results. One drop won't do it", I challenge him.

"Trust me. Give her one drop in a glass of Armand DeBrignac Demi-Sec tonight. She'll be waking you up for sex before sunrise."

"How many drops do I give her tomorrow?"

"It depends on how her pussy looks in the morning. Send me pictures. Make her touch herself. Time to orgasm is important. Let her finish." I start to object but he interrupts. "Trust me. You want to get this right. She may break before we have time with her. And if she doesn't, think of this as the setup."

"Alright. When do I bring her in for blood tests?"

"We'll start those when she can't come anymore. She'll need to stay at your place full time if it comes down to that", Harlan warns. I don't mind. I prefer it.

"Thank you. I'll message you tomorrow."

With that, I hang up and join my family, less Bethany. I'm angry with her. Teaming up with my own mom when she knows I'm mad just so she can avoid me pisses me off more. And my mom loves Bethany so she'd do just about anything for, especially if it meant she could get under my skin. Somehow, I need to get back in Momma's good graces.

The hardest part of when Bethany surfaces will be pretending that I'm not mad at her. I don't think she understands why I'm displeased. First, she's keeping secrets. Now, she's so caught up in whatever it is that she's hiding, she's not eating? She looked sick. I can't have that. I won't have that.

It doesn't take long before I'm brought into conversations and card games with my family. It's a nice distraction and all so I don't storm in that kitchen and interrupt heaven knows what they're talking about.

My phone pings in my back pocket. I don't have to look at the messages to know that our assistant already has the bottle of champagne chilled and waiting for us back at my house. I told her to throw in some flowers. Rose, lavender and poppy to be exact. I've heard her mention them. I think they mean something to her. What, I'm not sure.

By the time we're half-way home, she's falling asleep in the passenger seat.

"C'mon now. I have plans for you. Don't quit on me now, wife."

She rolls her head to the side to look at me. She hasn't even had anything to drink, and she looks exhausted. I bet I can wake her up though.

"Bethany", I fake chastise her, running my hand up her neck and fisting her hair. She opens her mouth in surprise. "Can I be sweet with you when we get home?" Her eyes widen a fraction more. She pauses to see if I'm being genuine.

"Yes. Please", desperation thick in her voice.

"So can you stay awake for me, darlin'?"

"Yeah."

She reaches out to touch me, but I don't loosen my grip. Her gentle hand starts on my cheek and then traces down my jaw, neck and then down my chest.

When she gets to my lap, I tighten my grip a bit more, but she doesn't heed my warning. Instead, she slides her hand under my shirt, undoes my pants and slides her hand inside to grab my hard cock.

The conflict running through my mind right now is like nothing I've felt before. She's my fucking wife. And I'm about to drug her. God...I love this woman more than she'll ever know but we don't keep secrets. That's something we discussed the second night we were married and back at my place. We were in air conditioning, and I could think. We talked and we agreed. No. Fucking. Secrets.

Darla J Michaels

I pull over and cut the lights. We're on a rode that doesn't get a lot of traffic anyway so it's private for what we're up to.

She's been stroking me for long enough that I need release. There's no turning back. I don't say anything to her. I simply guide her head over my cock as she takes it into her mouth. My head falls back on the headrest the moment her mouth is on me.

"Bethany", I whisper. God...the way she works me with her mouth. This is my wife...the wife I love...the wife that loves me.

I look down and the sight of my hand in her dark hair with the moonlight shining in the windows is enough to make me come undone. She's mine. Fuck. What am I thinking? She's mine to protect, I remind myself. Mine to love. Mine...

Her mouth sucks on me hard as I pull her head up. I've got her stuck here. Mouth hovering over my cock. Indecision swirling around me. The only thing I feel is her breath on the tip of me. She's that close.

"Wife", I croak out the word. "Do you trust me?" I need to hear her answer because I'm not sure I trust myself right now.

She nods.

"I'm going to let you go. Take your pants off. Leave your panties on."

She groans. She fucking groans. And I know why. My good girl loves having her panties slid to the side during sex.

"Fuck me all to hell", I breath out as she does what I tell her.

I don't even have to tell her to get on my lap. She sits right on top of me and kisses me like she's needed this. I'm sure she has. I've shown her interest but it's interest under the understanding that she will not receive pleasure. This has the promise of a reward for her.

"Beth..." I don't even know where to begin. I want to tell her that I've got her. That whatever this is that she needs to believe I've got her. She doesn't need to be afraid of it or me. Whatever it is, it'll be what it'll be, and we'll work through it. But I don't. I don't because she's so damn tempting there's no time for words.

As soon as I slide her panties to the side, she's lining herself up over me. I slide a very willing participant on top of my hard cock and the noise she makes upon entry is heaven to hear. It's a high pitch wine mixed with a heavy breath. It's the sound of us becoming one.

I take a handful of her hair once more and kiss her hard. I want her to know that she's mine. I've already claimed her and I'm never letting her go.

"You had a cigarette", she calls me out. "And whiskey."

I don't smoke regularly but I did tonight. I'm worried about my wife. My lips are on hers before I respond. It doesn't matter if I had a smoke or not tonight. I don't justify my actions to anyone, especially her.

I guide her hips up and down on top of me to the rhythm I like. When she keeps the pace on her own, I let go of her hips and move my hands to her face. She closes her eyes at my touch...or maybe it's the pleasure she gets from my cock. I don't know which but to be honest it doesn't matter. What does matter is that she trusts me. But she doesn't trust me entirely. God damn it.

I grab the hem of her shirt and pull it up over her head. She doesn't stop. With the flick of my fingers, her bra is unclasped. I slide it off her arms and throw it in back.

"Do you know what I love?" She shakes her head, then closes her eyes and swallows hard. "That I own you. That my tattoo is on your skin. That my last name is yours. That I'm the one your spirit sent to love you always, and I have." I kiss her once more and when I'm at my breaking point I slide her on top of me to the hilt and come so hard I leave teeth marks on her shoulder. She cries out but I don't let go. I sink my teeth in further, damn near drawing blood. And when I've stopped releasing inside her I kiss the bite until I have my answer.

"Beth...I will love you always." I search her beautiful blue eyes in the moonlight. "Love takes so many forms, doesn't it, darlin"?" She nods and bends down to kiss me.

"I love you so much, Archer", she whispers against my lips before slipping her tongue into my mouth. Her voice has so much emotion in it that my heart aches for her and whatever this burden is that she carries alone.

I allow myself a few more minutes to kiss my naked wife in the front seat of my car.

"Cold?" She nods and shivers, running her fingertips over the stubble on my cheek. I shift in my seat, grabbing the hem of my hooded sweatshirt as I lean forward, causing her to tip back without warning. She lets out a small scream, not anticipating the sudden shift of her body and wraps her arms around my neck before falling back against the steering wheel. "Come here", I softly order her wearing the devilish smile I know she loves. She smirks at me and pulls herself close enough to kiss me again.

"Now..." I let out a long exhale as I lift the sweatshirt over my head and she shifts to allow it. Then I bunch up the material and pull it over her head. She threads her arms through the sleeves and reaches back to pull the hood over her head. I laugh when I see all the stray hairs all over her face. I know she hates it when that happens, but I also know she loves the feel of my warm sweatshirt complete with my scent inside it. She tucks her nose under the collar to take a whiff while I gently brush the hair from her face. "How about I give you a little potion of my own when we get back to the house?"

She nods her head, and I think she thinks I'm talking about more cum. We can do that too, but I think it's time to show her what magic I can do.

5 Years Earlier- Mid-May

Chapter 13

Archer

It's been a couple of days since my tattoo with Bethany. I miss her.

She was so determined. Shit. The way she took her dress off. I've been replaying it every day since.

Those porcelain arms lifting the fabric over her head to expose the most beautifully pure body I've ever seen. She couldn't have been more perfect if she was made in a porcelain doll studio.

Not looking for anything more. She didn't even ask to take things further or to see me again. I wish she would have. I would have said yes in a heartbeat.

I wonder why she didn't at least imply she wanted something more. She took her dress off. I understood why. There was no other way to do it. I don't keep spare clothes here, so I had nothing to give her.

Her choices were obvious and few. If she wanted a tattoo, she'd need to get naked or reschedule.

She was so sweet in every way. So wide eyed when she entered my office. I'm sure my studio was the first she'd ever been in. Must have been intimidating for her. And she didn't even bring anyone with her.

In fact, when I suggested it, she looked surprised. I wonder if she has many close friends that know what she is.

It's easy to fear things you don't understand. I don't really know Bethany, but I do know she wouldn't hurt a fly. Just watching her walk around my office and check things out reminded me of a storybook character. You know the kind where they transfer magic onto everything they touch? She carries herself in such a way that makes me think she has great respect for the world around her. Most of all, herself.

But for practical purposes, do I think she can really do magic? No. I think we make our own magic. If we want something bad enough, we go out, grab it and don't take no for an answer.

If I had a second chance with Bethany, that's exactly what I'd do. I'd ask her out. No. I'd just tell her I'm taking her out. She belongs to me.

I know it's a crazy notion, but she does. I have never felt more complete kissing a woman as I did her. And when she slid on my lap...she felt different than every other woman who had ever done that. And trust me, there have been plenty. She felt like mine. Like a woman I could have on my lap every day for the rest of my life. Like a wife.

Fuck. I'm starting to get hard just thinking about it. I can't tattoo my VIP with a raging hardon. Time to think about something else. Like my art, for example.

Darla J Michaels

Tyler Maddox will be here any minute and I want this design to be perfect. He'll only see me, which isn't unusual for the rich and powerful. The thing is, I won't tattoo all of them. I interview them before I'll work on them. There's nothing worse than some rich prick sitting in my chair for hours while I try to pretend I'm interested. Tyler isn't one of those guys. I'm looking forward to our time together.

He's asked for a simple design. I wouldn't expect anything less from him. His request? A triskelion. A widely known symbol in the dominant community. And wrapping around two of the legs, he wants two dates. I'm guessing those are either the birthdates of his subs or the dates his subs were collared.

I look up when I hear Trix nock on the door.

"Mr. Maddox is here for you." She looks me over like she sees something that I don't.

"Is there anything else", I ask her, because she's clearly got something on her mind.

"Are you okay? You look kind of down today, Archer."

Whatever she's seeing must be real to her. She doesn't hand out sympathy regularly, even to me.

"I'm good, Trix. Thanks for checking in. Can you show Tyler back please?"

"Sure, Arch." She lingers in the doorway for a moment too long, looking me over and then finally stalking off.

I stand when I hear heavy footfalls returning to my office.

"Tyler", I great him enthusiastically. He gives me the same mischievous smile I'm sure I give him as we shake hands.

I don't have to prompt him to slide his sleeve up. He gets right down to business laying out his arm, rotating it so the underside is facing up for me to apply the decal. He has complete faith that what he asked for has been delivered.

I pass him the flash for him to approve anyway. While he reviews the design, I get my razor out knowing we'll move forward. My design is just what he asked for but with my signature elements. I add a hint of color around the dates and the center of the triskelion.

"Can you add one more thing?"

"Yeah. Sure." It doesn't matter what it is, I'll likely be able to whip it up without taking too much time.

"The Brotherhood."

"Alright. You want the words in the design?"

"Under it. Maybe curve it. Like it holds us together. Leave room for another date on the last leg though. I've got one more."

I finish shaving him and nod, wondering how it works. Curiosity gets the better of me.

"You have two subs?"

"I do."

"And they know about each other?"

"They do."

"How does that work exactly?" I know he can hear the disbelief in my voice by the smile on his face. "I don't know a woman who would let a man date someone else."

"I date six women, Archer."

I stop. Razor suspended in mid-air. Staring at him to see if he's fucking with me.

"Six?"

"Two are my subs. One didn't start out that way. The other sub did. The other four are women I date. They just aren't into the lifestyle."

"And all six of them know about each other?" I feel like I'm missing something important. This story has massive holes in it.

"Finish my art and I'll tell you about it."

Darla J Michaels

Damn. I never rush my work, but his story has me tempted. Tyler doesn't seem like a bullshitter to me. Which means whatever he's about to tell me is real and he really is fucking six women who all know about each other. There's either a lot of drama and hair pulling or they have some kind of crazy system or something.

I finish the flash to his liking and prompt him to continue his story. This is almost too good to be true. At least what little I know of it.

"Six women?"

Tyler chuckles. "You interested?"

"Is that an offer?"

"Possibly." Tyler takes a swig of his beer. He's the only patron I allow to drink in my chair because I know he can hold his liquor.

"I told the guys about you. We're looking to add more couples, but they have to be the right couples."

"What makes a couple right?" Sounds like a bunch of swingers to me. It would seem as though that would be the primary qualification.

"Well, you have to be willing to share", he starts with the obvious. "And follow the rules."

"Which are?"

"You can't fuck anyone outside of the group. So, if you're used to getting more pussy than we have access to now, it's going to be a problem for you."

"How much access would I get to the other six?"

"Whatever access their owner allows. We have a calendar, so everyone is in a rotation. When it's your day with a woman, you follow her agreement but really, her owner says what you can and can't do during your time with her. As long as it doesn't violate her agreement and her owner approves...have fun, man."

"What's the agreement for?"

"Sex. Think of it as the holy grail of how to please her. All her boundaries are listed in the agreement in explicit detail. Don't violate her agreement, don't do anything without her owner's permission and don't touch anyone outside of the group."

"Doesn't sound complicated at all. But um...why did I cross your mind?" I don't know Tyler that well. I like him but I really don't know much about him, and he doesn't know much about me.

"Honestly?"

"Yeah, man. Honestly."

"You don't look like you put up with any shit. These women are something else sometimes. We need someone who follows the rules, enforces the rules and makes the rules."

His answer makes me chuckle. Looks like this is right up my alley. "I get to make rules?"

"You get to make one rule. It's only for the women to follow and only after you've been through Introduction Night."

"Introduction Night?"

"It's when we get to have what's yours so you can have what's ours. Think of it as an offering. And once we're satisfied with what we've taken, we give back in kind."

I shake my head. This is fucking unbelievable.

"C'mon. You're not interested?" I don't answer right away. "What's your kink? We all have one. It's what makes The Brotherhood work."

Ah...now I get the addition to his tattoo. The Brotherhood...

"You know mine. In fact, if you meet our expectations, you'll know everyone's. It's how we plan dates. Women give

Darla J Michaels

back ten-fold what they receive. It's not a perfect system but it works for now."

"You found six women who were willing to agree to sharing and being shared? I can think of women who'd want to experience it but commit to it? Well...these women might want to commit to it but I'm not sure I'd be too interested in committing to them."

"It's more than just your interest. We must be interested too. And it is a commitment. Once they've agreed the only way someone can leave is if they violate a rule or if they decide to leave. So, once you pick a woman and she's in...there's no going back."

"I don't have a problem with commitment. In fact, that's my kink."

"How is commitment a kink?"

I can't believe I'm telling someone this. It makes me feel like the pervert I am. But I'm saying it anyway because maybe this could work.

"My kink is infidelity." Tyler takes a swig of his beer and looks me over as he considers my answer. "I want to get married. Then I want my wife to service others." Tyler smiles before he takes another drink from his bottle.

"There's just somethin' about telling your wife to get on her knees for another man that gets me going every...fucking...time."

"You've done it before?"

"No, man."

"Well, you talk like you have."

"That's how badly I want it."

"I'd be happy to be serviced by your wife at your direction...respectfully of course."

"How do I find a woman who will agree to marrying me just so I can order her to fuck my friends? Doesn't that seem a little farfetched to you? I think my chances are better having the tooth fairy come sit down in my chair for a skull tattoo."

Tyler laughs hard. "We found six. All you need is a woman who trusts you. It's that simple. Women are dirty. They just hide it better. Find a good woman. Get her to trust you. Find out her kinks. Then just tell her what you want to do to her. It's as simple as that."

"Hm...as simple as that, huh?"

Chapter 14
Archer

"I need a favor."

My oldest adopted brother's voice comes through my cell winded and rushed.

"Oh-kay?" I draw out my response because this man never calls me for a favor.

"I got called in for an emergency cardiac case."

"Uh huh?" I have no idea how I can help this man...now or ever.

"I promised Thomas that I'd come to his school today."

"Mmmmhmmm." I still don't follow. "Does he need a ride or something?"

"No. I mean yes. But I need you for something else before you pick him up."

"Damn man. Spit it out. What is it?"

"Just say yes first."

I cannot believe my very professional, very authoritative oldest brother is playing me around like this.

"Dante, what do you need?" My coffee has barely kicked in. I have no interest in his puzzles right now. He lets out a heavy sigh and finally comes clean with it.

"It's career day. Thomas asked me to speak at it so I agreed. I need you to go in my place." Before I can even start to object, he continues. "It's only fifteen minutes. You say who you are and what you do and invite questions."

I'm silent because I want to say no. But then Dante hits me with the one thing I can't resist.

"Thomas will be there. You're his favorite uncle."

I grumble because it's the truth. I am his favorite uncle. I'm the fun uncle.

We're in a silent stand-off until I finally relent.

"I'll do it but under one condition."

"Oh, thank goodness. Name it."

"I get to have him after school. You tell Terese that I'm taking her boy and we're eating sugar and gettin' into trouble. And I'm bringing him home past his bedtime."

I hear his heavy sigh on the other end of the line. "You know what...I'll deal with her wrath later."

Terese hates processed food and basically anything kids love. I love the look on her face when she learns I'm watching him. She knows she's going to have to undo whatever I've done later.

"I've got it covered. I'll show up for Thomas. Do the life savin' thing."

Dante thanks me one more time, tells me he'll text me the details and hangs up.

I wonder what it would be like to have kids. I know I'd be a good dad. My kids would want for nothing. Though I don't know how Dante does it. He's a cardiothoracic surgeon yet he still manages to have a close connection to his son. And Terese is an

OR nurse. How they even keep their schedules straight I'll never know.

The rest of the morning goes by painfully slowly. I finally got a chance to do the book work I had missed the day I covered for my sick tattoo artist. Thankfully, he's back now and balance has been restored.

I'm about to go stir crazy in my office when my alarm goes off to leave for the school. I'm nervous. I've never fit in with the crowd and the thought of going back to a place where you're made to conform from such a young age has me unsettled.

The public speaking part I don't mind, even though kids can be assholes sometimes. I'm curious if I'll be the only adult speaking who doesn't have a fancy degree.

I check in at the front desk under Dante's name. The lady looks at me skeptically but gives me a nametag and shows me to the classroom where students begin to file in. I'm not sure which would be more believable to her. Telling her I'm Dante, a heart surgeon, or telling her I'm Dante's brother who he called to take his place because he got called into surgery. Either way, she gives me the side-eye like I'm some kind of derelict.

A few more guest speakers enter with the kids. These adults are professionals. I stand out like a sore thumb. The difference between us is obvious. The man and woman are both in pressed suits. They look like they spent the day in their modern offices pushing papers, talking in web meetings and ordering people around.

I look like...a guy who likes fun. Ripped jeans, scuffed boots, t-shirt showing off my body art and muscular physique, spiked hair...I'm a father's worst nightmare...corporate America's too.

The suits start talking about how they got out of work early to come to career day and how glad they are not to finish the rest of the day at their office. Neither of them invite me into the conversation. They're probably assuming I don't have a career, even though I'm here speaking. But to them, I probably don't. I'm sure they're into making connections to build their status in the business world so they can get more status and privilege than they probably even deserve.

A teacher walks up to the front of the room and waves the three of us over to her. She's casual. More casual than any teacher I've ever met. Her long black hair is up in a ponytail. She rocks a t-shirt that says *Yes, I research...thoroughly...* She's got sneakers on that peak out under her boot cut jeans and a set of keys that hang around her neck on a hot pink lanyard.

"So, you'll each get about ten minutes. All you have to do is tell about what you do and then invite the kids to ask questions. And they will ask tons of questions. Easy peasy!" She smiles at us a little too wide like she's trying to convince herself she's telling the truth, and this will be easy.

"Excuse me, Ms..." She never introduced herself, so I have no idea what her name is.

"Oh", she rests her hand over her chest in embarrassment, then snorts. "Jennings. Ms. Jennings", she emphasizes the Ms. as color tints her cheeks.

"Ms. Jennings. Thank you. Uh...I'm taking Dr. Jackson's place", I start, when the guy presenting alongside me says to the woman in a low voice, *that explains it.* "I just thought you should know."

"Oh. Um...Okay. What do you do?"

"A tattoo artist. I own studios. The Ink Parlor...downtown", I start to explain to her but she cuts me off.

"Really? I've always wanted a tattoo." Her eyes get wide with wonder. I know that look. So many women have said that in my shop and those exact women are the ones who have no idea what they want and ultimately walk out with nothing.

"Okay. Well, you can go first and then we'll let the investment banker and accountant go next."

"Chief Financial Officer", the woman corrects Ms. Jennings in a cool tone.

"Oh. Yes. Sorry." She shakes her head as if she is ridding herself of the CFO's bad energy and then turns her attention back to me. "I never got your name."

"Archer Jackson, ma'am." I hold out my hand and she shakes it just a little too long. I nod at our now youthful audience. "Looks like we're ready."

I have to say that if there was anything Ms. Jennings was right about, it was the number of questions the kids ask. There wasn't one minute of dead airtime. And the kids were so fascinated with my work compared to the two degreed adults I co-presented with that I started going last just to make sure they got enough time speaking to the students.

Teachers rotated through the classroom, and I had yet to see Thomas. My assumption was that each class moved with their teacher to a different room until the end of career day. It was a cool concept that allowed everyone to see each group of presenters.

This last group is what I assumed to be the last class because we only had about a half hour until the time Dante gave me to pick Thomas up.

Kids fill the room once more and as soon as he walks through the room, Thomas' eyes land on me.

"Uncle Archer?!" Thomas' voice cuts through the room as he weaves through the kids to hug me.

Man, I love this kid. He's in third grade but I swear you can't get anything over on him. Tall, thin, probably because his mother feeds him twigs and berries, and smart as a whip.

"Where's dad?" I can see the worry in his eyes.

"He got paged. He asked me to come in his place." Thomas' eyes light up as soon as he makes the connection. I laugh hard. "Yeah. We're gettin' into mischief after school", I confirm.

"Yes!"

Thomas lets me go to do our special handshake. Damn this kid just makes my day.

"Alright. Go sit down before you get me detention", I tease him, looking up to find the most beautiful witch I've ever known looking at me from the back of the class.

I wink at her, and she laughs.

"Alright", Bethany claps. "Let's give our full attention to Mr. Caruthers, Mrs. Erickson and Mr. Jackson. Let's start from your right. Mr. Caruthers", Bethany prompts.

I stand back and pretend to watch the lackluster presentations by Mr. and Mrs. Superboring, but I can feel her eyes on me, and I love it. Their presentations drag on forever to me only because I want an excuse to look out into the audience and look at her.

"Thank you." The class claps and when their applause dies down, Bethany introduces me. "And to wrap up our presenter for the day, we have Mr. Archer Jackson, owner of The Ink Parlor".

"Thank you Ms..." I never got her last name when I did her tattoo.

"Everly."

"Ms. Everly", I finish thanking her, before I address the rest of the class. I scan the room before I begin making sure I have everyone's attention. It's unnecessary really. I get the attention of every room I'm in for one reason or another.

Women think I'm hot, moms sweep their kids away from me, guys looking for a tattoo are eager to chat and guys wishing they had a physique like mine can't seem to pull their eyes away.

"When I was about your age, the only thing I ever wanted to do was draw. It was a borderline obsession. I could be anywhere and find a canvas and something to draw with. And when I say anywhere, I do mean anywhere. I once painted a landscape on a fast-food wrapper with some ketchup, mustard and a French fry."

The kids snicker at this even though it's true.

"And I never let that part of me go. I was told that I'd never make a living with my silly pictures. I was told that those same silly pictures were no good. But I loved my silly pictures. Drawing made my soul happy. And I didn't care what anyone else thought. All that mattered to me was how I felt when I did it."

I look to the back of the room at Ms. Everly. Her lips are parted. Her chest rises and falls taking deep steady breaths. I smirk at her before I continue.

"And now people come from all over to have me tattoo my silly pictures on them. I teach other artists to sketch and tattoo their work on others and have several very successful shops of my own. I never gave up on myself when everyone else had. I never wavered in what I wanted when most said I'd be a failure. And most of all, I followed what moved me. And I can honestly say I've never worked a day in my life. Alright. I can see the questions forming." I motion to the front. "Let's see those hands." Mrs. Everly smiles at me, and I can't help but to smile back as a room full of little hands shoot up.

I point to a little girl in the front row. "What's your question sweetheart?" She's so wide eyed I can't stop smiling at her.

"Do people cry when they get a tattoo?"

"Well, I suppose some might but normally when they're in my chair they can take the pain."

"How painful is it?" Her eyes get even wider in anticipation, and I stifle a laugh.

"Some parts of the body are more painful than others. Your hands, feet, ribs, right over your sternum", I touch mine to show where it's located, unsure if they know what that is yet. Then I point to another child because I don't want us to get stuck on pain.

"Do you pierce people at your studio?"

"No. We do not do piercings." Before I can call on the next child, the boy continues.

"Because my dad's friend went somewhere to get pierced and he has a lot of tattoos. How many piercings do you have?"

"Nine."

The boy pauses and searches my face. "I only see two."

Shit. My Jacobs ladder has six and I have a tongue ring. I look to the back of the room at Bethany. Her eyes go wide. She's doing the calculation in her head too. I simply raise a brow at her. I could use a little help here.

The entire classroom looks at Bethany. She doesn't even notice because she's so fixated on me. So, I do the only thing I can think of to get her attention.

"Beth", I call her sternly. She snaps out of it, looks at me and squeezes her thighs together.

"Beth", one of the students repeats after me, questioning my use of her casual name.

Now I'm starting to get hard. She's attracted to me. I'm asking her out after the school bell rings.

"You know him", Mr. Superboring asks Bethany.

"I do", she answers breathily, and I can't help the smile that spreads across my face. This time she shoots me a look, and I

Darla J Michaels

laugh. Oooohs echo throughout the classroom and Bethany is back at attention. "Okay class. Archer...Mr. Jackson...does not do piercings. He does tattoos. So, let's keep the questions on tattoos, shall we? Now, who has the next question for Mr. Jackson?"

A hand shoots up immediately, so I address the little girl. She looks like a smarty pants. Sitting up in her chair nice and straight. She's got long hair that's nicely groomed even for the end of the day with two barrettes pinning up each side. Her button down has capped sleeves, navy blue with gold horses on it. I can tell she's going to ask a great question with the amount of enthusiasm she exudes.

"Mr. Jackson."

"Yes ma'am." I'm trying hard but failing to hold back my smile.

"What tattoo did you give Ms. Everly?"

Chapter 15
Bethany

I watch as the last child finally says goodbye to Archer. Thomas sits patiently at a desk, waiting to go home. He's such a good kid. Respectful. Smart. Great sense of humor. Just the way he looks at Archer, I can tell he looks up to him.

As soon as the last student high fives him and walks out the door, he turns his attention to me. I can feel my face heat. He's all I've been able to think about since my tattoo. In fact, since I took his sharpies, I've worn my hair up in the same way I did that night with the colors I stole...except for today. Today I let my hair flow down my back.

"Ms. Everly", he practically groans my last name. I can't help but to smile and roll my eyes. "That was...somethin' else."

I laugh. I can't help it. Wow. We both got called out by a bunch of third graders.

"How are you", he asks, stopping closer than acquaintances would stand but not as close as I'd like him to.

Darla J Michaels

I love how his eyes glitter with mischief. All hazel and beautiful. I miss his lips. I also miss his touch. And how he smells...like soap and nature.

"Beth?"

"Oh...um...I'm good", my voice goes up an octave and he smiles.

"I'm missing a few sharpies. I was hoping maybe we could meet up and I could get those back."

"Sharpies?"

"Yeah. Red and a light blue."

I cannot give those markers back. I picked them specifically for love, communication and trust. I picked them because I had a feeling that spirit brought him to me. What could be more obvious than a cancelation that brought us together? And now that he's here, by absolute chance when he shouldn't be, it only solidifies spirit's work further in my mind.

"Would you mind checking your work", I ask to distract him. "It's just me at home so..." He nods but eyes me up. I'm not fooling anyone. He knows I'm attempting to distract him. While there are some men out there who you can distract with shiny objects there are most definitely some you cannot. Archer seems like a very focused man to me.

I turn around, not wanting to invite more conversation about the thing I'm not going to give him. His fingertips sear my skin as he moves my hair gently over my shoulder.

"At least you have a zipper this time", he quietly chides me as he opens the back of my dress and parts the fabric enough to see his work.

"Cool", Thomas' voice startles us both and I'm reminded that we are at school...at my workplace. This has to be quick.

"Face forward, Beth."

I do as I'm told as he gently brushes the hair off my back that fell from acknowledging Thomas.

"Starting to scab. Looks good. Does it itch?"

"A little."

"It'll be worse tomorrow. Don't itch it. Just let it do what it's gonna do." He zips up my dress and I turn around to face him, then drop my gaze down to Thomas. He's slack-jawed.

I have no idea what to say to him, so I look at Archer for help. He is no help.

"Come out with me."

My face heats. It was an order. An order I want to follow without question. But when I wait too long, Thomas chimes in.

"I know my uncle looks kind of scary but he's really nice."

I palm my face because that was the most innocent thing a child could say in this moment.

"Say yes, Ms. Everly. I won't even ask for special treatment if you marry him."

This time, I'm shocked but Archer just smiles. Isn't he embarrassed by this?

"Seems fair to me, doesn't it Ms. Everly?"

"I suppose it does. And just what would we do when we go out", I challenge him. On the few occasions I have gone out with a man, they've all been dreadfully boring. I wonder if this one will be just like the rest. Dinner and drinks with the pretense of sex.

"I'll pick you up tomorrow and you'll see."

Who knew twenty-four hours could be so long? He's literally all I've thought about.

I met him at his shop at closing time. He wanted to pick me up at my house, but I didn't think that would be a good idea. Clearly, he knows what I am. I just don't want him asking questions. My answers could ruin this and I'm just not ready to let him go yet. I've barely even had my fill.

When he opens the shop door for me, I stop breathing. Holy shit. Archer stands there in a black fitted shirt, unbuttoned just enough in the front, exposing the gorgeous tattoos on his chest.

He's wearing fitted black slacks with a black belt. His hair is spiked, and he's got that devilish gleam in his eye.

"Ms. Everly." My name rumbles from his lips.

"Hi." My greeting comes out shy and wistful. Immediately, I want to take it back. I sound like a teenager because I feel like a teenager. Giddy with anticipation and flattered that someone cool like him would spend time with someone who's strange like me.

I'm the woman who just never quite fits in. It's not obvious to others but it's a feeling to me. Like most people aren't my people. Except for Archer. He seems like he could be one of my people.

"C'mon in. I want to show you something before we head to dinner." Archer holds the door open for me. It's in that way where his arm stretches across the door, and I have to pass him closely to get over the threshold.

He smells amazing. Just like he did the other night. I can't help but look up through my lashes at him when I pass him. He catches me and smiles.

"We're going back to my office", he tells me and takes the lead while my heels click on the floor behind his confident long strides. I don't mind walking behind him. It's not like I got to really look at him when I came for my tattoo. Now I have a different view. A view of his rear. My goodness this guy has a nice backside.

I bet he has muscular legs. He must work out in some way. I bet if he took off his shirt he'd have abs with that V thing below the belt.

The sleeves of his black dress shirt are rolled up exposing his muscular tattooed forearms and my eyes roam up his back to his broad shoulders. He's taller than me which isn't saying a lot because most people are...especially men. And his hair is styled neater...more formal than it was when he tattooed me. Looks like a fresh cut. I want to run my fingertips over the short hairs on the back of his head. He's perfect.

"See something you like", he asks me without turning around.

I bite my lip to try and stifle a smile, but I can't and when he turns around because I don't answer him, he smiles back at me.

I look away in embarrassment, my face getting hot as my cheeks pink.

"I want to show you something", he tells me as he motions me into his office. "Had it framed today." He nods at the wall.

"Why me?" I realize what I said. It might not be me. He might really like his work or really like witches. "Why frame it...I mean..."

Moving to stand in front of me, he tucks some hair behind my ear that doesn't need to be tucked. "I happen to really like you and there was a chance you might not come back. This flash was so I'd always have something of you here just like you have of me."

"The tattoo", I breathe, suddenly understanding how much feeling and soul he poured into his work that now lives on my body.

"I meant my markers, Beth", he gently corrects me, running his knuckles across my cheek.

Darla J Michaels

"I…" I'm just getting ready to play dumb when the place goes dark.

"Did you do that", he jokingly asks me. I never told him what I am and what I can do. It's a vulnerable part of me that I hide. It's just easier that way. If I keep my gifts to myself, I just feel like I don't belong on the inside instead of displaying how different I am on the outside too.

He drops his hand from my cheek and walks over to the window near his drafting table.

"Looks like it's more than us." I cross the room to stand by him and check it out. The few buildings we can see from his windows are without power, just like we are.

"What do we do now?"

"Wanna drink? I've got whiskey…and beer. We can leave for our reservations once the power comes back on. No sense in leaving earlier."

"I've never had whiskey", I volunteer.

"Whiskey it is. Have a seat", he motions to the table he did my tattoo on and pulls out some glasses from a cupboard. Once he fills our glasses, he's holding his out to me in a toast. "To power outages."

I clink my glass against his and take a sip. It burns as it goes down, and for a second it takes my breath away.

"You okay?" Archer grins at my reaction to the small sip. I nod, attempting to clear my throat but struggling. "It's an acquired taste. Take a few more sips. You'll see."

I do as he tells me, but it doesn't quite help me yet. He rolls over the stool he sat on to do my body art and I take him in. This is a different version of Archer Jackson. Different on the outside yet the same on the inside. No false pretenses. No games. Just a friendly, thoughtful, handsome man.

This is so strange. Since when does the power just go out? There isn't a storm. Maybe an accident somewhere? But for what is likely the whole grid? It doesn't make logical sense.

"What's on your mind, witch?"

I suck in a sharp breath, surprised he referred to me this way. No one has ever called me that and I can't tell if he's being playful or trying to insult me.

"Kitchen or green", he inquires when I don't answer him right away.

I take another sip from my drink and shake my head. This time the sip goes down smooth. How does he even know what that is?

"How do I get to know you if you don't answer my questions, Beth?"

I'm flattered that he wants to know me, but this topic makes me uncomfortable. Unless you are spiritual or practice magic, my experience has been that you don't get a lot of support. People mostly want to poke holes in your logic but what those people don't understand is that magic defies logic...their logic anyway.

"I don't think now is the time. I like you."

"I like you too. That's why I asked. Do you think I'll be scared? Or think you're strange?"

"I gather much doesn't scare you...but I'm not like other women." He nods as his eyes glitter over my face. "My values are...different. Tonight, for example. Were you taking me to a fancy restaurant before all this happened", I ask, motioning to the darkness.

"I plan on taking you to a very nice restaurant, yes."

"That's kind of you but we're not going." Archer furrows his brow at my statement. "Not because I don't want to but because it's not spirit's plan for us."

Darla J Michaels

He lets out a chuckle. There it is. The disbelief. It stings a little and he can see it on my face.

"I don't mean to offend you, Bethany. I just don't know if I believe in interference from a spirit", he tries to smooth over his reaction.

"Spirits", I correct him. "Someone else needed this power outage too." He looks even more confused, so I continue. "Spirit brings you everything you need exactly when you need it, and most people aren't even aware of it."

"That would imply that you have no free will. I make things happen. It's how I've managed to become so successful", he challenges.

"Of course. I'm not trying to imply that spirit pulls all the strings. What I'm saying is that spirit provides us opportunity to align with what serves us. Even if what serves us isn't as clear as money or a job offer. Let me ask you this...did you want to get dressed up tonight and go out to a fancy dinner? It's fine if you did but I suspect you did that because society says that's what you do when you want a lady to know you're interested in her. But I think you wouldn't have dressed up if you didn't feel obligated."

"I like my clothes just fine. But you're right. This wouldn't have been my first choice. Neither would the restaurant."

"Thank goodness. I would have been bored to tears and felt horribly out of place. See? It seems like spirit was serving both of us tonight." I raise a brow at him, and he chuckles. "What would you have done if society hadn't created this box for you to check?"

"I would have taken you for a ride on my bike. Then stopped for a beer and a bite to eat at The Crooked Chimney. We would have gone on a walk downtown and stopped at Moonstone Crossing where I'd hoist you up on the stone edge and get a look at you in the moonlight. Then I'd kiss you until you couldn't think straight."

I smile at him when he says the last part. "I would have liked that. I've never been to The Crooked Chimney. Would we play pool?"

"Depends."

"On what?" I'm smiling at him now because I can just tell he's being mischievous.

"On the cut of your top."

I laugh hard at him. I cannot believe he just said that.

"You asked, darlin'."

"So, what do you want to do now?" Our plans are shot. I know in my soul the power is going to take a while to turn on. We aren't going to that restaurant.

"Can you give me a minute?" I nod, excited about what's to come. Archer is improvising and I can't wait to see what he comes up with. He's clearly creative with drawing. Let's see how creative he can get with life.

I watch him move about his office. He clears off what little is on his tidy desk and then leaves me there with my whisky. He walks in and out of the room dropping off the things he'll need for his plan. I'm instantly comforted when he lights two tall black pillar candles on his desk. I can already feel the room being infused with opportunity.

It looks like he's carrying a pie. The paper plates are underneath it. He makes one more trip setting a paper towel roll down on his desk and then what I'm assuming to be silverware down next to it based on how it clanks together.

Finally, he grabs the carafe and his glass, then waives me over to his desk.

"I have been thinking about this pie all damn day. Just never got a chance to have a slice. But now, I wonder if it's because I wasn't supposed to have this alone." I smile at how he applies my belief in spirit without making me feel like a crazy person.

"Maybe", I hedge. "But the real test is what kind of pie is it?" It matters believe it or not. What's in the pie isn't a preference. It's a spell.

"Apple", he tells me with a gleam in his eye. "Will that do Ms. Everly?"

"That will do perfectly, Mr. Jackson."

"After you", he invites me, handing me a fork.

"I don't keep a pie cutter at my shop." He chuckles. "Hell, I don't even have a pie cutter."

"A fork is just fine", I tell him, genuinely not caring about how casual and unrefined this is. The whole thing is sweet and romantic. Pie and whiskey for dinner during a power outage. Who would have thought?

I dig in right in the center of the pie. Archer smiles at me as I work to get the first bite. When I lift my fork out of the pastry, caramel strings from it. I look at him, unable to hide my excitement in this new development. He chuckles and nods giving me permission to take the first bit.

It is heavenly and I can't help but to moan as I saver the goodness.

Archer takes a forkful and does the same thing. We sit in silence for a minute just eating and enjoying the ambiance.

"I think you might be right about this spirit thing", he concedes.

"Thank you."

"Do you think that's why I wound up at your school yesterday? Spirit brought me there?"

I nod while I chew. There's no way I'm going to tell him about my spell. That it was my desire. That I asked spirit to bring him into my life.

"I never thought I'd see you again", he admits to me while he eats another forkful of the delicious treat.

"Me too." I can't take my eyes off him. It's a pull that makes me never want to be with anyone else but him.

He chuckles. "I cannot believe your class called you out like that."

"That's how kids are. They throw you curve ball after curve ball. They're so much more observant than we give them credit for." Including Thomas. "Your nephew is a really good kid."

"He is. Momma and his parents see to that. They've done a great job raising him."

"What did you two do last night?"

"We bought a dog." My eyes go wide. "Yeah. We went to grab haircuts and some greasy food. And there was this lady selling puppies. Thomas wanted to take a look, and I couldn't deny him."

"He is such a sweet kid. One of the nicest in my class."

"So, we walk over, and these puppies are playing with each other all except for one. He walked over to the cage door, sat down and looked at us expectantly. It was like he just picked us instead of the other way around. And it was the craziest thing too. I lifted him out and he licked my cheek once. Let out a puppy bark at Thomas and then wiggled out of my arms to get down on the sidewalk. Then he just stood by me as if he was telling the lady who was selling him that he was leaving with me."

"Spirit", I tell him before taking another bite.

"Spirit", he echoes my sentiment.

Archer holds out his phone so I can see a picture of the dog.

"What kind of dog is it?"

"A cane corso."

"Beautiful. What did you name it?"

"I haven't yet. Thomas and I were throwing around names all night, but nothing seemed to stick. It'll come to me. I just need a little more time with him." Archer looks at my empty glass. "Would you like more?"

"Yes, please." Somehow that came out wistful and a little dirty."

"Could you not say it like that?" I laugh.

"I can't help it. Can I be honest?"

"That's why I offered you more whiskey. I'm hoping you'll tell me if you're kitchen or green?"

I roll my eyes and shake my head at him. "You make my day better. Every time I see you...or think about you...or hear your voice...my day becomes perfect."

He raises a playful brow at me and cocks his head to the side. I laugh hard as he slides my glass across the desk to me.

"I miss your lips on mine."

"Come here", he gruffly orders me as he slides his chair back to make room for me to sit on his lap.

I grab my glass and come around to his side of the desk.

"This is dangerous."

"You have more clothes on today than you did the other night. I think we'll be just fine."

"May I", Archer asks, looking down at my skirt. I nod and he grabs the fabric of my dress and lifts it up, so I don't have to set my glass down to climb onto his lap. He doesn't lift the fabric high enough to be inappropriate. I grip his shoulder to steady myself on the climb and leave my hand there when I settle in.

I could sit on his lap every day for the rest of my life. Not in a dirty way but to ground me. Because the vibes coming off this man are so safe and so secure, he feels unshakable.

I take a sip from my glass and roll the liquid around on my tongue before swallowing it down.

"I like your dress", he tells me while he smooths out the flowing fabric and his hands settle on my hips.

"Thank you." I wonder if he means it in a dirty way or if his words are genuine. The dress is nothing special. It's pretty but it wasn't like I spent hours in my closet picking something out.

I don't normally do that anyway and I certainly didn't feel the need when I knew deep down inside that this man was now mine. It's not that I don't care. It's that I'm being me because for the first time ever, someone just might be accepting me for who I am.

"You seem to like dresses. It's all I've seen you in. Do you own pants", he jokes.

"Of course I own pants. But dresses feel so magical. And people don't wear them anymore. Dresses make me memorable. Do you know how many looks I get when I go out in a dress? People do a double take, practically breaking their necks to look at me. It's because most people walk around in their pajama bottoms with their hair in a messy bun like it's somehow flattering to look like you rolled out of bed and got dressed from your laundry hamper." Archer chuckles. "Tell me I'm wrong", I challenge him taking a bigger drink from my glass.

"You're not wrong. But something tells me you don't do it for the stares."

"I don't. Dresses just fit me. They're who I am."

"And shoes? Do you have about a million pair of those?"

I laugh at him because of the stereotype.

"I have exactly enough shoes, Archer." He laughs at me now.

"Exactly enough. I'll remember that."

"And why would you remember that?" My heart is beating out of my chest right now. He'll remember it because he isn't planning on being done with me.

"Because I want more with you."

"More than tattooing me almost naked and eating apple pie in your office during a power outage?"

He nods, searching my eyes for an answer to a question he hasn't asked me yet. "More."

"I'm not so sure you could handle me Mr. Jackson. I'm a lot. And I come with spirits."

"Don't underestimate me, witch", he tells me in a low voice, like he's either trying to keep my spirits from hearing or he's talking to himself.

"You keep calling me that."

"I like it. I think it's beautiful that you believe in something others don't understand. I think it's brave. It's what makes you who you are."

"Do you mean that?"

He nods his head and leans forward to close the distance between us. "So far, I really like who you are", he tells me before pressing his lips against mine.

It's a sweet kiss. No tongue. Just brief and gentle contact. Grounded. Secure. Through that kiss, it felt like he was giving me some of the strength that he carries with him. But it's one kiss. And he stops.

I don't pull away from him because I want more.

"Archer." My lips are so close to his it's painful that we aren't touching.

"Beth."

The way he shortens my name like that. It's like a warning. Not in a mean way but a warning, nonetheless.

"Where's the rest of my kiss?"

"If I give it to you, does that mean you won't be sharing kisses with anyone else?"

I pull back from him, getting comfortable on his lap with the distance between us. I want to see his reaction when I answer him. "I teach kids to share in school", I let the thought that I'm not quite his dangle there to see what he does.

"How about a compromise? Do you teach that in school?"

"I do."

"You can share when I let you, Beth. Will that work for you?"

He's being coy. I nod and feel the short, freshly cut hair at the nape of his neck with my fingertips.

"Eyes right here, Beth." He smirks at me when I look into those gorgeous hazel eyes. "I don't dress up for many people. I don't eat pie in my office with women. And I surely don't sit a woman on my lap without intentions of sex."

I hope that's not what he's expecting from me tonight. He'll be sorely disappointed if he does. It's not that I don't want him. I just envisioned my first time being different...special. Not candles and rose petals special but significant somehow.

"But you're not just a woman. I get the feeling that you're a force of nature. And if my experience with forces of nature have taught me anything it's that you treat them with great respect. You don't fear them, but you honor them. You don't stand in their way but instead help them move obstacles. And you show up for them. Every day just like you promised. And when you create this unshakable bond, that force of nature that you happen to be so privileged to have in your life will always be yours even if she wants to share her kisses with someone else."

Darla J Michaels

"Archer..." He doesn't let me get out my rebuttal because his lips are on mine as though his kiss is his commitment to the vow he just spoke. I was going to tell him that I was only teasing. That I had no intention of kissing someone else. How could I when he's the one I'm kissing now? It would be completely ridiculous.

But there's no way he's breaking this kiss to hear what I have to say and I'm glad for it. I'm glad because I don't want to break it either.

It's not that I've had disrespectful men in my life. In fact, I've only had respectful men in my life. But how is it that he's respectful with the promise of being disrespectful in all the ways that might turn me on?

Like...I think he could order me around with the tone he uses when he shortens my name, and I'd follow every command without protest. If he told me to take off my dress right now, I'd do it. And if he told me to get on my knees for him, even though I've never been on my knees for another man, I'd sink to the floor without hesitation.

He's that guy. Gently commanding. Resolute in his expectations. A protector. A limit setter. A leader in a world of followers. And I'm sitting on his lap while he devours my mouth.

Even though he doesn't realize it, Archer created a spell with his offerings to me. The apples symbolize love, the cinnamon passion and prosperity and the whiskey symbolizes spirit connection and celebration.

My ears begin to ring when he kisses me deeper. You know, that piercing noise that only you can hear? That happens when spirit is trying to tell me to pay attention. It's that way for most people but they don't realize it. Instead of leaning into the noise, people try to get rid of it.

Tell Me Who You Go With- Archer & Bethany

Gram taught me to delight in it because when it happens, it means you get to know things that others don't. It means that spirit wants you to pay attention because something is there for you right in plain sight and spirit needs you to see it.

Archer breaks the kiss and tightens his grip around me, nuzzling my head to the side with his nose. I tilt my head for him, needing his lips anywhere he's going to put them.

The stubble on his face with his soft warm lips feels delightful. He's rugged and soft all at the same time.

I want more of him. This, I have a feeling, is a mere taste of Archer Jackson. I don't want a taste. I want all of him.

"Bethany", he breathes against my skin, shifting me once more for his pleasure. "The things I want to do to you..." His hand is in my hair. I left it down tonight. Something about meeting up with Archer makes me want to be wild and free. Not hide so much.

The ringing in my ears gets a bit louder, so I open my eyes to see what my shouty spirit wants me to notice. And my eyes land on a framed piece of art that takes my breath away. A double triqueta, or trinity knot, symbolizing individual souls uniting to form a powerful and eternal bond.

"Do them", I offer myself up to Archer as his teeth graze my collar bone. This is it. He is it. And I trust him. "Do all the things", I beg him in a breathy voice that makes me sound as desperate as I feel.

I realize I'm barely holding onto my glass of whiskey. He must notice as well because he stops worshipping my body to take the glass from my hand. Then he brings it to my lips for me to take another sip.

The way he looks as me...like he's full of devotion. But can you be devoted to someone you don't even know?

"That's it. I want you to take from me, Beth." He allows me a longer sip and then brings the glass to his lips for a taste. "And now I'll take from you."

The ringing stops. And my heart is racing at what we've just done.

The words. The sharing of a beverage that speaks directly to spirit...we've made a vow to each other. Even though he doesn't know it yet, we're bound to each other with something more powerful than a piece of paper. More powerful than a law.

Our souls have just agreed they need each other. Together our souls can rest. Apart will be utter chaos and longing far worse than we've ever experienced before.

Chapter 16
Bethany

I'm ghosting him. It has to be this way. I'm proving a point. I'm not sure if I'm proving a point to my mother, Gram or myself but a point is being proven.

Aside from Archer's texts and calls I haven't seen him once since our date. So maybe the tattoo and career day were just random coincidences.

And the ringing in my ears really could just be tinnitus. Right?

Maybe there is no such thing as spirit. Maybe my mother is right.

There is no such thing as magic, Bethany. She taps her fake French manicured nail on my tarot deck, and I cringe. Her negative energy on my cards makes me want to shove her out of my home. Literally shove her...

Believing in magic and spirits is for crazy people or children. Mother glares at me and wipes the fingertips she touched my deck with on her pressed slacks as though the cards somehow made her dirty. It's the other way around, actually, but she'd never believe that.

Both are tragic if you ask me. Mother turns to me like she's zeroing in on a target.

I think the greatest mistake I made in your upbringing is allowing you to spend so much time with your grandmother. She's filled your head with these silly little notions. Get rid of these. And for God's sake put a little makeup on. You'd look so pretty with a little mascara and eyeliner. Maybe by your next birthday you'll have a plus one.

These were the words my mother said to me after my birthday dinner. She claimed she needed to use the bathroom when they dropped me off at home. Dad and my twin sisters waited in the car. I should have told her to hold it.

In retrospect, I just should have met them at the restaurant but I'm also a grown adult who shouldn't have to hide things in her own home. Especially things I believe so very deeply in.

Which calls to question, if I believe so very deeply in my spirituality, why am I ghosting Archer?

Doubt. The seed of doubt that my mother has planted in my mind is exactly why I haven't contacted him. The seed I have watered more each day that I don't run into Archer.

It's been a week. We exchanged a quick text the day after our date. Archer had sent me a few pictures of his ripped-up couch, a coffee table with the leg about chewed off and a living room that looked like every pillow had been gutted and triumphantly strewn about.

We haven't spoken since, and I feel like I'm suffocating. Like a necessary part of me has been lost.

That night after my mother left, I cried. But the funny thing is, I'm not even sure what exactly I was crying about.

My mother is a hateful, nasty woman. If she doesn't agree with you, you're toast. She will obliterate you any way that she can to make her point or to get her way. Sometimes I wonder if I'm adopted. We are nothing alike.

I've lived with her remarks all my life, so I don't think I was crying over her. Maybe I was crying because I needed Gram. Gram would never speak to me the way my mother does. She was far from a pushover, and she gave as good as she got. But she had this way about her where every time she spoke, she seemed to make sense of people and the world in a way that was accurate even if she had no tangible proof that what she was saying was true.

Gram seemed to just know things. I think there is something to be said about people who have this gift. I find them comforting. Maybe that's what I needed...to be comforted.

Archer was comforting. I think him and Gram would have been friends. I could see them getting into mischief together. I could see Archer and I getting into mischief together.

Then why am I ghosting him? I pick up my phone, my finger hovering over the text message icon where his unanswered messages have accumulated. One hand stirring my simmer pot and the other at the precipice of a decision. Continue making my point or open these messages, fall apart and then apologize to the greatest person that has come into my life since Gram passed away.

What would Gram do? Not this. I'm sure of it. Gram would have told my mother to leave. Then she would have smudged the place and made herself a hot mug of tea.

But I'm not Gram. I don't come to this situation with all the years of practice she had. With all the experiences that gave her

Darla J Michaels

the faith she had before she passed. I'm new. A baby witch is what some call it.

So maybe I'm proving a point to myself. "If I did, in fact, cast a spell that brought my soul mate to me, then I'll see him today. I'll see him and...I have no idea what he'll do but I'll see him and know that I messed up."

And then I'll be heartbroken if he doesn't accept my apology. He has to accept my apology.

But for me to see him, unless he has a side job driving for delivery companies, I need to leave my house.

So, the plan is for me to be out all day. And I can't be at places where I think he'll be at. That will ruin the experiment. I have to be anywhere my mind takes me. If it drifts into my mind as something to do or be at, that is where I go. The point is that spirit will bring him to me if it's meant to be. And if it's not meant to be, I delete his number, drink a bottle of wine and burn my cards.

Okay...maybe not that last part but the wine for sure. The phone number will be harder to delete until I drink the wine.

I slip on one of my favorite dresses. The weather is starting to warm up so I can wear short sleeves without fear of freezing.

It's a cream-colored t-shirt dress. I add casual shoes with laces, pull my hair up into a bun so I can keep an eye out for Archer with an unobstructed view and head out.

I try my hardest to stick to the places that pop into my head and not the places where I might run into him.

The first stop is the farmer's market downtown. I go every weekend when they open. Most of the produce is organic and since I try to only use fresh ingredients for my meals, shopping here instead of the local grocery stores is perfect. Plus, I support the hard-working local farmers instead of the big chains.

I didn't plan this trip out the best though because now I need to take my purchases home, so they don't spoil. I decide that I'm going to get them safely inside but not prepare my purchases for the week until after I've seen Archer. I need to be out and about as long as possible for this to be fair. Afterall, it would be silly of me to do this experiment and not do it right.

I go grab some coffee and then remember the cupcake and visit Sinful. I know he might be there, but it did pop into my mind, so I give myself a pass.

When I step into the bakery I notice two things. First the smell. The store name doesn't do it justice. Second no Archer. I end up purchasing two jumbo cupcakes. One being pineapple upside-down cupcake and the other whiskey maple bacon.

I devour both at a park not far away from the storefronts. Eating my feelings has never tasted so good.

Then I decide to go shopping for my kitchen, even though I need nothing. I have every trinket and gadget they make but I still like to look around as though I don't.

The bookstores are next which takes me to lunch where I stop at the bar down the street from The Ink Parlor to grab a bite to eat and a beer. I order the same thing down to the number of drinks I had the night I got my tattoo in hopes of conjuring Archer up.

No such luck.

In an attempt not to be defeated, I continue my quest to test the very spirit I'm steadily losing faith in. But by the dinner hour, I have lost all hope. Spirit has not brought him to me. Which means I have created this romantic story in my head because of Gram and some tarot cards.

I feel like an idiot. I have probably lost the best thing that has ever happened to me because I believed in the divine. Because I believe in some unseen force that lurks about and helps people that call upon it. Maybe mother is right. Believing in spirits is for crazy people and children. I feel like both right now.

I need to get some air. I can't be here in this house with the so-called spirits and cards that tell my future.

I'm also a little tipsy because I've had about half a bottle of wine. Driving is out. I decide I'll go for a walk. I'll bring my picking basket and walk to my favorite spot to forage for herbs and flowers.

It used to be bigger, but someone built a house on the property. I was devastated that whoever bought that land had demolished so many trees and natural foliage. But I suppose people need houses and if I were going to have another home, that's where I'd want it. I can't fault someone for having good taste, now, can I?

The walk is just long enough to sober me up a bit. I clear my head, focusing on the sound my shoes make crunching on the gravel alongside the country road. I need the endorphins. That's probably what will carry me through the days without Archer. He's irreplaceable. If I ever did get a second chance with him, I'll never let him go.

"Why did you fail me spirit? I trusted you", I whisper to myself before I step into the lush green wilderness from the road.

I've picked here several times before. The land is ripe with wildflowers and herbs. Still trying not to feel betrayed by the spirits I've trusted for so long, I focus on the bounty at my feet. The darker it gets, the harder time I have at discerning what is good to pick. I should have brought a flashlight with me.

Out of nowhere, there's this yipping sound and what appears to be a ghostly creature darting across a wide expanse of lawn towards me.

Tell Me Who You Go With- Archer & Bethany

I realize that I've popped out at the forest's edge and what is likely the owner's dog is heading right for me...and so is the owner.

Chapter 17
Archer

What the hell is that? I'm drinking a beer on my back porch, relaxing from the long day of body art. Either I've had one too many beers or there's something in the woods. In my woods.

I take a swig of beer and keep on eye on the white creature moving between the trees. I've seen deer and other wild animals, but nothing like this.

So, I watch...and wait...and drink...and finally see the creature for what it really is...a she.

A she in a white dress that flows down to the ankles with long sleeves. She's carrying a basket full of greenery.

Now...I don't give a shit about that greenery, but I must admit, this is strange, and I want to meet her. She calls to me. For some reason that I can't quite place, I need her on my front porch.

I slowly get up from my chair and sneak to the door, so I don't alarm her...though I doubt she even sees me here with the massive sprawl of land.

"Spirit", I whisper. "C'mon boy." My new puppy jumps up from his bed and trots out to the porch. He's only been here about a week and has thoroughly explored my land. I let him roam because he doesn't seem to have an interest in being too far away from me. But the moment he sees her; he bolts off the porch.

I chuckle when her head snaps up to look our way and she freezes where she stands. I follow my dog. He's already reached her and she's crouching down to give him some love.

So, imagine my surprise when I get closer and realize the woman I've been chasing love from for the past week is on my property, stealing my foliage and petting my dog.

It's been a week since our date and she hasn't returned any of my calls or texts. I've been damned near out of my mind about it.

This week was her last week of school. Thomas said she was there all week. He teased me when I asked how he thought she was. Hell, I would have teased me too.

She was all I could think about. I replayed every moment we had together on our date and couldn't find one thing that would cause her to stop talking to me. And now she ends up in my backyard?

She's being licked to death by Spirit, so she hasn't seen me yet.

"You're trespassing."

She looks up in shock and Spirit takes the opportunity to jump on her, knocking her over backwards.

"Spirit", I call him, snapping my fingers so he knows I mean business. I crouch down and hold my arms out and he leaves her and rockets over to me, jumping up into my arms. My dog licks at my face as I try to hold onto him, so he settles down a bit and doesn't charge at Bethany again. She has some

150

explaining to do and I don't want her distracted when she does it.

"You alright", I ask her, holding out my hand to help her up while Spirit squirms in the crook of my arm.

"Yes." She averts her eyes and if I'm not mistaken, she's got tears in them.

"Bethany? Are you hurt?"

"No." She starts to chew on her lower lip, the tears in her eyes about to brim over. I reach down to pick up her basket of herbs. Most of it has been scattered onto ground, no thanks to my dog. But I can't imagine someone like Bethany tearing up over some greenery.

When I turn to her, she wipes a tear from her cheek.

"You've got two choices, Beth. You can either come back to the house with me and start talkin' or I'm gonna have you arrested for theft and trespassing."

She chuckles, then laughs and hiccups out a sob. I let Spirit down and pull her against me while the dog circles wildly around us.

"Thief", I murmur into her ear and then kiss her on the head.

We walk across the yard to my back porch. We're both silent even though we have so much to say. Well, I have a lot to say. I decided in the last week that if I did see her again and she doesn't share some reason that I've greatly offended her, I'm telling her what I want to do with her and asking her to marry me.

I know it sounds hairbrained and halfcocked because it is. But it's a hairbrained halfcocked idea that I can't get out of my head with her.

I have never thought about a woman like I have thought about this one. She consumes me. And it's not just my dick that's thinking this through. Although if I'm being honest, he's in my head much of the time. But it feels like we're something more. Like she was put on this Earth just for me and the day she walked into my office, it was like a match had been made.

I had only spent a few hours with this woman and my heart belonged to her. Every time my eyes met hers or my lips touched her skin it felt like something otherworldly.

And a reasonable person could challenge me and claim it's the way someone reacts when they start a relationship. I had thought about that too. But I've tried to start relationships, and they've never felt like this. I've never wanted someone as much as I've wanted Bethany.

I would even go so far as to say that I don't want her. I need her. And I mean that quite sincerely. When she stopped texting me back and didn't return my phone calls, I felt lost. I felt like this woman who had my heart was just gone. She had left me, and I loathed it. Before her, I never cared if someone ghosted me. There were plenty of women out there who were interested. I'd just pick the next one in line who looked like she'd put out. There wasn't even anything to get over.

But Bethany? I'd never get over her if she wasn't mine. I need her to be mine.

"Sit", I command her, pointing to the wood swing on my back porch. Bethany does as I tell her and looks up at me like an errant child. Spirit jumps up next to her and lets out a little whine.

I go inside and grab a beer for us and a dog bone for Spirit. I can't have him distracting me during this conversation and heaven knows if there's something for him to bother, he'll bother it. He's about cost me a fortune in furniture this week!

Darla J Michaels

Bethany is petting the silver-gold hair of my dog and he's looking up at her longingly. I shake my head. I think my dog has picked her like he picked me.

"C'mon boy", I motion off the bench with the bone in my hand. He doesn't give Bethany another thought as he follows his nose to the treat I have for him. I toss it off the porch, knowing it'll take him some time to finish it.

When I hand Bethany the beer, she glances at the label, then looks up at me and wipes another tear from her cheek.

"I could get you whiskey", I offer, confused as to why a beer would cause someone to be emotional.

"No. No...Brewed Awakening. I've had it before", he says with more emotion in her voice. "It's good", she chokes the words out and takes a swig.

"Did something happen, Beth?"

I don't know why, but she's laughing. It's the kind of laugh someone lets out when they're unstable. Like they've been pushed over the edge and instead of anger, it comes out in this maniacal fashion.

"I'm sorry." She wipes another tear from her cheek and faces me, swiveling her body so her knee is crooked on the seat and her other foot dangles over the bench not quite reaching the deck.

"For what?" I take a sip of my beer and wait. I want to hear the words. I don't think I've ever had a woman apologize to me in my entire life. In fact, I'm not so sure I can ask her to marry me anymore. I didn't think women did apologize and now that I've seen it with my own eyes, I'm not sure if she's even human.

"I should have called you back. I should have text you. I didn't and I'm sorry." She hiccups and I can't handle it. I don't want her to cry. I don't want her to think for a second that I don't want her.

"Beth, darlin'. I'm gonna kiss you and then you're gonna sit here and listen to what I have to say. And when I'm done, I want to know what you're thinkin'. Can you do that for me?"

She hiccups and nods and I turn towards her desperate for this kiss. But before I kiss her, I need to calm her down. I think she's panicking. She must think I'm going to break things off with her.

"Shhhh", I tell her and stroke her face with my fingertips, but she seems to be getting more upset.

"Shhhh...Bethany...darlin'. We're okay. Do you hear me? We're okay. Let me see those lips." She cracks a smile, and I can't help but to smile too. Then I kiss her. I suppose that's not really a fair description. What I do is more than a kiss. I love on her.

She needs loved on. Almost like I need to breathe life back into her. What did she do while she was away from me? This woman isn't the same force of nature that left my studio. It's like she broke after our date and hasn't quite put herself back together yet.

Even the way she touches me is different. On our date, her fingertips ran over my skin like she was exploring something that was hers. Now, she isn't exploring. She's almost rigid. Like her body is confused about what it's doing.

I wipe the last tear from her cheek and playfully bring her beer up to her lips. She gives me a small smile before she takes a sip.

"I don't know what happened to cause you to stop talking to me. If I did something, I want to know about it so I can fix it." I mean it. In all sincerity I do. I never want to do a foul thing to this woman that she won't enjoy. "Beth...come on out with it."

"I lost myself." She sinks her teeth down on her lip again and then takes another drink. I motion for her to keep going. "I

Darla J Michaels

stopped everything that I believe in because someone
challenged me."

"And I was part of what you believed in?" I don't
understand what she's referring to. "Did I give you reason not to
believe in me?" Her eyes get wide at my question.

"No. Never. I never should have stopped. It was foolish of
me. Gram would be so disappointed. I know better." I catch
movement peripherally and see that she's spinning a ring
around her finger. A thin silver band on the same finger I want
to put my ring on.

I still have no idea what she's talking about but it's clear to
me that she's learned her lesson. Whatever that lesson
happened to be.

"Who does this belong to?" I reach out and touch the band
she's been twisting around her ring finger.

"Gram. She gave it to me before she crossed over."

I take her hand in mine and twist the ring off her finger. She
starts to protest but I shake my head. "I'm moving it. Not taking
it", I reassure her. There's just one problem. The ring won't fit
on her other fingers. "We can resize it or you can wear it on a
chain", I offer.

"Why?"

"Because my ring will need to go here", I tell her. Her brows
raise in surprise. "I want a wife. I want you as my wife."
Bethany's mouth falls open.

"Okay."

I chuckle. "Okay?"

"I do." She shakes her head. "Yes. It's a yes."

Now I'm smiling so wide I think my cheek muscles are going
to get stuck like this.

"You do?" She nods, shifts in her seat and pulls her phone
from a pocket in her dress.

"Bethany, you need to hear what you're agreeing to first", I warn.

"You. I'm agreeing to you. Yes. I want you. Always. I never want to be without you again."

"I need you to want more than me." Her gaze meets mine and this time, she's confused. I never thought I'd get to have this conversation with her, so I didn't plan out just how I was going to broach the subject. So I just come out with it.

"I got an invitation to join The Brotherhood. It's a group of men who find a woman and we all date that woman within The Brotherhood." Her eyes go wide in shock. I'd be surprised if she responded any other way, so I try not to focus on her reaction and continue. "You'd be my wife in every way. The only difference is that instead of having a monogamous relationship, I'd share you with my fellow Brothers. I'd ask you to go on dates with them and do all the things you allow me to do to you as my wife. I'd want to watch them have you and tell you what to do to them. I want a wife to share however I please and I want that wife to be you."

Bethany looks down at her beer and picks at the label. I'm sure she's considering a lot of things about my offer now.

"Is it still a yes?" Now I'm nervous. I don't want to lose her. If she denied me this, I'm not sure what I'd do.

"Will it be a real marriage?"

"You bet your ass it would be. I don't believe in divorce. We'll have each other until our last breaths."

"Okay. I'm free for most of the summer. There's a week where I have the girls but other than that, any time before September will work."

Now it's my turn to be surprised. "Yes?" She looks at me and smiles. Then she nods. "Yes?!"

"Yes, Archer. I will be your wife."

Darla J Michaels

I set my beer down and reach for hers. She pulls it away from my reach. I don't give a shit about that beer. The only thing I want right now is her in my arms.

She shrieks when I grab for her and pull her onto my lap. This is my favorite place to have her. Right here. Looking into her beautiful blue eyes.

"I want my markers back, witch", I tell her playfully. She laughs triumphantly and takes a big gulp of her beer.

"I'm sorry", she tells me once more.

"Don't ever do that again. I missed you", I confess before pulling her to me for a kiss. "Don't hide from me, Beth. I want to know everything that burdens you so I can take your burdens away. That's my job now." She offers me her beer, and I take it, setting it down next to mine.

I kiss her. Not like I kissed her at my studio but softer. Because something tells me that she needs soft right now. She needs my gentle side. Bethany is a sweetheart. She's more vulnerable than she lets on and a part of me loves that about her.

"Are you going to call the cops on me now", she asks smugly.

"Naw...I've got plenty of ways to subdue you inside."

Chapter 18
Archer

"Tyler, what's up, man?"

"Hey Arch. What's goin' on?"

"How's the tattoo?" Tyler chuckles.

"Cut the shit man. You didn't call about my tattoo. Did you find her?"

Of course he'd know I found her. I never call him for anything and suddenly, I'm calling him out of the blue a week after his appointment?

"Yeah. I found her. She said yes. We have a date."

"A date? I think we give you the date, man."

"No, a wedding date."

"Damn. You serious?"

"Yeah. I told her what the expectations are, and she just pulled out her phone and started looking at the calendar."

"I told you. Look, I gotta go. I'll message the guys. Micah Stevenson will be in touch with next steps. He runs this thing."

"Damn. Okay. Thanks Tyler."

I still can't believe it myself. This is crazy. Never in my wildest dreams did I think I'd get married, and she'd let me share her.

I suppose it isn't that unheard of but it's not the norm that's for sure.

I need to figure out how I'm going to manage my personal affairs this summer. Joining The Brotherhood sounds great but that's not just one obligation, that's many. I bring one woman in and get six in return. That's six women I'm dating while running my studios and opening another across town. I'm going to be stretched thin but in the end it will all be worth it.

I ride the high of having a wife and a future rotation of pussy till the end of the day. Fuck. Could life get any better? Maybe. If I were married tomorrow with access to the pussy rotation that would be better than waiting.

I'm alone in my parlor. The staff and patrons are long gone for the day. After I shoot Bethany a quick text to check in on her, I pull up my email. As promised, waiting for my reply is Micah's email.

He's brief. I'm not surprised. His email asks me to provide them with the attached list of items to confirm I'm a good fit. Well alright. Let's look at this list.

Damn. The document is a full-page checklist, single spaced. Good lord. These men are not fucking around.

There are some financial statements I need to provide along with some medical information. Both of us have to test for disease and Bethany needs to have an exam. There's some medical power of attorney documents here that Bethany and I both need to sign off on. She releases all documents to Dr. Braden Hart and gives me all discretion with respect to medical decisions for herself.

There are some boilerplates that look like they make up a sexual contract of sorts. One for her and one for me.

Pictures of Bethany for their review and a background check disclosure.

I need to submit all documents in person to Micah at a mutually agreeable time. Once he's collected the information, it looks like we see Dr. Hart.

This process is something else. I'm not sure if it's just unfamiliar or a bit disjointed. Some of these things I'm not sure I can do before Bethany and I wed. We've both got a lot going on right now. She's trying to get ready to watch her younger twin sisters and for some reason, she's stressed about it. They're thirteen-year-old girls. How hard could it be to take a few young ladies for a week?

I message Bethany to see if she could stop by the shop. I'll have her sign these healthcare documents and hand off her boilerplate. She can work through it at her leisure and that will just need to be good enough for Micah.

Ever accommodating, Bethany stops by to pick up the documents.

"This one is for me as your husband to make decisions about your medical care", I explain, laying the paper out in front of her. "And this gives Dr. Hart permission to treat you and request your medical records." Barely looking at the documents, she signs and dates the bottom.

"And this one is the agreement. You can write your information in, and someone will make it official", I tell her, noticing her tense when she skims the document. "Is there a problem with that one?"

"No. No. I just...want to make sure I do it right", she tells me with a smile that feels slightly too big for Bethany.

I message Micah back about meeting. His assistant, Claudia, reaches out to finalize the meeting time. It takes Micah longer than I'd like to get on his calendar, but I don't exactly have a lot of free time myself. Really, it doesn't matter all that much, considering we aren't getting married for another month after I meet with Micah. As long as we're set on the first day I'm married, that'll do.

I'm so busy, time passes in a blur. It's finally the day I get to meet the rest of the guys and submit my information to be accepted into The Brotherhood.

Security shows me to Micah's office. He's not alone. I recognize Tyler but the other two don't look familiar.

They stand when I open the door. Tyler nods at me in greeting while Micah gets up to shake my hand.

"This is Dr. Jonathan Patino and Dr. Braden Hart." I shake their hands and we exchange pleasantries. I look notably different compared to them. Even Tyler could be considered a business professional because his tattoos are well hidden. I stick out like a sore thumb.

It seems like I'm the only one who notices because Micah just jumps right into the paperwork I brought them.

"Finances look excellent. Business owner. Expanding..." He pauses to look up at me. "You did all this yourself?"

"I read a lot." It's easy to assume I got lucky or a dead relative left me my money because of how I look. But behind the ink, I'm smart and driven. Those two components are lethal in business. I've done very well for myself to say the least.

Micah passes the medical documents to Braden. Braden looks them over to make sure he has everything he needs then he tucks them in his briefcase.

Micah pulls out the pictures of Bethany he had me include. "She's prettier in person", he comments before passing the photos to the others.

"What? When did you meet with Bethany?" I'd really like to know this detail since he made me go through the effort to get him the photos that he didn't even need.

"I never said I met with her. She goes to the farmer's market on the weekend. It was easy to check her out", he states plainly.

I try not to be annoyed by this. I'll be sharing her anyway, but I'm not a fan of the sneaking around. I want to be involved, not on the outside.

"When's the wedding", he asks, closing the folder and handing everything except my agreement back to me.

"July fourteenth."

"Where's it at?"

"We don't have the details worked out." Micah looks surprised by this.

"We're busy." I don't owe him an explanation about my free time.

"Do you have an officiant?"

"I have no idea. I hope Bethany's taking care of all that."

"I'll do it if you need one. Short notice and all", Jonathan offers.

"Alright. It would be symbolic to have someone from The Brotherhood marry us."

"Yeah. Happy to help. I'm on call that day so we may have to play it by ear", he tells me, scrolling through his phone.

"That's fine. We want it small. Just us."

"And a witness."

"Shit. I forgot about that. Okay. I'll remind Bethany."

Darla J Michaels

"Look, Grace can stand in if she wants to keep things quiet for professional reasons", Jonathan offers.

"I'll let her know."

"We'll need Bethany's agreement once you're married. We can't really start without it. Yours will do. I'll get the guys a copy and get you a copy of theirs along with the Ladies once you're on the schedule." Micah extends his hand to me, and I shake it.

"Welcome to The Brotherhood, Archer."

5 Years Earlier- Mid-July

Chapter 19
Archer

"Can I make you breakfast?" Bethany stands in her kitchen in a tank top and underwear, pouring herself a cup of hot coffee. I observe her as she adds a small pour of cream from the creamer pitcher, gently setting the porcelain dish back on the counter. She seems to be in great thought as she stirs the coffee, never taking her eyes from it as if what she's doing has great significance. I think it does, so I don't interrupt her but continue watching as she uncaps the dainty matching sugar dish, taking a pinch of sugar and sprinkling it in her brew. She looks down at her cup with a small smile and stirs clockwise once more. When she lays her spoon down on a napkin, she lets out a deep exhale. I take that as my permission to speak.

"I have never seen someone look at a cup of coffee with so much adoration as you Mrs. Jackson." She smiles, rolls her eyes up to the ceiling and takes a sip from her cup.

Darla J Michaels

"I don't eat meat", she volunteers.

"Excuse me?"

"Are you going to give me a hard time about this like everyone else? I mean...you caught me picking herbs from your property", she tries to defend herself, standing behind the counter as if it will protect her from my answer.

"Like...don't eat meat as in no meat? Like...no eggs, even?" I don't want to be mean but damn...this is probably something I should have asked about. She shakes her head, her blue eyes never breaking eye contact with mine. "Alright. Well...I can go to the store and pick up a few things. I do eat meat and if you don't want to purchase it, I'll have no problem doing so. Do you at least know how to cook it?" I realize I sound a little chauvinistic, but I wasn't expecting this one. It's more shocking than no air conditioning.

"No. To both", she tells me solemnly. To both? "I won't have that in my house", she clarifies in a gentle voice that somehow still conveys she's the authority. I tilt my head to the side in challenge. "We won't eat meat here", she tells me, swallowing hard at the finality of her statement.

"Even me?" She nods. "Even if I prepare it just how I like?" She nods again. "You sure about that?" A breathy yes is her answer as I slide my chair across her wood floor. I'm in boxers. It's way too stuffy to wear anything else in here until we leave.

She doesn't take her eyes off me as I walk to her. I like it. It shows she's got guts. Her actions are consistent with what I've seen from her so far.

I stop just beside her. She doesn't turn her attention to me. There it is. This is where her bravery ends. When I get close to her. I'm not sure how I feel about that. I don't want her scared of me.

"Darlin'." When she glances my direction and turns her attention back to her coffee cup, I grab her by the waist and hoist her up onto the counter. She lets out a shriek, not expecting me to get her attention in this way. I lay my hands on her knees and slide them apart, stepping in between them.

"Don't be disrespectful, Beth." Then my mouth is on hers. Damn. When we kiss, we're like live wires. I don't care that she doesn't eat meat. I don't even care that she doesn't want it here. I plan on spending almost no time here. In fact, I want to sell it. We won't need two places and mine happens to come with air and steak.

"I'm hungry", I tell her against her lips. She pulls back and furrows her brows at me. She thinks I'm telling her to cook for me. I place my hand on her chest and shove her back.

"Archer", she protests weakly as I hook my fingers in her panties and slide them down her hips.

"Shhh...don't interrupt me while I'm getting ready to eat", I gently chastise her, tossing her panties onto the floor and hooking her legs over my shoulders.

She's wet. I'm not surprised. While we didn't fuck last night, we did just about everything else until she couldn't keep her eyes open. She's an eager student. Eager to please and be pleased alike. I like that about her.

She whimpers when I kiss her slit. I can't help but to smirk. I love her little sounds. I lick my lips to find her looking down her body, watching me.

"You sure I can't eat meat in your house?" I give her a peck on her slit again and run my tongue from the bottom of her slit to her swollen clit, flicking away as she gasps. She takes a long hard breath as she groans and arches to me for more. "You don't seem to mind the meat I'm eating right now", I observe,

Darla J Michaels

rolling my eyes up to hers while I bring my mouth down right over her clit and tongue her relentlessly.

"Maybe I should stop", I tease her, pulling away. She grabs for me, knocking her coffee cup off the counter. It falls to the floor and shatters, splattering coffee everywhere.

"No? Well you said that I couldn't eat meat here...so..."

"Archer...", her eyes beg me, and I'm caught at a crossroads. I don't like being told no, especially by my wife but I want to make her come. She's so pretty like this. Pent up for me. Needy. Maybe even a little desperate.

"You have no idea..." I kiss her between the legs. "...how torn I am between fucking you..." I tongue her again. "...licking you..." I slide a finger inside her and when she whimpers, I give her clit a few pecks to punctuate my last option. "...or teaching you a lesson by not finishing my meal."

"Please."

Fuck if I love to hear her beg.

"Please what, Bethany."

"Don't stop", she urges me.

"So, you want me to eat?" She nods frantically, and I dip my head down to taste her again. She runs her fingers through my hair and her response makes my decision for me. She's so sweet...tentative...like her body is about to short circuit with everything she's feeling right now. I feel her tighten around my finger before she comes. She groans as her fingers slide from my hair to the stubble on my face. This is the first time I've truly loved how a woman has touched me.

This is the first time I have truly loved...

Bethany

"I just need a few things", I tell Archer as we walk through the farmer's market. He doesn't seem like he's in a hurry. I like that about him. It's mid-morning. We've showered, made each other orgasm again, showered again and had breakfast.

I look over at him in his t-shirt, jeans and leather boots he purchased before coming here. His clothes were too hot even for the weather this morning. He said we'd get to his place later. I have seen his place but haven't been inside. Based on size alone, it's much different than mine.

"What are we looking for?" Archer grabs my hand and pulls me closer to him. I stop and just look at him. Dark hair. The most beautiful hazel eyes. Dark stubble against his sharp jawline. He raises a full dark devilish brow at me and smirks.

"Bethany! You have a boyfriend?!"

My heart stops. Quite literally, I think. We both turn in the direction of the woman storming up to us, carrying a few bags in her well-manicured hand. She looks ridiculous for a farmer's market. Heels. Flowy floral dress. Big brimmed hat. Large dark sunglasses. I stifle an eye roll out of pure respect.

Archer smirks at me and looks back at the woman. Before I have time to tell him who this woman is, he's greeting her.

"Archer. I'm her husband. Not her boyfriend." He offers his hand to her, and she freezes where she stands but doesn't take the hand he offers.

I'm mortified as her eyes travel up his forearm. She's looking at the tattoos. It's clear she hates them. No. She's disgusted by them.

Once she's done looking my husband over like he's vermin, she turns to me. Her gaze lands on my gold wedding band.

"You didn't", she challenges, disgust clear in her voice.

I can feel Archer's eyes on me and my tears begin to well before I can stop them.

"And you are…", Archer asks, still being unnecessarily polite.

"Her mother", she huffs out, eyes like daggers at Archer.

Archer's eyebrows shoot up in surprise and I let out a teary chuckle. Even he can't believe we're related.

"Mom…", I start to explain but she cuts me off.

"You're a disgrace. A complete embarrassment.", she hisses at me, then looks Archer over once again before turning on her heel and storming off.

"I'm sorry", I tell him tearfully.

"No." He shakes his head and then wraps his arms around me. "You don't apologize for others behavior. I won't allow that."

I smile and pull in a few quick breaths to try and stifle a sob.

"Let it out. You don't want it to stay inside, witch. It'll eat you up."

He's right. It will eat me up. I'm sad for how they met but I can't say I expected it to go much differently any other time. Mother and I are nothing alike. She's such a snob. And mean. Such a mean bitter woman.

The way Archer holds me, it's like he knows heartbreak. Like he's walked side by side it for a good long time. It's almost like he's comfortable with it. And it makes me cry harder. We're nice people. Even though I don't know him, I know that he's nice. Spirit picked well for me. This I know deep down in my soul.

Tell Me Who You Go With- Archer & Bethany

I decide I like Archer holding me. Even though it's muggy out. I wonder if he's counting the seconds until he can get out of this embrace because of how warm it is. Being in his arms is something I could do regardless of the weather. He feels so good to me. Like any care I had in the entire world is just gone now.

I peek up at him when I untuck my head from his chest. His beautiful eyes scan my face.

"Let me see your mouth, Bethany." He doesn't let go of me. Just waits for me to tip my head back far enough to where he can dip his head down and press his lips to mine.

Kissing Archer is heaven. It's slow. He blocks out the world. It's like he could care less we're standing in the middle of a public place and he's showering me with affection. He isn't being indecent. His hands always stay at the most appropriate place. But he is loving me, and I must admit, I like it. I'd be willing to kiss this man anywhere, in front of anyone.

When he ends the kiss, he doesn't let me go.

"Bethany." I roll my eyes up to meet his once more. "It was just a moment, darlin'. Don't let it ruin your day." So simple yet so profound. And he knew my mother's words and the way she treated Archer would hang over my head, looming like a dark cloud. He's perceptive and I like that about him.

"Let's get what you came here for. Then we'll stop at my place and the shop. I took this week and next week off, so we'd have time to get things in order."

By the time we've walked from one end of the market to the other, Archer's arms are full of my purchases. Well...his purchases. He insisted on paying even when he couldn't access his own wallet easily. He simply handed me a wad of cash and continued accepting the bags I'd hand him.

Darla J Michaels

"You said a few things", he gives me a playful side-eye on the way to his Range Rover. I look over at him, now embarrassed that he's holding so many bags. "I'm not sure this will fit in my fridge with all the meat in it and all."

He's trying to tease me, but it won't work.

"It's not going to your house, it's going to mine", I tell him simply.

"No ma'am. We spent one night in that hotbox you call a home. I need sleep and I can't get it there", he clarifies.

"I can't spend all day with you. I have things to do." He looks at me and chuckles. "I'm serious. Things I'd like to cook. Daily rituals that keep me grounded. These are non-negotiables for me. If you drop me off at my place, I can come out to yours later. I'll even trespass so you can subdue me again Mr. Jackson."

Chapter 20
Archer

I get a text from Micah summoning me to his office this evening for my first meeting with The Brotherhood. That's great and all but I do have a life. A life with my new wife. He can't just spring a meeting on me same day and expect me to jump.

When I sent him a message back that I couldn't make it, he simply responds by telling me that we'll be on the calendar for next month's rotation. My call to him goes to voicemail. I'm pissed.

This is one of the things that bothers me about this group I have become a part of. I'm clearly not in yet. Now I understand that I've just come into this group but it's not like they only had a week to prepare for my arrival. They've had me jump through enough hoops that people as regimented as them should have given me a heads up about this meeting.

Unacceptable. Now I'll have to move my plans with Bethany. It would surprise me if she kicked up a fuss but even still, I never want to communicate that something or someone is more important to me than her. My fear is that by moving our plans, I'll be doing exactly that.

Darla J Michaels

We've only been married for three days. It's not long enough for her to be comfortable with my place or with me yet.

She looks my way the moment she hears my boots on the hardwood. Spirit jumps off the couch where he was nestled up next to her to greet me. I don't know what exactly I expect Bethany to do when I enter a room but right now, things feel weird. She looks uncomfortable clutching that mug of coffee like someone is going to swipe it from her.

"Hey", I try to greet her casually. She gives me a small smile then takes a sip from her mug. I have a seat on the coffee table right in front of her. "Everything okay?"

She nods even though she still looks meek. "Listen, I have a meeting tonight." I want to tell her more but it's none of her business. The guys were specific when it came to the need-to-know part of The Brotherhood.

"We could do lunch", she suggests even though I know it's not her preference.

"We could", I hedge even though my reservations were for tonight somewhere nice, and I'll have to cancel them. It's just as well because she doesn't like the fancy stuff anyway. Even still, it's effort and I want to put effort in as her husband.

"Don't you have this and next week off?"

"I do, but as a business owner you're never really off", I clarify. She has to understand that part of my success has been hard work. And while I make my own schedule there is still a lot that goes on behind the scenes in terms of my role at the helm of my businesses.

"So, what you're saying is you're kind of off?"

"Yes. I am kind of off. Maybe we could spend the day together until my meeting. I could drop you off at The Lux. You could grab a few drinks at the bar, and I could meet you after."

"Okay." She acquiesces, giving me a sweet smile.

Tell Me Who You Go With- Archer & Bethany

That was easier than I thought. Previous experience has taught me that women don't like their plans moved around. At this point at least, it doesn't seem like Bethany is like most women at all.

The day spent with Bethany is delightful. She's curious about me and my routines but for some reason, I think I make her nervous. I have to get to the bottom of that. Making her nervous is not my intention. I make a mental note to share my observation with her. I'm sure she'll tell me what I want to know.

As it turns out, my wife loves to cook. She took me into one of her favorite kitchen stores and informed me that we are in fact missing many staple gadgets at my house. When I suggested she move her things to my house and we sell her place, she looked as though I had just insulted her.

Despite my attempt to explain that we don't need two homes relatively close to each other in town, she was not agreeable to selling. I think once she realizes the upkeep on two homes is a big commitment, she'll probably concede to selling her place. Since I'm in no rush, I'll let things play out as I'm sure they'll play out in my favor.

We stopped at one of my favorite art supply stores where I introduced her to the owner and showed her around a bit. She offered to replace the markers she stole from me. The truth is, I already replaced them. I just like giving her shit about it and I like that we have a little inside joke even though we haven't known each other for that long.

She asked to stop by Sinful for another cupcake. This time she was not interested in splitting one. And since I have a sweet tooth like nothing else, I obliged.

It's delightful to be around her and when we're finally pulling up at The Lux, I'm reluctant to let her go in by herself.

174

Not because I think something will happen that she can't or won't handle, but because I just feel like she should be with someone. Protected...doted on.

"I shouldn't be long", I tell her as we pull under the portico. She's got her hair swept up in a much more formal way than she did on our wedding night. Even though I know it's not her style, I still had her dress up tonight. I like her dressed up. Smoky eyes. Nude lips. Black gown with a full skirt and a slit up the thigh. You can't tell the slit is there until she walks. Subtle but beautiful. It sparkles as she walks. The gown looks magical, just like she is.

It was a gift from our personal shopper. A congratulations gift of sorts among many other things. I also think our shopper was making sure she has Bethany's measurements correct for her upcoming dates. Just as I'll send our shopper to find clothes for the other women, the guys will do the same for their dates with Bethany.

Our kiss goodbye lingers. Neither of us really want to part from each other but she'll have to get used to this. I have a feeling meeting with The Brotherhood will happen off schedule from time to time. It's something we'll both have to deal with.

"Go on. Tell the bar who you are. They have your information on file and know to call me to confirm. You have your phones?"

She nods.

"Make sure you check them", I remind her, motioning to the attendant that we're ready.

I pull away when she's in the building and head to Micah's office. The drive does not help my irritation. Traffic is busy. There must be something going on downtown that I'm not aware of.

When I arrive at Micah's office, everyone is already there. In fact, it looks like they've been there for a while.

They're laughing, over drinks. Drinks I think I should have been invited to.

Micah stands to greet me when I walk into the boardroom.

"Mr. Jackson", Micah addresses me, meeting me half-way with his hand extended. I don't shake it.

"Is this the meeting before the meeting?"

Micah looks perplexed and then clarifies. "Some members of The Brotherhood partner with my firm. The other just trickle in. Since we have inherent trust and nothing is being discussed that could hold someone liable, I consider this time an open door. One you'll have in the future as well. I reserve time on Friday afternoons for personal matters unless for some unusual reason I happen to have court that day. You're welcome here any time in the afternoon on Friday as long as I'm here."

I feel like an asshole. He's since dropped his hand. I hold mine out, hoping he'll accept it as my apology.

He shakes my hand without hesitation. "You're new. Still learning. I get it. I might feel similarly if I didn't really know these men. What can I get you to drink?"

"Bourbon. Thank you."

"Please, have a seat."

I find an open seat at the table as Graham addresses me. "Bethany's on her first drink. The bar is trying to get her to order food with it. She's declined." He hangs the comment there waiting for some kind of decision from me. I'm not sure what he wants me to do with that piece of information. "Are you agreeable to her decision or do you want something sent to her?"

I let out a breath, not quite sure it's up to me to decide. "Yeah. Sure. Have a menu?" I can't have her sent just anything. That woman is rooted deeply in her convictions. She won't eat it if it goes against her faith that's for sure.

My phone pings. He's sent it to me. A quick read of the menu tells me her options are limited.

"Give her the mini falafel with tahini drizzle and the miso glazed eggplant bites." Sounds gross. I'm positive she'd eat it.

"Very well. I'll have the server make her aware of the expectation", Graham tells me as he types the order into his phone. "They'll message you directly going forward."

It's interesting that I now have control through people outside of The Brotherhood. I wonder if this will be the case wherever we're connected.

Micah takes a seat after serving me and we get down to business.

"How's the happy couple", Jonathan inquires.

"Excited to get things started."

"We are too", Micah cuts in. "I know it was short notice. We're glad you made it."

I hold my hand up to stop him. "We need to get a few things straight before any plans are made."

"Agreed."

"On my wedding day I was told my wife was still a virgin." Micah nods. "I shouldn't have left Braden's office without knowing that. I had a right to know. I jumped through all your hoops. You approved her." I scan the room to make sure everyone understands that I'm not happy.

"Archer, if you're looking for a welcome book you won't find it."

Now he's just being smart.

"How many secret sex societies do you know about, hmm? Gentleman?" They shake their heads. "What we do is different. It's unique. And while we have a set of rules established to keep order it's not a perfect system yet. And for every incident where there is conflict that's where we know a rule must be established. Look at these moments like opportunities. I can assure you on behalf of all of us, we're not trying to screw you. We're trying to screw your wife." He winks at me and the guys chuckle.

"Still as I left her", Braden asks me, referring to her virginity.

"She is." Many of the guys make noises in disbelief.

"Do you want help with that", Tyler offers. The guys laugh again.

"I don't know what I want yet. Right now, that's off the table."

"What are you waiting for", Graham asks the question everyone is probably dying to know.

"I'm not sure. It just doesn't feel right. When I look at her all I know is that the timing is off." They're looking at me like I'm not making any sense. "When you get time with her, you'll know what I mean", I tell them.

"Perfect. We want time with her tonight."

"Excuse me?"

"A gesture of good-will Archer."

"Micah, I have already given you a gesture of good-will. My wedding day should have about covered it."

"I think we'd like another opportunity to get to know her. Think of it as a test of sorts. You'll have to do this from time to time. Think of it as her conditioning."

"Conditioning?"

"Just like you, there is no guidebook for her. Your job at present is to make sure you get her accustomed to our expectations so they become second nature. This will be a first."

"What do you have in mind?"

"She's expecting you at The Lux, isn't she", Graham offers.

"She is."

"One of us could show up in your place."

I don't say anything at first because I really want to get back to my wife. If I had a choice between her or shooting the shit with these guys, I'd choose her. No offense but I'd rather take her to bed. I can get bourbon anywhere.

"I'll do it. Since I own The Lux, I'll just walk up to her and take her to a room. Simple as that. I have a lovely suite I keep there."

"No." There is no thought. It just flies out of my mouth. I don't want someone taking her somewhere I can't see them.

"Why not?" This time the challenge comes from Braden.

"She's nervous around me right now. I think the whole marriage thing is freaking her out enough. Adding someone else without me there might make it worse."

"I welcome spectators", Graham offers. "I think all of us feel the same way about that, don't we?"

"She doesn't know you. Don't you think an introduction should happen before you put your hands on her?"

"He's got a point", Jonathan interrupts the guys from talking over each other. "So, we pick from those of us she's met. That leaves us with Tyler, Braden and me."

Not Braden. I'm still not happy with him. He'll be last if I can help it.

"We also need to set up an actual date with her. We realize we're throwing you a curveball here with tonight's request but it's all in good fun."

"Good fun, huh? When do I get to have some fun", I challenge Micah.

"Well, that's what we're here to discuss. We've already got a schedule together, but we can move things around a bit depending on the commitment."

A calendar lights up on the wall.

"Claudia, would you mind highlighting the days where the plans are more flexible? Except for Jonathan, please."

"Of course,", Claudia's voice comes through the speakers in the corners of the room and the screen starts changing before our eyes.

"I'd like Jonathan to have the first date with her. Since he married us and all", I qualify so as not to be rude to the other guys.

"That actually works. Micah, if you want to swap your free time to take Morgan, that is."

"That'll be fine."

The screen changes again.

"I'd like to be with Bethany when she meets the others. Just like I was on our wedding day."

I look around the room for any disagreement with my request.

"Will it work Claudia?"

"Can I take some creative liberties without having a whole discussion about it?"

Micah smiles at her sassiness.

"By all means."

Claudia manipulates the calendar from wherever she happens to be. We all watch as dates appear and disappear. The color coding moves around the screen.

Within minutes the calendar is finished. "There. Will there be anything else?"

The guys look over the calendar. It looks fine to me. I see a few double dates Bethany and I are scheduled for. My first solo date seems to be with Kelly, which is fine. I've seen her picture. She's pretty. Other than that, I can't say I know too much about her.

Darla J Michaels

"And who is the lucky man tonight", Micah prompts since they never got an answer from me.

"Tyler. But on one condition. He does it at the bar and I get to watch from across the room."

Bethany

I'm tipsy I think as my phone chirps. Archer has been longer than I thought he would be. It was sweet that he ordered appetizers for me. Not sweet that he told me to eat them.

I got tipsy enough that food looked good though and it was sweet that he purposely ordered me vegetables.

When I flip my phone over, the text is from Archer.

AJ- He has my permission.

I don't pay the text much attention as I drain the rest of my drink and slide it to the back of the counter to signal I'd like another. I'm bored.

The bar has really picked up and I'm waiting to catch the bartender's attention. While I wait, I decide to text Archer back.

BJ- I miss you.

AJ- I'm right here.

What in the hell? I turn around and scan the room. He's not here. There's no way he has the wrong place, and I don't take him as someone who would joke around about something like this. So strange I think as I almost run into a man while sitting back down.

"Mrs. Jackson", the deep voice greets me.

"Shit", I breath out, surprised that Tyler is standing in front of me.

He bends down and kisses me on the cheek, then pulls my chair out for me like the gentleman he is.

"Where's Archer?"

"Here", Tyler answers, sliding my chair up to the bar for me. "Watching."

"Watching?"

Tyler swivels my chair, so I'm partially turned toward him. "He asked me to make you come."

I'm sure my eyes are popping out of my head right now. Intoxicated Bethany can be very expressive.

"Here?"

Tyler doesn't answer me. Instead, he finds the slit in my dress and parts it, allowing the fabric to fall over my leg.

"The sooner you come the sooner you'll see Archer. Also, the smaller the audience you'll attract." I look around the room and notice a well-dressed man taking in my exposed leg.

"Now...", Tyler runs his hand up my thigh and stops when he notices I stiffen. "...you may feel like fighting it, but I wouldn't do that if I were you." He continues his journey up my thigh. "Part your legs", he issues me the low order. I shift in my seat to obey him. "Come", he orders, motioning me toward him.

Tyler secures the palm of his hand against the back of my neck and pulls me the rest of the way to him. I knew he wanted a kiss, but he makes me so nervous. I've never been with anyone that' so dominating. I feel like everything I do is going to be wrong to him.

Oddly enough, when he kisses me, he leads, and I follow. It's freeing. I don't have to think because he's guiding me, which might be the entire point of what he does.

While I contemplate his ways, his thumb rubs over my slit. I moan into his mouth, and he releases me but continues rubbing me between the legs.

"Don't be too loud. You'll attract an audience."

"Another?"

I turn my attention to the bartender, leaning against the bar, finally attending to my empty glass.

"You know what...I think you should show your server what a good girl you are", Tyler suggestions. The bartender smiles politely, not understanding what's going on.

"Yes. Another please", I breathe, trying not to come undone around this man.

"Look at her", he orders the bartender. "Look at how pretty and put together she is." The bartender nods. "Now look at her hands." The bartender and I both look at my hands gripping the edge of the bar so tightly my skin is noticeably paler at the points that hold onto it. "And her mouth. Doesn't that mouth look like it's about make a noise so pleasurable you'll want her to sit here and make it all night long?"

I can tell the moment the bartender understands what's going on.

"Stay", Tyler orders the bartender. "In fact, I want you to tell her what a good girl she is." I whimper and look at Tyler. "Don't look at me." He nods his head to the bartender, signaling that I should be giving him all my attention. "He's going to coach you through it."

"Archer." I need to know where he is.

The bartender extends his hand to Tyler.

"Nice to meet you, Archer."

Tyler laughs. "I'm not Archer."

"Then who's Archer?"

"Her husband." Tyler nods over his shoulder. The bartender looks where Tyler nods. I know the second the bartender makes eye contact with my husband. I probably give Archer a similar look. It's a look of shock because he's strikingly handsome with a devilish gleam in his eyes. There's a flicker of concern. And finally, a calm acceptance that if Archer wanted to do something, he's going to do it and no one will stop him.

I look over my shoulder and can feel myself morphing through my typical response triad of what it is to be in Archer's presence when Tyler murmurs in my ear.

"You're mine. In front of him…", he nuzzles and then kisses my cheek. "…in front of this bartender…", he drags the tip of his nose down my cheek till his mouth is almost covering mine. "…in front of this whole damn room."

I want him to kiss me. He doesn't. Instead, his strokes between my legs become focused. There's a new pressure he's applying, and it takes my breath away.

"Look at him", he orders, his breath from the words he punctuates entering my open mouth.

What they're doing to me is unimaginable. I'm at a bar with my husband's friend touching me between the legs while my husband watches behind me. And now they want the bartender to watch?

"You close?"

"Huh?" I look at Tyler, the words being spoken around me are somehow harder for me to comprehend right now.

"Patrons are getting restless. Are you going to start calling her a good girl or will the crowd get bigger? I can guarantee no one will stop us."

My eyes dart to the bartender. He shifts his stance and starts rolling up his sleeves nodding to patrons down the bar from him like nothing unusual is going on here.

You gonna serve us or what?

Excuse me. Sir? Where's my drink?

They need more wait staff here.

Tell Me Who You Go With- Archer & Bethany

The people sitting around us are getting restless. People are going to notice that the bartender is paying attention to us any minute. I can see the man sitting on the other side of me turn to me in my periphery.

"Eyes right here", the bartender gently orders me. "How close are you?"

I can't answer. I'm close. Really close.

"Don't stop man", he tells Tyler. The bartender doesn't know this but I'm quite sure Tyler knows just what stage I'm at right now. It's the stage where there is no turning back.

I want this. If feels so good and he's rubbing it just right.

The bartender leans toward me, resting his elbows on the counter.

"What does it feel like? When it finally happens. When you do what he orders you to."

"No shit", the stranger next to me says to the bartender.

"You could help her", Tyler offers. "Gonna draw a bigger crowd if she can't get it done."

"You her boyfriend", the guy next to me asks.

"Yeah. Her husband's back there", Tyler offers. "Here", Tyler offers the guy sitting next to me, sliding his hand from between my legs, extending his glistening fingers to the man. "Smells good, doesn't she?"

I let out a breath and whimper. I'm throbbing harder now. Seeing my mess on Tyler's fingers and him being so casual about it. He's having strangers smell my arousal. Then he pulls his hand back and tastes his fingers.

"Jesus Chris", the stranger says next to me in disbelieve.

"You want them back", Tyler challenges me.

"Yes." I'm frantically nodding. "Get it done Bethany."

Still nodding, this time I open my legs wider for him. The moment he slides his fingers inside my panties and finds my clit I look at the bartender.

"Come on princess. Let me see you finish."

I grab Tyler's hand that rests on the counter. For a moment, I think he's going to hold my hand while I finish on his, but he doesn't. He moves my hand to the bartenders and now, I'm holding hands with a stranger while someone I barely know is getting me off in public.

"I want her panties after", the bartender tells Tyler. Tyler accepts his request. "Hear that princess?" He winks at me and turns his attention back to Tyler. "What's it look like? I bet it's pretty."

"It is. Pink. Bare. The tiniest little nub that gets so plump when you rub it."

I'm so close that if something interferes with my release, I'll probably cause a scene.

"Can I take her panties off? I'd give her a little kiss for doing such a good job", the patron asks Tyler.

That does it. I'm gone. I come hard as Tyler chuckles next to me.

"Fucking perfect", Tyler tells the guys as he continues to rub me while I ride out the pleasure.

Chapter 21
Bethany

I can't believe I insisted on having this meet and greet at my house. For the time being, Archer and I agreed to keep both homes. There were some critical things we did not discuss prior to wedding. Property was one of them.

When Archer informed me that he would be introducing me to the men I'd be dating, I wanted them to know exactly who I am. No holding back. No hiding. No changing to make others comfortable.

But now? I'm fighting the urge to beg Archer to message them and suggest we meet at his house.

"Bethany", Archer lays his hand on top of mine, stopping me mid-stir. "It's just drinks, Darlin'."

I get ready to tell him all my fears but a knock on the door stops me. Archer laughs at the look on my face. I'm sure he's seeing fear.

"You're beautiful, you know that?" He gingerly takes the spoon from my hand and places my hand over his heart.

"What if they don't like me?" It's a fair question.

188

"They do." He grabs my hand and pulls me across the small space to the front door.

That's another big difference about Archer and me. My house is small. Cozy. Quaint. His space is large and luxurious. I never would have guessed for such a casual guy.

This is one of the fun parts about our relationship. It's new, which means we get to learn about each other. Typically, this is done before marriage. Typical has never been a word used to describe me.

Archer lets the first of them in. There's a handshake. A muffled greeting I can't understand. A chuckle and then Archer turns to me.

"Landon, this is Bethany. Bethany, Landon."

Landon's eyes glitter over me. He looks nice. It's also very clear that he's assessing me.

"Micah was right. She is prettier in person", he tells Archer over his shoulder as he takes a few steps to stand in front of me.

"It's nice to meet you, Bethany." He bends down and kisses me on the cheek, then he touches a finger under my chin and tilts my head up to look at him. "Would you like a membership at Momentum for her", he asks Archer, who stands behind him.

"She can have one if she likes. I doubt she'll use it. Just a hunch."

"What's Momentum", I ask him, curious that I get a choice about something. I haven't gotten to make many decisions since the marriage. I think that's more of a Brotherhood thing than a marriage thing though.

"I own a few gyms. If you aren't interested in a gym membership, I have nutrition packages. One of the girls uses both. If you aren't interested in working out, the nutrition package is fantastic. I'm sure she'd tell you all about it."

I laugh. He furrows a brow.

"Beth", Archer chastises me.

"I...no thank you." I wonder what this man knows about me. Probably not the most important things. Landon looks behind him at Archer.

"Beth", Archer prompts me.

"I eat a plant-based diet of all natural foods." Landon immediately starts shaking his head in disapproval. "I'm not vegan but I do limit dairy and I can assure you, I have a very healthy diet."

"Can you get her to eat meat", Archer chimes in.

"Why", Landon asks me pointedly, ignoring Archer's request.

Now it's my turn to be taken aback. Landon has absolutely no tact with his question.

"I prefer eating fresh food. Eating plants speaks to me spiritually."

"Spirits won't fix a nutrient deficiency", Landon challenges me.

"Who has a nutrient deficiency?" I look up to find Braden walking toward us.

"Oh. Hi." I raise a nervous hand at him. "No one has a nutrient deficiency", I tell Braden confidently.

"Yet", Landon challenges.

"No thank you", I tell Landon firmly. "To all of it", I clarify so as not to be misunderstood. I'm not changing how I eat for them and if I was made to join his club I'd look at is as a form of punishment.

"Bethany", Braden calls my attention to him as Jonathan walks through my back door, greeting Archer.

"When I'm here for you...", he moves Landon over with just his presence alone. I'm thankful. I've had just about enough of Landon for one evening. "...you'll greet me with a kiss." I look over at Archer to make sure it's okay, but Archer is busy talking with Jonathan.

"This is customary. Anything short of a kiss is disrespectful." I hesitate. This is so strange.

"It's a kiss. Not cock", Jonathan tells me, stopping next to Braden. "I'm next so if you could..." He motions with his hand to move it along. "Can I help", Jonathan suggests.

Braden lets out a heavy sigh. "Do you mind?"

They're communicating about something that is totally over my head.

"Not at all", Jonathan tells Braden. They shuffle around me. Jonathan steps behind me as Braden steps up to me. Instinctively I take a step back. Jonathan's hands are steadying my hips. "You're making this harder than it needs to be."

"Right here, Bethany", Braden calls my attention to him. "This is a kiss. Albeit a meaningful way to connect, I almost had your cherry last week. And I do believe I made you come."

I blush at the memory. I haven't seen him since. Archer has control over who I see when. In the last week, it's just been Archer and I. Aside from sweet text messages on the cell I got on our wedding day, it's been easy to forget this marriage was a package deal.

"Maybe, if your husband allows it, I'll make you come again tonight." He dangles the idea out there but, in this moment, I'm too nervous to be interested in pleasure. "But I won't please a disrespectful woman, Bethany."

Jonathan's hands gather my hair into a low ponytail. I decided not to wear it up for no other reason than not wanting to be ready to get on my knees for them. I'm still getting used to Archer. I don't want to add anyone else into the mix quite yet. Plus, swallowing is not my favorite.

Jonathan tightens the grip on my ponytail as Braden leans in for a kiss. It's sweet. Oddly enough, I feel cherished, and I find it easy to fall into a rhythm kissing him.

"She's got a line", Jonathan says behind me.

"Fine", Braden concedes against my lips.

Jonathan spins me around to face him, still fisting my hair. "I don't have rules about how you greet me", he tells me, tightening his grip and securing me for his kiss. "You'll know what I want when we're together. I'll make it clear", he tells me before bending down to kiss me on the lips.

"This one is not a whore", he says over his shoulder. I can't see who he's talking to because Tyler is blocking my view.

"How can you tell", Tyler challenges Jonathan.

"Here", Jonathan doesn't let go of my hair but moves me in front of Tyler, holding onto me so Tyler can have a taste.

"She came pretty hard for me on her wedding day."

"You fingered her. That's basic shit, Tyler. I sure hope she came for you."

I blush at Jonathan's assessment. How can these men be so comfortable talking about sex like this? And in front of my husband?

I don't have any more time to contemplate it. Tyler's lips are on mine. I get lost in the kiss. The moment I reach my hand up to rest it on his chest, Tyler grabs me by the wrist, preventing me from touching him.

"You're right. She's a romantic."

"She is a romantic", Archer confirms.

Are they unhappy about this? I'm so confused. But my confusion doesn't last long because Tyler walks off to talk with Braden and Landon, and Jonathan releases my hair when the most intimidating man I have ever met steps in front of me.

"Bethany." He gives me a small smile then he leans in and kisses one cheek and then the other. "I happen to like romantics", he tells me quietly in my ear. This man makes me smile. "Micah Stevenson. It's a pleasure to meet you. Thank you for inviting us into your home."

Oh wow. I think I just fell in love twice. Aside from Archer, I like Micah the most.

Just when we're about ready to sit, the door opens once more. A man in a pressed gray suit strolls in. He looks formal. So formal if the guys didn't acknowledge him, I'd think he had the wrong house.

"Apologies for my tardiness. For you, Bethany." He kisses me on one cheek and then the other, extending a bouquet of flowers to me. As soon as I reach for it, I pause. Calla lilies. Archer gives me a curious look. The others are staring at me as well.

"Um...thank you", I tell him, hesitating to take the flowers from him.

"Allergy", he guesses. "Her medical records didn't indicate a floral allergy", he looks over at Braden who is the keeper of my records.

"Uh...it's just that those flowers"...I point to the bouquet, still not taking it from him. "...they are...um...associated with death", I tell him, not yet reaching for the bouquet. "I'm so sorry...", he didn't even get to introduce himself so I can't even apologize correctly.

"Graham."

"Graham. I apologize, but I..."

"I'll find something to put these in", Archer interrupts, taking the flowers from me as the crowd looks at me curiously.

"Please, make yourself comfortable", I motion to what little room there is left in the living room.

The men take up every stitch of furniture. To say the space is cozy is an understatement. The guys look cramped. If their places are anything like Archer's, I can understand why.

In fact, we're so packed for space, I end up sitting on Archer's lap. I don't mind. Since the day we met, his lap has become one of my favorite places to sit.

"You look uncomfortable", Tyler calls me out.

"I'm nervous." It's the truth and I think they should know it if they don't already.

Tyler nods but does not provide me any reassurances.

"May I", Tyler asks Archer, motioning toward me. Archer hesitates for a moment before he agrees to Tyler. Tyler pats his leg with his large palm and looks at me.

"Beth." Archer said it as a warning. I may test Archer in private but in front of his friends? I'm not stupid.

I rise and cross the small space to sit on Tyler's lap.

"Archer tells us you're a teacher", Micah mentions, hoping this starts the conversation between us.

"Elementary."

"We're talking it over", Archer tells the guys.

"Talking what over", Micah asks, taking a sip of his drink.

"Archer bought me a greenhouse as a wedding gift", I start before Tyler cuts me off.

"He bought you supplies for a greenhouse and hired a crew to build it. Don't make Archer's gift sound like some thousand-dollar greenhouse you got off the internet."

I look at Archer in disbelief. "He told me he hired someone to put it together."

"He hired an architect to draft a blueprint and a contractor to build it."

"Why?"

"You told me the maturity level was on the floor where you worked. You deserve better than some shitty little beds."

"So, you want her to quit", Micah asks, leaving me out of the conversation entirely.

"I want her to enjoy the breaths she has. If she can say that she'd rather be in a school working alongside people who think small compared to her versus working in her own greenhouse then she can stay right where she is. It's just a year she'll take off and then she'll see."

Micah nods, seeming to understand his logic.

"I'm not quitting." All eyes are on me. "It's not a gift if you're forcing my hand somewhere else", I point out.

"Please don't encourage the whole vegetarian thing. Unless she's going to raise livestock in there."

Archer and I both shoot Landon a glare for the sideways support.

"Materials delivered today. First shovel goes in the ground tomorrow. You'll be up and running after the weekend. Just want to make sure the foundation sets before you start planting and watering", Tyler informs me.

"I'm not quitting", I say once more so everyone is clear.

"What do you plan to grow", Tyler asks me. I'm shocked that he's even curious.

I turn in his lap to address him instead of talking with my back to him. He allows me to lay my hand on his arm. "Just some herbs."

"What kind of herbs?"

Archer snickers from across the room. "She's not growin' pot man."

"I didn't think she was." Tyler raises a brow indicating he's waiting for my answer.

Tell Me Who You Go With- Archer & Bethany

"I like to cook. It's healthier than eating out. It tastes better too."

"My crew is building you a greenhouse with automated climate control, smart irrigation, nutrient systems and self-cleaning glass so you can cook?" Tyler turns his attention to Archer but doesn't say a word.

"I mentioned that I purchased raised beds when Archer was tattooing me. I never asked for a greenhouse. I wouldn't even know how to work that." Tyler exchanges another look with Archer.

"The greenhouse will go up as planned tomorrow", Archer confirms.

"Let's see your tattoo", Landon changes the subject.

I can feel my face turn red. This wasn't something I wanted to share in front of a group. I'm not ashamed. I just think I'll be scrutinized and I'm not good at defending my beliefs yet. It's why I don't share my spirituality with just anyone.

Jonathan gets up from his seat next to Archer. "I could use another drink." I rise from Tyler's lap, eager to help so I get out of showing them my body art.

"Of course,", I tell him. I like Jonathan. I'd make him as many drinks as he wants.

When I grab for his glass, he hands it off to Archer and takes my outstretched hand in his.

"You don't mind, do you", he looks back at Archer.

I'm not sure if he's asking about the drink or me.

"All good, Brother", Archer answers.

Jonathan turns to me. "Take off your clothes."

If I was embarrassed then, I'm mortified now. I take a step back from him. This is not what I expected.

"It's on my back. Between my shoulder blades."

Jonathan doesn't respond. He just waits.

"Beth...", Archer starts to correct me, but Jonathan holds his hand out to stop him.

"What's the problem, Bethany?" Jonathan waits while I consider what I tell him. "We don't rape women. But we do hold them accountable to our rules. I'm giving you a simple order. So, what's the problem?"

"Well, it can't be her pussy. She has nothing to be ashamed of in that department", Tyler reasons.

I decide to trade one insubordinate act for another. I don't answer Jonathan. Tyler is right. I'm not self-conscious about my body. My body is beautiful. My body art is beautiful. I just don't want to face judgement.

I turn around and pull my hair to the side. "Would you mind", I ask Jonathan for his help with the zipper.

He unzips my dress. We let it fall to the floor together.

"Turn around", he gently orders me, and I do as he says, showing my tattoo to the rest of them.

"It's a witch's knot", he tells the room.

There's a moment of silence and then the questions start flying.

"You married a witch?"

Landon is suck a jerk.

"What kind of witch?" Interesting question coming from Tyler.

"Kitchen with a little green. They mix together", Archer explains it to Tyler like I explained it to him.

"That explains a lot", Landon chimes in.

"It sure does", Graham agrees with Landon. "I'll be more mindful of my gifts going forward. My apologies."

Jonathan tilts my chin up to look at him while they scrutinize me. Not only the physical me but the spiritual me. When he offers me a sip of his drink, I take it. And as the commentary continues, he watches my reaction. This is my worst nightmare come true.

"I don't believe in witchcraft. I believe in God." Braden isn't disrespectful but I hear him loud and clear.

"Like spells?" This time the question is addressed to me. I may as well be out with it.

"Spells...potions...cards...yes. All of it."

"You've gotta be joking." I hear amusement in Micah's voice.

Archer chuckles. "No man. She ain't joking."

"Limits", Jonathan asks Archer.

"No fucking. Other than that, enjoy.", Archer tells Jonathan with a smile in his voice.

I feel like I'm going to fall apart. Jonathan is the only one who can see my face. I cannot believe he's going to do something sexual with me. What a monster.

"Take me to your room." With my head down in shame and my dress on the floor, I do as he orders.

Jonathan is all business when he shuts my bedroom door.

"Do you have a deck in here?"

I can't speak. I'm humiliated. They think I'm a joke. And the worst part? Archer is part of the they.

"Bethany?"

I can't look at him. He's probably going to continue the torture. I feel gutted.

"I've never had my cards read. Would you read mine?"

I'm so upset I'm shaking, covering my mouth to try to stifle the sobs.

Jonathan sighs. It's heavy and full of frustration. I thought he was going to leave and send Archer in. He did not. Instead, he grabs me from behind and secures me against his chest with one arm and covers my hand over my mouth with his own hand.

"I believe in you." The room is silent at first. Then it's not so much. "I believe in you, Bethany." Jonathan covers my mouth because he's trying to mute my muffled sobs. "It doesn't matter what anyone else thinks...including me...but just so you know I believe in you."

What he says sinks in. I'm not alone. He knew that I needed someone to support me, and he gave me an opportunity to escape when I needed it most. When I start to calm down, he moves his hand from over mine. I wipe my eyes and face him.

"Thank you."

"Don't thank me. I've had some experiences that I can't explain. I don't doubt for a minute that what you do is real." I smile at him. Other than Grams, no one has ever told me that.

"I don't read my cards in here", I tell him.

"Where do you read them?" I can tell he's curious. I wasn't expecting this at all. I appreciate how nice he's being. He values me.

"In the woods. Past the stream."

"Why not in here?" Jonathan takes a seat on the edge of my bed.

"I have a larger space to work with, and I use the ground to lay out my cards. The spirits communicate better with me outside."

"Like a wifi signal?" He chuckles.

"Kind of."

"So, is it a no or is it I'll do it because you asked nicely but understand that the reading might be a little off because we don't have the best signal?"

"Have a seat", I tell him, grabbing a deck I think will work well. "I don't use this one often", I begin to explain grabbing a deck I used when I first started reading tarot.

"I want the deck you normally use. This is serious." He's not being funny. I can hear it in his voice. He wants a real reading.

Letting out a heavy sigh, I grab the deck from Grams.

"You don't like people touching this deck, do you", he observes, when he sees how old Grams' cards are. "It's why you wanted to use the other cards?"

I'm in shock. How does he know this stuff?

"I won't touch it. You have my word." He settles in on my bedroom floor but before I sit down, he motions for me to come closer to him. "You won't need these", he tells me, hooking his thumbs on each side of my panties and sliding them down to my ankles. "Tarot card...spiritual wifi issue...I think...".

Chapter 22
Bethany

What a witch. I look around the room at my handywork. One, two, three and four grown men all out cold on my living room floor.

I look down at Micah, asleep on the floor. *You've gotta be joking.*

No Mr. Stevenson. I am far from joking.

For a moment, I consider drawing a sigil on their foreheads. Not only am I not familiar with harmful sigils, but I also don't work with them. It goes against my fundamental beliefs as a kitchen witch.

Drugging dickheads, however, does not go against my fundamental beliefs as a kitchen or a green witch. Besides, I wasn't sure if it would work.

I guess now I know.

"Not bad, huh, Grams?"

The only thing is, I don't know how long they'll be out. So, I ensure my peace and take their car keys. I grab their fobs from their pockets and their wallets. While this won't hurt them like they hurt me, it'll take up most of their day tomorrow. Quite honestly, it's not good enough compared to how they hurt my feelings but it's all I have to work with.

I toss a change of clothes and my cards in my satchel and dump their keys and wallets in the side pocket of my bag. Swiping my keys from the counter, I head out, not bothering to lock them in. I never lock my doors, and no one ever bothers me.

Shrugging any cares away about my decision, I close the door behind me and dispose of a few things before going back to Archer's place.

I hold onto the wallets. On the way to Archer's place is a corn field. They have quite the crop this year. I can dispose of the keys there.

I grab them from my bag, including Archer's and walk right into the woods. As soon as I get to the stream I cross to read my cards I start walking along it.

"I am not a joke", I state, hurling the keys to Micah's Bentley into the stream.

I walk down the stream a bit. Wouldn't want to throw them all in at the same point. Landon's keys are next. "I hope this explains a lot." His keys land in the stream with a satisfying plop.

Walking the entire opposite direction of my normal crossing point, I grab Braden's keys. "I hate to break it to you Braden, but God is a spirit, so therefore, you believe in spirits." I don't even waste the intensity on his set of keys. He may have been the least offensive of all but he's still not finding his keys.

But I save the best for last. Archer's Hellcat. My heart races in my chest. He broke my heart. I never would have expected him to laugh about me. I'm a joke to him. I'm a joke to my husband.

Darla J Michaels

I swallow back tears and focus on the task at hand. I'll get rid of the other key when I make it to his house.

"Am I funny now?" I put everything I've got into that throw. His keys sail through the air, glinting in the moonlight as they land into the stream.

I get into my car, and head to our marital home, but before I arrive, I take care of the last task. The wallets.

I've never looked through a man's wallet. There's nothing interesting in any of them. I take the cash and consider what I should do with the rest. Should I pull everything out and frisbee each card or chuck the entire wallet? Either way, they aren't finding these.

I decide on the entire wallet. Then I can get to bed early, get up early, and head out for the day. This witch has seeds to plant.

Spirit greets me enthusiastically as I enter Archer's place. I give him some food and we fall asleep snuggling in Archer's bed together. He doesn't even notice that Archer's gone. I should be sad about that, but I'm angry so I'm not.

Even more outrageous than the blatant disrespect from them, they actually thought I was going to put them in my mouth.

I suppose I'm partly to blame. I did Jonathan's reading, and he was so appreciative I got overwhelmed with emotion. Not only did he believe in me, but he gave me an escape from the criticism I've always struggled to defend. Instead of crying I asked to taste him, just like I did Archer on our wedding day.

"Only if I can taste you after." I nod, closing the distance between us. He gathers my hair as I undo his pants.

The moment my mouth is on him, he's full of praise for me. "That's it, pretty girl." He's already leaking in my mouth. I find myself wanting more so I go deeper and gag.

"Look at you...", he comments, his voice full of wonder. When I look up at him, he groans. "Such a pretty witch."

I love how he calls me this. He appreciates me for who I am. I don't have to meet his expectations because I've met them, just by being myself.

"Get on the bed, Bethany." He guides my mouth from him and helps me to stand. I do as he tells me while he gets up from the floor and follows me.

I'm surprised when he climbs on top of me. "Do you trust me", he asks after kissing me, laying his body down on top of mine. I nod. "Good."

I groan as he slides his hard cock back and forth along my slit. This is heaven. He is one of my people. I trust him implicitly.

"Comfortable?" I nod in answer because words have escaped me. He feels so good between my legs. "I'm going to fuck your mouth now. And while I use your mouth for my pleasure, I'm going to lick you. And Bethany..."

"Hmmmm?" I moan, dazed by the pleasure he's giving me.

"There is nothing more...and I do mean nothing...that I love more than eating pussy."

I'm panting, laying on the bed while he switches positions on top of me.

He doesn't say another word as he slides himself into my mouth and plants what I can only describe as a loving and enthusiastic kiss between my legs.

I love this. I love that he's loving me and using me in equal measure. I'm dying to know what he tastes like but I'm also nervous. What if I can't swallow? What if I gag?

The door clicks open. Jonathan stops for a beat to address whoever is at the door. "We're busy."

"I can see that." It's Archer. I tense underneath him and Jonathan ups his game. He slides into my mouth deeper at the same time as he adds a finger inside me. He presses a finger against the spot Archer finds that feels so good. I whimper against his cock in my mouth. When he's satisfied with my response his tongue massages my clit and I'm digging my fingernails into his backside.

"She's gonna spit it out", Archer offers.

Jonathan lifts up for a second to answer him. "No, she's not." Then he continues his work between my legs.

I'm trapped beneath him in the most fantastic way. And even when my own husband doesn't have faith in me, he does. Suddenly, I want to swallow for Jonathan. I want to make him proud and piss Archer off.

Jonathan stops tonguing me and pulls his finger from inside, moving it on top of my clit while he addresses me.

"Alright beautiful girl." I gag around him as he continues to fuck my mouth. This is the hottest thing anyone has ever done to me. "You are going to gush for me. You're going to want to fight it. Just remember who's cock is down your throat."

I moan around him in response because I can't make actual words.

"You're going to make a mess on your bed and I'm going to make one down your throat."

I hear footsteps and mumbling. "Damn…", a deep voice that must be Tyler says from the door.

Jonathan slides his fingers back inside me and hits the spot with determination.

"Don't focus on them. You focus on me." I moan around him and suddenly, there's nowhere else I can focus. Because within a matter of seconds, I have the urge to pee. I start to struggle underneath him, but he pays no attention to it and doesn't stop rubbing me with his fingers and his tongue.

And that's it. My body gives up and releases. At first it feels like I'm going to wet the bed but then I orgasm and a release so big and so wet comes flooding out of me while Jonathan continues to lick and massage me inside. I come harder just listening to the sound my release makes against his fingers. And not only are my thighs wet, but I can feel the soaked fabric of my bedding stick to my skin.

I come again as another wave of pleasure hits me and another gush of fluid pours out from between my legs. That one feels bigger than the first.

Without warning, Jonathan comes down my throat. I don't gag. Instead, I suck hard, bobbing my head up and down as though my only job in this moment is to wring every bit of pleasure from him like he did for me.

And that's what led to Archer ordering me to service them. Like I said, it was my fault. But now that I think about it, maybe it was Jonathan's too.

The most powerful people are always doubted first. That's how they become the most powerful. No one even looks their way until it's too late.

Sleep tight, Bajora.

I felt like Jonathan was trying to tell me to pay them back for how they treated me. So naturally I translated that into drug them.

I kissed Jonathan goodnight and turned my attention to the eager men left at my home.

"Let me make you some drinks."

"We're good, darlin'. I think we want to give you a drink instead", Archer chuckles.

"I insist. This is one of my favorites", I tell them, even though it's taking every atom in my body not to tell them to leave my home.

Darla J Michaels

"Make it for me on our date. Gotta gets out of here. I have an early day with one of the crews tomorrow."

He's going to pass on me sucking him? No way. I don't know how long it's going to take for this to kick in, but I need him until the guys start to get tired. I'll gladly suck him off if it means I'm killing enough time not to give the rest of them pleasure.

"I can't stay long either but I would be delighted to try your drink. I could even help make it", Graham offers.

Despite his poor choice in flowers, Graham is kind. I kiss Tyler goodbye but don't take Graham up on his offer. Instead, I make him one.

"That's so kind of you. But I've got it." I bite my lower lip and look at him with the most innocent stare I can muster. "Maybe there's something else I could give you to try", I hedge, giving him a shy smile and then looking at Archer for permission. Keep your eyes on the prize, Bethany. Worst case scenario, your tonic doesn't work and you're giving a bunch of assholes head. Best case scenario you put them all to sleep and get out of here.

"I like her. Beautiful. Intelligent. Dirty. Sweet. You've got the whole package." Graham addresses me next. "Make your drinks, darling. Of course, I'll wait for you...and take your offering." Graham gives me a wink and has a seat in the living room with the others.

As soon as they're out of eyesight, I get to work. Some might like sweet, and some might not, but I have to take a chance. I don't have a lot of time and this needs to be quick, considering it's one of my favorites. I need to hurry before someone catches on that I'm up to something funny.

Considering they all went with whiskey earlier; I decide to avoid putting anything sweet in the glass. Țuică it is. I'll add a little tonic water to make it look like I did something special. And because I have no idea what I'm doing for a dose, I'll give them an eye dropper each. Maybe an eye dropper and a half.

Archer comes around the corner as I'm capping the bottle. If I had my favorite dress on, I'd drop it in the pocket. But I have a nightgown on. Jonathan insisted I make a dignified exit. Again, he didn't say that, but I know why he was insistent that I put clothes on after we cleaned up.

My only alternative is to grab the drink tray and hand it to Archer before he steps up to the kitchen counter.

"Thank you, Beth." He eyes me and for a moment, I think he knows I'm mad at him or at least that he's done something to hurt me. But his words confirm he's clueless. "I'm so lucky you're mine, darlin''."

I give him a small smile, touch him on the cheek like a loving wife would but do not return the sentiment. I'd rather deepthroat a cactus than lie to him.

"I made this for Graham. It doesn't fit on the tray. I'll bring it to him in a moment", I explain to Archer.

Thankfully, he leaves with the tray, allowing me enough time to clean up and return to the living room with Graham's drink.

"This has to go", Graham tells me after I hand him his drink. He grabs the hem of my nightgown and lifts it over my head. I am, once again, naked in front of them.

I look over my shoulder at the guys. "So...what do you think", I ask them. When they don't answer but ogle my naked body I prompt them further. "The Țuică. It's Romanian."

"Strong", Archer comments. "Good...but strong."

"Surely it's not too strong for you guys", I comment, further encouraging them to drink the brew.

I unzip Graham's pants, reaching inside his boxers to pull him out.

Not wanting to waste any time, I grab him firmly with one hand and start to stroke him. I have no idea how long it's going to take for the tonic to work or if it even will. But I didn't drug Graham's drink, which means I need to service him before the guys pass out but not early enough to kneel for them.

"Eyes up here, Bethany." Graham looks down at me like he's in heaven. "I think I am going to take my time with you. Such a lovely mouth you have." He lets out a groan and touches my cheek.

No Graham. You have it all wrong. I'm going to take my time with you.

Chapter 23
Archer

"Hey asshole. Wake up."

Tyler? I open my eyes and immediately shut them. Sun streams in the windows temporarily blinding me.

I hear groans all around me as I sit up, trying to recalibrate myself to what's going on. It's unlike me to sleep during the day. And while I don't know the other guys too well, something tells me they didn't become successful by sleeping in either.

"What the fuck?" My phone says it's almost noon. I scan the room, and the guys don't look much better than I feel.

"Dude...you pissed yourself", Tyler tells Landon.

"Shit", Landon exhales, still waking up from his slumber.

Still bleary-eyed, they're rubbing their eyes, clearing their throats and rubbing their necks. The telltale sign of falling asleep upright.

"Where's Bethany?" I don't have any missed texts or calls from her.

Darla J Michaels

"I thought maybe you knew. But when you didn't call me back and neither did anyone else, I thought I'd head over to check on you."

"Where's Graham?" He's the only one who stayed for another drink and head, but he isn't here. Seems odd to me.

"Working. How much did you guys have to drink last night?"

"I don't know. Not much. The whiskey and then Bethany's favorite drink…" The words die on my tongue. She wouldn't…would she?

"My clinic closed today because the doc was missing. I'm going to kill her." Braden lets his head fall back against the couch with a heavy sigh.

"No, I'm going to kill her. Slowly. I missed court. Do you know what happens to a lawyer when they miss court? They get fined. They could be charged with contempt. I could be reported to the bar."

Micah looks like the devil right now.

"And that doesn't even include the reputation damage. I own the fucking firm!"

"Now wait a second. You don't know that what Bethany served us knocked us out."

"Heads up!"

I turn just in time to catch the bottle soaring in the air across the room from Tyler.

"So what? She's got stuff like this all over." I refuse to believe my wife knocked us out.

"Go ahead then. Take a sip."

The room is quiet as I consider the likelihood that what they're accusing my wife of doing is true.

"While you ponder that, check your wallets. When I didn't see your car in your driveway but saw hers, I went to check on her. She was sound asleep with your dog. And right next to her on the nightstand was a stack of money. Had to have been about a couple thousand. Does she typically carry that kind of cash with her?"

We all start feeling around for our wallets. I close my eyes in defeat.

"Where are my fucking car keys", Micah growls. I'm missing mine too. After a moment, we realize we all are.

"So, Brother…how do you want to handle this?"

"How does he want to handle this? No, no…we're all handling this, Tyler."

I understand that Micah is upset but Bethany also belongs to me. So I get the final say. "It doesn't make any sense. Why would she do this?" If something happened yesterday, I missed it.

"You called her out", Tyler volunteers, looking at Landon.

"About what? Not eating meat? If she wants to be a part of this, she's got to get thicker skin."

Landon is clueless sometimes. I didn't realize it at the time, but I knew she was self-conscious about being a witch. I just didn't think it would extend to us. We're her people now. She's in. She should walk around confidently about who she is.

"Kitchen or green", I tell Landon. He still has no idea what I'm talking about.

"Us thinking what she believes in is ridiculous is not a reason to drug people", Braden rationalizes holding his hand out for the bottle. I toss it to him, and he uncaps it to take a sniff. He pours a little on his palm and rubs it around with his index finger. "I wonder what she put in here."

"Yes, Tyler", Jonathan's voice comes through Tyler's phone on speaker.

"Hold on, Jon." Tyler taps the screen of his phone. "Graham?"

"Yes, Tyler. What can I do for you?"

"You're on speaker with Jonathan. I'm at Bethany's house. She drugged them."

There's silence on the line. "Bajora", Jonathan murmurs in frustration.

"Bah what?" That better be complimentary.

"Bajora. It means the curse. She's kind of a mix between a Drabarni and a Chovihani", he explains.

"What in the fuck are you talking about?" My patience is getting thin and none of those terms sound nice to me. That's my wife he's referring to.

"She's a Romani witch. A Drabarni is an herbalist...a healer. She uses potions and remedies. But a Chovihani is focused on divination and enchantments. She's a blend of both so I called her Bajora but maybe she's more like...a Dravahani? Hm...I kind of like that. It rolls off the tongue...", Jonathan muses to himself.

"How do you know she's Romani?" We haven't covered that yet. I suppose we have a lot to cover but how does Jonathan know he's right?

"How do you not know she's Romani? Dark wavy hair that curls when it's humid out. The blue eyes threw me for a loop but look at the shape. She's got that wide-eyed look without even trying. Strong cheek bones. Her face is expressive as hell. I could tell right away that she was upset last night."

"Why didn't you say anything?" Who is his allegiance to? Her or us?

"I honestly thought she'd tell you. I guess she did tell you. She must have felt threatened if she couldn't be direct. Interesting that she let Graham go though."

"Threatened?" Now I'm starting to take offense to his assessment.

"She met most of us for the first time. You had her show us her tattoo. She was feeling vulnerable enough as it was standing there almost naked. But the tattoo...it's a spiritual part of her. You mocked a part of what she deeply believes in."

I look at Tyler. She let the three of them go. "And you three were the only ones who didn't mock her, which is why she didn't do anything to you."

"I made her come so she definitely wasn't doing anything to me. I also told her I believe in her."

I let out a chuckle laced with disbelief.

"Look Archer, whether you think you insulted her directly or not, you didn't stop it. She wanted you to stop it." Jonathan seems sincere but why didn't he tell me?

"Is that what she told you?"

"She didn't have to. She was facing me. She was upset."

"So upset she sucked your cock", I challenge. I won't tolerate disrespectful behavior. Bethany crossed the line and she's going learn her lesson.

"She cried, read my cards and then yeah, she sucked my cock."

I'm about ready to turn my molars into dust. How can he be on good terms with my wife and I'm not. We've barely been married, and she drugged me because she was mad?!

"Well I say we drug her back", Braden offers, holding up her bottle of tonic.

"I don't think I'd do that", Jonathan warns.

"She isn't getting this back. What's she going to do", Braden asks the room in challenge.

"Nothing. I say we get rid of all her herbs too. She can't be trusted. That's the only way we can trust her", Micah throws in for good measure.

"Guys, I gotta go. I'm just...don't fight fire with fire. Apologize. Please."

Has he lost his mind?

"Message me and let me know what happens."

The call disconnects and everyone is looking at me. I have no idea what I want to do. Part of me feels bad that I made her feel bad. But part of me is also pissed that she did what she did.

"I think we drug her back and see how she likes it", Landon offers.

"Any other suggestions", I offer the group.

"Drug her and burn her witch stuff", Micah adds while typing furiously on his phone. "All of it."

"Seems like a suitable punishment", Tyler offers, even though nothing has been done to him. "But it's your choice. She belongs to you."

I could tell them no, but at the same time, their recommendation seems justified. "It's suitable." I wish it didn't have to be this way.

Braden holds up the bottle and tilts in in the sunlight to see through the amber colored glass. "The only remaining question is, what do we use to drug her?"

Bethany

I've tried not to look at my phone. They've either woken up by now or I've killed them.

Shit. I almost hope my phone is blowing up over this. Truly, I had no idea it would work which means I have no idea what dosage is best. And by best, I mean not harmful.

Reluctantly, I power my phone on. The workday is almost done. Archer works later but I have to face him eventually anyway. Maybe it will go better if I'm facing him in the middle of his workday?

There are two messages. One voicemail and one text. I open the text from Archer.

AJ- Dinner at 7. My place. Love you.

I tell him I love him back and confirm that I'll be there. I'm not sure if this is going to be a good dinner or a bad one.

Next is the voicemail. It's from Jonathan.

Bajora. I heard. Call me.

If he has heard, then that means they're mad. At least mad enough to talk about it. I trust Jonathan so I call him back right away. He picks up on the first ring.

"Bajora", he greets me.

I smile at his name for me.

"Hi."

"You had to do it, didn't you?"

Just hearing his question brings me back to last night. It was torture.

"They hurt me. I wanted to hurt them back", I offer, even though it feels like a weak argument when I say it out loud. "Will you be at dinner?" Please say yes. Please say yes. Please say yes.

"I'm working."

He offers no reassurance to me. That's fine. I can take it. It's Archer. He's reasonable. I hope. I'll just tell him the truth, and we'll move on. No harm no foul.

I didn't use all the cash I took from the guys. In fact, I barely put a dent in it. I have everything I need already.

But there is one purchase I could use for tonight. The dress I bought. I think Archer will love it. It's a simple sundress with short sleeves. It comes in tight around the waist and then flares out to a fuller skirt. The material is black with red poppies and there's a triangular cutout just above my breasts to expose my skin. I'm not sure if I have shoes there, but I'm not concerned. I just won't wear any since it's just us and his place is my home now too.

I manage my time so I can arrive precisely at seven. I'm a punctual person, however, I also don't want to poke the bear more than I already have.

I pull into the driveway beside his Hellcat and my pulse starts to race. He got it home. I wonder how much trouble it was for him. The main thing is that he got it home. I try to take comfort in that at least.

When I open the back door, Spirit doesn't come to greet me. Strange. I also don't smell dinner. Even more strange.

The house is quiet. A few dim lights are on.

"Archer", I call out to him. There's no sign of anyone. I dig around in my bag for my phone to make sure I didn't misread the text. It's ringing.

Jonathan. He was working tonight. Now I'm really confused. "Jonathan?"

"You're safe Bajora. Just relax."

I drop my phone when someone grabs me from behind and covers my mouth. Before I can bite down and fight, I feel the sting of a needle in my neck. Archer's angry face is the last thing I remember before passing out.

There's laughter. A fire. Then I hear my name. It's Archer I think. My brain is all foggy from whatever they gave me. And when I try to answer whoever is calling me, I can't because there's a ball in my mouth.

My muscles hurt. So does my skin.

"Oh, look who woke up", Landon says with a sweetness that's too sweet to be genuine.

As my eyes focus, I realize I'm off the ground. I'm also only wearing panties. And I'm tied to a tree.

The guys walk toward me. All dressed in black. All furious looking except for Tyler and Graham. They don't look mad. Just observant.

Tyler has his phone out. I can tell it's unlocked from the illumination of the screen. He's filming me. I try to yell at him through the gag, but I can't. It's impossible.

"Look at me." My head is the only thing I can move. I look at Archer as tears start to fall. I'm terrified. "Every action we take has a consequence. It's either good or it's bad and I'm sorry to say that for you, right now, it's bad."

Archer motions Micah over to take his place in front of me.

"All criminals deserve to understand the charges they are being accused and convicted of before their sentence is carried out. We have assault by drugging, robbery, theft and destruction of personal property and false imprisonment. Please speak now if you object to these charges against you."

218

I try to talk around the gag but it's no use. Micah smiles at me in this sinister way that makes the hairs raise on my arms.

"Alright. Since Bethany has nothing to add we will proceed with the consequences for her actions." Micah motions for the first member of The Brotherhood to step forward.

Braden takes Micah's place and gets closer to me than I would allow an angry person to. Then he tugs on one of the ropes tying back my arm and I groan in pain. Between the rope burn, the tree bark against my back and my straining muscles, I'm miserable.

"How'd you like being drugged? Was it everything you ever hoped for Bethany?" I shake my head at him, tears streaming down my face. "I thought you might say that. But I will say this, just like you slept soundly in Archer's bed, we enjoyed ourselves watching your naked body out here tied to this tree over dinner. This makes you and I even."

Landon takes Braden's place. He's holding my new dress. "This looked amazing on you. When you walked into Archer's house, I almost felt bad about destroying it." He walks over to the fire and tosses it on the flames. It lights up instantly. Disintegrated in minutes. "I should keep you there until you piss pants."

I sob. He looks mad enough to do it. I look to Archer, but he doesn't give an indication one way or another if he'll leave me tied here as Landon suggested.

Micah steps up taking Landon's place. He holds the amber colored bottle out to me that holds the sleep tonic I gave them.

"This works well. Really well. Not as fast as the meds Braden gave you but it does work longer. Definitely convenient to have around, though."

He spins on his heel and in a graceful arc, tosses the bottle into the flames. Braden and Landon begin loading boxes on top of the flames, destroying whatever is in them.

"Now, in exchange for criminal charges and jail time, I asked for your herbs, tonics, potions...basically anything you use to do all the witchy stuff you do. They're in those boxes."

It feels like he punched me right in the gut. It's taken me so long to make those things. To collect and dry the herbs out alone is an art. I'm openly sobbing at the grief I feel because of the loss. If my grandmother's grimoire is in one of those boxes I will throw up. It's old. From my great, great grandmother who practiced too.

I'm sobbing around the gag and crying so hard I can barely see. Spit is coming out around the gag and dripping down my chin. If I could beg them to stop, I would. I'd promise them anything just to stop.

"Almost done, Beth." Archer steps up to me, holding my grandmother's deck of tarot cards. "I trusted you. We trusted you. That trust has now been broken."

Archer drops the deck on the ground and extends the High Priestess Card out to me. He reaches in his pocket, pulls out a lighter and starts the corner of the card on fire.

That does it. Burning my grandmother's cards would break me. I thrash against my bindings and yell as loud as I can through the gag. Spit is flying out of the corners of my mouth and snot is bubbling out of my nose.

And then something happens. It's a gentle breeze that feels like it only reaches Archer and me. He looks into my eyes and his go wide for a fraction of a second. Archer pulls the lighter away. Fanning the card, he puts out the flame.

"Take the gag out", he calls to someone over his shoulder.

Tyler steps up to undo the ball gag fixed to my head and that's when I see that he wasn't recording me at all. I was on a video call with Jonathan.

"Bajora", Jonathan says to me, sadness in his eyes at the sight of me.

As soon as the gag is off my mouth, Archer is palming my face. I sob, heartbroken that he would burn one of the most sacred possessions I own.

"What just happened?"

I can't speak. I ugly cry, snorting as I gasp for air.

"I heard a voice."

I don't know what he's talking about.

"Guys, you do know she doesn't need any of those things to practice witchcraft, don't you", Jonathan warns over the phone.

Chapter 24
Archer

I fucked up. I've been married for one week and I fucked up. Big.

So big that I'm not sure what I can do right now to fix the damage I've done. I let the guys have influence over me that I might not have otherwise allowed.

Was I mad about what she did? Steaming. Did she embarrass me by acting out in this way? I was mortified. Did I give a shit about my car keys and wallet or the guy's stuff? No. It was all replaceable. As my wife, the money was hers anyway. If I was being honest, I thought it was funny that Landon pissed himself. Kind of served her right that he got it on her couch.

The stuff she gave us was far from the worst thing I've ever had. I'd had more than my fair share of alcohol that's left me feeling like shit when I woke up. This stuff knocked us out but personally, there were no side effects. My memory was intact. Nothing hurt. I didn't feel sick. She could probably sell the stuff to people who had trouble sleeping and make a killing.

Darla J Michaels

Not today though. Today my wife is a shell of the woman I first met and it's my fault.

That voice that whispered in my ear was the only thing that made me stop.

You're hurting her.

The words were right in my ear. A chill came over my body in the middle of a muggy July night.

The most terrifying part of that voice was that it was right. I was hurting her. She had scratches and bruises for sure being tied up to that big tree and all. But that wasn't what the voice was talking about. The voice was talking about her head, her heart and maybe even her soul.

Bethany looks at me warily when I sit on the coffee table in front of her. This has become commonplace but now, she shrinks away from me instead of reluctantly looking up at me.

I hold a hot mug of coffee out to her. She swallows thickly before she accepts it.

She sips her coffee with one hand and cradles the tarot card I burnt with the other. Her thumb rubbing over the burnt edge as if she's soothing it.

Never in my entire life did I think I'd mistreat someone like I did her but it's worse because she's the person I vowed to protect.

I need my mom right now. I need to look at her and tell her about my wife and what I've done but I can't. The shame that rolls off me because of my behavior is almost suffocating. We went too far, and I let them.

The guys have been calling and texting, but I haven't responded to any of them. I have nothing to say to them and anything they have to say to me won't make any of this better.

Bethany's sobs haunt me too. I couldn't get her untied quick enough after Tyler removed that gag. I helped get her up there, but I was following direction from Tyler. He ties women up. It's never been my thing. When I want to subdue a woman, I use an order or my hands.

You need to follow my directions or you're going to hurt her.

Those minutes where we were getting Bethany down safely were the longest minutes of my life.

She fell forward into my arms, her legs still bound to the tree. Her strength was impressive as she fought against me while Tyler untied one leg and Graham untied the other.

Bethany! Beth! Settle!

At first, I thought she didn't want me to touch her which would make perfect sense. But then her hand shot down, reaching for the cards she had no chance to get in her current state. I realized that she didn't want to get away from me. I was just a barrier to something she needed.

When Tyler and Micah freed her, I helped her to the forest floor as gently as I could manage. But she managed to push herself out of my arms enough that she fell the last couple of feet, landing on her hands and knees.

We all stood back and watched her in silence as she scrambled to pick up the cards. Some had started blowing in the wind. Landon bent down to stop one, picking it up to hand to her.

Don't touch them!

Her words were spoken in a shrill voice as that cool breeze I felt moments earlier falls over my body once more.

We hear Jonathan's phone go off.

Fuck. I gotta go.

He disconnects the call. The only thing you can hear is fire and Bethany's sobs.

I got it.

When I wave the guys off, no one moves.

224

Darla J Michaels

I said I got it!

I bark the words out, but they all look reluctant to leave.

Give us updates. Micah issues the order as though I work for him. *Archer, she dates all of us. We deserve to know.*

These are the last words spoken before they leave me with my wife, scrounging around on the forest floor in her panties while her most treasured belongings burn.

After she collects her cards, she stands, wiping the snot from her face onto her forearm. She looks around to get her bearings and walks off without giving me a second thought.

I have never chased after a woman in my entire life but last night...I did. I called her name. She didn't answer. I grabbed her arm. She shrugged me off.

Bethany had no regard for me at all and it had me wrecked in a way I never thought a woman could wreck me.

So, I kept pace with her as the thick summer air clung to us. It wasn't until we got to her front door that I had really looked at her. She had gashes on her knees from the fall and collecting her cards. A few broken nails with dirt darn near under all of them. Leaves in her hair which was now curly and wild from her struggle and the humidity. Her legs held the chalky brown dusting of the dirt she had crawled around in.

This was what I had reduced my wife to all to make a point to her. The point that she is to obey me and my Brothers. It's ironic that now, all I want to do is fall to her feet and beg for her forgiveness.

Her sobs start up again when she realizes the door is locked.

We're goin' to my place Beth. C'mon.

I try to gently encourage her to leave with me, but she ignores me once more.

C'mon darlin'. Let me cover you and get you home.

The chill falls over me once more as she screams. It's not like anyone can see us out here. She's at the end of a very long road. The only house out here. Other than her, I bet no one comes down this road regularly but the mailman.

I do the only thing I can think of which is grab her and carry her to my truck. She screams like a lunatic the entire time. Scratching and clawing at me to be put down. By the time I have her in my truck, I'm not only wearing her snot and blood, but I can feel where she's scratched me through my shirt. It burns something fierce. Nothing about the scratches felt normal though.

I talked to her nonstop while we drove to my house. It was a short drive. She said not one word back to me. Just sat there, clutching her cards.

When we got home, to my surprise she got out of my truck without any prompting at all. I think she knew she had nowhere to go like she was. I was just grateful because I was desperate to start fixing what I had done.

Her progress over the gravel drive was slow because she was barefoot. This time, when I picked her up, she didn't struggle. She also didn't look at me. This was the worst.

Reluctantly, I set her down at the front door. When I unlock it and motion for her to step inside, she does.

Let's get you cleaned up.

I walk toward our bedroom. She doesn't follow. As soon as I touch her, that coldness creeps over me again until I release her.

I don't know what happened. I don't know if she did a spell and unlocked something or what happened but it's creeping me out.

I grab some bourbon and a few glasses. She looks at the third glass I pour and then at me. What I see in her gaze chills

Darla J Michaels

me to the bone. It's as if her eyes alone are saying *that's what you get husband.*

I knock back the first glass and pour another while she sips from hers.

I won't go in with you. I'll get it ready. You have to clean up or those cuts will get infected. She starts to cry, clutching her glass in one hand and her cards in the other. My perfect bride has cracked, and I was the cause of it.

I won't touch them again. Cold comes over me once more. *Ever. I won't touch them ever.*

She looks at the glass once more then directs her stare back at me. When I look over at the glass of bourbon, I see that it looks like there's less in the glass. I poured the same amount in all the glasses. I could probably do it with my eyes closed. I'd venture to say it's precise. But now, only half of what I poured remains.

When I look back at Bethany, she's walking toward our room.

I do as I promise. Start her shower and get it ready for her just how she likes it. She keeps the cards clutched to her chest even when I walk out. And the look she gives me is one of pure hatred. The scariest part? She doesn't bother locking the door. We both know we're not alone anymore. She has protection now.

Pounding on the back door gets my attention. I want to just leave it. If I don't answer, whoever is there will go away. Then I hear footsteps. Shit. It's one of us.

"I haven't looked at my phone since we got together last night", I start to defend myself to a very worried looking Jonathan.

"Don't explain yourself to me. Save it for the others." He disregards me after his response, sitting down next to Bethany.

"Bajora." She leans against him and falls apart in his arms.

I'm pissed. She willingly gives him affection and completely shuts me out. I get it. I hurt her. I'm trying to fix it.

"Where does it hurt", he asks her.

"Everywhere", she sobs.

He kisses her on the head while she shakes in his arms.

"Have you slept?"

"No", she answers into his chest.

"Can you grab her something else to drink. Some tea. Lemon balm with lavender."

He's shitting me right now. Is this a fool's errand?

"Did you want me to call Suzette", he offers when I don't move to do his bidding.

"No. I..." Suddenly, I feel like an intruder in my own home. Maybe I need a little air to think clearly. I grab my wallet and keys prepared to search the web for where I would even get something like this.

I drive two hours one way to find this tea. I got the eye from the clerk. Wouldn't surprise me if they were witches too. It felt like she knew exactly why I was picking this up.

By the time I get home, Bethany and Jonathan had fallen asleep together on the couch. This was the most peaceful I had seen her since last night. I was glad he could help her in this way, but I was also jealous it wasn't me that could do this for her.

I did get her the tea though. I could at least make her some. I bought more than the tee. They sold me a tea strainer, a kettle, some crystals, some candles and a few bundles of sage. I don't think I've ever brewed tea in my life. I've seen Momma do it a few times, but I must admit, I paid almost no attention to how she did what she did.

228

Darla J Michaels

I get the kettle on and rush to pull it off the burner when it starts to whistle. I look over to see if I've woken them to find Bethany looking at me with interest. Except it feels like she isn't quite looking at me. Like she's looking at me and something else. Something I can't see.

The hairs on my arms stand up but there is no cold that casts over me this time.

When Bethany untangles herself from Jonathan he grabs for her, causing her to chuckle. I let out a sigh of relief. I thought I broke her. Thank goodness she's still in there somewhere.

"Go", he tells her, playfully swatting her on the backside. I can't help but to watch her as she gingerly steps into the kitchen to see me.

"I'm sorry." Fuck. I can't remember the last time I cried but now...I'm tearing up.

She tears up too but before she comes to me, she asks me something that breaks my heart.

"Do you believe in me now?"

"I do." The words barely get out before I'm a blubbering mess. She practically runs into my arms, and we sob together.

Her heartbreak wasn't entirely about the disrespect, or her things being destroyed although, I know that was part of it. It appears she cared most about what I thought about her and if I believed in her the way she believed in herself.

I'd be lying if I said I believed she could cast spells or if I even believed in magic at all. But I can't explain some of the events of last night and even this morning. There's no doubt there's something here with us. If there wasn't, that lady at the herbal shop wouldn't have given me sage.

"Will you drink the tea", I ask, although it really comes out sounding more like a plea. She's got this ashy color to her that I don't like. I don't think the tea will fix it, but she might feel better.

"Okay." She sniffles a little, still not done crying yet.

"The tea was actually for me", Jonathan calls through to the kitchen. I give him a look to express my displeasure and he smiles and winks at me. Such a bullshitter. "I do still want some though."

These two are going to be the death of me.

Chapter 25
Archer

I promised Bethany that I'd introduce her to Momma today. I've been trying to drag my feet because I want Bethany back to how she was before I hurt her. If anyone will know something isn't right it'd be Momma.

Not that I'm trying to hide what I did but I also don't want to highlight it the first time they meet either. I think about that night all the time. And as odd as it sounds, whatever she let out has been following me around. I have no physical proof, but I can feel it that's for sure.

"Are you nervous", Bethany asks me from the passenger seat of my truck.

"I am." Her eyes go wide, and I laugh. Is it that incomprehensible that I would be nervous about something? "I am human, darlin'. And if there is one person who I know loves me beyond reason it's Momma. But I also know she's gonna be hellfire pissed that I wed without her present."

This time Bethany laughs. I'm grateful every time I hear her laugh now. I feel like we're not out of the woods yet. We're still making up. We've been together almost two weeks, and I haven't taken her virginity or decided on who will. Teaching her a lesson put a halt to even thinking about sex.

We've done other things but not like we were before the forest. I've been more sweet and less dirty. She seems too fragile and part of me doesn't feel right about doing anything more at present.

This is a big day for both of us. Aside from sharing the big news with Momma, we have a date tonight...with Micah. He seems fair but right now, I'd put him in the bottom of the six of the men I want her with. She needs someone who will be sweet with her. I get the feeling he doesn't do sweet, if his behavior the day of Bethany's punishment was any indication.

"At me", Bethany asks, preparing for the worst.

"No. At me. You know she took me in barely having enough money to feed the mouths she had. She's going to be heartbroken." As soon as the words come out of my mouth, I realize I will have broken two hearts today. They're the most important hearts you never want to break.

I let out a heavy sigh and Bethany grabs my hand to show support. I don't exactly live around the corner from where I grew up anymore so it's a bit of a drive. Almost an hour to make it out to her. I thought the drive would give me plenty of time to figure out how I was going to tell her without making Bethany look like a shameful secret.

Even as we pull into her driveway, I knew that was wishful thinking. I've thought about it a lot. Since the day I proposed. It's been weeks and I'm no closer to a good way to tell her than I was when Bethany agreed to marry me.

"Let's go. She may kick me out, but she'll give you a seat at her table."

Darla J Michaels

Bethany looks worried. There's nothing I can do to comfort her. Momma is Momma and if something gets her attention heaven help whatever it is.

I knock before entering.

"Momma!"

The house is silent. I'm glad there are no visitors. One of us is always visiting Momma. Especially my siblings with children. Momma cooks a fantastic meal and bakes just as well if not better. Someone would be crazy not to take a seat at her table.

"Momma!"

She comes around the corner on her cell phone and gives me a stern look for bellowing through her house. But as soon as she lays eyes on Bethany her tone changes. I laugh and she hushes me audibly this time.

"Mary I am so sorry to interrupt but I have to go." She's nodding and smiling. "Mary...look it's Archer and he's brought a *woman* home." I can hear Mary cackling through the line. "Yes, yes, I'll call you back after they leave. Bye dear."

She pockets the phone in her apron. She must have been cleaning or beginning to start some food before we stopped by for our visit.

"Archer." My name on her lips couldn't be wrapped in love more as she comes in for a big hug just like she always does when she sees me.

I'm glad I'm getting a hug. She might not be so happy after I introduce her to Bethany.

"And who is this", she asks, looking at Bethany, taking Bethany's petite hands in hers.

"Bethany, ma'am."

Momma turns to me and winks. I laugh at how cute Momma is being toward her. I'm holding my breath because she's almost touching Bethany's gold band.

"You can call me Momma Jackson."

"Momma", I chastise her. She pays me no attention until she brings Bethany's hands up like she's going to kiss her knuckles. She sees the ring immediately. I can tell because her eyes widen, and she looks at my left hand to see if I'm wearing a matching one.

For once, Momma is at a total loss for words, so I step in.

"Momma, this is my wife." The words were easier to get out than I thought they'd be. It's the first time I've introduced her to anyone in this way. I love how the words feel on my tongue.

"Well, welcome. Come on in. Let's...um...are you hungry? Thirsty?" Momma ushers Bethany through the house toward the kitchen. I hope Momma can get her to eat. "I have sweet bread. Oooh...and lemon bread with vanilla frosting."

I walk behind them as she ushers Bethany through the house. This feels so good. So right.

Momma gets her seated at the small table in her kitchen instead of taking her to the formal dining room. I still can't believe I grew up here. She didn't have a lot of money, but she did have one hell of a house. Said there was some sort of secret there, but she could never tell it. Fine by me. Her house was by far better than the one I lived in before she took me in.

Momma bustles about the kitchen and waves me away when I try to help her.

"Sit with your wife", she tells me, putting extra emphasis on wife so I know I'm in trouble.

Bethany looks at me nervous for what's to come. I reach across the table and grab her hand. She smiles at me and somehow, getting the gift of her genuine smile makes not telling Momma worth it. She still loves me and for that I'm blessed.

"You have a beautiful home Momma Jackson." Bethany lets my hand go so Momma can set down the desserts.

"Thank you. It's a lot of upkeep but I'm blessed to have it just like I was blessed to have my boys." Momma gives me a pointed look while Bethany stifles a smile.

"Coffee or tea dear?"

I know what Bethany is going to choose before she says it.

"Tea would be lovely. Thank you."

I can't take my eyes off Bethany as Momma prepares her tea, bustling around in the background. When Bethany notices, she gives me a shy smile and looks away.

"Don't do that, darlin'", I gently correct her. "I like looking at what's mine." Her cheeks turn pink as she looks across the table at me.

"Archer", Momma calls my attention over to her.

"I have a few things downtown I committed to picking up before I knew I'd have company." She's referring to our drop in. I'm afraid I won't be able to get them later and I'll need one for dinner this evening with Miss Mary", Momma hedges.

I look at Bethany to make sure she's comfortable being here alone. I'm still worried about her.

"It's fine, Archer", she affirms in her delicate way.

Momma is already writing out where I need to go and what I need to pick up. When she hands me back the list, a quick assessment tells me this isn't going to be a quick run downtown.

I let out a breath and look at Momma, who's got an eyebrow cocked at my response.

"I'm happy to grab these things for you, Momma". I lean in to kiss her on the cheek how I normally do, but she turns at the last second, leaving me there kissing the air.

I glance at Bethany, and she's got her brows raised and her mouth in that overly nervous smile like an emoji.

Tell Me Who You Go With- Archer & Bethany

I let out another audible breath and stalk over to Bethany for a kiss. I should be respectful in front of Momma but Bethany is my wife. Momma already knows what husbands do with their wives. So, I kiss her and to my surprise, Bethany allows it. If I'm not mistaken, it feels like she needs it by the way she kisses me back and her fingertips linger against my stubbled jaw.

Momma clears her throat, signaling that we should break it up. We both break the kiss and smile. If Momma is breaking up a kiss that must mean it looked like the kiss was meant to be more than that.

"I need these things to prepare before dinner with Mary."

I give Bethany one last peck on the lips and then I'm off. I wish I could say I'd hurry, but I know some of these people. It is not in their realm of possibility to be quick. This list is going to take me hours.

Darla J Michaels

Bethany

Momma Jackson is polite, however, any woman with a working pair of eyes can tell she's not happy with her son. I can't say that I blame her. Don't they say that a son's wife is a mother's replacement? Not only do I not have the intention of replacing anyone, I'm also no replacement for Momma Jackson.

I sip from my tea, wondering how Momma Jackson knew to put this together. She either knows witches or is one. Or she's an herbalist. Quite honestly, I wouldn't discount any of these scenarios.

I'm considering how I ask her about her knowledge to blend nettle, sage, rosemary and cinnamon together, but she beats me to it as soon as Archer closes the door.

"You brought something with you." It's a simple statement and she pulls out a chair to sit across from me. She's talking about the spirit that's been with me since my punishment.

This has never happened. I have never attracted nor conjured up a spirit before. I never thought I was powerful enough to do it, but I did and now, this entity watches over me wherever I go. Sometimes I can even see shimmers of it.

"Bethany."

I realize I'm staring into my cup of tea when Momma Jackson calls my name.

"Please take it with you. It can't stay here."

"How do you know?" I swallow thickly as I look into her eyes, trying not to be ashamed of who I am and that I'm not afraid of this spirit that never leaves my side.

She plates a slice of each bread for me as she considers how she'll respond to my inquiry. I note she stalls a little as she takes a bite of the lemon bread and sips from her tea without hurrying to answer.

"I grew up in Savannah. My childhood home was also home to those I could not see. Some I could see. But when you grow up in a home like I did, you can walk into a place and feel things that want you to feel them and even some that don't. Yours wants everyone to feel it."

I nod. It's true. The spirit by my side makes everyone hesitate just a little. Momma Jackson is just the first to call it out. Other's hesitation is unknown. They pause before they approach without any awareness of why.

"I'd ask if you're okay, but I already know the answer." Momma Jackson lets the statement hang there. I can't tell her what happened. In fact, I can't tell her anything about Archer and I's arrangement. It wouldn't be right, and I wouldn't tell her anything I wouldn't tell my own family at this point.

"Did he hurt you?" My eyes go wide at her question I'm in shock she would ask me something like that.

"No", I tell her firmly because I think she means physically. "He would never."

"I didn't think so, but I had to ask. Even I can see the circles under your eyes. You look worn out, sweetheart."

She's observant, I'll give her that. I am worn out. All I can think about is when I can rebuild what was taken from me and how I'll go about it. And the grimoire. It's gone. I feel absolutely lost without it. I'm grieving.

"Do you know who it is?" She's talking about the spirit that follows me around.

"No. Maybe...I don't know." I know who I want it to be, but I don't think the spirit world works like that. But then again, no one really knows how it works. "Does it bother you? You must know what I am because you can see it doesn't bother me. And the tea…", I trail off, not wanting to say the words just in case she doesn't know.

"No. I could tell the moment you walked in you wouldn't harm anyone. I could also tell you're not one to be played with…with or without your invisible sidekick."

I laugh at her reference to my attachment being a sidekick. Then I laugh again. This is so crazy. I'm married. My heart is crushed. And there's a spirit that has felt the need to stay by my side from the moment Archer untied me from that tree.

I give her a small smile. Talking about me right now isn't any fun.

"Can you tell me how you met Archer? I'm sure it's a fantastic story." Archer had told me bits and pieces, but he was pretty guarded. I think he still hurts more than he lets on.

"I'll talk as long as you're eating. I've got more tea for you too."

I nod and make good on our deal, starting with a bite of the sweet bread first.

"Do you like it?"

I nod while I chew. This is heavenly.

"The story is simple. He ran into me. Literally. I caught him stealing."

My mouth falls open. Archer?

"Ugh…and the smell. That little boy was dirty, dirty, dirty!" This I laugh at. She has no idea how dirty her little boy really is.

"He cleans up nice though", I tell her wistfully before she continues her story.

"The store owner comes barreling out of the front doors yelling at me that my son stole from them. I was shocked that the man thought he was mine. I mean…we look nothing alike!"

I laugh hard at Momma Jackson's reaction decades later. She's not wrong. They do look nothing alike.

Tell Me Who You Go With- Archer & Bethany

"I could have adopted Archer, that's true. But why would a stranger assume a little white boy was mine? But the damndest thing happened when I looked down at Archer. He smiles that mischievous smile up at me. I leveled him with a stern look and that was it. My son was coming home with me after I paid for the loaf of bread he stole and apologized to the manager."

"That's it?!" There's got to be more to the story than that.

"I had a home full of foster children already. Adding one more to the bunch wasn't going to hurt anything. The biggest trouble I had doing it was from Archer though. He wouldn't tell me his name. Child Services came out and he wouldn't tell them his name either. We tried to see if anyone knew him at the schools in town, but no one recognized him. To this day he won't tell me where he came from. He was like someone who fell from the heavens. We had to go through the court system and everything just to get him an identity. He was a vault."

"I think he was hurting. And I think a big part of him wanted to leave that hurt behind. He said his parents left him. Was carrying around a metal box with drawing pencils in it. That's all he had aside from the clothes on his back. I have a connection that helped me expedite everything. They couldn't put him in school until he had an identity, and no one claimed him, so time was of the essence. It took me months to legally adopt him and give him my name. They gave him a temporary last name of Doe so he could see the doctor and any other matters that required a record. Stubborn then and stubborn now. But I'm sure as his wife, you already know that don't you?"

"I do." I do and I love how stubborn he is. "And you took him in already having eight boys?"

"I did." She starts chuckling. "You should have seen their faces when I brought that dirty little kid through the door that looked nothing like the rest of them." I smile, imagining it. It must have been a sight to see.

"My boys looked at me and said...Momma...he's white." We both laugh this time. "So, I did the only thing I knew how to do. I gave my boys a hard time about it, so they'd learn their lesson." She winks at me conspiratorially, but I don't follow.

"How so", I lean in, reaching for another slice of her sweet bread.

"I told them he wasn't white. They thought I had lost my mind. I kept it up for days...with conviction too. Then I sat them down and simply said...he's part of our found family. Just like the rest of you. You're brothers now. Nothing else matters."

Momma Jackson gave me chills. Found family. I've never heard that sentiment before. It's beautiful.

"Now that didn't stop them from doing all the things that brothers do. They picked on each other and fought like hell. But they grew up with love in their hearts for each other in their own ways and that's all I could ask for."

Chapter 26
Bethany

Archer has a lot of nerve. We're on our way to meet Micah for a date. My first date and it's with him. He was probably the ringleader who got the guys to destroy all my things.

"This is going to be a nice night, Beth. Try to look like someone who is going on a first date. For reference, first dates are normally happy occasions."

I'm not sure if that was a dig at me or if Archer was trying to make a joke to loosen me up.

I don't respond. Anything I have to say would be disrespectful. The only one of them not on my shit list right now is Jonathan. He wasn't even there. Well, he was on the phone, but I feel like that barely counts. Why couldn't this date be with Jonathan?

"You look lovely."

His compliments won't help. Of course I look lovely. It's not hard when a stranger who knows your exact body proportions buys clothes for you.

"It's also customary to say thank you when you get a compliment."

"Thank you." I give him that one, but I sound like a brat when I do it.

Archer chuckles in that way I've learned means that he's frustrated with me. It's that low chuckle with a little hum at the end of it. I look at him and smirk.

"We're even now, Beth. We're dropping it. You need to drop it." He shivers a little after his order. I know exactly what's happening. My little attachment is mad at him. I don't know how I know that it's there when it doesn't show me it's there, but I do. It's just a feeling.

Not even close Archer. We're not even close to being even.

Archer tells me that Micah asked for this first date. That makes me madder. I'm confident that he hates me. I smile a little. It was worth it.

"See there. You have some happiness in there somewhere", Archer encourages me. He has no idea.

Micah stands when he sees us following behind the waiter. He shakes Micah's hand, then kisses me on the cheek how I'd imagine royals do it. A hand on the arm and a peck on the cheek before I sit.

"Dom Perignon", Micah tells the waiter before I'm fully seated.

"Yes, sir."

"Bethany, how are you", Micah asks, his voice full of concern.

"I'm fine." Micah and Archer exchange a look.

"Beth", Archer warns.

"You said we're even", I tell Archer simply. "Right, Micah? Even?" I look at Micah and wait for his response. He was livid at me for missing court. I suppose I can't blame him but if Archer says we're even, all that evenness should include Micah too, shouldn't it?

Micah chuckles and it sounds like he doesn't have a soul. I thought I was going to like him. No wonder he's here by himself.

"Bethany, I'm going to give you a piece of advice that has always served me well. Find the one thing your opponent can't afford to lose and aim straight for it."

The waiter delivers our bottle and pours us each a glass with a flourish. Micah raises his glass, and we follow his lead.

"To trying your best. Because the difference between winners and everyone else...is knowing exactly what to take from them."

He clinks his glass against mine but just as he's about to take a sip, he squints and looks next to me. I follow his gaze and there's nothing there. Archer seems just as clueless.

"We don't know each other yet but contrary to what you believe, even after that little stunt you pulled, I do like you. You've got backbone. It's admirable."

"You called me a joke." Saying these words out loud hurts. I feel vulnerable about the whole thing all over again.

"I never called you a joke. I was surprised by what I learned about you, but I can assure you that I", Micah touches his fingertips to his chest, "...would never be in a relationship with someone who is a joke."

"I liked you", I tell him simply.

"Beth", Archer warns from across the table. I don't acknowledge him.

"I thought you were sweet." Micah laughs and my face heats with anger.

"Trust me. No one has ever called me sweet. Side note, you wouldn't want that. You think you do but sweet won't make your pussy come."

My mouth falls open that he would be so blunt as to call that out. He also might be right. I'm getting turned on just by the mere notion of being used for pleasure.

"May I touch your witch? I'm curious." Micah addresses Archer as though I'm not able to give permission for myself.

"I'd like that...very much." Archer calls my attention to him. "Beth, be a good girl for Micah."

"Here?" I don't want him touching me at all let alone in public.

"Look at me", Micah gently commands. "He owns you now. Legally and otherwise. Which means he has the right to give you to me anywhere in any way he chooses." Micah rests his hand on my knee and his eyes dart next to my seat. His hand stills on my bare skin and his eyes meet mine. Slowly, he pulls his hand away.

Micah and Archer exchange a look. Archer looks confused. So am I.

And as if Micah has lost interest in touching me all together, he flags down a waiter so we can begin our meal.

Chapter 27
Archer

"I made a decision."

Jonathan continues scrolling through his phone while I wait for his attention. This is important. I need him to focus.

"I heard about your double date with Micah. I already submitted the paperwork to the courthouse. You might be able to annul it if you haven't fucked her yet."

"That's what I want to talk with you about."

"An annulment? I'm a surgeon. You've got the wrong Brother. Call Micah. From what I heard; he'd be happy to get that paperwork going."

"It wasn't that bad."

"He said he saw a dead woman next to her at dinner." I don't say anything because I'm at a loss for words. I didn't realize he saw a dead person at dinner. I just thought he was worried about Bethany's mental status after we tied her to that tree and burnt her witchy things. "Do you see dead people around her?"

"No. I think I feel them though." That would explain the chill I get a lot when she's around. It would also explain the lights flickering and odd noises that I either never noticed before or were never there until recently.

"I told you. I told all of you. Now look what you've gone and done."

"I didn't do anything!" Well, I kind of did something. I burnt the edge of one of her cards and I have her grimoire.

"Well, I don't do ghosts either so you're on your own. But for the record, I told you not to."

How did this get so messed up? This was supposed to be a marriage. It was supposed to be *I do* and a happily ever after. Instead, I have a wife I don't feel right fucking and a spirit on the loose.

"Is that it because I gotta get to the gym." He's sitting there in his scrubs just getting off a long shift and still has the will to work out. Just one more reason I like him. He's badass.

"No that is not all. Look, I came here to ask you to fuck my wife."

Jonathan's brows raise in surprise. "No." He gets up and starts to walk out of the room.

"No?"

"Roughly one hundred languages translate this word the same."

Jonathan is being a smartass. I don't have time for this.

"Is it because of the spirit thing? I mean, we could sage it or whatever people do to get rid of them", I offer.

"No...but I must admit I'm not too excited about having a dead woman watching me make your wife bleed."

"Then what's the problem?"

"The problem is she cares about you, and you broke her heart. You really think having me come in and fuck her before her own husband does is going to make that better?"

"I can't."

"Because of good ol' Gertie?"

"What?"

"Gertie the ghost." Jonathan chuckles.

"Stop callin' her that. And no, it has nothin' to do with Bethany's...friend."

"Attachment", Jonathan corrects me.

"Whatever."

"No. Not whatever. She's got an attachment who's protecting her, and it sounds like that attachment isn't too keen on you and Micah."

"That's why I need you to do it. She likes you. She trusts you. In her eyes, you're the good guy."

"So, you want to take me down with you guys? I don't think so. Go fuck her yourself. You want a coach or something? I can be there. I'll even fuck her right after you. But not first." He starts to walk down the hall but turns around. I'm hopeful he's changed his mind. "You know what? Have Braden do it? He was ready on your wedding day. I'm sure he'd still do it."

Jonathan continues down the hallway, not bothering to show me out. I hate that I'm admitting this but if it's the thing that gets him to agree to my request, I'll do it.

"She said your name in her sleep", I call out after him. He stops but doesn't turn around. "She was in my arms, moaning in her sleep and she said your name."

"Moaned it or said it", he asks, still showing me his back.

"Moaned it." Jonathan spins on his heel, now facing me. He motions for me to continue. "Twice."

Darla J Michaels

"Yes", he hisses while he makes a downward fist pump. "Text me the details."

He spins around and walks off without another word.

Chapter 28
Bethany

"Bajora."

I love how Jonathan purrs my nickname.

"I hear you have a new friend." We're at his place having after dinner drinks.

"I do?" He must be mistaken.

"Gertie?"

I laugh. "Who?"

"Your ghost. Gertie."

I roll my eyes at the name.

"Have you seen her?"

"How do you know it's a her?"

"Micah saw her."

"What? He did? What did she look like?" I cannot believe my sidekick showed herself to him.

"You haven't seen your own spirit friend? Man. Maybe you aren't as tight as you thought", he goads me.

"Stop dodging the question. What does she look like?" I'm dying to know if it's Grams.

Darla J Michaels

"I don't know. Some old lady with a bun in her hair. Heavier. Micah said she looked hauntingly displeased."

I laugh hard at this. I'm not sure who I'm maddest at. Archer and I are on the mend, but my heart still feels broken.

"Do you have your cards with you?"

"No." This surprises him. "They're safe. I don't think Gertie is going to let anything happen to them.

This time Jonathan laughs.

"That's too bad. I was hoping you could give me a reading."

"You just want back in my mouth", I tease him. My God that was hot.

"I don't need your cards to be back in your mouth, Bajora."

His dress shoes click across the floor as he crosses the room to me. He takes my glass from me and has a sip of my drink before setting it next to his. I get it. He's in charge. I'd like to think our relationship is a little different though. We have something more than the others. It's like the connection that Archer and I have. On a spiritual level, Jonathan understands me. Where Archer is concerned, spirit understands that we need each other. I don't understand much more than being very unsettled when Archer and I are not together at some point during the day.

Jonathan reaches behind me, unzipping my dress. He brushes the fabric over my shoulders. It pools onto the floor, exposing my naked body for him.

Archer wouldn't allow me to wear undergarments today. He said I'd be coming home in something else anyway.

I'm still getting used to the guys dictating so many things in my life. Clothing is an odd thing to choose. Maybe in a kinky way I understand choosing a woman's undergarments, but these men go all out. The dress pooling on the floor must be worth a pretty penny. The shoes are red bottoms. I looked these up.

Tell Me Who You Go With- Archer & Bethany

Who would spend so much money on something that touches the pavement?

"I like you, Bethany." Jonathan using my given name sounds weird. Suddenly serious. "What?"

"I like it better when you call me Bajora." It reminds me that he understands a part of me that others don't. It's our thing. I feel special when he calls me that.

"On your knees, Bajora."

I sink to my knees awkwardly. The heels are so tall, and the fabric of the dress is bunched underneath my knees. When I reach back to remove a heel, Jonathan corrects me.

"Leave it."

I look up at him, my mouth falling open in shock.

"Look at that. You're all ready for me you greedy, greedy little witch." He winks at me, and my mouth drops open further. "Hold that right there. You have such pretty teeth against that lipstick", he tells me, taking it upon himself to unzip his slacks and pull himself out.

"I have something for you."

"Cum?" I used to blush when speaking this way, but it's become more commonplace since marrying Archer.

"Lots, and lots of cum, Bajora", Jonathan confirms as he slides himself into my mouth.

I can already taste him on my tongue. I want more. What's leaking out for me isn't nearly enough. In my hunger for him, I'm a little overzealous and gag myself. Jonathan seems to delight in it. He finds this time appropriate for instruction.

Placing his palm at the back of my head and one holding my jaw, he begins to instruct me.

"I love fucking a woman's mouth like this." I roll my eyes up to him and he leaks into my mouth once more. "It's about control. See..." He slides in farther and I gag around him, drool dripping from the sides of my mouth as I press against his legs. "...you can't interrupt my rhythm like this." He gags me again. "You're right where I want you. Good girls get on their knees and open their mouths for their boyfriends. Better girls swallow."

And with that, he throws his head back and releases into my mouth.

There is a literal heartbeat between my legs right now. When Jonathan finishes in my mouth, his entire member pulses with his release. It is the hottest thing to watch let alone feel in my mouth. And I can't quite explain it but being on my knees for him and even Archer, feels like a gift they give to me.

"Bajora...now I want you to tell me why you don't swallow for your husband." Jonathan slides himself out of my mouth so I can answer him even while he drips onto my thighs and the inside of my bunched-up dress.

"He tastes like meat."

Jonathan's laughter fills the room as I shift uncomfortably on the floor. I haven't been in this position long but I'm starting not to be able to feel my toes in these heels.

"And what do I taste like?"

"I don't know. Sweet? Salty and sweet?"

"I'll let Archer in on my little secret. Bajora, promise me you'll swallow for him tomorrow morning. Even if you're mad at him."

"Why?"

"Because he loves you and he shows it sometimes in some really fucked up ways, but he does love you."

I take his outstretched hand and grimace as I stand. He lifts me up and throws me over his shoulder, heels and all.

"What are we doing?" I gasp as his large palm comes down hard on my bare backside.

"You'll see."

That's all the information I get as he walks down the hallway.

"You're mine tonight", Jonathan tells me as he enters what appears to be a spare bedroom.

"You won't get much sleep", he tells me, setting me on my feet again.

"Can I take off the shoes?" He looks me over thoughtfully before he answers.

"Under one condition."

"Okay." I put my hands on my hips, and he smiles at me. I'm naked except for my shoes. I have no power here. My attempts at copping an attitude are even weaker like this. If I were him, I'd look at me like that too.

"I need to be honest with you. And you can't be mad at me."

"For the honesty? How is that fair?"

"Good point. You can be mad for the honesty, but you must forgive me. If you don't, we're done here tonight." Whatever this is sounds serious. "I care about you, and I can't do this if there's part of you that's holding a grudge."

"Fine. Now can I take off the shoes?" He shakes his head and shrugs out of his shirt after setting his cuff links on a nightstand.

"That night when the guys burned your stuff...I gave them the syringe with the drugs in it."

My heels click on the floor as I take a step back. Jonathan doesn't reach for me. He doesn't even call my name. He simply waits.

"Are you joking?"

"No."

"I trusted you..."

254

Darla J Michaels

"And you should trust me. But you should also know that every time I will choose them. They are my Brothers. We support each other always. Even if we don't agree. They asked for the meds, and I handed them over without hesitation. Anything they ask, I will do it because they will do the same for me."

"I need to think."

"Take all the time you need with those shoes on." I walk to the bed and sit down. "Standing." Shooting Jonathan a glare, I stand and grimace at the discomfort. "Your legs look fantastic in those, but I'd think quick if I were you. Those look dreadfully uncomfortable."

This feels like a slap in the face. I trusted him and he betrayed me. While that's not okay, my rational brain knows they would have taken me kicking and screaming regardless of the drugs the guys got from Jonathan. Either way, I would have been tied to that tree. The difference is between me being awake for it or knocked out.

He's also being honest. I never connected him to helping even though Tyler had him on a video call. They probably assumed I knew they all had a hand in my punishment in some way. Wondering who was responsible for what never even crossed my mind.

Jonathan now stands in front of me completely naked. I smile when I see that he's still wearing his shoes too.

"Solidarity", he says, winking at me.

"I forgive you, but I don't like what you did."

"I can accept that. I didn't like what I did either but...alliances and all", he remarks sarcastically, bending to untie his dress shoes. "Get those off and get in bed", he orders playfully.

Tell Me Who You Go With- Archer & Bethany

I have never been more excited to follow an order from one of these men. I don't care if I ever put those shoes on again. I hope Jonathan donates them.

I watch Jonathan as he sets his shoes near the wall on the other side of the room.

"Damn, Bethany. You have no intentions of sleeping, do you?" I have no idea what he's talking about. "You didn't even pull back the covers", he clarifies, taking the duvet and pulling it back as far as my body will allow it. Then he climbs on top of me, wraps me in his arms and rolls us over onto the sheets.

I'm on top of him, laughing as he slides the decorative pin out of my hair.

"Heirloom", he asks holding the vintage bronze fillagree hairpin between us.

"It's Gertie's", I tease. This time he laughs, gingerly placing the pin on the nightstand and rolling me over onto the sheet.

"I like you, Bethany. And I wish I could do sweet but sweet's just not my thing. But I'm going to make up for it", he tells me, now sliding his hard length through my folds, rubbing over my sensitive flesh.

"Make up for what?"

"For this", he whispers against my lips, catching my cry in his mouth as he slides inside me to the hilt without warning.

I'm stunned.

"Orders", he tells me, looking into my eyes, which are quickly welling with tears. "Bajora, try to relax. Let them get used to each other. This is all so new to them. Let me see your mouth", he gently orders me.

I turn my head when he tries to close the gap.

"Bajora", he gently chastises me.

"He ordered this?"

Darla J Michaels

Jonathan doesn't answer me right away. He kisses down my neck and my shoulder as far as he can go without shifting inside me, then repeats the process on the other side.

"He did. But it wasn't without careful consideration. You must believe that if you don't believe anything else."

"Because I haven't forgiven him?" Jonathan shakes his head and begins to slide out of me. I grip his hips, trying to stop him but he continues.

"Look." He's looking between our bodies where we connect. "Tell me what you see." I see a mess. Jonathan's hard length is covered with my arousal and my blood. "Go on. Tell me", he urges.

"Blood."

"And?"

"I was wet."

"You are wet." Jonathan slides back inside me. It's painful. "I know, Bajora. I know. And so does he." I don't follow. "Archer knows things too. He knew giving me the one thing no one else can ever have would mean more to both of us than if he had taken it for himself. And I can tell by the look on your face that you know I'm right. You don't have to admit it to me. Your pussy will do that for you."

The next day, Jonathan drops me off at Archer's place. I was given a trench coat and the same pair of shoes to wear. If I thought it was hard to walk in these heels before, it was nothing compared to having sex all night after losing my virginity. Jonathan didn't allow me to shower even after he had me a few more times this morning. When I objected, all he said was orders.

When I enter, Spirit has extra energy. As kindly as I can muster, I motion for him to sit and slide off the torture devices on my feet.

Padding into the kitchen to find Archer, I hear Spirit licking. I turn around to find him licking what is likely Jonathan and I's mess off my shoes.

Archer's cell vibrates on the counter. It's Jonathan. Archer doesn't lock his phone, so I slide the bar over and open Jonathan's text message.

JP- Done

There are some bubbles dancing across the bottom of the screen and then another message appears. Pictures...of me.

I open them and scroll through. One is of us joined together, his cock bloody. Another of my broken hymen. The rest are of his release either leaking from me or dripping down my thighs.

A final photo comes through. He took the picture selfie style. I'm asleep in Jonathan's arms. I'm out cold and he's glowing from a post orgasm haze.

"How you feelin'?"

"Oh shit", I gasp. I'm so caught up in what I see that I didn't notice Archer enter the kitchen. "I'm sorry."

"Beth."

"Hmmm?"

"I asked how you're feelin', darlin'."

It takes me a moment to formulate an answer. I'm sore. I'm tired. I need a shower. And although Jonathan explained it to me at his house the best he could, I'm hurt by Archer's decision.

"I need...to be alone for a little bit. It's a lot to process", I tell him as I walk past him to shower and change. This is me trying not to fall apart. Pretty diplomatic considering. But diplomacy isn't something I find I can hold onto when Archer grabs my arm.

"I asked you a question, Beth."

"Okay." I answer him in a low tone because I'm trying not to be emotional.

"Okay?"

But when he copies me in an incredulous tone, diplomacy exits stage left. I whirl around to face him, and he blanches at the sight of me. Silent tears stream down my face, and I'm so angry it feels like I might be having an out of body experience of some kind.

"You want to know how I feel? I'm heartbroken. You gifted me to someone else. For what?" I shove him and to my surprise, he lets me, taking a step back from the impact of my hands on his chest. "What did you trade me for?" I shove him again. "Was it better than my virginity? It must have been. I bet you had well trained pussy last night", I seethe.

I get no reaction from him. He looks me over and waits.

"Oh. I remember. I suppose a promise is a promise", I tell him as I untie my trench coat and toss it to the floor. I turn around for him so he can see the cum dripping down my legs at all angles. Then I grab a few hand towels and place them on the floor at his feet. I kneel just as I promised Jonathan. Swallow like the best girl...

When I look up at Archer, he's angry. Probably because I'm waiting for him to take himself out to be serviced. I reach up for the button on his pants and he catches my wrist in his hand.

"Get up", he grits out. I try to pull my hand from his grip, but he won't let go.

"Let go." I'm still struggling against him.

He does not let go. Instead, he bends down and lifts me up as I struggle against him. It takes him no effort at all to set me on my feet and back me against the wall.

Tell Me Who You Go With- Archer & Bethany

You would think I would have learned by now, but I haven't. Screaming and struggling won't get me anywhere because once again, I find myself subdued by one of these men. My hands are pinned over my head, my legs are spread apart on each side of his heavy boots and his free hand is now around my neck, firmly securing me to the wall. That hand applies pressure when I struggle.

I'm sobbing. Not because I'm scared, because I'm humiliated.

"I need you to listen to me, very carefully Beth." I sob harder. "I'll wait. Get it out, darlin'. Get it out."

I sob until I feel a little better. He's right about not holding in emotions. It feels horrible. Even though this feels horrible too, bottling it up would have felt worse.

"I didn't trade you. I traded me. I didn't deserve you. What I did...how I behaved...how I let my Brothers behave...I'll never forgive myself for that. That behavior shouldn't be rewarded. Jonathan did right by you that night, so I knew he'd do right by you last night too. I didn't have a date last night because I knew all I would be able to think about was you. I'm tryin' to fix it Beth. I don't want this thing between us that I created and I'm tryin' to fix it."

Chapter 29
Bethany

I'm showered, in a bath robe, sitting in the living room when Archer walks in. We both needed some space after I got home from my date with Jonathan.

I needed time to realize that what Archer had done was the sweetest most fucked up thing a husband could do to their wife. He needed space so he didn't strangle me. So much space, he got in his car and left.

The things I accused him of were so disrespectful. I hope he can forgive me. He's been gone a while. It's past lunch time and I'm wondering if he plans on coming back.

I could message him, but I don't. If he didn't message me back, I think I might fall apart. And maybe that's why I'm so upset in the first place. Because I love him. And I don't understand how he loves. It's twisted and messy but oddly well-meaning. What I do know for sure is that he's got my heart and my head all mixed up.

Gram would probably say that makes it the real deal. I wonder what Gertie would say.

Tell Me Who You Go With- Archer & Bethany

The fact that they saw the spirit that somehow attached to me and gave her a name makes me smile. And I hate to say it, but it makes me even happier that the spirit scared the shit out of Micah. She must really dislike him.

And then it dawns on me. If Gertie follows me, she must like Jonathan. She must have approved of him doing what he did. He never once complained of being cold or seeing anything. I wonder if he would have. Could Jonathan's duty to Archer have been more important than seeing an apparition?

Since I have no expectations that Jonathan will text me back immediately, I fire off a text to him. Inquiring minds want to know. I think it says a lot if Gertie just sat back and watched. Hmmm...maybe that's weird too. Never mind...

To my surprise, Jonathan texts me back right away. I love how playful he is even though he doesn't answer my question. Or maybe he does. It's hard to tell. He sends about a dozen ghost emojis and then follows it with a picture puppet, which is one of my younger sister's names for a GIF. The picture puppet is of a hot guy winking.

I message him back a quick thanks and resume sipping my tea.

Normally not a daytime napper, I managed to fall asleep on Archer's couch. I haven't gotten a lot of sleep lately and the emotional toll of everything that has happened over the past few weeks has exhausted me. My body must have needed the rest.

I wake up to the smell of food cooking. Archer can cook but it's mostly meat. I'm not sure what he's working on in the kitchen but it smells amazing. Definitely not meat.

I rub the sleep from my eyes and let out a yawn. And my eyes land on the coffee table.

My heart stops. Either Gertie is fucking with me, or it's real. And if it's real, where has it been and how did it get here?

I reach out and run my fingertips over the leather cover of the grimoire. "Dinner will be ready soon."

Archer leans against the wall with a dish towel over his shoulder and his arms crossed over his chest. I'm speechless.

"The lady at the store recommended white wine to go with dinner. I got a little of everything if you want to look. You can pick a bottle and I can pour you a glass", he offers.

"How..." The words are literally stuck in my throat as I flip through the pages. It's all here. My grandmother's elegant handwriting covers the pages. Everything is intact just as it had been the day they burned it all.

"I hid it. I knew taking that would cross a line."

"There was a box", I start to explain, hopeful that he grabbed that too. He nods. I start to sob. He saved my grandmother's letters to my sisters and me.

"Bethany, darlin', I thought you'd be happy." I stand and stumble to him, falling into his arms. "I'm tryin' to fix it."

I nod against his chest because this is just one more of the fucked-up things he did because he loves me.

Chapter 30
Archer

I called a meeting at my house. It's late. Bethany and I have had dinner. She's not expecting company.

Footsteps sound in the hallway as my fingertips trace up her bare arm. She never changed from her bath robe. No make up, dark long curls flowing over her shoulder as we sit in silence, sipping our drinks.

Bethany looks over her shoulder as Tyler enters the room, taking a seat next to her. He slides his hand under her legs and pulls them onto his lap, resting one hand on her thigh and grabbing her foot to massage it.

More footsteps echo down the hall as the rest of the guys file in. Bethany gives me a worried look, attempting to pull her foot away from Tyler.

"Settle, Beth. We need to talk."

Micah, Braden, Graham and Landon find a seat across the room, looking me over.

"Darlin'', I called this meeting to set some things straight."

Darla J Michaels

She tries to snug her robe closed tighter under Tyler's palm but instead of closing it further, Tyler stops her and slips his hand underneath the fabric to rest on her thigh.

"Today we'll add my rule. It requires you to resolve whatever disagreement you have with my Brothers and I immediately. No lingering grudges."

She beings to protest but I stop her.

"I won't allow disagreements to go on longer than a day. It's been long enough. We're here to resolve this and resolve it now. Speak your peace."

Bethany looks around the room, unsure if she should really speak up.

"You won't be punished for your honesty", Micah tells her.

"Remember what we talked about the first night here? I can deal with anything but secrets. Dishonesty is one in the same for me. Go on. Say all your things and we'll work it out."

"Where's Jonathan?"

She feels safe with him. He couldn't be here, but we met anyway because he's the only one she doesn't have issue with.

"He's not available and he isn't needed here tonight."

"I don't feel safe with you." Bethany directs her statement at Micah, Braden Landon and Graham. "I have never drugged anyone before. I didn't even know if it would work."

Braden shakes his head and smiles.

"I just needed to stop what was about to happen. I didn't want it. I wasn't trying to hurt you like you hurt me."

Micah raises a brow at her.

"Those were things", she tries justifying her actions. Micah shoots her a stern look. "I have never done anything like that", she confesses, sudden remorse in her voice.

"You wanted to change what I ate and put me on a treadmill", she tells Landon. "And you two regarded me as though I was crazy for believing in something you don't believe in. I wanted to hurt you back. To show you that I'm not insignificant. That I should be taken seriously and respected."

"What's it going to take to fix it, Beth?"

"Time." She sounds sad. I know she's still hurting but that's not how this works. She's on our schedule now.

"Let me be clear, Beth. I will give you to these men. We're on the calendar. You have said your peace."

"Will I get an apology?"

"Will you be giving one?" She doesn't answer me. "I didn't think so. Now kiss and make up", I order her, shooting from the hip.

This can't be resolved. They hurt her. She got back at them. There is no amount of apologizing in this moment that will fix this.

I move Bethany from her comfortable position laying against me. Before she stands, I untie her robe. "Leave it", I order her when she moves to close the fabric.

Bethany shoots me a glare and turns to address everyone but Tyler and I. She isn't sure who she should go to. Micah helps her by holding out his hand to her. I'm curious how this is going to go. She's angriest at him.

"Come sit", he gently orders her to sit on his knee. To my surprise, she complies without fuss, her face softening when she turns to him. He turns her face so she's looking at him.

"I don't like what you do. It bothers me."

"The spells?"

Micah lets out a heavy sigh. "I'm not a threat to you. Respectfully, I'm asking you to get rid of the woman."

She shakes her head. "I don't even know how she got here. I wouldn't even know how to do that."

Bethany's honesty warms my heart. She's being vulnerable with someone she regards as her biggest adversary.

"She won't allow me to touch you." Bethany smiles. Micah sighs once more before he confesses something that I'm sure takes a lot for him to admit. "You've made me a believer. Is that what you want to hear?"

Her smile gets wider. She nods and Micah shakes his head at her tenacity. His hand drifts to the edge of her robe, pulling it open to further expose her nakedness underneath to the guys. He's testing the waters. Probably to see if her little friend is going to stop him.

He turns her head to kiss her, and she kisses him back. By the looks of them, forgiveness has been achieved. So far, this has worked better than I could have imagined.

I nod at Micah when he breaks the kiss to look at me. He takes my silent permission and returns to kissing Bethany. She moans when he slides his hand between her legs.

"I want you willingly", he tells her between kisses. "And believe it or not, I want you to want me too." He kisses her once more and her legs spread further for him.

"Just like that", he croons to her.

I'm so fucking hard it takes all my self-restraint not to interfere. I want to touch her. I want to tell him to do more than touch her.

Landon clears his throat. "Wait your turn", Micah tells him between kisses. Micah stops kissing Bethany but he doesn't let her go as she settles in his embrace. "I want to come in your mouth. On your knees sweetheart."

She leans in and kisses him again, then carefully slides off his lap and onto her knees.

Micah looks across the room at me, looking for my okay.

Tell Me Who You Go With- Archer & Bethany

"Be sweet with her", I warn. I'm not sure how I'll take someone gagging her other than me.

"We're going to take our time, Bethany", he tells her as he guides her hand to the zipper of his slacks.

Chapter 31
Archer

If anyone understands unusual family dynamics, it's me. But this takes the cake.

Not only was Bethany's mother ungodly rude to me when we first met, I found out just before Bethany had said yes to my proposal, her mother was the reason she ghosted me.

"I think this is good", Bethany says in the passenger seat.

I'm trying not to make a face that conveys how delusional I think her statement is but it's hard. My face generally reflects how I feel. And how I feel right now is annoyed.

"You know I won't allow her to disrespect you, right?" We need to be clear on this. She's my wife and she will be treated with respect.

"I think once she gets to know you and my dad meets you and sees how great you are she'll cool down a little. Put yourself in her shoes. How would you feel if your daughter got married out of the blue and you met him at a farmer's market on a random Tuesday?"

"How would I feel? Well, I'd like to think I could be the bigger person. And while I wouldn't insult him, I would make him think long and hard before he did anything to hurt my little girl. Your mother was not protecting you. She was humiliating you and she did it by trying to humiliate me. Can't be done, Beth. It just can't be done."

"Remember the girls will be there."

"Nora and Noelle." Those poor girls having to live under the same roof as that mean woman for another five years. The week with us will be a reprieve for sure. "What are they like? Are they like their mom?"

I glance over at Bethany and she's smiling at me. This is not funny to me. The way that woman came at her daughter was inexcusable.

"They're too young to be like anyone. They're still figuring life out."

"I think you should have them over a lot. Get them out from under that woman's thumb."

"I'd like that. I miss them. I'm just so busy during the school year and so are they. Then I feel like the summer just flies by." Keep going Bethany. Make my point for me. "And the girls have their friends they want to see in the summer. I worry that they won't have time for me because I haven't made time for them."

"That could happen. Teenagers are funny like that." She looks sad when I glance her way again. "You know, I know someone who could free your time up so you could see your sisters more. He's a very generous and reasonable man who would give you just about anything you asked for."

She throws an irritated look my way.

"Teaching is important to me."

"Is teaching more or less important than the relationship with your sisters?"

"That's ridiculous. You can't compare the two."

"You're right. You can't. I know what I'd choose if I were in your shoes. When you choose one thing, you're not choosing another. There will always be something more important in your life by the priority you make it." She scoffs at me. "It's not a criticism, Beth and it doesn't make you a bad person to want one thing more than the other. I'm just trying to get you to choose the thing that you really want instead of the thing you think you might have to choose."

When we pull into her parent's driveway, I think Bethany is relieved she doesn't have to defend the topic of wanting to return to work at the school. She gets out of the car and shuts the door.

"Beth, back in the car."

"Oh, come on. She's probably watching."

"I hope she is. I hope your dad is too. Now." I open the door for her and wait for compliance. We've tested each other a lot over these first few weeks. I'm sure the trend will continue until we reach common ground.

She rolls her eyes and gets back into the car. I shut the door and signal for her to wait. And when I estimate the time it would have taken me to get to her car door to open it, I open the door and offer her my hand.

"You are the most important person in my life now. I will not compete with your ego to treat you like you matter to me."

I shut the car door and pin her against it. "You matter to me, Beth. From the moment you walked into my shop, you mattered to me." I kiss her softly to make my point. When she doesn't rush me or push away for fear her family is watching I know she's in a good place. Whatever happens during dinner is inconsequential to our story. I don't want her to ever feel a bit of worry or concern now that she's mine.

When I step back, she looks up at me starry-eyed.

"Mrs. Jackson." She takes my hand as we walk up the driveway to the back door.

Bethany doesn't even get a chance to knock, and her sisters are there. Their mouths fall open when they see me. I laugh. I can't help it. They're cute. Suddenly, I'm feeling much better about this dinner. These girls are sure to be entertaining.

"Nora and Noelle", Bethany points for my benefit to address them. "May we please come in?"

The girls giggle and move out of the way to allow us entry.

"They look just like you", I tell Bethany. My goodness. If there weren't an age difference, the three of them could be triplets. I'm guessing when Nora and Noelle get older, people will make that mistake with them a lot.

"Is this him", Nora asks Bethany all wide-eyed and full of wonder.

"He has tattoos", Noelle remarks to Nora as if she can't see them herself. "Can I touch one?"

I laugh at her question. It's adorable and kind of reminds me of Bethany. The day we got married she spent a lot of time looking at my body art. She'd run her fingertips over the images that color my skin with rapt interest. No one has ever treated me with that kind of sweet affection. I gather Noelle will be a lot like Bethany when she grows up.

"I don't think so, darlin'." Noelle's mouth falls open and Nora giggles. Bethany nudges me playfully and I just shake my head and smile. "It's nice to meet you both, though. Looks like we're family now."

"We are family now", a stern deep voice with notable warmth cuts into the conversation.

Darla J Michaels

"Dad." Bethany walks over to him and gives him a great big hug. I watch as Bethany's father soaks in her affection, shutting his eyes and squeezing her tight.

"How are you Snuggle Bug?" He's holding her at arm's length and looking her over.

"I'm good, dad." Bethany looks over her shoulder at me.

"Mr. Everly." I walk up, intruding on their moment and extend my hand. His handshake is firm, and his eyes are kind. There's no warning there. Instead, there's respect. I wasn't planning on that tonight. Perhaps he has the influence Bethany alluded to on the way over.

"Archer, right?"

"Yes, sir."

"Ted. It's great to meet you. Won't you come in? There's more to the house than the foyer." He raises a brow at the twins, and they instantly talk at once to show me around.

I get the tour but oddly enough, Mrs. Everly is nowhere to be found.

"Dad, where's mom", Bethany finally asks, while her father attends to the roast in the oven.

"She had a meeting that ran late. She's wrapping up a few loose ends and will be on her way in time for dinner."

"Can I help with anything...that's not meat?" Her father laughs at Bethany's offer but takes her up on it. I don't think he really wanted her help, but I do think he wanted time alone with me. It was the perfect request to get me alone before her mom got here. I don't blame him. I'd probably do the same thing but I wouldn't be so discrete about it.

Bethany smirks at me as Ted makes us drinks and leads me out to The Thinkery as he calls it.

Aside from our visit to Momma's house and the run in with Bethany's mom day one of our marriage, we hadn't exchanged much information about each other's family. We've been busy. I took a few weeks off to be with my wife, but the time hasn't gone as I planned it. We've done some Brotherhood stuff but mostly, it's been her and I working through the dynamics of our relationship. Her punishment took a toll on her. Working with her through the aftermath took up most of my second week with her.

"Come on in. Make yourself comfortable", he waves me in. I playfully give him a doubtful look. He laughs it off and waits for me to enter, shutting the door behind us.

The Thinkery is nice. More than just a large shed with a concrete floor. I don't know the specific tools a woodworker uses, but it looks like he's got damn near all of them. There's a shelf full of cans of paint and stain. On the far end of the space, he's got finished bookshelves, some statues and smaller boxes that likely hold smaller sentimental gifts.

The place smells of wood shavings though there's barely any dust on the floor. Ted is neat. I like that. It shows discipline. I'm not saying his daughter is messy, but she isn't neat like her father, that's for sure.

"Is this the part where you threaten to kill me and hid my body if I don't treat your little girl right?" I want to get right to it. While I won't be telling him my intentions with his daughter, he doesn't have to worry about me mistreating her. At least from this point forward.

To my surprise, Ted laughs. "No. You don't strike me as someone who would hurt my daughter."

Guilt floods over me the moment he shares his sincere assessment of me. I have already hurt her. Not physically but she's been on the mend emotionally.

"I just want to get to know you and I thought maybe you'd want to get to know me."

274

This guy seems so different from his wife. I wonder how these two even got together.

"I would like that. Yes." It's nice to be welcomed into their family instead of looked at like I'm vermin.

"How did you and Bethany meet? We didn't even know she was dating anyone let alone married."

"Bethany came to my shop. The artist she had an appointment with was sick, so I covered for him." I'm not sure how much Bethany wants her father to know about getting a tattoo, so I decide to share what I'm asked.

"And that was it? You fell in love?"

"Is that so hard to believe? Your daughter is beautiful. Smart. Funny. A genuinely nice person. I've never met someone with a heart as big as hers."

"What kind of art was she there for? I've never known Bethany to be interested in art."

"I own several tattoo shops, sir." Where I thought he might express his displeasure, he smiles. "What?"

"Do I want to know?"

"Can't tell you that, sir. Body art is personal. Ask her about it. I'm sure she'll show you."

"Her mom is going blow a gasket." I laugh at how he calls his wife out. "And stop calling me sir." Ted thinks as he sips his drink. I look him over, noting that the only feature his daughters share of his are his eyes. Their other features come from their mother. Thank goodness they haven't seemed to inherit her behavior too.

"What about you? I'm assuming this is a hobby", I motion around Ted's workspace.

"Why would you say that?"

"Well, you have a modest amount of finished projects." I nod to the other side of the workspace. "None of it is packaged or tagged and as far as I can see, there are no packing materials here. No computer or space that appears designated for a desk. Looks like your work is finished but not for sale." I walk over to the space where he keeps the finished products. "Damn...these are nice."

"Thank you."

He doesn't correct me, confirming I'm right. This looks like a lot of work. "Why do this if you aren't going to put yourself out there and sell it?"

"Why do anything?" I don't follow. "We do things out of obligation, need and if we're lucky out of love. Why would I want to sell the things I made from love?"

"Is this about Bethany?" Ted chuckles at my question.

"No. I have a feeling if Bethany agreed to marry you, you're great guy. Her intuition has always been spot on. I'm talking about passion. The things that light you up when no one else is around."

"Art is my passion and I sell it", I challenge him.

"It's not the same. You're giving a customer something that was already theirs." Now I'm really lost. "When an idea drops into our minds, it's ours. We own it. And if we act on that idea, it's already done. It might not be done immediately but it's done in the future. Our present self needs to go out and make it happen."

"Customers come to me to fulfill their idea. So, you're saying art isn't my passion because it's not mine?" I disagree but I want to see where he's going with this.

"No. I'm telling you that you aren't giving away the work you're truly passionate about. Do you have a piece of art you would never part with at home? Something you made that you would never consider giving away let alone putting the image on another?"

"I do."

"That's passion. That's love. The rest is business. We need both to be complete human beings. Something that we work for...a duty...a vocation. And something we could do for hours where time is meaningless, and our mind pauses so what's in our soul can manifest in physical form."

There it is. This is why Bethany and her dad get along. Soul. They acknowledge it. They feed it. I thought I fed mine but in comparison, I'm a little off track. I haven't drawn just for me in a while. No...it's been years.

"You're deep." I don't want to admit that I have lost this part of myself.

"I hope so. I'm a professor of Ethics and Philosophy." And it all comes together. "Obligation and need take over from time to time. If there's a drought in the well where your passions are, give it some water. It'll spill over into everything else in no time. I know things. I'm tenured." He jokes about the last part, and we share a laugh.

I like him. Seems like a good guy. A level-headed man.

Our laughter dies down when a car pulls in the driveway.

"You ready?"

"Let's do this", I tell him with a smirk.

"I'd give you advice, but I get the feeling you don't need it", he tells me as we step out of the space that gives him joy. It's then that I realize all my space is shared now. Maybe I need a space just for myself, I consider as we head toward the house. Bethany has her greenhouse.

I should allow her to get started in the greenhouse. That's a task for later. Maybe she can get it set up with the girls when they come over later this week.

We step inside the kitchen expecting to see the ladies but it's empty. Completely cleaned up leaving a trail of the smell in its wake. I follow behind Ted, heading toward the voices of the ladies in the dining room.

"He's so hot, Bethy."

"Mom, you should see him."

"I have seen him."

"Do you sleep in the same bed with him?"

"Oh my God...do you see him naked?!"

Jesus. These girls are making me blush. They're barely teens.

"Hello", Ted calls out before we get to the dining room. I'm not sure which one of us he was saving from embarrassment, me or him. "How'd it go, Viv", he greets her, kissing her on the cheek as their daughters ogle me.

"They're thinking about it", she tells him, putting the emphasis on thinking as though whatever they're pondering is a no-brainer.

"It'll work out. You going to change before we eat?" Ted looks at the spread on the table. "The ladies did a great job. Looks amazing. Thank you."

"I was on my way to do that when I was stopped by these boy-crazy teenagers of ours." She shifts to look at me, shaking her head with a much milder disapproval than she did the first time we met. That's something, I suppose.

"Girls, grab something to drink and have a seat. Refill", Ted asks me. I simply nod and he takes my glass with a smile. He manages her well. She must not pull that shit with him.

Bethany and I are left alone in the dining room. She smiles at me, and I can't help but to return the smile. This woman lights me up like nothing else. I have heard of couples loving and adoring each other. I just didn't think it would happen to me.

"Isn't he the best", she brags stepping up to me and raising up on her tiptoes to get a quick kiss.

Darla J Michaels

"He is the best, yes." I'm glad she has him in her life. I've never had much of a father figure in my life. Maybe we could be close someday. He seems like someone I could have in my circle.

Ted and the girls file back in with the drinks. Noelle hands me mine.

"I'm older so dad said I could bring it to you", she tells me as though being slightly older than her twin somehow gives her more maturity and the ability to handle more responsibility.

"Thank you." When I clink my glass against hers, her eyes go wide in surprise. I almost spit out the sip I took. Her reaction is comical but a little worrisome. I realize that I may have to make myself scarce when the girls are staying with us. It might be easier that way.

We're all seated with Viv, who still hasn't introduced herself to me yet, glides into the room. She went from business professional to slacks and a cashmere cardigan and heels. I wonder if this is to put me in my place or if this is how she always dresses. No one else is dressed this nice at the table.

"Shall we say grace", she asks the table, holding out her bony manicured hands for each girl to hold during prayer. Interesting. I could see Ted saying grace but Viv? I think she speaks straight to Satan himself.

The room is all business after prayer, which was lackluster and unoriginal compared to Momma's. Viv checks a box. Momma speaks to the Lord.

We pass dishes around the table and for the first few minutes, the only sound in the room comes from utensils clanking as we eat the delicious meal.

"This is excellent", I compliment Ted and the ladies.

"Do you cook?" Viv is laser focused on me across the table.

"Yes, ma'am."

"Boxed dinners?"

"Actual dinners...not in boxes."

"Mom", Bethany tries to intervene.

"Beth, it's okay. Nora and Noelle will be staying with us for a while. Viv is just making sure they won't come home malnourished. Aren't you, Viv?"

I think I saw actual fire in her eyes but I'm not sure if it's because I shortened her name, her daughter's name or both.

"Are we staying at your house", Nora asks. "We'd be on the floor if we slept at Bethy's", she clarifies.

"We haven't worked those details out yet, but I'd assume so."

"Aren't you getting your house ready to sell Bethany?" Viv puts emphasis on her full name and all I can think about is not smiling.

"Oh, no mom. We're keeping both", she tells her simply.

"Why? Is this a real marriage? What is going on here?"

"I can assure you it is a very real marriage, Viv."

The girls giggle at the innuendo.

"Archer why don't you tell us about your line of work", Ted volunteers. I'm not sure if Ted is trying to push ol' Viv over the ledge or if he thinks this will be safer territory but I indulge him all the same.

"I'm an artist. I own several tattoo shops in the area." This time I do chuckle. Viv's mouth has parted, showing the partially unchewed food in her mouth. As if she already knows, she turns to Bethany, her look holding a silent question.

Bethany looks at her father and I laugh hard when her father sets down his fork, rests his elbows on the table and steeples his fingers, looking her in the eyes right back.

Viv gasps. The girls have no idea what's going on at first.

"What is it? Where is it?"

Darla J Michaels

Bethany's cheeks turn pink and that's when I decide to intervene like I should have with the guys.

"Viv, tattoos are private. When she wants you to see it, or even know about it for that matter, she'll let you know. Until then, the topic is closed."

"You have a tattoo", the girls yell in unison.

"Can I have a tattoo", Nora asks me.

"No", Viv and I answer in unison.

"You'll show us, won't. you", Noelle presses Bethany.

I wait for Bethany to answer for herself. She doesn't need me for this one, but I can tell she's still uncomfortable.

"Probably."

The girls giggle in delight as Viv shoots Bethany daggers. Ted is eating again, and I can't take my eyes off my wife. I'm proud of us. This is a big step in the right direction.

When Viv gets up to grab a glass of wine, I decide this meet and greet is going to be one hell of a great time after all.

Chapter 32
Bethany

Hiding my witchcraft from the twins has proven to be impossible. At first, I thought it would be no problem. What I didn't account for was how interested they would be in me and my new life...especially Archer.

And while I hate that Archer has decided to become very busy while we have young houseguests, I couldn't be more supportive of his decision.

We aren't used to having kids here. While they are teens, who are easier to care for than smaller kids in some ways, in others they are a handful. The first night the twins stayed with us, Archer took a shower and walked out to the kitchen in a towel to grab a glass of water. He had come home from the gym and was hungry and thirsty after his workout. The girls were slack jawed as I put the finishing touches on dinner.

Archer took one look at them, turned to me and walked out of the kitchen without another word. Nora and Noelle exchanged not so discrete comments about his physique. I tried

282

to ignore them. But some of these things you just can't unhear. So, the moment Archer suggested he focus on his personal projects for the week I was beyond encouraging.

It also gave me time alone with the girls to show them some of my practices. It's easier without Archer. The girls are curious. Archer is leery. Especially after everything that happened at my house. He hasn't let me go back there until today.

"You look sad", Noelle remarks while we sit on the floor around the coffee table in the living room.

"Do I?"

"Where's all your stuff", Nora asks. They haven't been here often, but the guys took every herb I had collected. All my tinctures, salves, oils, and the like are gone. Someone has even been by to clean out the perishables in the fridge.

I'm not hungry anyway but I could use a drink. I let out a breath as I open the cupboard I kept my liquor in before I got locked out of my home.

"Girls", I bellow from the kitchen floor. "Grab some glasses." Their eyes go wide when they see me hold up the bottle of wine. "It's sweet. You'll like it."

I figure we could all use a little something, considering I'm a little emotional and it's showing and they're curious but not quite believers yet.

Nora jumps at the chance for a drink while Noelle gingerly lifts the pages of grandma's grimoire.

"You can give me hers", Nora volunteers. I shake my head and roll my eyes. I can't get them drunk but I do want to create some memories. Plus, I know they'll keep our time together a secret. I told them I'd show them my tattoo and we'd do witchy things. I think they know they have this side of them but mom or Viv, as Archer now calls her, snuffs that intuition out at every breath.

"Why didn't Gram do witchy stuff with us", Noelle asks from the living room. If I'm not mistaken, she sounds hurt about the notion that Gram would leave her out.

"You were young. Maybe too young." Noelle shakes her head and taps the page she's stopped at with her index finger. "It's because of Viv, isn't it?"

I laugh even though I shouldn't. "Don't be disrespectful", I gently chastise her as I hand her a small glass of the wine.

"Tell me the truth", she demands, setting the glass down in front of her and turning the page.

"The truth is that I don't know. I don't know why Gram worked with me and not either of you. Maybe she wanted me to teach it so her work wouldn't get lost? It's hard to say."

"Are you going to teach us? Or are you just showing us your secrets?"

"Do you want to learn? It only works if you want to learn."

"Does it work? I see this stuff in movies and it looks stupid", Nora speaks freely. She's not wrong. It does look stupid in movies.

"It's how I got Archer", I tell them. Their eyes go wide, and Noelle reaches for her glass. "It's true. Gram told me to do a spell when I turned twenty-three and I did and now...I'm married." I tell them simply, feeling giddy just saying the words. I haven't told anyone yet. Mostly because I don't really have anyone to tell but still, it's the first time the words have slipped from my lips, and I like it.

"Can you teach us how to find our true love", Nora asks.

"Later. When you're older. Out of your teens", I clarify.

"That's so lame", Nora sulks, taking another sip.

"Alright girls, here are the most important principles of spell work. Above everything else, you must be intentional. You can't be half in. If you're asking the universe for something, you have to want it. Really want it."

"How does the universe know", Noelle asks. She isn't challenging me. I can see she's grappling with the same thing I did when Gram taught me.

"It's a vibration. A frequency of sorts. A physical need that you can't feel except in your heart. It's like a piece of you is missing or something isn't quite right."

"And then you just ask", Noelle clarifies with skepticism in her voice.

"And then you just ask. It's literally that simple."

"Are you going to send us home with candles and incense?"

"No. I'm not sending you home with anything", I confirm over their grumbles while I refresh my glass. "Viv will have a coronary." This time the girls laugh.

"But there are things you can use that aren't as obvious and you can find them around the house."

"Oooh...like what", Nora asks holding her empty glass out to me. I pour her a bit more and continue my lesson.

"Like buttons, twine, paper, garlic, water, hair..." Their eyes widen when I say hair.

"Are you teaching us with those things tonight?"

I shake my head, looking at the girls in the candlelight. They groan at my answer.

"I thought we could look through the book and I could give you more background. We can do spell work in a few days once you understand the general principles."

"Can we at least see your tattoo today?"

"I thought you'd never ask. Unzip me", I playfully order. I wore my black dress for this occasion.

Nearly spilling their wine, the girls rush to check out my body art.

"Woah. Viv is going to be pissed", Nora remarks in admiration.

"What is it", Noelle asks.

"A witch's knot."

"Super pissed."

"I want one."

"Me too. Would Archer do ours?"

"I don't know. You'll have to ask him." I'm sure he'll just love that. While they know he won't tattoo them now, I'm sure they'll do just about anything to be in his chair when they're legal.

It's late when we return to Archer's place. The girls are tired but still on watch for him.

"He's probably working", I tell them when they don't find him in the usual communal spots of his home. "Go to bed. I'll see if I can get him to squeeze in time for breakfast tomorrow. I'm sure he'll make bacon and eggs and all the things you both like."

They accept the promise of breakfast with Archer and stalk off to their rooms.

I'm exhausted. It's been fun having the girls around, but it's still been work. Now that I don't feel the need to hide things from them, the time I have left with them will probably be less tiring, I think as I get ready for bed. Archer doesn't look like he's been up to our room. His cars are here so I know he's home. I'm just not sure where he's hiding.

My phone pings on the bed.

AJ- Meet me in the greenhouse. I've got candles and wine. ☐

Darla J Michaels

Say no more. I'm never too tired to decline an invite from my husband. He is the best thing that happened to me even though sometimes he's also the worst.

I slip my shoes back on and quietly sneak out of the house so the girls don't notice. If they know where he is, they'll surely come out to catch a glimpse of him.

The night is humid. Archer must really be looking to sneak away from the girls if he's willing to be in the greenhouse which is muggier than it is outside.

"Darlin'", he greets me as I step through the door. He had given the girls and I one of his cards to go shopping for seeds, soil and everything else we thought we'd need to start growing plants. We spent so much time selecting the things we would need we only had time to unload our purchases. Tomorrow is when the real fun begins. Although, I'm not sure the girls will see it that way.

"This thing should have a lock", Archer tells me as he passes me a glass of wine.

"Oh, come on. They're not that bad."

"I agree. It's just...there are things I want to do to my wife that impressionable youth should not be privy to." Archer clinks his glass against mine and takes a sip. He's got that devilish look that thrills and terrifies me at the same time.

I look down, feeling a little self-conscious. We haven't been all that intimate since they punished me.

"I know you've been getting..." Jesus this is weird to say. "...you know...your needs met..." I motion to his crotch. He laughs and I shush him.

"I have. But there's one need the others won't come close to meeting. That's my need for you."

Now I take a sip of my drink because I feel the emotions from when I was at my house come flooding back.

"You're not just a meaningless fuck to me, Beth. And I have not, nor will I ever, pass you around. I give so I can receive. And you give so you can receive. It's not complicated. It's all just a moment. But this...", he motions between us. "...this is forever. You can't turn this off. You can't substitute it."

Now I'm crying. I really wanted to avoid crying today. Figures Archer would make me all emotional. "And I gave. So tonight, I want to receive", he tells me, carefully taking my glass and setting it on a nearby wooden crate next to his.

"The girls", I object before his mouth is on mine.

"Shh...wife", he whispers as he unzips my dress and slides the fabric over my shoulders.

My hands fall to his waist where I toy with unzipping his pants before he allows it.

"Shoes", he orders me, stepping back to allow me space to slip them off. When I start to slip my panties over my hips, he stops me. "Not yet."

Archer reaches one hand behind his back between his shoulder blades, pulling his shirt up and over his head. He tosses it on the floor of the greenhouse without a care where it lands. Then he works off his pants and shoes, standing there in front of me in a similar state of dress.

"Kneel."

The way he says that word with commanding power has my brain all foggy. I sink to my knees and look up at my husband. He stands before me, sweaty, tattooed and ready to be taken care of.

But there's a difference tonight. He made me nervous before. Tonight, I feel the full weight of his protection and his support. The energy around us feels like the intention I spoke about earlier with the girls. A soul's submission to something that's so right even if others cannot see it.

"Go on and get it, Beth."

I no longer have shaky hands like I did all the other times I had him in my mouth. Tonight is different. I think it's because tonight, we're different.

I stroke him, missing the way he feels in the palm of my hand. Heavy. Warm. The piercings messing with my rhythm as I get used to them again.

"I miss this", Archer breaths as I stroke him. Precum drips from his cock in clear streams. I wonder how much he's going to give me today.

"Suck on it, Beth", he urges, sliding his palm to the back of my head and gently guiding himself into my mouth.

His precum drips down my chin. He leaks so much, there is no way around wearing some of it when I put him in my mouth.

He lets me set the pace. It's slow. I still haven't mastered giving him head yet with all the piercings. Archer says that will come in time.

"Tastes good, huh", he asks sweetly. I swallow around him in answer. He does. He tastes different compared to the other times I've had him in my mouth.

"Damn, darlin'. I want to give you to my Brothers so much. I want to watch you on your knees for them. Encourage you from across the room and tell you how good you're doing. I want to make promises to them about when they can have your pussy and what they can do to it when it's theirs."

I whimper about him giving me to his friends. It's a turn on for sure even though I haven't quite forgiven all of them yet.

"But I can't do that until I get between those legs of yours. Fuck", he breaths out, then secures my head unloading into my mouth.

I swallow every spurt, massaging his hard cock with my hand since I can't move my head. He doesn't gag me. He simply looks down at me in adoration as I continue to give him pleasure.

"On the bench, Beth. I'm hungry and I need to eat."

He helps me from the floor of the greenhouse. When I stand, he slides my panties over my hips and down my legs.

"This is mine to kiss and play with", he tells me, sliding a finger inside me as I stand before him naked, clutching his arms while he curls his fingers inside me. My head drops to his chest, and I let out a groan at the pleasure he gives me.

"Jonathan said you were perfect", he tells me. "Is it wrong that I don't regret it? That I couldn't have this yet because my only right was my last name?"

My knees are close to giving out. The way his finger strokes me on the inside feels so good it's almost unbearable.

"My wife", he says, kissing the crown of my head. It's all he can do because he's got one arm between us and one around me to keep me where he wants me. My face is still buried against his chest, which is slick with sweat from the humidity, but when I finish on his hand, the heat, the sweat and the hurt feelings of the past no longer matter.

"That's my good girl", he tells me as he slides his hand from between my legs and backs me toward the wood bench in the center of the greenhouse.

He isn't slow. He isn't sweet. He's just Archer. A man who takes when he's ready and gives in equal measure.

There was nothing more he could have done to prepare me for him. Even though Jonathan had me multiple times, he wasn't pierced.

Archer does nothing to soothe me. Not like Jonathan did. He doesn't talk me through it. He doesn't even pay attention to

Darla J Michaels

how I struggle a little beneath him. It's as if my trying to close my legs and press against his chest are just the way it is.

"Let me take Beth." It's the only thing he says to me as he begins fucking me on that bench. He doesn't stop. Just listens to my groans and occasional sharp inhales after he's slid in a little too rough or a little too far.

I don't finish. I don't think I was meant to. The way he covered me with his body gave me the impression that my body was to be used in service to him.

And when his body decides release is immanent, I whine as he slides in farther than he has before to finish inside me.

"Beth." My name quivers on his tongue before his mouth is on mine. His kiss isn't sweet. It's possessive. And I must admit that I like it.

A thump outside of the greenhouse gets our attention.

"Quiet"", a hushed teenage voice hisses while a light moves around wildly on the other side of the glass.

"Shit", Archer barks out as I chuckle beneath him.

Present Day

Chapter 33
Archer

Micah chuckles. It's not a happy chuckle. He's frustrated. And if I'm not mistaken, he thinks Jonathan's plan is stupid.

"Create a list", Harlan orders his virtual electronic assistant. The moment the words leave his lips, the screen is changing to formulate a checklist. "We'll need a lookalike." All the components to finding a lookalike appear in sub-bullets below the main bullet. "A country Jonathan can volunteer in. Sub-bullet", Harlan corrects the assistant when it makes this bullet a main one instead of a sub-bullet. "Incentive...sub-bullet. Which means a full file background on him." More bullets drop below. "Cell. Untraceable."

"Wife", Jonathan volunteers.

"Add it", Harlan commands the screen. "Alibis. A man on the inside. I can employ them, or it could be one of us."

Darla J Michaels

"Arms."

"No. No. No. No. No." We all turn to look at Micah. "You're going to get caught. Is that what you want?"

"I'm not going to get caught because you're going to help me. That was five no's. So tell us, counselor, where are the holes?"

I get why Jonathan is asking Micah this. He's the one who knows where Jonathan will likely get caught up if we move forward with this plan.

"Who are we getting on the inside to drug their doc?" Micah wastes no time poking holes in our plan.

"Add it", Harlan tells the room. "Color code the concerns and start sub-lists for each."

Micah glares at Harlan. His participation was not meant to problem solve. I'm not sure if Micah is unaware, but just one look at Jonathan tells me he's already made up his mind. We're here to help him work out the details.

"And how do you even get into the community", Micah continues.

"I have employees that can hack their systems. I also have employees who can be very persuasive", Harlan offers.

During the debrief, we learned there is a small operation where these predators are vetted and tracked. Jonathan clearly doesn't have a history as a predator, nor will his fake identity but there will be some things that will make him appealing to these people. We can easily manufacture that into his background.

"Create a profile to make Jonathan the perfect fit for their seedy group. Provide a short list of my best staff to taint their resident doctor's food." These orders appear on the list. "I'm assuming you have a drug of choice?" He aims this question at Jonathan.

"Get me the guy and I'll get you the drug with instructions."

"We may have a few experimental things we're working on." Jonathan shakes his head.

"It has to be something dependable. A long enough timeline to make it look like a doctor is legitimately sick but a short enough one to get me in the door before they replace him with someone else."

"You think this guy is the only doctor", Micah challenges.

"He is. Of course, there are other docs in the area but he's the only one who is allowed to touch the members of their church." Harlan clicks a button, and a screen pops up, scrolling through the church's members, each with the doctor's name and credentials next to them.

"That's illegal", Micah points at Harlan.

"Have you ever considered that much of what I do is illegal?" Micah pinches the bridge of his nose. Looks like he did not. "Oh, come on counselor. You've never walked the line? You may not break laws like I do but I'm sure you're not squeaky clean", Harlan challenges.

"Let's focus", I bring the group back. I can't have Harlan in a pissing match with Micah. We're the only ones who aren't fighting with anyone and I'd like to keep it that way.

"The Chamberlain Society", Jonathan tells the room and nods to Harlan.

"Note it", Harlan orders the screen.

"What the fuck is that?" Micah is steadily losing patients.

"My escort service", Jonathan answers like it's nothing at all. "Well not *my* escort service but the old service I used", he clarifies.

"I think we have big enough problems without adding prostitutes", Micah fires back. "Take that off." When nothing happens with the screen, Micah directs his glare to Harlan, but Harlan is unfazed.

"I'll get my wife from there. I'm sure Vee will know just the girl." Micah tilts his head and furrows his brow at Jonathan. "Woman. Come on. She employs young beautiful women...and some great looking men."

"Do you trust her?" I have to ask the question. It's been a while and the more people we add from the outside the more liability we have. Right now, the trust in this room is hard enough between friends without adding people who are just collecting a paycheck.

"Vee? Yeah. She won't be a problem. Neither will the girl...woman, I mean..."

"Note it." Harlan makes the decision on behalf of us.

"You can't fuck her. You can't even touch her", Micah cuts in. "How are you going to make this work and follow our rules?"

"This is for Linea. And I assure you, Grace doesn't care who I fuck."

"Add communicable disease tests under Vee's lady."

"Un. Fucking. Believable." Micah takes a sip from his whiskey glass.

"I'm not out whoring around. I'm taking care of business, Micah. And if that means showing my fake wife some attention in front of monsters to take them down then so be it. I'm not asking for permission. I'm giving myself the authority to do what I know is right even if I cross the line. And you know what? If Grace were here...if she knew about all of this...she'd be on board. She'd be on board because it's for Linea."

It's quiet. Jonathan is right. He's right about all of it. And I understand why he can't let it go. She was first. They were responsible. He knew. He knew something bigger was wrong but there was nothing he could do to get her to talk. He was trying to make his part in all this right. In a way, I could understand where he was coming from. It's an awful feeling that never really goes away. It just lessens a little after you do whatever you can to fix things.

"He's right", I tell the room in a voice so low and emotional I don't recognize it as my own.

"I know."

We all turn to Micah in complete shock. He agreed with me. No...Micah agreed with Jonathan in the weariest voice I have ever heard from him.

"Fuck", he hisses the word and knocks back the rest of his drink. "I don't want to make this worse. She needs all of us."

It's the first time I've seen Micah become emotional about Linea's past. Even when he explained it to us at the meeting, he was all business. I suppose he had to be. Even though he was to be impartial, in some ways, he was representing Braden and Linea.

"Micah, if you do not want to make this worse then help. Whatever this thing is between you two...it doesn't matter. She matters."

We all wait for Micah's decision after Harlan speaks. Micah is in an impossible position. For the first time, I think we all feel the full weight of it. He will betray his best friend to avenge the woman they both love. It's tearing him apart now but if this goes wrong, it may destroy him.

"This is my family. Okay. I'm all in." As the words leave his lips, he seems sad. This is tough stuff. Whoever thinks being in these relationships is all fun and games has never entered one. We do have a lot of fun, but we also have some shit decisions to make sometimes.

"I'm all in under one condition. If this blows up..." Micah scans the room. "...I'm the one who tells Braden."

Darla J Michaels

Chapter 34
Jonathan

Reaching out to Vee felt...oddly enough, just like old times.

I'd like to fund a scholarship. Know anyone who can help with large cash donations?

I wasn't sure if her personal cell had changed. It's been almost seven years since I said goodbye to Vee and her girls.

I also wasn't sure if she'd pick up. When I called Vee to let her know I would no longer be donating to The Chamberlain Society Foundation, I thought she'd cut me off forever. That call felt like a breakup. Especially since I was leaving the ladies for a virgin. Nothing about the situation set well with me. But I'm the guy who follows through on his commitments come hell or high water. So, there I was, ending a relationship with the best underground escort service I could have ever imagined for uncharted territory.

The only reason I did it is because I was curious if we could share her, and if she would let us. And I must admit, I like uncharted territory. I make my best decisions spur of the moment. My intuition always serves me well.

When I ended it, I think we were both heartbroken that day even though she laughed when I called her.

You called. I take it you didn't think you could tell me in person? Afraid you might be too weak and need to make one last donation?

It was my turn to laugh. She knows once something leaves my mouth it's as good as done. There was no chance I was changing my mind. I think maybe she was hoping that this once I would make an exception.

I look at my wristwatch. She's kept me waiting for a half hour in her office. She's pissed. Showing me who is in charge. I'll wait here all damn day if she'll help me.

Looking around, I note the place hasn't changed a bit. Not because she doesn't have the money. Probably because she doesn't want people poking around. If I were her, I wouldn't feel any different.

As close as Vee and I were, she never gave me any of her secrets. She did give me a birthday gift in her office once. Had me sit right in front of her desk while I got head from Nico.

There was a mix-up the first time I met with a society member. I got a man. I was horny. He was attractive. So...what the hell, right?

I came so fucking hard I asked to meet with Nico regularly. I never said anything to Vee about the mix-up. I just kept requesting him. Imagine my surprise when Nico walked into her office carrying a slice of birthday cake with a candle in it. He had me blow it out. Vee fed it to me while Nico got me off.

Best fucking birthday ever. That's the day I learned that Vee sent Nico on purpose. Her explanation?

I thought you'd like him. It was a hunch. Exquisite, isn't he?

Behind me sounds the click of the door handle. This place hasn't changed one bit.

The moment her shoes land on the hardwood, my heartbeat picks up. God...the memories of this place. I didn't realize how much I missed it until now.

I want to turn around, but I don't dare. Not because that's the expectation but because I don't want to ruin the surprise. The surprise of her.

She's twice my age and but even more attractive than most women younger than her. And the confidence and class she carries is tenfold of any woman I have ever met...including Grace. Nothing intimidates this woman. Nothing shakes her. She is unbeatable. An absolute force to be reckoned with.

Her cadence slows a bit as she rounds her desk. Rarely have I ever seen her in white but today, she wears a pant suit. White pants and jacket, buttoned, exposing a red satin blouse underneath. She's also exposing cleavage that is starting to make me hard. God. Damn it.

Her glacial eyes meet mine. She's mad. I know because the corner of her red lip doesn't tilt up the slightest bit at seeing me like it used to. Stopping beside her chair, she tilts her head to the brown leather chairback and trains her stare back on me.

I was wrong. She's pissed. I smile and shake my head as I sigh, rising from my seat to pull out her chair for her. If this is how she wants to play this, it's fine. I can play. Besides, this is just for show. Deep down she's happy to see me. I know it.

I look at her appreciatively. Why not? Women who are stunning love it when a man's gaze lingers. Regardless of the airs she's putting on, I know she loves my eyes on hers.

I slide her chair in for her after she sits, noting her signature scent hasn't changed in all these years. Christ, that makes me miss her more.

Darla J Michaels

Vee waits until I take my seat before training her cool stare on me.

"A scholarship fund." She lets my request hang there, waiting for details.

"I need one girl. Exclusively. To take with me." She starts laughing before I can even finish. "Vee…"

"Don't Vee me. You walk in here after all these years and ask to have one of my girls?"

"I know…", I start but she interrupts me again.

"No, my honest man…you don't."

I sit back in my chair and watch her. For a second, her eyes soften as she looks me over.

"You missed me." Her gaze turns colder.

"And you didn't even think about me. You gave me up for a virgin…to share", she says virgin with disgust, and it makes me chuckle.

I never told her that. "How'd you know?"

"My business is knowing."

This is exactly why I need her help. She's the best at doing things secretly. The best at hidden requests. The best at getting people to trust her and relinquishing control. I mean, I'm alright at getting people to trust me but I swear, this woman is magic. I need some of her magic.

"Why? What could one of my girls offer you? As I hear, you do quite well for yourself these days. You're fucking more than the virgin. So why do you need one more?"

I wasn't prepared to share my plan with her. I was only prepared to walk in here, ask for a girl and get her.

"I need her to be my fake wife."

Vee is trying to stifle a smile, but she can't contain it. Her smile gradually turns into a laugh. The longest, hardest laugh I think I have ever heard come from her.

"No."

Alright. This isn't going well. New tactic.

"The virgin was raped. By her family. Her brothers. Community members. They abused her before we got her out of there. She was pregnant. They killed it. They were going to force her to fuck for money for the rest of her life." She cocks a brow at me as to say...that's what we do here, remember?

"Not for her to keep. She'd be their sex slave. They have an entire operation going where they groom young girls to grow up and serve the men for the rest of their lives. I'm going to stop it. But to get in, I need a wife. And it can't be someone who's afraid to suck a cock. I won't let anyone else have her but me. And truthfully Vee, I'm there for business, so I won't be having her either. I get the impression showing her public affection will be more than enough to satisfy the curiosities of our relationship."

Vee trains her gaze just over my shoulder. Frozen like a statue, she's thinking. I follow her hand moving to the signeted ring on her finger and observe her delicate, manicured hand rotate the ring as she thinks.

This is awkward. Seeing her distracted but composed bothers me. It's uncomfortable. Vee doesn't get distracted.

She inhales a shaky breath and gracefully slides her chair out. When I stand to help her, she pays me no attention. It's as if I'm not even in the room.

I stand there, feeling entirely out of place as I watch her take out two crystal tumblers. At least I know she's still in there. She just assumes I'm drinking. Which...fuck...I may as well.

Just like she does everything, slowly, gracefully and full of intention, Vee pours our drinks.

I come to her. Something about her seems fragile and I'm concerned about it. I've never seen her shaken. She hands me a glass and pauses a beat too long before picking up her own.

"Vee…are you alright?" I'm concerned. She isn't cool and efficient like I know her to be. Right now, under that calm exterior, I think she's barely holding it together.

"My honest man…I haven't been alright a day in my life."

I tell her what I can while we wait for the ladies to join us. It's been almost an hour since she sent a message out via cell.

"What's your plan?"

"Get inside and make them pay."

She's shaking her head.

"I won't compromise the safety of my girls." I start to interrupt but she holds up her hand to stop me. "These aren't puppies. They're people. And if you go in there without a plan, not only do you compromise one of my girls, but you compromise every girl in that disgusting community."

I nod solemnly. I had only thought so far as making the ones who hurt Linea pay. But sitting with Vee, I realize this is more.

"We could free them. Christ, Vee…I don't even know what I'm dealing with yet."

"If you free them, consider what's next. They have no job, no education, no money. Now they're on the street and damaged."

"So, they're fucked either way?"

"Maybe."

A knock sounds at the door. I straighten my posture. After a few drinks, I'm relaxed in my chair. Vee looks just as poised as she always does.

A woman walks through that could be the spitting image of Vee. Blonde hair. Blue eyes. Tall. Slender. Impeccably dressed in a pressed navy suit.

"Madame, they are waiting for you. How shall I send them in?"

"One at a time. We'll know immediately." Sabine nods and exits the room.

"Stand up. In the center of the room. You're about to meet your wife."

Thank fuck.

Vee doesn't move a muscle. One after another, a woman is ushered in and stood next to me as Vee scrutinizes us. One after another, each woman is sent away...until her.

The moment she walks in, I know she's a perfect fit. Long wavy dark brown hair, amber colored eyes, a natural bronze skin tone...she's slender, taller than an average woman but not eye level with me. Her plump nude, glossy lips give me a small smile.

"How much is this one going to cost me?"

"My honest man, as with any long-term patronage of this nature, the foundation will require a substantial contribution to meet your very specific needs. We simply account for the six years you've been underpaying me."

I shoot her a look. Underpaying her...

"Plus, interest." Her smile is soft and a little cutting. "The recommended charity donation for someone at your level would be eight hundred sixty-four thousand, Jonathan. Plus, seventy-five for the transfer. Legal fees, training and discretion are factored in."

"Training?" Now she's fucking with me.

"After that, your monthly patronage is eighteen."

"Over a million dollars?" Vee doesn't even flinch.

"Oh Jonathan...don't pretend that you don't have it. Don't pretend that it isn't worth it. And don't pretend for one moment that laying down with Seraphina won't make you question the very vows that you took."

Now that gets my attention. How in the fuck does she know?

"Do we have a deal, my honest man?"

Chapter 35
Archer

"You don't need to take notes, Micah. My assistant does it for us", Harlan reminds him.

"It helps me think. I don't want to stop the flow of conversation for my list. Keep going. I'll share after you all are done."

This is the most focused I think I've ever seen Micah. I understand why people pay top dollar for him and anyone else at his firm. He's sharp. He misses nothing.

"Seraphina is perfect. I've trained with her a few times since we've met. She'll play the part well."

"Did you fuck her?" I have to ask. We all recognize Jonathan will have to cross some lines to make this work.

"Yeah. We've done everything."

If I'm not mistaken, he seems bothered by it, which is strange considering how convicted he was a few days ago.

"I wasn't going to, but Vee was right. If I want it to be believable, we can't be strangers to each other."

"She good?"

He nods.

"At everything?"

He lets out a sigh and says, "Yeah." I can tell talking about it makes him uncomfortable. "Look, sex isn't the point. Can we just move on?"

"I need a few more weeks to secure the agents I've selected. They're finishing a job for me and need some rest before I call them in to debrief", Harlan informs us.

"I'll put in my sabbatical notice this week. The hospital needs ninety days", Jonathan explains.

"That's perfect."

Harlan has a fair amount of people behind the scenes to help us pull this off. He needs time to get them up to speed, polish off the intel and set the stage for Jonathan and Seraphina's arrival.

"Agreed. We have quite the list of loose ends to tie up from a legal standpoint. Is there anything I don't know that may become important later?" Micah scans the room. We've all been open books. No one volunteers anything new.

"Alright. From a legal standpoint, if we get caught, it's easier if the people involved only follow orders."

"But from a tactical standpoint, if they don't know the background and need to improvise, they may compromise the mission if they don't know enough information", Harlan cuts in.

"Well, how confident are we in the people we've selected? The only one I know is Jonathan, so my money is on him. But if this goes south, he could get hurt or go to prison...or both. So, the question is, who is your money on?"

I'm directing this question at Harlan. We're all friends here. No one wants to see this end badly. But he knows most of the players. We all bring an expertise to the table. Not being at the top of our game or trusting others who aren't at the top of theirs isn't an option.

"I can tell you this...if anyone in my employ crosses me, I'll personally gut them", Harlan tells the room. "Bold...italic...highlight...", he orders his virtual assistant for dramatic flair.

"That's real sweet of you Harlan but this is death or prison. If your people cross you, I'll gut you." Harlan's eyes widen at how casual my comment is. "We need to be sure. Have you communicated with any of them?"

"Of course not, Archer. I'm not a rookie. I've got toys, connections and a whole fleet of people willing to do my bidding."

"That's great. I say we get the intel, review it and look at your people's profiles to match the best." Harlan shakes his head.

"I promise them anonymity."

"Change their names then. I don't care. But we're all scrubbing the information together." I turn to Jonathan. "That includes Seraphina and Vee."

"Fuck. I have already paid a fortune for this. You know that, right?"

"I do. But you want justice, don't you? You walked in here talking about freeing those women who don't want to be there. If you want this to work, we need to make sure no details are overlooked." I turn to Micah this time. "I think we need Linea." He closes his eyes and shakes his head. "We'll be careful. Whatever we say to her and whatever information she gives to us, we'll be careful."

"Take her on a date. You have a date coming up. You know the information we have just as well as everyone else. Do it then."

"I think it would be best if she comes here", Harlan offers. "We can bring her right into this room. Don't you think a part of her wants them caught? Punished even?"

"I think she wants to forget", Micah counters.

"She can't." We all turn to Jonathan. "You don't forget that. You can't even fix it. I think we bring her here. We ask her some questions. Then we ask for her silence so we can bring justice where it's due."

"How do we explain the schedule change?"

"We shouldn't need long with her. We'll need to figure out what to do with our dates while we're with her", Harlan states the obvious.

"We shouldn't add anyone else yet", Micah cautions us.

"I think we should." All eyes are on me. I know it's risky but there is one part of this plan we have not considered. "Who do we have for body disposal? Know any guys with access to heavy machinery and cement?"

"Makes sense. Our dates can stay with Tyler. It's been a while since he's been with three of them. I'm sure it wouldn't be an issue. We can stagger picking them up and the ladies will be none the wiser."

"Show The Brotherhood calendar for the next month", Harlan orders to thin air.

We quietly scan the calendar and consider our options.

"Can we get Tyler here for the next meeting?" He has to agree to this before we go asking our Brothers for permission to change things up. If he's not in on it, our request will be cause for questions. We need this to be nothing more than Tyler's thirst for sex and maybe trying out some new toys.

"Call Tyler Madox."

The line rings on the speakers overhead. Just when I think it's going to voicemail, Tyler picks up.

"What's up, Brother?"

"I need a favor. It's...to be kept quiet."

"Alright." Tyler seems like he could care less about the secrecy.

"We're meeting at my place next weekend. Early. Can you be here?"

"Who's we?"

"Be here before six. Don't tell anyone. It's important, Tyler."

A heavy sigh sounds through the speakers. We all wait for his affirmation of attendance.

"This better be fucking good."

"It will be. I'll send you the details. Thank you, Tyler."

"Now, all we need to do is figure out how we're going to get away so we can review the details against the final roster", Micah wastes no time after Harlan disconnects the line.

"One thing at a time, Micah. One thing at a time."

Chapter 36
Archer

I had one request of Braden before my date with Linea.

I want her nice and pent up. So wet and so tight she can barely see reason.

Braden laughed and agreed. He likes to get Linea all wound up and since he married her, he seems to have even more fun doing it than he has in the past. Funny how a little mindset shift can make all the difference.

When I walk through Braden's back door, I can hear his deep voice. While I can't make out what he's saying, I can tell he's talking to her by the cadence and tone. He's giving her limits she doesn't like. I know, because I asked him to do it.

When they come into view, Linea looks over his shoulder at me and then back at him.

"Check her. I think you'll be pleased", Braden suggests to me, stepping from in front of Linea to allow me access to her.

"Linea, darlin'." There's still fire in her eyes from the cake tasting and the wedding. I smile as I reach down and slide my hand under her skirt. My fingertips glide over her panties and she closes her eyes, taking in a deep breath.

"I bet..." I run my thumb over her lace covered slit. "...it wants to come." She's nodding. "I don't think I can help you with that tonight, though."

Her eyes open and if I have ever seen a look of despair, she's wearing it right now.

"You haven't been a nice girl since that cake tasting. Braden, do we reward brats?"

"We do not." Braden kisses Linea on the cheek, pats her behind and leaves the room.

"We do not", I affirm, looking her over. "C'mon." I won't say anything more to her. We have a date and I need her to think she isn't going to get pleasure. The needy are so much more generous and I need her mind buzzing for this meeting.

The weather is starting to warm a little. It's good for Bethany. Allows her a distraction while the drugs work. I'm glad to be on the same side as Harlan. I'd be out of my league going against him.

"Where are we going", Linea asks from the passenger seat. Normally, I wouldn't respond to her inquiry. But I'm going to give a little since we don't have much time. If she sees that she gets a little latitude maybe she'll work harder to come up with details we need to know.

"Harlan's." Her eyes widen a fraction. She hasn't spoken with Francesca since the day she had with Hadley. "She won't be there." When Linea looks down and starts picking at her nails, I stop her. "Don't you think you've punished yourself enough", I ask, laying a hand on hers.

"I feel awful."

"Don't. Francesca knew what she was getting herself into. She was part of the story. You weren't intending on outing her. Think about your intentions."

Linea doesn't argue with me. Instead, she sits there and waits the drive out. It's like a part of her might be shutting down out of defeat. Or maybe it's exhaustion. I can't imagine how tiring carrying this burden around has been for her let alone the changes after.

Her and Hawk have been at it. She's tested Braden at every turn. She's even mad at Micah. This behavior isn't normal for Linea, but I can't say that I blame her. She's working through some heavy stuff. I just hope our meeting with her tonight doesn't add to it.

As soon as we pull into Harlan's gates, Linea recognizes the cars out front.

"What's going on?"

"Darlin'...we just want to talk. If you help us, I'll lay you out right there in Harlan's conference room so you can make a mess on that glossy mahogany table of his."

I cut the engine and open her door. Since Harlan's house staff have been ordered off the premises when we meet, except for his kitchen staff, I let myself in.

Linea has been here several times but there are parts of his home that even she has never seen. We'll be in the secure conference room, just like all the other times. Harlan meets us outside the door. He needs to credential Linea for her to enter. I watch patiently as he scans her thumb in the reader and has her walk through the full body scan to satisfy his upgraded security measures.

The doors open with a woosh, and we step through to find the guys hard at work. They don't bother covering up the screen. There's no point after today.

"Linea", Micah greets her. He looks so fucking in love with her. No wonder he's been wrecked about this plan. We all care about her but not like Micah. Micah cares for her bone deep. I wonder if Braden knows. I'm sure he does if it's obvious to me.

When Linea doesn't answer Micah back, I prompt her. "Linea, bein' a brat won't get you that orgasm", I remind her.

"Hi." It's pouty. I can't help but smile. Jonathan can't contain himself. He laughs hard. Linea looks over and smiles at him.

"I hope it was worth it, darlin'. Have a seat", I order her, pulling out a chair at the head of the table for her. She's next to Jonathan and Micah. I take a seat across from Harlan. "Counselor", I prompt Micah.

"Linea..." Linea's eyes shift from Micah up to the screen, which is now dictating the meeting. "We need information from you. It's extremely important. And we know you may not have it, but we need you to answer our questions and tell us everything you know even if you think it might not matter."

Linea swallows thickly as she reads the heading on the screen. Her hometown is listed at the top. Just above the dictation is the hierarchy we put together the best we could with the information we have.

"You're safe, Linea", Micah reassures her when he sees her delicate index finger tap gently on the glossy table. "Let's start with the chart. The religious head is at the top. There is Dr. Petersen. Then some families listed below him."

As Micah goes through this, I realize it's a pathetic chart.

"Are there others in church who might be close confidants?"

"The Shepherd", she whispers.

"Who is that?"

Hearing Micah like this is interesting. When we have a new Lady, it's common for them to be concerned about Micah. They think he's intimidating. But when he's in lawyer mode, he's calm and encouraging with a kind of gentle curiousness about him.

"Elias. Shephard Thorn." She shivers when she says the name.

"Shephard Thorn. That's good. Does Shephard Thorn have any help?"

"Jonas." Linea scans the room. "Evangeline."

One look at Jonathan and I can tell he's shocked. She's telling us things she didn't tell him. I'm sure he isn't mad, but I know he's wondering why she didn't share these things weeks ago. It makes me wonder if their deal is off. No one knows what it is. I hope for the sake of this truce, he'll forget about it.

"Tell me about Jonas." Linea looks around the room once more and clears her throat. Micah stands to grab Linea a glass of water, holding it out to her. When she brings the glass to her lips, her hand quivers.

"I think he's mean." Linea takes another sip of water. "Father never let me near him. Wouldn't even let him look at me."

"What does he do?"

"He's always in church helping Shephard Thorn."

"And Evangeline?"

"She's pretty. The men like her. Father liked her."

"How did your father like her?"

"I don't know, exactly."

"Tell me what you do know. It all matters, remember?"

This time Jonathan gets up and pours a glass of bourbon. We all thought it was going to be for him until he slides it in front of Linea.

"I know it's hard, Linea. We're here to make it better", he promises her, nudging the glass a bit closer to her once again.

"He had her over for my brother's birthdays. At night. When each turned sixteen. I heard them. But I don't know what they were doing. It could have been…"

"Linea, you're not at a hearing", Micah reminds her. "Grab your bourbon and come here", he coaxes her cooly. I watch as she moves under his spell. He slides his chair out and he offers her his hand, guiding her onto his lap. "That's excellent bourbon. Go on. Have a sip."

Once more, she does as he orders her, clearing her throat after the burn of the drink.

"Is there anyone else that helps Shephard Thorn?"

"I don't think so." She looks as weary as she sounds.

"Look at the names below the clergy. Who are we missing? We have watchers and helpers listed. Family members."

She doesn't offer anything more.

"Let's look at your brothers. They're all married now. Most with children. And we have your former fiancé also married now with a child and one on the way."

Linea takes another sip from the glass.

"Most of the children are little girls."

I'm not sure if Micah is a genius or a total douche bag. I'm sure we'll know any minute.

"Why are you doing this?" The first tear falls. Micah wipes it away with his fingertips, motioning for a cloth napkin at the other side of the room kept at the bar.

"Would you believe me if I told you we're going to fix it. We're going to make this all better."

Linea scans the room, and her eyes meet mine. I simply nod, affirming Micah's words.

"When?"

"Linea", Micah says her name in that way he does when he chastises one of our women. "Since when do you get to know things?"

She takes another sip from her glass and offers up one last detail.

"Rebel, Gabe and Solomon are The Shepherd's sons."

I look at Jonathan and he pales in his seat. The good shepherd might have access to his fake wife after all. This will be tricky for Jonathan. Seraphina is stunning. And so are the wives of the husbands Shephard Thorn knocked up.

"What?" Linea sees the concern on Jonathan's face. Jonathan gives her a fake smile.

"You did good. You did really, really good", he tells her from the other side of the table.

"Here", Micah takes the glass from Linea. "Finish up", he coaxes her with the elixir while wiping tears that fall. "I bet you and Archer are going to have a lovely time tonight." Linea sucks in a few breaths, trying not to sob. "You're okay, Linea. We've got you."

We say our goodbyes and I take Linea out for dinner. She picks at her food, mostly interested in my alcohol. When she orders a glass of wine with her meal, I tell the server she cannot have it. It's for safety reasons.

"You'll like what I have planned better", I explain even though I don't have to. She's fragile and she did such a good job giving us a piece of the puzzle we wouldn't have anticipated. I'm sure the guys have already figured out a way to leverage the information about Shepherd Thorn's illegitimate sons.

I can't think about our plan though. My only objective is to return her how I left with her. Horny. I'll even go with happy. But I know she can't come back to Braden like this.

"I'm not going to say anything", she tells me in this new bratty way she has about her since getting married.

"I know you won't", I challenge her. She cocks her head to the side in disbelief. "You want this as much as we do. And I know you don't know what *this* is but trust me, things end with us", I promise her.

She looks off into the sea of other diners, clearly unhappy with my refusal to give her more alcohol.

"I have a surprise for you tonight. It's a surprise that will scratch that itch of yours." Her eyes dart to mine. "Aaah...now look whose attention I've got. Let me tell you what's going to happen from here. You're gonna eat your dinner and your dessert. Then I'm gonna take you back to my place and introduce you to Loretta."

I watch Braden check in with Linea after I drop her off. He's sweet with her. I think he can tell something's up.

"Look at me, baby."

She tilts her head up to look at Braden. He searches her face for something he doesn't find, then brings his lips to hers before telling her to get ready for bed.

"She's tired", he tells me when she's out of earshot.

"She got a lot of fresh air tonight. I introduced her to Loretta. Took her out on Blue Bird Pass." I laugh when Braden shoots me a glare. "We were careful, man."

"Were you trying to frighten the brat out of her?"

"No. I thought she needed some endorphins."

"Ah. So, she was not a good girl for you?"

"She was alright. A little sassy from time to time but she was alright."

"That's it?"

318

Darla J Michaels

He's gonna be pissed but I'm not going to lie to him even though I doubt Linea would tell him.

"We went out to that nice stretch of quiet road, and I pulled over and had her get on the front of the bike."

"You had her drive?" He looks furious.

"Loretta? No, man. Nobody drives Loretta but me."

"I don't follow."

"I had her lean back against the bars and wrap her legs around me." I pull her panties from the pocket of my jeans and hand them to him. "You should have seen her come. Hair blowing around her face from the wind. My God, Braden. You think her noises sound heavenly in bed you haven't heard anything till her cries collide with the Loretta's engine."

"Have you lost your fuckin' mind, Archer?"

"Shhh...keep your voice down." The last thing I need is Linea getting freaked out because she thinks we're arguing. If she gets upset, who knows what she could tell Braden.

"You could have killed her!"

"She was safe the whole time. Nothing was going to happen to her except for that orgasm...or three." I smell my fingers. They still smell like her.

"Don't ever do that again." I shake my head at his overreaction. "Archer, I mean it. She is the most important thing in the world to me and I will not have her safety put at risk."

I nod, understanding where he's coming from. She is the most important thing in the world to him. He's gone to lengths he probably never thought he'd go through to commit to her and keep her safe.

Just like I have and continue to do with Bethany. I respect it. I don't regret making her wet pussy come on my bike, but I respect that it'll be the first and last time she does it.

Tell Me Who You Go With- Archer & Bethany

"Is she good?" I hate that Braden asks this because I don't know. But I can't tell him that so I say the only thing that will get me out of here without telling him more than he needs to know.

"She's good, man. Go fuck her and she'll be even better."

Braden laughs and shakes my hand. For the first time, I feel like things are starting to come together.

Darla J Michaels

Chapter 37
Bethany

One week later...

Something is wrong with me. Archer says I'm fine but I'm pretty sure something is wrong.

All I can think about is sex. Not in my mind but my body...it wants to orgasm. A lot.

I'm soaked. So wet that I'm considering removing my panties, but I'm worried I'll start to drip down my thighs.

I'll be home for lunch. I think I'll have a taco.

That's the crass sentiment Archer left me with before heading to the shop. I have no idea what time lunch is for him, but if it's noon, I have about three more hours to go before I get relief.

He isn't giving me permission to get myself off without him in the room and he swears he's not punishing me. Instead, he claims he wants to be a part of how I worship my own body. How special it is when a woman touches herself and how he wants to be there in case I need help.

I just need to finish before you leave. I beg him.

I have to go. You be good. I'll be back to eat you later.

I would just do it. Before the implant I'd just touch myself and get off. But now they know. They'll all know, which means I'll be disobeying a direct order.

The only thing I can think of to occupy my mind is to go out and work in my greenhouse. When seasons change, I do more maintenance inside. It's just as well anyway. Maybe if I'm thinking about something, else, I won't be thinking so much about all the ways I want Archer to fuck me when he comes home.

Tires sound on the gravel driveway and stop me in my tracks. They don't sound like Archer's tires. I look out the back door and realize the car in my driveway is Jonathan's. Why would Jonathan be here now?

So strange. I enjoy seeing Jonathan. It's always a pleasant surprise when he stops by. Especially if he's stopping by for me.

Figuring I'll catch him on the way out to the greenhouse, I run up to change clothes and shoes. If I thought Archer had given Jonathan permission to take care of me, I'd be waiting next to the door like Spirit.

Bounding down the stairs to greet Jonathan, I am stunned at who I see standing in the living room.

"Linea?"

"Hi. I hope I'm not interrupting anything", she starts.

"Where's Jonathan?"

She suddenly looks nervous.

"I came here to see you", she dodges my question.

"Okay..."

"It's just that a few weeks ago...I didn't realize that you knew about Archer."

She knows about Archer too? Maybe that makes sense since Hawk is with her all the time. Now that I think of him, I'm realizing Hawk isn't on her heels right now.

"Does Braden know you're here?" It's a fair question. So far, there's no indication any of the guys are with her. Rumor has it, Linea is always accompanied by someone since her wedding to Braden. A little overprotective if you ask me but to be fair, I could see Archer assigning something like that to me, especially when we have kids. He's hinted around about staff from time to time. I hope that's all his comments amount to are hints.

"And then I went on a date with him, and it all clicked", she continues.

I am so lost right now.

"And then I realized I have bigger problems than trying to figure out how to be a good wife for Braden", she rambles. "You were right by the way. You were wife of the year. I didn't know he missed clinic because of you. But all that makes sense now", she thinks out loud to herself.

"Anyway, so I had a date with Archer and Micah asked me all these questions about my family. And there was a big screen on the wall with one of those professional graph things." She motions her hand around in the air as if she's drawing it out for me and I'll be able to make sense of her gestures.

"And they were all on there. All the people who hurt me were up on the screen and they told me everything would be alright, but I couldn't say anything. Not even to Braden. But then I realized that you knew. So, it would be fine if I stopped by and talked with you because you've known all along."

She looks like she's going to throw up.

"Linea, do you want to sit down?"

"Yes, please", she breaths, laying her hand against her chest as though she's just finished running a marathon.

"It's all I can think about. And I'm a processor. You know. I need to think out loud and Francesca hates me now because I had her get a pregnancy test for me in secret."

What??!

"And I mentioned it because it was part of the story. So, I don't have her to process with anymore but now I have you."

I nod. She's always had me as someone to talk with, although I haven't been her first choice because of Francesca. I happen to really like Linea. She's really nice. It's not normal for a woman to be that nice to other women who fuck your significant other.

"They said they're going to fix it to keep me safe. And all the other girls safe too."

I'm still completely lost. I never knew she was in danger. And which girls are in danger? Some of us?

"Linea how did you get Jonathan's car again?"

"I took it when he got in the shower."

"You what?!"

She makes that nervous emoji face and I chuckle because she's adorable in her own way when she does it but holy fucking shit she cannot be here.

"You have to go. Go back to Jonathan and return it. Apologize. And do not tell him where you went."

"I won't tell him. I swear. This is our secret. It has to be. They made me promise I wouldn't say anything to anyone about their plan to go after my family and the congregation."

I think we're talking about different things. It's either that or she's lost her mind. There is no way she knows what I know and everything she is telling me is news to me. Any other time I would get the details from her but under these circumstances, I'll pass. I'll find her later and get the whole story from her.

Darla J Michaels

"Linea, sweetheart, you're not hearing me. You have to go back to Jonathan right now. Get in the car, go straight to his house get down on your knees and service him like you have never serviced another before him. And please do not mention my name."

I'm almost begging her to get out of my home. If Archer finds out about this and thinks I was part of whatever this is with her, he won't even attempt to let me finish today.

"You don't seem worried at all that they won't come back. I'm going to try not to worry too. Thank you. This helped. I really needed this." She kisses me on the cheek and leaves me dumbfounded with a whole new set of concerns.

Chapter 38
Archer

Harlan installed a new camera system in my house so I can see what Bethany is up to when she's at my place. It's not that I don't trust her. I need to know things and if she's insistent on keeping this secret, then there is no stone I won't leave unturned.

I leave the shop and log into the camera system. She's pacing in the living room...and she looks miserable. It's probably because not only can she not touch herself without permission, she also can't finish.

That's what the drug does. It gets you to a point where every orgasm is better than the last. Then every orgasm after takes longer and longer to have until finally, you can't have one.

There is no amount of stroking, buzzing or fucking that will make it happen. But she doesn't know that. For the last six days I've managed to slip her the drug.

Holding her down and injecting the medicine would have been a last resort for me, but I would have done it without question if it came down to it.

Darla J Michaels

I'm giving her one more chance tonight. Tell me what I want to know or I'm sending someone to get it out of you.

My cell rings and I pick it up on the car audio.

"Hey Hawk."

"We still on for tomorrow morning?"

"I'll text to confirm. She'll get one more chance tonight."

"What does she know?"

"Nothing yet. I'll be watching the whole time."

"Can you get it on tape?"

"Yeah."

"She's gonna run, Archer."

"If I can't get it out of her tonight, the whole point is that you scare her enough that she calls me."

"And if that happens, just to be clear, I'm to stop and call you?"

"No. I'll call you. Every room has a camera in it. We can test them tonight. You have the logins. Message me confirmation and we'll be good to go for tomorrow."

I finish the rest of my drive in silence and try not to feel guilty about what I'm about to do. I'm already drugging the woman I love. She's almost out of her mind with need. At first, I thought that was as questionable as it got.

I learned to look past it. Bethany and I were enjoying her needy little pussy. She already loves sex but adding this drug makes her love it tenfold. Unfortunately for her, now we're at a point where I'm the only one getting off. She gets so close and either has a weak orgasm or can't push herself over the edge.

I can hear Spirit when I cut the engine to my truck. Here we go. One more round before I bring in the big guns.

To my surprise, Bethany walks straight out the door following my dog. Her eyes have this wild desperation in them.

"Hey darlin'", I start, trying to ease into the evening.

Tell Me Who You Go With- Archer & Bethany

She walks up to me and kisses me as Spirit circles around us. There is no hello. Just a kiss from my very eager wife.

"I need you", she whispers against my lips.

"And I need you", I tell her playfully.

"Archer", she warns. I cock my head to the side and give her a devilish smile.

I kiss her and walk her backward to the stairs that lead to the back porch.

When we get inside, she's leading me upstairs to our bedroom. I can't help but to chuckle. I'm not fucking her tonight. In fact, I'm going to fuck with her until she tells me or until Hawk comes for her.

I let her help me undress. There's no need to help her undress. She's so urgent about it, if she could just cut her clothes off she would.

"I love you, Bethany."

"And I love you, Archer."

"And because I love you, I'm going to warn you."

"Hmm?" She's barely listening.

"If you don't tell me this big secret you've been hiding, I'm sending someone for you tomorrow morning. I haven't met him officially. I've only seen him briefly and heard things about him from my Brothers. But I can tell you this." I grab her by the shoulders and focus her on what I'm trying to get across. "He has my permission, Beth. You can scream. You can fight. You can use your safe word. But he has my permission. And I happen to have it on good authority that he likes the fight."

Her eyes widen a fraction. She gets it but she still doesn't talk. So, I push her a step further.

"You know this little problem you've been having?" I reach between her legs and start stroking her. "Well, I have potions and tonics too." Her eyes widen and then narrow in anger. "I can keep this up as long as you can. In about a week, I'll have to start testing your blood and then weaning you off, but you'll go right back on again. So why don't we stop all this and you can just tell me what's going on."

"You drugged me", she asks in outrage.

"I did. We don't keep secrets, Beth." It's one of the things I've been clear and consistent about since we married. Hell, I've fostered a relationship of openness since I met her. Opening up is important to me. As important as not harboring anger with your loved one.

And this whole thing has been fun from a sex standpoint. Everyone who's been with her for a date this past week has said she's come harder than she ever has. But I'm tricking her. And in the end, tricking someone, even if you have good intentions, never ends well.

"Isn't it irresponsible to put my wellbeing in the hands of a stranger?"

"I would never put you in real danger, Beth. And you control this. It all stops when you tell me what happened."

"What if it breaks you?"

"Tomorrow might break me." She squeezes her thighs together and I smile. "I had cameras installed, Beth. I'll be watching the whole thing."

She swallows thickly, starting to understand the seriousness of the lengths I'm about to go through for the information she's harboring.

"Here's how this could go. I'll run you a hot bath and pour you a drink. Then you tell me. We'll apologize to each other. And then we'll make up until we can't keep our eyes open."

Bethany starts to tear up. This isn't a show. She isn't the type of woman to play someone...in this way or any way at all really. But she knows what I require of her.

Tell Me Who You Go With- Archer & Bethany

She wipes a tear from her cheek and clears her throat. "What should we make for dinner?"

Chapter 39
Bethany

I was going to try to stay awake. And one would think with the way I'm dripping between the legs and the constant need for an orgasm, it would be no problem. But the body needs sleep. And I nodded off.

And now I'm in Archer's house. Alone.

I could leave. But he'd just find me. He'd make it more creative.

We're both stubborn. I wonder whose stubbornness is going to cost our marriage more. I'm more afraid that the truth will do more damage. That's why I didn't tell him last night.

For a moment, I wonder what would happen if I just let this guy do what he's going to do. It's sex. I have it with a fleet of men now. What's one stranger that my husband added into the mix going to hurt?

Archer would never let someone hurt me. I'm sure this guy has been through all the same tests that the guys have been through.

Even still, I'm not making this easy on him. I get up and lock the door to our bedroom. Archer didn't exactly tell me when he'd be here to assault me, but I'm sure he's not waiting around all day just to play with me.

I'm only a few steps away from the door, when it unlocks from the other side.

I freeze. Nothing happens.

The nob doesn't turn. There are no footsteps. No creeks in the floorboards. Not one sound except for the pounding of my heart and the whooshing in my ears.

"Archer", I call out, backing away from the door.

"He's not available."

As soon as the first word is out of Hawk's mouth I bolt for the door. He was in our room this whole time. I don't even have to turn around to know it's him. The few words he did speak just weeks ago have been burned into my brain.

This cannot be happening. No. This cannot happen.

Hawk is quick. He grabs my long hair and the scuffle begins.

"Let me go", I order him in a shaky voice that sounds nothing like my own.

He says nothing. He doesn't even acknowledge me.

"Archer!"

I swing at Hawk, my fist making contact with his chest. He just tilts his head to avoid getting hit in the face. My attempts to harm him barely get his attention.

With every second that passes, we're getting closer to the bed.

"You don't want to do this", I try to reason with him.

"I actually do want to do this", he corrects me, tightening his grip on my hair and yanking me against him so I can feel his erection against my back.

"You don't know what you're doing."

Darla J Michaels

He laughs. It's a sinister laugh...just like Archer.

"Why don't I let you be the judge of that?"

I do my best to fight him as we move across the room.

"I hear you've been soaked lately. Let's check."

In one fluid motion, Hawk is bending me over and shoving my face into the mattress. I scream into it while Hawk pulls my nightgown over my backside.

I didn't bother putting on underwear last night. What's the point when you just soak them? I also thought I'd have more time before this went down today.

But now, Hawk is looking at my bare pussy, dripping wet, thighs a mess with my arousal.

I reach behind me, grabbing at him. Trying to stop him by any means possible even though I know it's hopeless.

Archer has beaten me at my own game. If this were anyone else, I'd be in this for the long haul. But it's not anyone else. This...the very man who is going to fuck me...he's the secret.

I manage to turn my head when I hear the teeth of his zipper slide down. The hot lump is in my throat. This is happening. The potential fall of everything Archer carefully constructed over the years.

I sob before I say the words.

"Bethany...", Hawk starts, just as I feel the tip of him at my entrance.

"You're his brother." I heave in a breath and sob. Not because of what Hawk is to Archer but because of the destruction I fear will come from this. I wanted all the pieces before I told Archer but the guy I'm working with doesn't have them yet.

Hawk pauses, not moving a muscle.

"Who's brother, Bethany?" When I don't answer as quickly as he'd like, he slides the tip inside.

"Archer's. You're Archer's brother. Don't do this. Please don't do this."

When Hawk doesn't move, I continue. "He's got a tattoo of his mother on his chest. Have him show you. But don't do this. Not until you see it at least."

There's a long beat of silence. I don't know what else to say. I don't think going into the fact that his voice sounds exactly like Archer's when he says my name, that his eyes are replicas of my husband's and that his mannerisms are so similar that to me, the lineage is undeniable will result in him removing himself from between my legs.

Hawk shifts behind me. Then the door opens. I breathe a sigh of relief at the sound of Archer's footsteps.

Neither of them says a word while I remain bent over for Hawk's pleasure.

"Archer", I croak. He does not answer me back.

I turn my head this way and that, until Archer finally comes into view. He tugs his shirt over his head to reveal the tattoo of his mother.

"That her?" Archer is pissed.

"Yeah."

"Did you know?"

"No."

"Get your cock out of my wife."

Hawk releases me and removes himself from inside me as I hear Archer's footsteps retreat. I sob as Hawks' hand grabs my nightgown and covers me back up.

I lay there and listen to his zipper. I don't know what to do. This wasn't how I wanted any of this to go. I wasn't even going to say anything to Hawk. I was going to let that be Archer's choice. But I couldn't knowingly have sex with my husband's brother either. I just hope I chose the lesser of all the evils, especially now that I know Archer is involved in something that may mean trouble for him.

Chapter 40
Jonathan

Grace, I vow to annoy you for the rest of your life.

That's good. I got an eyeroll.

I vow to fix your problems, or at least make sarcastic comments while I pretend to.

Chaplain Sal laughs. He's worked with me too long. He knows that vow is sacred and unbreakable. I deliver on this regularly with my co-workers, including him.

I vow to always be honest—except for the stuff I can't be honest about.

Really? I don't answer Grace's lackluster challenge. I told her we didn't have rules yet and I just want to cover myself. We have no idea what in hell we're even doing other than fucking. We're definitely doing a lot of fucking. I shrug and move on.

I'll protect your secrets better than I protect my own. And if I ever lie, it won't be about loving you. That part's non-negotiable.

"You're burning the candle at both ends", Grace attempts to lecture me. "Don't you have to leave for your flight in six hours", she asks, pulling me back into the present.

No. The answer is no. I do not. But the internet says I do so to her, I do.

I told her I'm doing charity work on Island Vienta in the Caribbean Sea. Well, that's what I told everyone. Gotta keep up the ruse.

Really, my doppelganger, courtesy of Harlan, is getting on that flight as me. I hate two things about this plan. The first is that someone's working under my license. They better not fuck me over. And a close second is that I've had to break The Brotherhood's most sacred rule. No touching anyone outside of The Brotherhood. I didn't think it would bother me but now that I'm doing it, my actions don't sit well with me.

Where will I really be off to in six hours? To pick up my fake wife so we can take down a disgusting organization and I can finally write the wrongs of these assholes.

But before I start my real journey on my fake life, I'll be sleeping in a private room at The Chamberlain Society Foundation. I need rest before we get behind the wheel and begin acting like Mr. and Mrs.

"I don't have time for sleep now. Too much to do", I tell her, hinting that she's the one I want to do.

"Why do you have to do this? Can't you let someone else go?"

"You're going to miss me. That's sweet. We don't even live together, Grace. What's there to miss?"

"Your tuck-ins and wakeups", she tells me. That's true. I do great tuck-ins and great wakeups. But with the time difference and my fake surgical schedule, contact will be limited. It has to be this way. If we have too much access to each other Sera and I will get caught. And these people don't play with a full deck. I suspect if they thought we were compromising their operation they wouldn't hesitate about getting rid of us. They'd probably delight in it.

"Stop stalling and play", I order her. We're in her living room. She's wearing panties and socks. I'm still fully clothed. "You don't have a good hand do you?" She shakes her head.

"I fold", she tells me, laying her cards down and motioning to her panties. "These?"

"The socks can go." This surprises her. "What? When I win this next hand, I want to fuck you with your panties on."

"You'll ruin them."

"I hope so."

Disobeying the order, she slips her panties off along with her socks.

"Why don't you just fuck me?"

I toss my cards behind me and Grace laughs as I reach for her, pulling her close but making her stand. I hunch down and burry my nose in my favorite place on the planet. Grace's pussy. Damn...I'm going to miss this. And then I start my last tuck-in with her.

"Have I annoyed you today", I check in with her.

She lets out a breath as I tongue her.

"Yes." Her reply is clipped. I can't tell if she's answering my question or responding to my mouth.

"Fix any problems today or provided sarcasm at every opportunity?"

"Oh God. If you don't get me off, you're going to have that problem to fix", she warns, looking down at me while I refocus my efforts.

"Have I been honest with you?" This one eats me up a little because I haven't been. But I quickly give myself absolution here because I never promised honesty. I promised honesty when I could be.

"Does cheating at strip poker count?"

I tongue her harder and pull back when I think she's close. "I don't cheat. You're awful at cards", I correct her and go back in for the kill.

"And did I protect you today", I ask after she comes on my tongue.

She gives me a weak nod. "Who's going to protect me when you're gone?"

I know what she's asking. She wants to know who she'll be transferred to. The guys asked me who I wanted her with. I told them I didn't want to know.

"You meet with Micah tomorrow." It's all I say. She knows my lack of information means she should drop it. And she also knows that I know that she has an appointment with Micah to discuss the matter. The topic is closed.

I pull her on top of my lap. Still fully clothed, I just want to kiss her. I want to memorize everything about her because after tonight, it's goodbye. And Grace is tough. She isn't someone I would expect to sit around and mourn me. But she is someone who could be deeply hurt from everything I've done and everything I'm about to do.

I intend to send people to jail but I also intend to kill some. I have no remorse for those on either of the lists. In my mind, it's as good as done.

"What's going on?" Grace cradles my face in her hands and looks into my eyes. She knows.

"I'll always be honest—except for the stuff I can't be honest about", I tell her, repeating the vows I made to her over six years ago. She lets out a heavy sigh and drops her hands into her lap.

"Grace." I take her hand in mine. "I'm coming back. I'm not finished annoying you for the rest of your life and I always keep my word, don't I?"

Epilogue
Jonathan

Vee slow claps from across the room.

"How does he look, Seraphina?"

I came inside her, unable to look away from her beautiful amber colored eyes.

"Guilty", she whispers between us.

Vee groans at Seraphina's assessment. "Well, he looked good from back here. If I weren't looking at his face, he'd look like he was really fucking the love of his life. We've been at this for almost three months, Jonathan. You two are supposed to leave this afternoon for your new life." Her patience are wearing thin.

I'm fully aware of exactly how long we've been at this. I'm also fully aware of how I probably look when we are at this...because the look on my face is exactly how I feel. Guilty.

Every time, I remind myself that I'm doing this for the right reasons, but it doesn't help.

"Can you tell her?" I don't answer Vee right away, so she clarifies. "Not the virgin. The woman who's yours. Can you just tell her?"

That I'm fucking an escort? No.

"Jonathan", Vee sternly uses my given name instead of the pet name she has used since I became a donor. "This isn't just about you. Look at the woman you're lying on top of. You're responsible for her. And while the service she provides is sex for me, I have people to vet the people who want to fuck her. You do not. Which means if you can't make this believable...if you can't make someone understand that they can have anyone else but her, the security that I promised her...that *we* promised her is gone.

"I won't let anything happen to you, Sera."

"What happened to the Jonathan I met years ago? That man wouldn't have felt guilty", Vee challenges me.

She's right. That man would have fucked whatever pretty unattached thing was in front of him, thrown a stack of bills on the bed and went back home to study. But that man didn't have a woman he called every morning and every night. This man does.

"Let's try it again", I suggest to Sera.

Vee's heels sound on the wood floor from behind us. She stops at the head of the lounge she had us fuck on.

"No." It's one word and by the tone of her voice, I know she knows. "You don't have that kind of money so get it out of your head."

But she'd be perfect, and I like her.

Sera's brow creases as she looks at me, trying to understand Vee's remarks.

"Wrap it up. You're going to be late", Vee orders us as she leaves us alone in the suite, our naked sweaty bodies still molded together.

I look down at Sera and gently brush some hair away from her face. Sera and Vee are right. I do feel guilty. But I don't want to feel guilty anymore.

"Do you trust me?" I have to know. Because if she doesn't, this whole thing may not work. But if she does, I no longer will be able to trust myself.

She cranes her neck up to brush her lips against mine. "Yes."

She doesn't relax back against the pillow. Instead, she waits.

And I think she thought I was going to kiss her. Instead, I start to move inside of her. I'm still hard. She's still swollen from orgasm and the second I slide in deep her mouth falls open.

"This...Sera...is how you fuck your wife."

Archer

How did things get so fucked up? I managed to do it again but this time, wronging my wife was entirely my fault.

There is no one else to blame. I get all the credit for this one.

You'd think I would have learned my lesson. Nope.

Instead, I hired a man to rape my wife or at least scare her enough that she'd tell me the secret she's been hiding. And that man turned out to be the secret.

My parents left me. I had no means and they left me to care for myself. They never came back. They never called someone to help me. They just left.

And the kicker? They started a new family. Not separately. Together. My parents split. My mom left me. Then they got back together and had Hawk according to the information Harlan pulled up for me.

No wait. That's not the kicker. The kicker is that I hired the brother I didn't even know I had to assault my wife.

Jesus Christ. My wife was terrified. But it wasn't of the sex. She was terrified of me. Not that I'd hurt her but terrified of my reaction.

Bethany knew that when this secret got out, it would tear me apart. She knows me well. I'm in my Hellcat trying to keep it together.

I just got in my car and started driving. Turned off my phone and just started to cruise.

How do I come back from this?

Darla J Michaels

Check out the Bonus Scene!

Archer finally orders Bethany to service one of his Brothers.
Get social with Darla and ask for the Bethany's Act of
Service bonus scene.
Email Darla at darlajmichaels@gmail.com or message her
on Facebook.

Don't forget to write your honest review on GoodReads!

Sneak Peak
Jonathan & Grace's Story

Prologue
Jonathan

"You can uncuff him", Micah tells the guard. "He's not a danger to me."

The guard releases my shackles. I rub my wrists and get a good stretch in before we start the talk about how disappointed Micah is in me.

"They're charging you with murder. First degree. Sexual assault. Sexual assault of a minor."

I'm not surprised by any of this.

Darla J Michaels

"Jonathan. Now is the part where you say, Micah, I'm innocent."

"Really?" I'm offended that he would even feel he needed to ask if I did any of those things. Well, the sexual stuff I'm offended by. There's no way I would do that. The murder stuff? That's fair.

"Yes, really."

Micah is here in a suit. I'm his friend. This feels ridiculous to me. He closes his eyes and lets out a heavy sigh.

"Just tell me what happened."

"I didn't do it."

"Any of it?"

"I'm innocent." I have no idea if there are cameras on us or if there's audio going. There's no way I'm saying something that could be damning later.

"You could be in prison for life without parole for these charges."

"I'm not going to prison."

"And why is that", he prompts me, his question sharp and ripe with frustration.

"Because you're the best lawyer there is. Now do your fucking job and get me out of here."

Grace

"Ma'am you have to wait here", a security guard yells following me. "Ma'am...ma'am!"

I don't respond to him. There's no reason to. He can't help me. The only one who can help me is the man in the glass office and I'll be damned if I do this over the phone.

I see Micah in his office. There are two men sitting across from him at his desk. He looks up at me as soon as I reach the door handle.

When I open the door, security is there.

"You cannot go in there, ma'am. You have to wait."

Micah signals for the security guard to let me in. I glare at him as I enter Micah's office.

"Grace is everything alright", Micah asks me, standing when I approach his desk.

"Where is he?"

"Will you give us a minute", Micah asks the gentlemen in his office. They must be employees of his. They look too relaxed to be clients.

The men exit quickly at Micah's request.

"Grace, what is the matter", Micah asks me, rounding his desk and stopping to lean against it.

"Where is my husband?"

"Your what?"

I'm stunned. Jonathan promised he wouldn't tell anyone and by the looks of Micah's face, he didn't.

"One more time. Your what?"

Darla J Michaels

"Jonathan. Where is he?" I can see Micah's mind reeling with this new piece of information, but he still doesn't answer my question. So, I do the only thing I can to move this conversation along. I reach in my purse and pull out the positive pregnancy test I just took, tossing it onto his lap.

"God! Grace! Is there pee on this?"

He grabs a tissue from his desk and picks up the test. Then he looks at the result.

"What happens now?"

20 Years Earlier

Chapter 1
Jonathan

I have wasted half of my summer break going through my parents' affairs trying to get as much of them in order before I start med-school.

Of all the things my father left to me, he left his entire firm. I have no business running a law office. Mostly because I know nothing about the legal system but equally as important, I could care less about it.

Between his assets all over the globe, his business that I'm running while unqualified to do so and this damn financial ledger that I cannot reconcile, I'm beginning to think this is some kind of cruel joke.

Well, it can't be any worse than it already is I think as I take file after file from his desk drawers and plop them out on top of his desk.

Darla J Michaels

Frustration gets the better of me and I'm not careful. When I start tossing them on his desk, one slides off the haphazard pile, and spills onto the floor.

I have got to get it together. Making a bigger mess isn't going to help me fix this one. I'm beginning to think nothing can. Besides, I decided to devote the summer to reviewing my parents' medical records and learning from them so their deaths wouldn't be in vain. So much for that, I think as I round the desk to gather the contents of the file.

There, on the floor just outside of the file's envelope is a black card with gold lettering. The Chamberlain Society Foundation.

Well, I'll be damned. The missing piece to one of the accounting puzzles...maybe. I dial Ned, my father's accountant. We have spoken so much since his death I now have his number memorized. The phone barely rings and he picks up.

"Mr. Patino. How can I help you?"

"For the last time Ned, it's Jonathan. Look, I think I found something to help me with my parent's financials."

Now, you'd think my parent's accountant would just tell me everything I needed to know, but my father had no desire to make this easy on me. His wish was that I review every stitch of his life on my own and use the resources at my disposal. The reason? Once you work to understand something it's harder to get rid of it.

He didn't want everything he had carefully put together torn apart by someone who didn't understand it's value. His genius was incredibly maddening.

And he didn't do this with just his finances, he did it with everything. The only kindness he did was provide me with a contact in each major area of his life to bounce things off and provide a bread crumb here or there when I got too stuck to move forward.

Since my parent's death, I have learned a lot about investments, accounting and running a law firm. It's monopolized almost all my time and I'm trying not to be resentful.

"Please, go on Jonathan."

"A business card. I think it explains the large transfers to The Society. But what I don't understand is why he would make regular donations. And why would he have an entire account that has transactions for a single charity."

"I find that if you want answers to questions that may be complicated, you visit the source."

I chuckle. Of course he would say that. There's no address or phone number on the thick plastic business card.

"Will there be anything else?"

"You wouldn't happen to have an address for this place, would you?"

"No. But you do. Will there be anything else, sir?"

I hang up on him.

"Fuck!" I'm in their gigantic house screaming obscenities like a teenager. He taught me better than this. I don't think I have ever heard my father yell in my entire life and here I am losing my shit over a business card.

A chuckle escapes from me. And then another. And now, I'm laughing maniacally. I wish I had a sibling. Then I wouldn't be doing this shit alone.

After my laughing fit, I relax back in my father's plush leather desk chair.

"How do I figure you out", I say to the card, holding it up as if some clue is going to jump right out at me.

It's such a funny card. Thick, black plastic with gold letters. Who hands out plastic business cards? I tilt the card, admiring how substantial the card is and notice that at just the right angle, I can see through it.

Bolting upright, I hold the card up to the light, tilting it this way and that. The logo disappears and in its place is everything I need to follow the next clue.

"Mother...fucker..." An address. No phone number. No personal contact.

I know The Chamberlain Society Foundation is entirely philanthropic. It's run by Genevieve Merchand-Wren. Her information is all over the web. She's pretty. She also looks like she wouldn't give me the time of day.

Fuck it. I grab my keys, my wallet and the card and head out. If I give her money, I'm sure she'll tell me anything I want to know.

The drive takes just under an hour. I pass by the building, marveling at how large it is. The place reminds me of one of those historic monuments about the size of a courthouse built fifty years ago.

It's stone. I'd estimate there to be four stories with a basement. Grand stone steps cascade from the front doors where pillars stand. Quite a remarkable looking building. But it doesn't make sense to me. Why would a charity be in this kind of grand structure? Don't charities set up shop in modest buildings?

Finding a spot on the street isn't hard. It's still early in the day. A Tuesday in a business district isn't all that busy before lunch.

I welcome the walk outside. Physical activity will help me release some of this pent-up energy I've been feeling. So will putting another piece of this puzzle together.

When I enter the building, I'm even more perplexed. The only person in the expansive entryway is a receptionist. It's so quiet, you could hear a pin drop.

"Welcome to The Chamberlain Society Foundation. How may I be of service", the young woman behind the counter inquires of me.

She's striking. Very well put together. Tailored navy suit. Dark hair pulled back into a bun at the nape of her neck. Pearl studs in her ears that match her pearl necklace. Red lipstick.

I hand her the card. "I'm here to see Genevieve Merchand-Wren."

The woman takes the card and hovers it over her laptop keyboard. "Hmmm..." She opens her desk drawer and places it inside. "She's unavailable today."

There's no offer to see her later. This woman just looks up at me serenely like she's waiting for my next move. Of course, this wouldn't be easy too.

"It's either me or she can speak with my attorney", I threaten. I have a right to know where my money is going. The woman doesn't even blanch at my threat. There's no scramble to call someone or nervous typing on her laptop. It's as if I've just thanked her for taking my card and telling me to go fuck myself.

"Okay. Let's try this another way. I'd like to make a donation." She nods, giving me a small smile.

"A very large donation. And I would like to speak with someone about how I can go about this."

I have no fucking idea what I'm donating to but if it gets me in the door I'll take it.

"Look, I'm not someone you want to turn away. I've got more money than I know what to do with and something tells me, this place could help me spend it." I scrub my hands over my face and pull out my wallet, tossing a card onto her desk. "Fifty grand. Just to talk with someone. Put it in any fund you want. I just need someone's time and I need it now."

She takes my card, holds it over her laptop keyboard just like the business card, opens her desk draw and places the card inside. What in the hell?

Footsteps sound to my right. A middle-aged man dressed in a suit with polished shoes and a pocket square greets me.

"Mr. Patino. We've been waiting for your arrival."

"And you are?" How does this man know who I am?

"Cassian Knox. Please...come with me and we can discuss the package you're most interested in. We have many donor options available. I'm quite confident you'll find something that speaks to you personally."

Chapter 2
Jonathan

"Prostitutes?" Cassian must be fucking with me.

"Escorts", he corrects me. "Although we refer to our staff as Companions when you fulfill your donor commitments at The Society", he explains.

I'm at a loss for words. "My father..." I'm not even sure how to ask this question it's so far outside of the realm of possibilities in my mind. "Roman..."

Cassian raises his brows and leans forward as if to say, spit it out already.

"The transfers are for...sex?"

"Companionship", Cassian corrects me.

"There were multiple donations from my father's account", I state as if he would know or even care. "How could he have worked so hard and have had that much free time to come here?"

"Might there have been another donor?" I shake my head. "Perhaps someone close to Roman", he hints.

356

I chuckle. "The only one close to my father was my moth..." Cassian smiles when I look up at him, confirming that I have uncovered yet another mystery.

"Now that you've gotten to the bottom of that, we've already charged your account. Your father provided us all the information we needed ahead of time."

What in the actual fuck?

"It's not unusual for donors to continue through family generations. The donations are so...fulfilling to our members."

I laugh. I cannot believe my parents came here for sex. I would have never guessed.

"Is this an actual charity?" Cassian doesn't answer my question. He breezes right past it as if I hadn't asked.

"I have selected some lovely ladies for you to choose from today. Your taste will help me better understand your preferences for your donation portfolio."

The door to his office opens and another woman in a sharp suit walks in. She's all grace on her high heels. This woman is wearing a cream-colored suit in a similar style as the woman at the front desk. Her heels are a powder pink color. She is also wearing pearls.

"Send Isla", Cassian orders the woman who is closing the door behind her. She pauses and looks between us.

"Genevieve will take over from here Cassian."

I'm not sure which of us is more shocked, him or me.

Cassian clears his throat and rises from behind his desk.

"A pleasure to meet you, sir." With a nod, he leaves the room.

The click of heels replaces the sound of Cassian's dress shoes on the polished wood floor.

Well I'll be damned. She really is here to see me. Trailing her are three beautiful women. They aren't in lingerie. In fact, if they walked out of this building right now, you'd think they were just like anyone else on the street.

One wears a mid-length sundress with ballet flats. Her hair is long and wavy. A sun kissed blonde with a natural tan to boot. Two brunettes stand next to her. One wears a skirt with a modest button-down top that isn't quite long enough, allowing her bellybutton to peek out just above the waist of her skirt. The neckline falls over one shoulder. She wears strappy sandals. The kind you'd see a woman wear if they were outside walking around with a coffee window shopping.

The other brunette wears pressed dress shorts. Her shirt also isn't quite long enough to cover the waist of her shorts. It's a knit short sleeved stripped shirt. Her hair is pulled back in a bun. Tan legs. Neutral makeup. Bright white slip-on casual shoes.

"Ladies." When Genevieve speaks, all eyes are on her. "Jonathan has given a generous donation today in good faith that we will leverage his funds to make a difference. Please show him how The Society takes care of such generosity."

What transpires before me is like nothing I ever imagined I'd see in person. The woman in the sundress brushes the woman's hand in the skirt. They share a look that seems to take forever as I hold my breath.

No, I think as their lips meet. No fucking way. It's a tender kiss. They've done this before. There's no doubt in my mind. Either they've performed for many donors in the past or they're actual lovers.

A hand lands on mine, and I realize, I'm gripping the arm of the chair. White knuckling it actually. It's the girl in the shorts.

"What's your name?" Genevieve laughs. Damn it. I'm nervous and she knows it.

Darla J Michaels

The woman at my side makes a show of looking down at my pants. I'm hard just like they knew I'd be.

"Don't overthink it, Jonathan. I assure you that your parents didn't."

The woman runs a delicate, manicured finger over the outline of my cock. Oh God. I need this. I haven't fucked a woman since final exams.

I look up at Genevieve. She has no shame, standing there leaning against the desk Cassian recently vacated, just watching. She doesn't apologize. She doesn't explain herself. She simply stands there, the picture of power, analyzing my every move.

I look over at the ladies kissing. They're only wearing panties now. Watching them is exquisite. They look like lovers. Each kiss...each touch so tender.

The woman who's name I don't know slides my zipper down. When she frees me, I'm harder than I've ever been in my life.

Genevieve's designer heels click against the floor as she comes closer to inspect me.

"Very nice." This woman has no shame at all. I shouldn't be surprised. She runs an escort service under the guise of a charity.

The woman kneeling between my legs opens her mouth above my cock, letting a stream of spit fall onto the head. She watches it slide down my shaft and looks up at me, more spit spilling over her lower lip and onto my cock with precision.

A moan sounds from across the room. I look away to see the two women naked, laying on a lounge in full view, sliding their bare pussies against each other as the woman at my feet begins to stroke me.

"Isla loved fucking your father. I wonder if she'll like fucking you as much", Genevieve tells me.

I look down at the woman stroking me.

"Who liked fucking my mother", I ask, not because I really want to know but because I'm hoping that if my father was unfaithful, my mother was too. It would serve him right.

"Also, Isla." Genevieve's laugh cuts through the moans on the other side of the room. "Your mother could eat a pussy like it was going to be her last meal."

Jesus. My mom?

Genevieve walks over to the women. They pause when she approaches them like she's done this before. Her manicured hand reaches between them. She rubs over the woman's bare slick mound laying on her back, then flips her hand and does the same with the woman on top.

When Genevieve turns on her heel, the ladies resume rubbing against each other.

She's holding her glistening fingers out to me in offering and my mouth opens like I'm a God damned puppet.

I groan at the taste of them. Slightly salty. Slightly sweet. The smell of sex on her fingers makes my brain foggy and pliant.

When she steps away to wipe off her hand I'm only after one thing.

"Suck on it", I order the woman.

Genevieve laughs again as the woman dribbles more spit onto my cock, never faltering in her rhythm.

"Jonathan", she chastises. "Do you know why these women look so beautiful and healthy?" Fuck. I have no idea, but this better have to do with the cock she's about to put in her mouth. I shake my head and slide my hand behind her head. "Drop your hand or it will be the last time you set foot in here", Genevieve warns.

Darla J Michaels

Without hesitation, I comply. There is no way this is the last time I'm setting foot in here. If she told me to walk around this room and cluck like a chicken to stay, I'd do it.

"She's here to collect a sample from you. When we know you're safe, you can play any way you like." She steps up to me once more. "Have some patience. This is just the beginning." The sound of her heels fades into the distance, then stops at the threshold. "Jonathan, welcome to The Chamberlain Society Foundation. I'm afraid there's no going back now."

Acknowledgements

I wanted to release another book on Halloween. For reasons I don't quite understand, it's my favorite holiday. The challenge with this release date was that it was tight. The kind of timeline that required me to question my entire process to ensure I could make my own deadline. But we managed to pull it off and I couldn't have done it without...

My husband. There were many days he would come home from a long day at work and take our kids out as late as all of them could muster so I could have some quiet time and get this story on paper. He never complained once and for that I am grateful.

A big thank you to our kids, 4, 8 and 10. This past summer they had some very feral days out in the neighborhood and more screen time than I'm proud of. While I had huge mom guilt, they were probably having the time of their lives. Thank you for rolling with things while I figure out all this author stuff.

When I told my cover artist, Kristina Bates, that I needed a cover quick but didn't have the whole story written I can only imagine what was going through her mind. But she rolled with it, indulged me and quite honestly, I think it's the best cover she has done for me to date.

Stephanie Barenz, you pulled a rabbit out of your hat reading my very rough chapter drafts while traveling on vacation. You are amazing as always and I appreciate you for putting up with my timeline antics.

My coach, Clayton Snyder said two things to me when I told him I wanted to publish a third book along with three companion stories this fiscal year. First, he said that's awesome. If anyone can do it, you can. Second, he said, how long do you think you can keep this up. Well played, sir. Well. Played. He was the perfect blend of *I have faith in you* and also, *woah sis settle down*. I appreciate your encouragement and the level-headed perspective you bring into my life. You're the best.

And finally, to my readers. Thank you for your support. I realize that writing a witchy book could be a turn off for some. So, you might be wondering why I did it. That's simple. The story was in my heart and when a story is in my heart, I can't just leave it there.

Even still, some of you might be wondering...does she believe in magic? Is she a witch? Could she have been Bethany in this story?

Maybe the truth lies somewhere between starlight and shadow, tucked inside whispered spells and half-kept secrets. Magic has a way of blurring the edges between what is tangible and what is only felt. Magic doesn't always need an answer...only belief.

About The Author

Darla lives in a tiny little town in Wisconsin with her husband and three small children. Her favorite thing about Wisconsin is fall because hello...the beautiful colors, caramel apples and Halloween of course!

Darla is obsessed with everything organic and homemade, natural products, and making her own lotions, scrubs and soaps with herbs and oils. Darla loves cooking, chardonnay and rainy days where everything seems to slow down a little.

A perpetual optimist, Darla strives to inspire others. She wholeheartedly believes that everyone has a genius somewhere within them and anyone can achieve whatever they want if they put in the work and never give up.

www.ingramcontent.com/pod-product-compliance
Lightning Source LLC
Chambersburg PA
CBHW060223030726
47499CB00004B/1164